The Envoy

THE ENVOY

George Brown

ARROW

Published by Arrow Books in 1996

1 3 5 7 9 10 8 6 4 2

First published in the United Kingdom in 1995 by
Century Books Limited
20 Vauxhall Bridge Road, London, SW1V 2SA

Random House Australia (Pty) Ltd
20 Alfred Street, Milsons Point, Sydney,
New South Wales 2061, Australia

Random House New Zealand Limited
18 Poland Road, Glenfield,
Auckland 10, New Zealand

Random House South Africa (Pty) Ltd
PO Box 337, Bergvlei 2012, South Africa

Random House UK Limited Reg. No. 954009

A CIP catalogue record for this book
is available from the British Library

Papers used by Random House UK Limited
are natural, recyclable products made from wood grown in
sustainable forests. The manufacturing processes conform to
the environmental regulations of the country of origin.

ISBN 0 09 933761 4

Typeset by Deltatype Ltd, Ellesmere Port, Cheshire

Printed and bound in Great Britain by
Cox & Wymand Ltd, Reading, Berks

This is for my Aussie mates,

DETLEF AND KERRIE THINIUS

And their family and many, many friends
who showed a couple of Poms exactly what
Australian friendship and hospitality is all about

Author's note

To thank people in helping in the construction of a book of this nature is one of the pleasures, as an author, I relish. However, in some instances the injudicious mention of a name can seriously jeopardize the security of that individual. For this reason, whilst I would like to offer my thanks to a number of people, particularly those in the Middle East who 'returned past favours', prudence dictates that they be satisfied with this expression of my gratitude. *They* know who I mean.

But I have no such qualms in mentioning Alan Mahoney of ANTROPOS who rashly made himself available whenever things went wrong. Captain Tim Holt, ex-10th (PMO) Gurkha Rifles who supplied the *falaful* and *kadayif*, and my stepdaughter Veronica Kingston who provided some new variations on an old theme.

Then, while we're on the subject, there's Oliver Johnson whose editing makes my books readable, and after butchering four such offerings we still remain, I hope, very good friends!

And lastly, but, as they say, not least there's Paula for whom mortal thanks cannot repay the suffering she has to endure as an author's wife. Her reward will come!

G.B. Feb '95

Death is not oblivion: it is not the end –
it is the beginning of a true life

Hezbollah creed

PART ONE

Prologue

It was the only way he could tell that a new day had started.

He forced his eyes down as far as they would go, following the needle-thin shaft of sunlight that cut across the side of his face and settled like a laser target on the left side of his chest. It wasn't going to last long; he knew that. He'd been waiting for it at this time every day, longing for it for what he estimated was nearly one and a half years. He managed to move his head just three inches – but that was enough. He was improving every day – this day his forehead actually touched the grill just a few inches above his face and he was able to follow the shaft of light and watch it until the sun, moving fractionally on its upward path, shifted away from the tiny crack it had found in the wall and left the room in total darkness. For the thousandth time he tried to move his hands and arms; there were only two inches of space on either side. For his feet there was neither space nor feeling. There was no need to reassess his prison, he knew its dimensions and its shape exactly. He was wedged upright in a coffin-shaped niche crudely gouged out of the damp clay wall in a crumbling cellar below one of Beirut's shell-torn streets. He was imprisoned in this dank coffin by a roughly constructed wooden panelling which held him in place in the wall. His only contact with the outside world was through a six-inch-diameter circular hole cut out of the wood, level with his nose and mouth. But he wasn't alone. Somewhere in the dark emptiness he sometimes heard a monotonous, moaning chant. It was a very small comfort that nearby was a fellow sufferer.

As on every day before it, when the infinitesimal contact with an outside world abandoned him his head went back to the slimy wall behind him and his neck muscles relaxed as he allowed the tears to flow freely through the grime of his face and disappear into the filthy matt of an eighteen-month-old beard.

When he'd first woken up in his coffin eighteen months ago he'd prayed it was a nightmare. His prayer wasn't answered. He tried to turn his body. There was nowhere to turn to. He tried to move his legs. There was no reaction, no feeling – just excruciating, mind-screaming pain. His feet – the same, but no pain. They were dead. But it wouldn't have mattered, they weren't touching anything – he was suspended just three inches off the ground by the pressure of the wooden panelling. The nightmare progressed. He flinched, and his shoulders touched the sides. He began to scream and didn't stop until, through the sheer horror, he fainted.

But the relief was short lived. He woke up still screaming and kept it up for two days until his bowels and bladder emptied and there was nothing in his body to respond to his claustrophobic hysteria and he collapsed into a coma. It didn't last long enough. Water gushed from somewhere behind his head. It poured over his face and body, half filling the tomb and leaving him shivering with cold and fear until everything flushed through a hole near his feet. He gibbered and shouted and screamed but nothing was said and after a few moments a flap was dropped over the opening and he was back in the dark claustrophobic uncertainty of his grave.

Every so often – he estimated every twelve hours – the flap was lifted, his lips and teeth prised apart and several handfuls of a cold mush of mashed beans moistened with a foul-tasting peppery gravy was spooned into his mouth. It was swallow or choke and it ran straight through his system to be flushed out with the daily sluice until, through hunger and thirst, he forced his body to retain it.

After several weeks, although fear and horror still bubbled dangerously near the hysteria mark, he became calm enough to consider his situation. Perhaps someone would come and explain; perhaps tell him the length of his sentence – everything must end some time. It was the only thing that kept him alive – although his sanity was another question.

After a while the routine forced feeding became the high point of his daily existence; an event he craved, the one indication that he was human and that time hadn't stood still. It kept his will alive. He wondered why he bothered. And still every day came the sluice. It was his only pleasure in life. He took to talking to himself. At times he sensed the presence of the other person again, someone who might live and tell the world how he suffered.

After a while he prayed only for death.

1

Washington, DC

Thurston Macauley checked the time then moved out of
the central heated foyer of the Hay-Adams and on to the
portico. He waited at the top of the steps, shivered with the
change of temperature and thrust his hands deep in the
pockets of his dark grey overcoat as he studied the evening
traffic crawling through the rain along 16th Street.

The black limousine slid into place dead on time.
Macauley nodded to the driver and climbed into the back
seat. His uncle, Joe Doerflinger, grunted an indecipherable
greeting and moved slightly to make more room. It was
necessary. Doerflinger was a tall man, well built, heavy
around the waist with age. He would have been an
extraordinarily fine specimen at his peak – football,
basketball, Army – anything physical. Special Forces –
inevitable – right up in front of the front, then OSS and
CIA – again inevitable. And even more inevitable, at the
soggy end of his life, Personal Security Coordinator to the
President – a sinecure for an efficient blameless career and a
long personal friendship with the present President.

'You stay there often?' he asked nodding at the imposing
edifice of the hotel.

Macauley nodded. 'It's quite comfortable.'

'You ever thought of staying at your mother's place? It'd
make her happy.'

'Sure I've thought about it. But you know how it is, Joe.
When I'm in Washington it's for business, not family.'

'Make time, son. She worries about you. She thinks I'm responsible for your well-being. Try and see her soon.'

Macauley shrugged in the dark of the car. 'OK. And thanks Joe. I'll make a point of it when I get time.'

They lapsed into silence as the car crossed Pennsylvania Avenue and turned on to West Executive Avenue. The security guard at the gate held the car just long enough for him to recognize Joe Doerflinger then, with a finger wave at the Secret Service driver, urged him, with a slight nod of the head, towards the west portico of the White House. Two young Marines saluted Doerflinger stiffly. Another Secret Service agent slipped from the shadows of the pillars.

'Good evening, Mr Doerflinger,' he said, looking quizzically at Macauley as if not expecting to see Doerflinger with someone else.

Doerflinger caught the line of his gaze. 'It's OK, Sam, the President's expecting him as well.'

'As you say, sir.' Sam didn't ask for an introduction. Doerflinger was an intimate, a regular. He belonged. The agent led the two men through the foyer to the West Wing Reception Room where he handed him over to another similarly dressed young man. He studied Macauley for a moment, frisked him visibly and exchanged glances with Sam before escorting them to a gilt-enclosed elevator set into the wall. They rode up in silence to the West Sitting Hall, where the two agents departed, pressing the elevator buttons. The doors closed with a sigh and Doerflinger and Macauley were left on their own in the elegantly comfortable room on the family floor of the White House.

No further security was obvious, and Doerflinger said, 'Wait here, Thurston,' and with easy familiarity he strode across the thick carpet to one of the doors leading off the sitting hall. He knocked solidly on the door and without waiting for a response opened it and walked through.

Macauley gazed about him. This was the private part of

the White House, no one was ever going to get this far uninvited, but even so, he thought, as he picked his way carefully round the perimeter of the room, its ornate beauty seemed wasted. He ran his fingers across the early English satinwood commode and admired the seventeenth-century workmanship, then lowered his head and studied the two fine French porcelain vases standing on the commode. He shuddered at the desecration in converting them into lamp bases. He moved on quickly, past a Maryland bookcase secretaire with an ornate gold eagle finial and recalled that that great draper's wife, Bessie Truman, was responsible for acquiring most of the fine furniture. He was absorbed in William Ranney's masterpiece *Boys Crabbing* when the door opened and Doerflinger beckoned him in.

The President sat at a large Georgian bureau writing notes in a small ordinary-looking pocket diary. Macauley felt a sudden onrush of nerves but Doerflinger was his usual urbane self.

'This is my nephew, Mr President,' he said. 'Thurston Macauley.'

The President finished his notes and looked up – a tired, thoughtful scrutiny. 'How are you, Thurston?' he said, standing up and offering his hand. Macauley took it without thinking, the President's informality putting him at ease. 'Let's go and sit over there by the window. Joe, d'you want a cup of coffee?'

'No thanks.'

'OK. So you're Joe's nephew.' The President studied Macauley intently.

'Yes, sir.'

'I've heard good things about you. Sit down. I've heard some of it from Joe, now let me hear the rest from you. Start at the beginning.'

Thurston cleared his throat. He wasn't a White House man. Thurston Macauley came from a different world: he

8

was Defense Intelligence Agency. Meetings with the President weren't normally on the agenda and he wasn't happy. Although he'd never had a *tête-à-tête* with him, he was an expert in Middle East affairs and as such was used as a high-grade courier on sensitive security exchanges between the President and America's main ally in the Middle East, King Hussein of Jordan. The fact that he was the nephew of the President's personal security adviser had no small bearing on the sensitive nature of his assignments. But he was well equipped for it in more significant ways. Macauley, like his uncle, had gone through the system – West Point, the Army, Special Forces, Vietnam, CIA Bangkok; Beirut; Baghdad and most of the world's tinder-boxes, concluding with a clandestine mission with the British SAS behind Iraqi lines in the Gulf War. He was confident, and competent, in his present status; his missions on behalf of the President he considered a reward; he enjoyed them, they were untaxing. His recent return from Jordan and the report he had made to Joe Doerflinger was the reason for his exceptional late-evening meeting with the President.

Thurston Macauley marshalled his thoughts.

'Two nights ago, sir, I was the Ambassador's guest to a reception at the Japanese embassy in Amman. It was a large gathering: the usual thing, everyone from everywhere, but there was one guy who got my interest straight away. Kamel al-Majid. I'd noticed him when the Iraqi General Staff were negotiating terms at the end of the Gulf War. He's Saddam Hussein's son-in-law and a general in the Iraqi Intelligence Service. It seemed we were both manoeuvring towards the same end and, after a bit, I found myself rubbing shoulders with him as we helped ourselves to the smoked salmon. We had a couple of drinks together and became quite chummy.' Macauley didn't alter his tone or his expression. 'At first it was small talk, pleasantries, but then we got on to the UN nuclear inspection of Iraq and the trade sanctions and how these sanctions are ruining the country. He started to go into detail of how it could be if Iraq played ball with the West. Then he went coy and started looking over his shoulder as if his father-in-law was hovering in the background. He guided me to a corner, turned his back on the room and suggested we continue our chat at a little private club he knew. I agreed. We left the Japanese embassy at different times and I joined him about an hour later.'

The President and Doerflinger watched Macauley and listened without interruption. At one stage Doerflinger made as if to hurry his nephew to the point but was restrained by a slight movement of the President's hand. He was absorbed, his eyes fixed on Macauley.

Macauley sensed his uncle's impatience. He met his eyes. 'It gets better. Installed in a corner table, a couple of double whiskies inside him, he got pretty tactless and went on at great length to tell me about Iraq's nuclear potential. I got the feeling that our meeting at the Embassy wasn't a chance encounter, he'd been waiting for it. Then the feeling changed to certainty – he was angling for some sort of deal. I let him do it his way . . .'

'What sort of deal?' asked the President.

'Can I lead up to it, sir?'

'Sure. Go ahead.'

'He said the nuclear installations that were left in Iraq are peanuts – a blind. There's nothing there of any substance, just a few protected sites for the interest of the UN's inspection teams. He said they're happy for them to find these little bits and pieces and Baghdad'll hiss and piss about violation of their sovereignty and the indignity inflicted on their nation. He reckons the UN'll finally give up and go home.' He looked significantly at the President. 'But it's a blind. Al-Majid told me there's documentary proof that

Saddam had the tacit approval of Jordan's Hussein to choose three sites in the Az-Zarqa region of east Jordan for storing advanced nuclear components, including a significant amount of plutonium-239. Majid reckons Iraq has, in these safe dumps, everything required to construct nuclear warheads and a short and medium range delivery system. All Saddam needs is a quiet UN inspection-free period – which he's expecting to get when there's nothing more for them to find in Iraq – and he'll be in the position to scatter warheads all over the Middle East. Israel's the definite number one target – '

'Why did he tell you all this?' the President asked. Macauley looked at Doerflinger. His uncle nodded for him to continue.

'Sir, I'll get to that in a minute, with your permission, but first a little bit more background on Majid. Majid is not a run-of-the-mill revolutionary; he's no Saddam sycophant. He's watched Saddam's adventures with growing disillusionment and this came to a climax with the Kuwait disaster and defeat in the Gulf War. He realized then that the Allies were only playing at war. If Saddam went on the warpath again and we took it seriously it would be the end of Iraq as he knows it. And . . .' Macauley paused a moment to read the President's expression, but it offered him no clues. 'Saddam is definitely set on going on the warpath again. About this Majid is definite. He's convinced Saddam knows there's nothing he can do politically, or economically, to bring Iraq back into any form of contention in the Middle East, so he reckons Saddam will gamble everything on possession of a nuclear armoury. He's going to go to war again, Mr President, and this time he reckons we wouldn't risk a nuclear challenge. General Majid wants to maintain the status quo and he's prepared to betray his country, its leader, and his wife's father to achieve that. He's offering us the locations of these three sites, plus their present

11

production capacities, their projected target of nuclear warheads and their present state of preparedness. He's offering us the wherewithal to wipe Iraq for ever off the list of nuclear nations – but at a price.'

'What price?'

'He wants $150 million.'

'Anything else?'

'Asylum and a safe house in the US.'

'We could put the Israelis on to it and let them go and bomb these places to hell – '

Macauley shook his head before Doerflinger could reply. 'Nothing doing, Mr President. General Majid is quite emphatic on this point. They're all substantial underground bunkers. Well-constructed installations and totally undetectable from the air, by satellite or anything else. Nobody outside the Iraq inner circle, that's Saddam's clan, the latter-day Iraq royal family, knows the full extent of the Jordan project.'

'That leaves us with Majid – is he to be trusted?'

'It's got to be worth the gamble – ' Doerflinger took over – 'with every possible safeguard, of course.'

'Such as?'

'Thurston goes back to the Middle East – gets photographs, does a bit of camping around in Jordan to see if any sand's been moved. He's qualified. They won't object – it'll justify his stay there and he'll be on the spot when Majid makes his play.'

The President nodded. 'Thurston,' he said. 'You've done a great job here. I'd like you to continue with this to make sure you're getting the genuine article. OK?' He turned back to Doerflinger. 'Joe, make the necessary arrangements. OK, Thurston, perhaps you'll allow Joe and me a few minutes in private . . .'

When Macauley had left the room the President got up

from his chair by the window and lowered himself into the armchair opposite Doerflinger.

'This thing has a couple of alternatives that ought to be aired. One – ' he lowered his voice and drummed his fingers on the arm of the chair slowly – 'I can't afford to go to the UN with this. Jordan's too important an ally, so we'll have to do it all softly-softly, from start to finish. But if the negotiations go wrong, if this is some Iraqi plot, it could go badly. A hundred and fifty million bucks for information about a non-existent nuclear installation supplied by Saddam's son-in-law. For Christ's sake! And in Jordan. Jordan's the only goddam Arab friend we've got in that area and, apart from upsetting 'em, this'd be worse than the Iran/Contra thing if it turned out to be an Iraqi set-up. They're capable.'

'If that's how it ran, Mr President, I guarantee it wouldn't get as far as the White House steps . . .'

Which is exactly what Mr President wanted to hear.

'How would you go about that, Joe?'

Doerflinger formed his fingers into a spire and balanced his elbows on the chair-arms. He touched the spire gently to his lips and pursed them. 'There's only three of us going to know about it. You, me, and the guy waiting outside for my orders. Once he gets involved there will be no discussion on the technicalities of the undertaking other than eyeball-to-eyeball with me – no phone contact other than for the basics or emergency but no mention at all of anything that will finger his mission . . .' Doerflinger hesitated. 'I would ask you, Mr President, with respect, to agree with this stance.'

The President gave him a narrow smile but otherwise said nothing. It was understood. Even in the White House one had to watch one's tongue. 'What about this Majid – Saddam's son-in-law?'

'Anything that comes from the other side will be

considered just a typical load of anti-American bullshit. It wouldn't take five minutes to refute anything from them. Macauley's the only one on our side who could put his foot in it, but he's much too good a man to make a slip.' Doerflinger held the President's eyes. 'I have no worries about Thurston Macauley, Mr President.'

'You sure about that?'

'I'm sure – he's my nephew. He's not going to be letting anybody down. Take my word for it, sir, from this point of view this Presidency won't be involved in failure –' Doerflinger lowered the spire from his lips – 'only in success.'

2

Lieutenant-General Kamel al Majid unfolded the map in front of Thurston Macauley in the hotel room in Amman. It was the only time the map had left the inner cabinet room of Saddam Hussein's Revolutionary Council in Baghdad; it was the first time it had seen the light of day − anywhere. Only a close member of the Leader of the Revolutionary Council's immediate family would have had solitary access to it. Macauley studied it with incredulity.

Everything was there: the highly secret locations, the capability and current stage of development of each installation − everything, right down to the establishment and sizes of the hand-picked special garrisons. Macauley looked for the sting. There wasn't one. This was real − it even had Saddam Hussein's signature in the 'agreed & approved' box. ORIGINAL NO.1/TOP SECRET/ACCESS RESTRICTED. There was no doubt about it: the signature was genuine, original and in ink. This was definitely the Real McCoy.

Watched by Saddam Hussein's son-in-law, Macauley walked thoughtfully across to the bed where he'd left his briefcase. He opened it with a solid click. Majid's eyes narrowed as he studied Macauley's back poised over the open briefcase. He was like a stretched spring, tense and wary. And well he might be. For what he was doing, death would be a light sentence in Baghdad.

When Macauley straightened up and turned to face

15

Majid he had in his hand a flat, miniature Nikon camera. He was still adjusting the lens.

'No camera,' hissed Majid. 'No pictures . . .'

Macauley stared at him.

Majid's eyes refused to meet his. 'You look at it – that was the arrangement. The map is authentic. It's the only one . . .'

'OK. No picture. A question – '

'Quickly!'

'How did you get it to Amman?'

'That's not part of the business, either. You look at this map and you note what you want. The references you put up there – ' he tapped the side of his forehead with a long slim finger. 'Anything else can be traced back if you are taken. Pictures or notes – no. Forbidden.' He repeated, 'That was not part of the deal.'

Macauley kept his mouth shut. He replaced the camera, flattened the map on the bed and stared hard at it, concentrating on the enhanced area on Jordan's eastern border with Iraq – the featureless, uninviting region of the Ash-Sham desert. Macauley had no difficulty with figures and location. His ability of total recall was one of the attributes that ensured his place among the top executives of the Defense Intelligence Agency. It didn't take long. But it seemed like a lifetime to Majid as he paced the room, chain-smoked two cigarettes and alternated between peering out of the dirty window and standing near the door listening for movement in the corridor outside. When Macauley turned away from the map and sat down in one of the room's two chairs Majid was beside him in a flash.

'OK?' he hissed.

Macauley nodded and Majid, now slightly calmer, began carefully refolding the map. When he'd finished he placed it in the slim, leather folder he'd brought it in and, zipping it up, slipped its thin strap over his wrist. He raised his eyebrows at Macauley. 'The arrangement . . . ?' he whispered.

'Agreed,' said Macauley. And held Majid's eyes. The Iraqi's breathing had settled to a more even tempo; the earlier sickly, fear-induced pallor had receded and he looked his normal suave, urbane self again. 'But with a small proviso,' added Macauley.

'Proviso? What proviso? You said you agreed.' Majid stopped in his tracks, his eyes suspicious again. 'The map is produced; it is right. I have fulfilled the agreement . . . What is this proviso?'

'I must verify these references,' Macauley said patiently.

'What do you mean, verify? How verify? You have seen the map; you have read the signature – you know that signature. It is Saddam Hussein's. There is no question about its authenticity . . .'

'It could be an authentic ruse,' said Macauley quietly. 'I need to make sure that at least one of these installations is where the map says it is, at the very least . . .'

'You do not trust me?'

Macauley looked him in the eye. 'No – not one little bit.'

The Iraqi didn't take offence. 'I cannot help you with this.'

'I don't need your help. But you're going to have to wait for the transfer of account and the other arrangements until I've done a little bit of research.'

Majid's face clouded again. 'How long?'

'Give me a week.'

'That wasn't the agreement.'

'The deal is still there. It's solid. The money's in place in Geneva, all you have to do is collect it and then transfer the deposit into your own name. The other arrangements have been made. You've a secure identity and a house in the United States. Everything is on tap for you. All you've got to do is wait one week while I take a little trip into the desert, then find yourself a safe phone and ring me – ' he glanced down at the watch on his wrist and studied the magnified date – 'on the 23rd here at the embassy.'

'You'll leave details of the deposit with your people?'

'No. I'm the only one who knows those details and that's how it stays until I come back.'

'And if you don't come back?'

Macauley studied the Iraqi's concerned expression for several seconds. 'Then we've both got problems!' he said.

3

Lieutenant-General Kamel al-Majid, in light-coloured cotton slacks, a white short-sleeved shirt and a tie, stood on the steps of the hotel and studied the immediate surroundings. With his slim, expensive folder-size wallet dangling casually from one wrist he looked in every way the character he had assumed — that of a senior bank employee visiting a private client in his hotel room. There was no trace of his earlier agitation; he was a man in complete charge of the situation. His confidence showed. He was shortly to be rich and safe, beyond his wildest expectations. Satisfied with his inspection of the area he crossed the road and climbed into the taxi at the head of the queue.

He was photographed three times — on the steps of the hotel, crossing the road, and getting into the taxi.

Thurston Macauley was also photographed, but this time the photographer, dressed in an ankle-length *shamise*, his head covered with the traditional *shamargh* and *aqal*, left his table outside the café and, handing his camera to his companion, strolled casually on the opposite side of the road in the same direction as Macauley.

He had no difficulty keeping in touch with the American. He blended into the background as, like a thousand other bearded Arabs dressed for Friday mosque he wandered without apparent purpose in his wake until Macauley, equally aimlessly, arrived at the American embassy. The Arab watched him enter, studied the Marine

19

further. He looked up in anger as the two men walked into the room and closed the door behind them. Removing his finger from the intercom switch, he scowled across his desk. 'How dare you walk into my office without permission . . .'

But something wasn't quite right. There was a lack of deference from the brigadier who strolled across the room and lowered his tall frame into one of the scattered armchairs. Casually he lit a cigarette and crossed his legs, taking care not to disturb the razor-sharp crease in his pale linen trousers. He gestured languidly at the major, who remained standing: he could begin talking.

'My name is Sa'dun Shakir,' he said tensely. 'I'm from the GID. If you wish to establish my credentials I have no objection to your using the phone – ' He gestured nervously with an elegant hand at the telephone. His fingers were adorned with a variety of jewelled rings, of which he seemed very proud. He allowed the hand to retain the gesture so that Majid could study the rings.

But Majid wasn't studying rings. Majid was trying to sort out his stomach, which had thumped solidly on to his bladder. GID – the three letters seared into his brain like red-hot bullets – Da'Irat al Mukhabarat al-Amah, the secret police and intelligence organization responsible for the maintenance of the Revolutionary Republic. Saddam Hussein's personal Praetorians directed with ruthless efficiency by Majid's own uncle by marriage, Saddam's half-brother, the cold and merciless Sabba'a al-Tikriti. Majid's stomach refused to budge. Fear dried the saliva in his mouth and replaced it with hot desert sand. He shook his head and managed to meet the major's eyes.

Still standing awkwardly, Major Shakir produced a long envelope, opened it and with deliberation selected from it a 10cm × 15cm coloured photograph. He studied it for a moment, then flicked it across the vast desk like a croupier

21

dealing a card. Leaning forward he placed his finger on its corner.

'Will you identify that man for me, please, sir.'

Majid lowered his eyes from the centre of the major's forehead and stared with horror at the clear, sharp image of Thurston Macauley leaving the hotel in Amman. At the bottom of the print was a small box with an electronic digital timer facility. The date and time of the picture's origination was clearly imprinted. He looked up. 'Who is it?' he asked, trying to keep his voice steady. But it didn't work. It sounded as if his voice belonged to somebody else; it was so high it was almost feminine.

The major made no reply. His eyes were like ice, unmelting.

Majid lowered his eyes as if to study the photograph again. 'I've never seen this man before, Major.'

The brigadier expelled a thin stream of smoke from between his pursed lips with a gentle whistle. It was the only sound in the room as Majid once again locked eyes with the major and forced himself to keep them there.

In place of a reply the major's fingers went back into the envelope and sent a second photograph skimming across the desk. He reached over and with great deliberation lined up the two pictures. They were identical in size; the setting was the same, with the hotel entrance forming the background. Only the times when the pictures had been taken differed, and then, only by minutes. The second one was a picture of himself. The time shown was eighteen minutes earlier than the picture of Macauley.

Majid's eyes broke contact with the major's of their own accord. Majid had lost control of them; he pressed his knees together to stop the jelly-like shaking and to prevent his bladder from bursting over his beautiful and much-loved carpets. He reached for a new cigarette, the finest tobacco blend that money and position could buy, and with difficulty held the flame of a gold lighter to its end. He sucked deeply, noisily: the smoke tasted like burning goat droppings in his dry mouth.

'So?' he asked. It was the only word he could think of. His brain had died. It refused to function. He tried again. 'What is this supposed to mean?'

Major Shakir smiled. It was a genuine smile. 'It means, sir, that his excellency, Sabba'a al-Tikriti, would like you to come to his office and talk about it.'

Majid stubbed out his cigarette. He knew what he had to do. 'I'll phone him.'

The major shook his head. 'He said I was to show you these photographs so you could think about them on the way to his office.' He picked up the two photographs, shuffled them in his hands and placed the one of Macauley on top of the deck again. 'This man,' he said, 'is an American agent. Probably CIA. I've no doubt that your close proximity to this enemy, and spy, has a simple explanation. I think the reasoning behind Tikriti's instructions is that he won't have to go through all this again when he sees you.' The smile had long since vanished. The major had got over his nervousness at being in the presence of one of the great. He now looked like a happy python studying its breakfast. 'Will you come now, sir?'

'Very well,' said Majid resignedly. 'Will you wait outside while I make a telephone call to my father-in-law?'

'I was told no phone calls.'

'You know, of course, who my father-in-law is?'

'Yes, sir. I know also that Sabba'a al-Tikriti has already spoken on the subject to him. Now I'm to take you to GID HQ where Tikriti wishes to discuss this matter with you personally.'

It was the word 'discuss' that put the final pressure on Majid's bladder. Sabba'a al-Tikriti's name was a byword for sadistic cruelty. He was in the right job. He enjoyed his work. This was the man who, had the Americans carried the war to its rightful conclusion, would have been at the top of the War Crimes Commission's list. Saddam Hussein might have been second, but he would have been a very poor second to Sabba'a al-Tikriti. The fact that he had taken this 'discussion' on himself was, for Majid, the toll of the death sentence. There would be no trial. There would be nothing left to send for trial after Tikriti had finished with him. Majid levered himself out of his chair.

'I have to wash my hands.'

The major met the eyes of the brigadier, who gave a fractional nod.

'Leave the door open, please.'

Majid made no reply. With difficulty he walked stiff-legged across the beautiful giant-sized Bokhara rug that covered most of the room, to his private dressing room. He did as he'd been told. With the door open, he washed his hands noisily then leaned over the lavatory and flushed the cistern. Unobserved from the office, he crept across the dressing room and silently slid back a section of the louvred wardrobe that ran from one side of the room to the other. The Russian-made 9mm Makarov was in its shiny leather holster on one of the shelves. With a single movement he grasped its butt, slid it out of the holster, cocked it and put the muzzle into his mouth. He bit hard on the unyielding metal, closed his eyes and, after a moment's hesitation, squeezed the trigger.

The major had just reached the dressing-room door when the explosion blasted his eardrums. The brigadier, shaken out of his casual manner, moved up quickly behind him and gazed at the mess over his shoulder. The cigarette was still pursed drily between his lips as he studied Majid's twitching limbs coolly for a moment then touched the major lightly on the shoulder. 'If I were you, Sa'dun, I'd pick up that gun and do the same for yourself. Our beloved

Tikriti was rather lookng forward to an afternoon's sport with his niece's husband; I think your news is going to somewhat ruin his day!'

The brigadier had underestimated Tikriti's anger.

After he'd demoted the major to the rank of corporal and had him posted to an anti-aircraft battery in the northern wilderness of Mosul he called in Abu Dahti, one of the top killer specialists of the GID. Dahti had more than proved his value in the tracking down and elimination of British special force infiltrators during the late Kuwait adventure and Tikriti wasted no words on his brief. Simple. Track down the American spy, Macauley, and find out what were his dealings with General Kamel al-Majid. Then kill him.

Sabba'a al-Tikriti stared at the thick dossier in front of him. It was all there – the extent of Majid's involvement in state affairs; his knowledge of sensitive issues; the enormity of the damage he could have inflicted on the regime. Tikriti's face was set for thunder. It went deeper than that. The nature of Majid's dealings with the representative of the 'Great Satan' – and it hadn't been a problem to identify who and what this particular representative, Macauley was was of more than academic value. Tikriti opened the dossier at random and glanced at a list of the confidential and restricted files that had passed through Majid's hands. Details of any one of them would give untold political and military advantage to the Americans. But it was more damaging than that – as if that wasn't bad enough. It was the spectre of a gloating Western world and the ridicule of the Arab Muslim over one of the Family treating with the 'Great Satan'. That, in itself, should have cost the traitor several days of unremitting pain. But it must never come to that. The announcement of Majid's death would have to be withheld until the extent of his betrayal could be established. It would have been better if he'd been thrown into the desert where the hyenas could have picked over his rotting flesh. Tikriti gave himself some small satisfaction in relishing the picture. But his satisfaction didn't last long. He knew that when the time came Lieutenant-General Kamel al-Majid, the great revolutionary leader Saddam Hussein's own son-in-law, would have 'died bravely in action defending the Homeland and the Revolution'. The bile at the thought of a hero's state funeral for the treacherous pig would stick in the throat of Sabba'a al-Tikriti for a long time.

Abu Dahti set about his mission with enthusiasm. The thought of coming to grips again with an agent of the Great Satan generated a feeling of warm anticipation. He hated America. This was personal; it was going to be a labour of great love.

'Confidential' had been Tikriti's admonition. No inside help; no contact outside the iron doors of GID HQ. But he couldn't do it alone. It took less than a fraction of a second's reflection to disobey the first of Tikriti's edicts. He sent for Abdul Qasim.

Abdul Qasim was no ordinary agent. Dahti's right hand, closer than his brother, the name Abdul Qasim had been buried in the vaults of GID Baghdad's headquarters since the end of the Kuwait war. Now, blessed with the codename 'Razak' for the rest of his life, he was building a new reputation for cold, efficient cruelty. He'd made himself a target for American and British retaliatory measures following his activities as Dahti's deputy in the Iraq Special Group concerned with Allied infiltration into the Iraq homeland. He had excelled in the inhumane treatment of captured British SAS members on long-range penetration operations. His handling of prisoners of war had been brutal and incisive and at least two deaths were attributed to his hand. The interrogation and torture of those who survived the ordeal was a nightmare that would haunt them for the rest of their lives.

Held in high esteem by Saddam Hussein himself, every step was taken to protect Qasim from the retribution of the British government. His next assignment, to penetrate Iran's intelligence service the SAVAK, he had done with such success that his new masters appointed him to an operational role with the SAVAK-inspired Hezbollah in Lebanon.

Dahti had no difficulty in tracking him down. Razak had made hostage-taking his new speciality, but at a word from his erstwhile friend and commander he left his current commitments in Beirut to a deputy and attached himself temporarily to Abu Dahti's new mission. Under instruction from Dahti he made arrangements to leave for Amman that day.

4

Mohammed Faruq took his job very seriously. After twenty-three years as a chauffeur at the American embassy in Amman he was considered honest, trustworthy and a loyal servant of the US Mission. He was all of these things, which is why the Ambassador had no hesitation in entrusting the president's personal representative, Thurston Macauley, into his hands.

With two Arab Legion NCOs as escort they left the embassy compound early in the morning in a solid six-seater Japanese four-wheel drive and headed into the rising sun for the parched and arid area of Az-Zarqa and the beginning of the Ash-Sham desert. Had Macauley been an ordinary American tourist his chances of being granted permission by the Jordan military authorities to wander off into the desert in the direction of the Iraq border would have been precisely nil. But Thurston Macauley wasn't an ordinary American tourist, he was a noted Arabist, and they were hard put to refuse a direct request from the US Ambassador for Macauley, as he put it, to spend a few days in one of the world's most interesting deserts. Finally they agreed, but with limitations and the insistence that he be accompanied by bodyguards chosen by them. The bodyguards were well briefed by their superiors.

Faruq welcomed the trip. He warned his wife that he'd be away for three or four days and nights with an American VIP tourist who wanted to see the country. Faruq could afford to be cynical. There wasn't much there for the American to see, he told her, except sand, hills, uneducated Bedouins and filthy camels ... Very funny people, American tourists! She didn't mind. There was nothing unusual in Faruq staying away overnight; it happened at infrequent intervals and she was accustomed to it. It was his job. He was well paid. Who was she to object? Her sister, who lived in central Amman, thought it would be a good time to spend a night or two away from her husband. It showed them, she told her sister, what it was like to live for a night or two in a house without a woman. Not too long, mind you; not long enough to feel the freedom of a man unattached. Two nights were enough. Her husband was not displeased. He could spend a few more hours in the evening when the bank closed sitting in his favourite café – a game of cards, a few glasses of coffee, a couple of *shwarma* – fresh bread stuffed with slices of newly grilled young lamb – and a rekindled interest in looking at the girls from the offices on their way home. He agreed with his wife's unspoken philosophy. It was nice to be free – but not for too long. An empty bed was a cold and empty place once the novelty had worn off.

He was quickly joined by three unmarried friends who mocked his new freedom. The jokes and banter came fast and furious.

'How can you be sure your wife hasn't gone to spend a few days with her lover?'

'My wife doesn't need a lover with me around!'

'So where has she gone, leaving a great stallion like yourself on the loose?'

'To keep her sister company.'

'A likely story. Your brother-in-law needs someone to keep his wife company. He's such a bore? Doesn't he talk to her?'

The waiter, a taciturn, middle-aged Iraqi, refilled their

glasses with coffee and hovered to enjoy the fun. He stayed listening and smiling at the appropriate times until the party broke up and the little gang of friends went on their way. Early in the morning, after he'd helped close the now empty café he made his way down Abdullah Isa Street and drew up a plastic chair at a table of one of the all-night stalls. Smoking a cigarette, he sat under the flickering pressure lamp sipping a glass of thick sweet tea. Soon he was joined by a man of similar appearance: dark blue baggy trousers, white shirt open at the neck and scruffy, broken down-at-the-heel once black shoes, no socks. On his wrist he wore the essential heavy, artificial gold bracelet of an imitation Rolex 'Oysterdate Perpetual' which flopped loosely round his wrist like an identity chain. He glanced down at this before ordering coffee and taking an unopened packet of cigarettes from his shirt pocket. He stripped the cellophane and threw it on the dusty floor. It didn't look out of place – the surroundings of the stalls hadn't been swept or tidied since the beginning of the Gulf War. When he'd lit his cigarette he passed the packet across the table.

'I have a request from Abu Dahti,' he said from behind the hand holding the cigarette at his mouth.

The waiter threw his almost spent cigarette on to the ground and selected another from the packet, lighting it with a cheap disposable lighter.

'He's looking for an American,' continued the new arrival.

The waiter inhaled deeply. This time he held it, allowing the smoke to escape only when he spoke. 'One thing Amman is not short of, my brother, is Americans. Is there anything special about this one?'

The other man shrugged his shoulders. 'There must be if Abu Dahti has taken an interest in him. I have seen this American, I have watched him, and I have photographed him. I walked with him to the American embassy. He was allowed in without having his identification checked, which means he is important, very important. But he is not on the list of embassy staff, permanent or otherwise. He is, therefore, here in Amman on a mission . . .'

'When did you last see him?'

'Friday. I watched him from the grounds of the mosque.'

'How did he become your target?'

'He wasn't. He appeared in the same place as the person I was studying; a routine watch. But things have developed from this meeting, if indeed meeting it was. It might have been coincidence but obviously it wasn't, as the great Sabba'a al-Tikriti has taken a personal interest.'

'And Abu Dahti is his instrument? Who was this person you were watching who has coincidental meetings with official Americans?'

'I cannot say.'

The waiter studied his companion's face by the light of the flickering, hissing lamp while he ran things over in his mind. Tikriti, Dahti, embassy Americans . . . the mixture made an intriguing plot but he slapped his curiosity back into the recesses of his mind. The actions of Tikriti and Dahti were not for the interest of a low-rank agent sleeper in cooperative Jordan.

'Anyone else?' he asked at length.

'Razak.'

'Ahhh — the full set.' The smoke from the glowing cigarette hissed into the waiter's lungs again. 'What makes you think the American in question is still in Jordan?'

'I've been watching the airport since yesterday. Our people working in Jordan immigration have copies of his photograph. He hasn't left the country and as far as I can find out he's not at present in the embassy confines. He is somewhere on the loose.'

The waiter sipped a new glass of tea and closed his eyes.

31

He was tired. He'd done a long day's menial labour – GID was a hard taskmaster. But a thought had come to him.

'You don't like coincidence, my brother?'

'I view it with suspicion.'

'Then try not to let suspicion cloud your judgement. Listen. There's a man who works in the Royal Bank of Amman, comes regularly to the café, stays no longer than an hour in the evenings and then goes home to his wife. He has several friends who do likewise. This evening the bank clerk stayed late because his wife has gone to stay with her sister . . .' he paused again as if wondering himself whether this had any relevance to his colleague's quest. 'The sister's husband, I gathered, has gone away for a few nights so the wife sought her sister's companionship . . .' he stopped again. The other man had had enough.

'How does this idiot who leaves his wife for several days become involved in Dahti and Razak's search for an American embassy official?'

'The idiot who has left his wife for a few days is a permanent member of the American embassy drivers pool. He drives American officials and VIPs around the city, and into the *badw* when the urge to go and look at the poor of the country milking their camels strikes them,' he said acidly.

'How do you know of this?' The cynicism had gone from the other Iraqi's voice, replaced by a sharp edge of interest.

'The bank clerk's friends were making fun of his plight. I stayed nearby to enjoy the fun – if fun you can call the idiotic banter of immature *badawi*. May I continue . . . ?' He didn't wait for the other man's permission. 'This driver has been ordered to drive an American on a sightseeing tour of the sand. The American is a visitor to Jordan – Amman. If this man has access to official American embassy transport and chauffeur he must be an official, possibly VIP.

32

Coincidence, my friend, that you mistrust. But how does that match the description of Abu Dahti's American?'

The other man studied the waiter's face for several seconds then bared his lips in a smile. 'Brilliant!'

But the waiter wasn't interested in commendation. He continued sucking at his cigarette and closed his eyes again. He'd got a job. He'd got two jobs. He was an agent of Iraqi Intelligence and he was a waiter in the popular café in the *souk*. In his mind he did both jobs well. Sabba'a al-Tikriti knowing about it wouldn't make him any more proficient at either.

Abu Dahti and Razak brought the entire GID Amman apparatus into play. The embassy driver's house was put under twenty-four-hour watch and a description of the vehicle he had left in obtained by the waiter. The American embassy and the main routes into Amman from the east were watched continually, and the airport staff employed by Iraq Intelligence was reinforced by a sophisticated watching team. Once back in Amman Macauley would never be allowed to move without Razak and Abu Dahti knowing every step he took.

Three days after the waiter had passed on his information to GID's Amman resident agent the 4 × 4 truck was spotted and tracked back to the embassy. On its way through the city a series of profile photographs were taken of Macauley and the Jordanian driver. From these the resident had no difficulty in identifying the man he had photographed at the hotel and followed to the embassy.

Razak and Dahti decided to take Macauley on his way to the airport.

But then things started to go wrong for them.

Macauley had seen everything he needed to see to convince himself of what he'd been fairly sure of in the first place –

that Majid had been on the level and the map was totally authentic. He was even more convinced that the West had got themselves a problem; a much bigger one than they'd ever thought possible. Saddam Hussein hadn't got a nuclear bomb – but he wasn't far off it. Without making a nuisance of himself Macauley had confirmed one of the map references, and the signs were all in place that Saddam Hussein's nuclear weapons industry was alive and with very little effort would be thriving. Macauley reckoned that with the details of progress supplied by Majid and a definite sighting of nuclear manufacture installations in the Ash-Sham desert it wouldn't take more than a couple of years before there were some very heavy Iraqi fists being banged on the table in New York. George Bush was going to regret for evermore that he hadn't allowed Norman Schwarzkopf to march into Baghdad and dismantle the whole bloody shooting works – Saddam and all.

Twenty-four hours before his scheduled contact with Majid, Macauley was summoned to the embassy basement communications centre for a scrambled link with the White House in Washington.

Joe Doerflinger wasted no words on civilities or greetings. 'Mac, Majid has gone out of circulation. There's a sudden shyness around the Ministry of Defence in Baghdad and our contact reckons there's something ominous about Majid's non-appearance at yesterday's emergency council meeting. His family's gone too. His town house is empty except for an increased guard presence. Looks like he's been split open. How did you leave it with him? Have you exchanged contracts?'

Macauley stared, expressionless at the blank concrete wall. His thinking was already ahead of Doerflinger. 'No – like I said, he put his stuff on the table. I held everything back until I verified it.'

'And?'

'It's all here — like he said.'

'OK, then. We'd better assume Majid has talked to GID. I don't think they'll do anything — there's not a lot they can do short of moving these places around the desert like chess pieces — and that's what they ain't. So, Mac, I reckon they'll hold off, just to make sure that something did pass. Majid may have died before he compromised you.'

'That would be the good news, Joe,' said Macauley without feeling.

'Sure. Even if Majid did talk the Iraqis won't tell Jordan what's happened — they'll just go in quietly and start moving stuff around. Importantly, though, Mac, we've got to be kept right out of it if possible. Are you following me?'

'How're you going to keep Jordan out of a thing like this? The bloody thing's going on in their back yard.'

'Not your problem, Mac. We have a President who's elected and paid handsomely to work out that sort of detail. I'm more worried about the immediate. That means you — '

'I've got the message, Joe. I'm moving out now.'

'Get rid of everything first. No papers, no notes. Nothing. Don't leave anything around in the embassy. Just make sure everything's in your head. Got it?'

'It's a very clear picture.'

'Good. Can you ship out of Amman with another name — just in case Majid described you to GID?'

'No problem. I'll go out domestic and change to Pan Am at Rome. If they have marked me and I start jumping in and out of an airforce bus they'll know for sure that I've got something. When I get to Rome I'll act the innocent abroad for a night and revert for the trip home. If they're on to me they'll expect me to make a dash for the States; a night in the Rome fleshpots'll throw them. One thing, Joe . . .'

'Go on.'

'No friends here or Rome. They attract attention. I can

35

look after myself better than with some Charlie tagging along in the background. OK?'

'OK. Ring me from Rome.'

'Why?'

'No reason. Don't get lost.'

The following morning Thurston Macauley, casually dressed, joined the members of the Marines detachment returning to the States on rotation in a small unmarked twelve-seater bus. He made no attempt to conceal himself and to his fellow passengers he was just another guy catching a lift to the airport. For anybody outside the embassy who might be interested he had nothing to hide; he was on a routine passage. The bus pulled out of the embassy compound and slowed down to walking pace to negotiate the 'Khomeini stepping-stones'. It gave the GID watcher ample time to study all the occupants. He had no difficulty identifying Macauley.

But Razak was taken unawares. They had been expecting Macauley in a lightweight suit, as befitting an official of the American embassy, briefcase and official embassy car with a middle-aged Jordanian chauffeur. What they weren't expecting, and hadn't catered for, was Macauley and several members of the toughest fighting force in the world. It threw all their plans into the nearest dustbin. Even if they were able to re-muster at nil notice a fighting force large enough to ambush the bus it would still be a non-starter. An accident on the way to Amman's international airport and the disappearance of a solitary American tourist would raise little dust among the world's media; but the ambush, pitched battle and killing of a party of United States Marines of the embassy detail on their way home and the abduction of an American civilian would bring not only the wrath of Jordan's establishment on their heads but the wrath of their own people in Baghdad.

'Get in touch with your people at the airport,' Razak demanded of the man helping him. 'Find out where they're going and then get word to Dahti.'

After several minutes the Iraqi agent rejoined Razak. 'Dahti has reached the airport,' he informed him. 'He is now aware that your plan has failed.' There was a hint of reprobation in his voice but Razak ignored it.

'Never mind that. Has he been told that there are now several passengers?'

'Yes. He said you are to join him at the airport without delay. Meet him at the main concourse.' He stood his ground as Razak marched towards their battered car. 'What do you want me to do now?'

Razak didn't slow down. 'As Dahti said. Don't waste time. Drive the car. Go as quickly as possible but don't break any laws.'

Dahti had taken it all in his stride. He looked totally unflustered when Razak spotted him. There was a moment's visual contact; a brief eye message, and Razak followed him into the washroom. They occupied a basin each leaving an empty one between them, turned both taps on and began washing their hands. Nobody stayed long enough to disturb them and as they talked they looked not at each other but into the mirror, all the time studying the washroom activity behind them.

'All the Americans you saw,' murmured Dahti with hardly any lip movement, 'are booked Royal Jordanian to Rome. All except one have an outward connection with Pan American to New York after a two-hour delay in Rome. Macauley has a single ticket. Rome. No onward booking. I've arranged for a team of our people to take him at Leonardo da Vinci.'

5

This time it went without a hitch.

The man standing in front of Macauley in the queue for taxis at the main entrance to Rome's Leonardo da Vinci airport raised his hand and waggled his fingers at a taxi. As if from nowhere an aged, two-tone blue and white Mercedes 230SE with heavily smoked-glass windows cut in front of the slow-moving taxi and stopped at the head of the queue. The taxi's horn screeched indignantly and the driver's arms flailed in the air. The man with his hand raised ignored him and climbed into the back seat of the Mercedes. He left the door open. Macauley felt the muzzle of the gun grind alongside his spine just above his trouser waistband and was pushed bodily into the back of the car. Before he could recover his balance a hand grasped his shirt and he was pulled further in. There was now a revolver in the passenger's hand which was jammed into the side of his neck as the man behind him crowded into the car. Macauley was sandwiched between the two men, his hands between his legs, a revolver in his neck and an automatic grinding into his side.

As the Mercedes pulled away the irate taxi driver gave another toot on his horn. But it lacked venom. The driver had just seen something he didn't like and quickly looked in another direction. By the time he'd taken the place of the Mercedes at the head of the queue and opened the door for the waiting passenger the Mercedes had filtered unobtrusively into the mass of traffic heading out of the airport going towards Lido di Ostia. Macauley's abduction in the full glare of an international airport, in broad daylight, had taken less than thirty seconds, and nobody had noticed it except a taxi driver who didn't want to know.

The Mercedes did a tour of Ostia before cutting back towards the airport and turning off the road. It circumnavigated the extreme perimeter of the airport surroundings and approached the southern extreme along a disused road that led into an area of the old airport now awaiting redevelopment. The driver pulled into a large, derelict hangar. Their nearest neighbour, a good mile across the old runway system, was a private flying club, its presence defined only by dim lights reflected in a rain-filled crater.

Macauley was dumped roughly against the rusty metal wall. He was unconscious. There had been no finesse about it; the Iraqis used the short method — they had beaten him around the head and face with their pistols until he passed out. They weren't worried about a bit of blood. By the time Dahti and Razak arrived Macauley was curled up on the floor, his hands and legs tied tightly behind him and his three abductors standing over him smoking and laughing at their own private jokes as they gave the occasional absentminded kick to the unconscious American's body and head.

Dahti took charge. He greeted the three men with a casual nod at Macauley's body. 'Israeli,' he explained. It was the only explanation they were going to get. Their interest revived, the men studied the American again and this time, jamming their smouldering cigarettes into their mouths set about kicking his head with purpose and renewed vigour. The driver, braver than his two companions, grabbed the bound man's hands, pulled him on to his front and searched with his pointed dirty shoe for Macauley's crotch. Having

39

located his target he brought his foot back and with a triumphant cry of 'Yehudi, kiss im'mak!' kicked him with all the strength of his stubby legs. The others liked it. They joined in until Dahti, impatient to get on with his part of the job, broke up their game and dismissed them. The driver who had brought him and Razak to the hangar was ordered to leave with the men after concealing his car. His disappointment showed, but there were no arguments – Abu Dahti was a name of consequence. His word was not for questioning.

When the four Iraqis had left, Dahti and Razak set about bringing Macauley back to consciouness.

They squatted him on his knees, hands still tied behind his back and roped to his ankles. The position was excruciating and as he came round he did so with a low moan which intensified as his consciousness slowly returned and became a full-throated scream of agony.

The unholy noise echoed hollowly around the vast area of the hangar, but it didn't disturb the two Iraqis. Before his eyes began to focus they covered the top part of his face with a metre of oily cheesecloth then stood back and leaned against the wall smoking cigarettes while they waited for the screams to abate.

Razak was the first to lose patience.

He placed the sole of his shoe against Macauley's face and slammed his head hard against the wall. The shock cut Macauley's scream to a startled choke. Then silence.

'Who's there?' gurgled Macauley. His mouth wasn't working properly; his tongue felt like a piece of uncooked liver. The words refused to form, his teeth were loose and his brain beyond reasoning. He moved his head this way and that trying to locate the presence of other beings. 'Say something, for God's sake – ' he managed to articulate.

'What is your name?' asked Dahti.

'Who are you?'

40

Macauley felt his head slammed back against the metal wall, then a hand grabbed his hair and his face was pulled forward and pointed upwards.

'Don't ask questions – answer them. What is your name?'

Macauley made no reply. The sigh from Dahti was almost one of pleasure. 'Pull his trousers down,' he said to Razak.

Macauley felt himself roughly handled, thrown on to his side and his belt loosened. His trousers were dragged down over his hips to his knees. As one pair of rough hands left him another took their place and he felt the sharp point of a knife touch his stomach. As he tried to pull away there was a downward cut and a ripping sound as his underpants were sliced open.

The next moment he was hauled up and rammed against the wall. As he slithered downward a foot in his chest arrested the movement so that he was propped up on his knees. He shivered at the cold vulnerability of his exposed genitals and opened his mouth ready to scream when he felt the blade of the knife against his thigh as it sought, found and then raised his penis.

'Name?' repeated Dahti, casually.

'Macauley.'

'What are you, Macauley?'

'American citizen. Tourist – '

The toe of Dahti's shoe caught him just below the left eye and slammed his head hard against the wall behind him. The second blow landed on his mouth: with his head unable to ride the force of the kick he felt two of his teeth dislodge and rattle around inside his mouth. His head came off the wall and hung on his chest allowing a mouthful of blood to cascade down his chest and into his groin. He was allowed five seconds' reflection before his head was thumped back again by a third aimed kick across the bridge of his nose. More blood gushed. It splashed off his chin and,

41

like a small waterfall, poured in a stream to join the earlier puddle formed between his clenched thighs. But it hadn't finished. Over the agony of the repeated blows he felt another, sharper, more frightening pain. The knife was being drawn slowly across his penis. He felt every fraction of every millimetre as it sliced a shallow cut through the sensitive skin. He screamed at the top of his voice and fainted.

The faint didn't last long and Macauley began screaming the moment he came back.

The sharp edge of the blade was placed across the top of his open mouth. The scream choked into the back of his throat and he felt a gush of foul breath close to his face.

'You are a spy,' Dahti hissed. 'You are a spy, you are a spy, you are a *spy*!' He shouted the last word into Macauley's face, stared at him for a moment then took a deep breath. 'You are going to talk to me about your spying or suffer untold pain. So far I haven't even begun to hurt you. You may think about it while I smoke a cigarette.' He turned his head and smiled mirthlessly at Razak. 'Light me one, please.'

Razak did as he was asked. The half-smoked cigarette that Dahti already had he placed carefully on an unbloody portion of Macauley's quivering thigh. It took a second or so for the burning sensation to work its way past the other pains Macauley was suffering. He opened his mouth and screamed as the skin bubbled and burned under the red-hot ember, helpless to dislodge it. After a moment, Dahti picked up a bundle of dirty cotton waste and rammed it hard into Macauley's gaping mouth. The noise died to a whimpering, snotty, unbroken groan from behind the mouthful of greasy waste which worked its way down his nose as the two Iraqis squatted on their heels enjoying their cigarette as they studied the progress of the burning ember on the American's thigh.

42

When it had almost burnt itself out Dahti got to his feet and put his face close to Macauley's.

'Macauley,' he hissed. 'I will continue to hurt you and it will get worse. What you have received so far is very light punishment – a little girl's chastisement for being naughty. My friend and I will now start to really hurt you unless you tell us everything about your business with General Kamel al-Majid.' He stopped to see whether his words were going in and, satisfied, glanced at Razak and nodded. He continued. 'When I take this stuff out of your mouth you will start talking. If you say you know nothing about our General Kamel al-Majid I will not play games with you but I will give you such a half-hour that you will wish you could crawl back into your mother's womb. Understand – your mother's womb ... You will not get a second chance.'

He stood up, balanced his foot over the smouldering cigarette then lowered it and ground the ember into the burnt skin of Macauley's thigh. Macauley's head jerked up like a puppet on a string and crashed noisily against the metal wall. He almost ruptured his throat trying to scream, but nothing came through the dirty cloth in his mouth and, mercifully, he fainted again.

The next time he came round the cotton waste had been removed from his mouth. His arms and legs were totally numb but his face was racked with pain. The incessant banging of his head against the wall behind him had partially dislodged the blindfold, sufficient for him to see a half-inch crack of light when he forced his eyes downwards. When they became accustomed to the light he could see his bare thighs, the red and black scars from the cigarette and, most pathetically, his blood-soaked crotch. But he'd got the message. Majid had been marked. It had always been on the cards. But worse, they'd got his name; and they'd got it right. It was now a question of how much, or how little, these people would accept – and, more importantly, how much, or how little Majid had been made to tell them.

They'd noticed a twitch, and gave him a kick in the side to see if he was receiving. It was a gentle nudge compared with what he'd already received, but it was a little reminder that no man could bear the unrelenting infliction of pain. They were going to get it eventually; he might just as well see how little they'd be satisfied with before they did the final screw. Another kick. And another. Funny, these kicks weren't hurting as much. Maybe their feet were beginning to ache! Maybe he was getting used to being kicked. Another kick –

'Talk!' A dirty black shoe appeared in his slitted vision and rested casually on his thigh. It was almost as if the owner was taking the weight off his other foot while he chatted about the state of the world with his friend. But that's as far as it went. The foot pressed harder, moved slightly to find the centre of the burnt area, then moved from side to side in a scraping motion.

'Talk,' the voice repeated.

Macauley tested his mouth. He was surprised that there was still feeling there after the battering his face had taken. Apart from the odd fit of choking when blood found its way through the nasal passage into his throat his voice came out quite clear.

In halting tones he told the questioners as little as he thought he could get away with; he told them that in repayment of $150 million he had bought Majid's defection to the United States. At the mention of the sum the two Iraqis exchanged glances. Nothing was said. No change of expression. Just a glance – but each man knew instantly what the other was thinking.

'What did General Majid offer to bring with him for this sum?' asked Dahti.

'Nothing. The money was just for his defection. It was to be a political coup for the US. The defection of one of the most senior military members of the Revolutionary Council, Saddam Hussein's own son-in-law, would have shown the world that the President of Iraq was losing control of the Council; that the government was about to crack. That would have given encouragement to anti-Saddam factions to increase their activities – '

Dahti aimed another kick at Macauley's head but there was no venom in it. It was a purely reflex action. He was shaken by the closeness of his country's betrayal by one of its leaders – but the shock, and his contempt for Majid, was overpowered by another emotion. He put it into words.

'Has he been paid this money?'

Macauley shook his head.

It wasn't enough for Dahti. He jabbed his heel into Macauley's groin and put his weight on it. Macauley howled in pain.

'Answer!' screamed Dahti.

'The money wasn't paid.'

'How was it to be paid?'

Macauley hesitated, and got another heel jab.

'Answer immediately. Don't think.'

'It is in a Swiss bank account. The transfer was to be made when Majid arrived in Washington and had given his first press conference . . .' It was spur of the moment but Macauley thought he could live with it.

Dahti and Razak again exchanged glances. They held each other's eyes for a long moment then Dahti jerked his head in the direction of the other end of the hangar. Macauley heard footsteps echo and resound off the tin walls then fade into silence as the two Iraqis stopped, lit cigarettes and squatted on their heels. Macauley strained his ears through the hollow silence but could hear nothing. He had a good idea what was being discussed: $150 million was a sound basis for a very detailed conversation between two Iraqi agents. He also knew that he would live just as long as he held on to the Swiss bank account number and the secret combination giving access to the account. It was a question of how long his body, and his mind, could sustain the form of torture at which these two were obviously very adept.

By flexing his muscles he tested the binding round his wrists but realized immediately he was wasting his time. He shook his head vigorously up and down in an effort to dislodge a little more of the blindfold, and wished he hadn't when the blood began pounding once again through his fractured nerves. Clenching his eyes tightly to try and stem the slicing pain that was cutting through his head, he wriggled himself into a more comfortable position and waited for the next round of punishment.

'Is the pig telling the truth?' whispered Razak.

'Wouldn't you?' Dahti made a rare movement of his lips and exposed his yellow teeth. It was as near as his face would ever come to showing humour. 'He knows he has more punishment to come. What is the point in further lying. Why should he? What can he gain?' His eyes hardened as he studied his old friend's crafty face. 'A hundred and fifty million dollars American,' his voice, low and harsh, took on a note of incredulity. His eyes never left Razak's as he waited for his reaction.

'You think the Americans would pay that much money for the treachery of one man?'

The fencing had begun.

Razak held his gaze. 'There must be more to it – '

Dahti nodded in agreement. 'But one thing at a time, my brother. The American money is a fact. Let us concentrate on that.' So now they were 'brothers'. Razak got the message: they were going to share it. Dahti was on fairly solid ground; he knew Razak well – they'd been through much together. Brothers! Razak's face remained expressionless. 'A man could live the life of several pashas on a fifth of that amount . . .'

'I'd be very happy with such an amount.' Razak had laid his cards face upwards on the table for his 'brother' to see.

'Then we understand each other,' said Dahti.

Razak dropped his cigarette on the dusty floor and ground it underfoot. He studied the mess for a moment then looked back into Dahti's face. He didn't need to say anything. It was all there in his greedy expression.

'Let us continue, then.' Dahti led the way back to where Macauley was lying. He noticed his changed position, tested his bonds and without removing the oily cloth around Macauley's eyes tightened it. He kicked him to let him know the interrogation was about to start again.

'Macauley?'

'Uhhh . . .'

'He offered no exchange for this money?'

'No.'

'No secrets, no documents — nothing?'

'Just himself.'

The two Iraqis exchanged glances again. They'd done their duty for their country. Its secrets were safe. Now for the life of pashas. 'Do you know who we are?' Dahti asked Macauley.

Macauley shook his head once.

It was enough for Dahti. 'We are officers of the Iraq Intelligence Service. We intend taking you back with us to Baghdad where you will be further interrogated and then brought to trial for the attempted corruption of Iraqi military personnel. The sentence in my country for such crimes is death.' Dahti paused and studied the thin hair on top of Macauley's bowed head. 'Or we could kill you here and now.'

Macauley made no movement.

47

Dahti kicked his head. 'Do you hear me, Macauley? We could kill you here and now.'

'I hear you,' mumbled Macauley.

'There is an alternative.'

Macauley knew what the alternative was. He didn't hold his breath. He'd spent many years in the Middle East, he knew his Arabs; and he knew the words to the music – it was a common tune – it was called graft.

'You tell me how and where this money is lodged; how it was to be transferred to General Majid's name; what name the account is in and the number of the account.' He waited again, then glanced sideways at Razak.

'Macauley, we are offering you your freedom.'

Like hell you are! Macauley kept his head lowered and, as far as he could, out of the line of fire and waited for the kicking to start again.

Nothing happened.

'Do you understand what I am saying?' insisted Razak.

Macauley kept his head down. 'I can't help you.' He wished he could see what was happening. The silence was oppressive. It went on for quite a long time – until Razak spoke again.

'Why do you want us to hurt you more? You are going to have to help us in the end. You know that. No man can stand the amount of pain that we are capable of inflicting on you, so why don't you help us so that we can send you back to the airport and you can catch your aeroplane home . . .' Razak's voice took on a wheedling tone. He couldn't understand why a man would allow himself to be hurt when it would be so simple to get it over quickly. He put his thoughts into words. 'It's only money, Macauley. And it's not even yours . . .'

It all sounded so reasonable and logical to Macauley in his painful and dark world, but he knew he'd given them the reason to keep him alive. It was now a simple equation –

48

tell them nothing and be beaten to death slowly and
painfully, or give them the money and die quickly with no
pain. Razak was being generous. But Macauley wasn't
made that way – he chose the first option.

'I can't help you.'

The two Iraqi agents took off their jackets slowly and
went to work.

After twelve hours all they'd succeeded in doing was to
reduce Macauley to a blood-splattered wreck.

He'd told them nothing more. The periods of unconsciousness were becoming longer and more frequent and it
was taking longer to bring him round. His screams were
becoming weaker and more difficult to force through his
swollen throat but the two Iraqis, although running out of
ideas, were nowhere near to giving up. They squatted with
their backs against the wall, smoked cigarettes and stared
morosely at the unconscious figure curled up beside them.

'He will talk,' Dahti was reassuring himself rather then
Razak. 'Nobody can stand this treatment. He must talk . . .'

'I know,' said Razak and spat into the dust at his feet.
'But when?' He glanced casually at the watch on his wrist
and sounded the first note of caution. 'And what about
Baghdad?'

'Baghdad?' Dahti turned his head and frowned into
Razak's eyes. 'What about Baghdad?'

'They'll be expecting you to report. Al-Mukhabarat's
Rome centre will have reported this afternoon's happening
to Control and they will have by now passed it on to
Tikriti. He will want to know what's happening to this – '
he gestured with his chin at Macauley. 'He's probably
sitting in his office this very minute waiting to hear from
you . . .'

Dahti stared at him. He was exhausted. It had always
been one of his failings, the inability to delegate; the inner

49

compulsion to administer the punishment himself. This American had met them head on. He hadn't broken – and at this rate he wouldn't. But Dahti knew that time was his mistress; all he needed was time and he wasn't going to get it here in this rusty hangar on the outskirts of Rome. 'I'm not concerned with Baghdad, at the moment,' he said after a while. 'But I am concerned about the security of this place. It was not the intention that we spend this length of time here.'

'Then we'll have to move him,' said Razak.

'Where do you suggest?'

Razak had worked it all out. But he had to make it appear as if it were reluctantly being dragged out of him. 'Somewhere with a hole in the ground; somewhere where this creature's friends can't come looking. It has to be Iraq.'

Dahti shook his head. 'No. Somewhere out of reach of Tikriti. Somewhere where GID is not welcome. Do you know such a place?'

Razak nodded seriously. 'Yes.' He paused. 'And so do you.'

Dahti wasn't in the mood for conundrums. 'No more games, Razak. Make your suggestion.'

'Beirut.'

Dahti hawked his throat and spat in the dust again, but before he could argue Razak added '. . . I have a loyal team of Hezbollah already there guarding a prisoner in a place unknown to anyone else. It is as safe and secure as the bunker under Tikriti's own building in Baghdad.' He prodded Macauley's body with his foot. 'This will never be traced to Beirut – ' he glanced at Dahti's sceptical expression – 'and neither will we.' He returned his gaze to Macauley as he spoke, '. . . but one thing is certain, my friend, we can't stay here indefinitely.'

Dahti was already aware of that. He'd also given thought to the reach of Tikriti's influence. Tikriti was a man who could inflict the most severe punishment at great distances and Rome was but a spit from the Ministry building in Baghdad. Not only could they not stop here; they must make sure that when they left no one knew where they had gone. Not easy. 'Beirut is over 2,000 kilometres away,' he said grudgingly.

Razak pointed his thumb at the east wall of the hangar. 'Flying club,' he said. 'Less than two kilometres.'

'– and will leave a trail directly to Beirut.'

'No, my friend. You forget, whilst you, an Iraqi of GID, have no influence or welcome here, I am now an Iranian and a trusted member of Iran's SAVAK and Rome looks upon us kindly . . .' He glanced sideways at the scowling Dahti. 'Tread carefully, my brother, and put your trust in me.'

'Stop talking, then, and say something.'

Razak smirked contentedly. He had established his leadership. Dahti would do as he was told. 'Iran has a strong apparatus in Rome with close Hezbollah connections. I know personally the SAVAK resident at the Iranian embassy. A short word and he will arrange for us to fly out of Rome in a private aircraft.'

'And tell him you have a captured American you wish to bury in Beirut!' snapped Dahti. 'You're talking like a fool, Razak.'

Razak smiled through his tiredness. 'I have a captured Israeli I wish to bury in Beirut – for barter purposes!' He stretched his foot out and jabbed Macauley's battered body several times in the back. 'And this is the Israeli – '

The Iranian SAVAK organization within the Rome embassy did its stuff with no more than a slightly raised eyebrow.

A light Cessna aircraft, privately logged, was waiting just

off the end of the runway in the club area of Leonardo da Vinci airport at eight the next morning. Razak and Dahti smuggled Macauley's unconscious and battered body out of the car and bundled him on to the two rear seats at the back of the aircraft.

'We're going to Cyprus,' Razak told Dahti when they were installed in the plane. 'Getting clearance for Beirut was too risky, and besides, the Israelis have a continual watch on that area. They consider all Lebanese air space as theirs.'

'And at Cyprus?' Dahti was only half serious. They were now in Razak's territory. He could afford to play second fiddle and let Razak take the weight.

'SAVAK has a boat at Larnaca, but this is under continual survey by Mossad elements. It has been arranged for the boat to put to sea and when out of sight to come back and wait for us near a place called Mazotos. There'll be a car waiting at the Larnaca flying club to take us to this village – it's about twenty kilometres south-west of the harbour and from there it's a short sea trip of about 250 kilometres to Al-Batron.'

'How far is that from your place in Beirut?'

'About fifty kilometres. But no problems – a clear road, no blocks, a straight run into the north end of the city. Be happy, brother, our problems are almost over.'

'So you say,' murmured Dahti, his voice thick with scepticism. 'What about Israeli gunboats?'

'They don't patrol that far north, which is why we're going slightly out of our way. Leave it to me . . .'

Dahti studied his friend for a moment then closed his eyes and didn't wake up until the small aircraft touched down at Larnaca. Keeping well away from the main airport it taxied, without attracting interest, to a slot in the area reserved for private aircraft. There was no interference or curiosity from Cyprus's pro-Palestinian customs and immigration department or its non-existent anti-terrorist organization.

Macauley's body, now wrapped tightly head to toe in grey plastic tape with a small opening at his nose for breathing, was left in the Cessna's small luggage hold until darkness fell over the airport surrounds. When the time came, and with the Italian pilot entertaining the airport police, the two Iraqis manhandled the bundle into the boot of a waiting car and, avoiding the Larnaca motorway and main road, the SAVAK-employed Cypriot driver followed the secondary road signs to the unmade-up track that descended to Mazotos.

The boat was already there. Nothing pretentious. If it was going to draw attention to itself it would be by decrepitude. It was nothing more than a peasant fishing boat with a solid engine, one-man crew and enough netting and gear to justify to an Israeli gunboat that it was on a peaceful and innocent fishing expedition.

There was a special compartment below the water line and under the engine-room planking – a six-foot-long, twelve-inch-high by two-feet wide slot between the secondary ribs of the hull. It was into this claustrophobic nightmare that Macauley's body was jammed. Any air that filtered through the boards was saturated with diesel fumes and the clankety clankety clank of the big Perkins drowned out all other sounds. Macauley, nearer dead than alive, was unfortunate to remain sufficiently awake to be fully aware of his position. But he couldn't even cry or fight his horror by shouting and screaming; he had to lie, unable to move any part of his body; unable to breathe; unable to see. All he could do was pray for death or unconsciousness. A corpse in a coffin would have been more comfortable.

As soon as the engine room was restored and Razak and Dahti installed in the cabin and out of sight, the boatman

53

cast off from the rough jetty and headed quietly away from the shore and into the open sea.

Abu Dahti sat at the stern of the boat and stared morosely at the phosphorescent wash sent up by the Perkins's screw. A thin watery moon slipped in and out of black clouds, giving little illumination to the surrounding sea. Boats were not Dahti's thing. He preferred dry land. This stuff gave him an inferiority complex; he was totally dependent on another person's ability. It didn't suit his temperament.

Razak studied the back of his friend's head from his reclining position on the bunk in the dirty cabin and wondered what was going through his mind. His own thoughts were of no particular surprise to him; they were inevitable once the figure of $150 million had been pronounced. It was a lot of money, and now the question that ran through his mind was where friendship ended and partnership began. Partnership meant equal shares; it also meant that two people shared a secret that would be much safer in the mind of just one of them. But the money . . . He could live a most interesting life with a sum of that magnitude; it would more than make up for the vicissitudes of a lifetime dedicated to the dictates of the Revolutionary Council and would in some small way help him live with the stigma of desertion. Having readjusted his conscience Razak closed his eyes and thought about what had to be done.

It didn't take long.

Through hooded eyes he studied again the back of his friend's head. The solution was a simple one – Dahti had to go. Razak's eyes glowed with resolution as he turned his head and studied the figure of the boatman in the ramshackle wheelhouse. There was a small problem with a simple solution – he could go overboard as well. But who then was going to put this stinking tub through the

treacherous waters off the north Lebanese coast? Not
Razak. He was no more of a sailor than his old friend and
co-conspirator Abu Dahti.

OK. The boatman lives and Abu Dahti has an accident.
Subtlety. A silent accident. Razak continued to study the
man in the wheelhouse. From where Razak sat he looked
asleep; he was lounging in a grimy wicker chair, his bare
feet propped on the ledge beside the wheel and throttle.
Every so often the wheel creaked and complained and a
black, oily toe reached out and inched the wheel back into
line. He, at least, knew where he was going; he was the
only man on the boat who did and he was literally doing it
in his sleep.

Razak dismissed the boatman from his thoughts and
turned his head back to Dahti. He hadn't moved. Maybe he
was sleeping too. Unlikely. Without moving from his
position Razak reached for the heavy service 9mm Beretta
lodged in the mattress beside him. Silently he eased the slide
back a fraction and checked there was a round in the
breech. Dahti's pistol was where he'd laid it earlier, on the
gallery above the back of the opposite bench seat, which left
him with only his bare hands. But Dahti's hands weren't
ordinary hands, any more than Dahti was an ordinary man.
With several senses and the instincts of a jackal at bay, his
ability to stay alive had been honed to a fine edge by a life
of murder, cheating, torture and intrigue. Abu Dahti would
be a very difficult man to take unawares. But Razak had a
small point in his favour. Abu Dahti trusted him; he was
his friend.

Razak's hands were steady as he tucked the Beretta into
his trouser band; it was a last resort — silence was the key
and it would have to be quick. There must be no chance
for Abu Dahti and nothing for the dozing boatman to talk
about later.

He stood up and stretched, then, as a second thought,

55

reached for a packet of cigarettes and the disposable lighter
sitting on the ledge, before padding in his bare feet across
the cabin. He stopped at the door and waited, leaning
against the after cabin and studied Dahti's back. It was the
perfect target.

But he'd been right about Dahti's senses.

Even as he stood contemplating the back of Dahti's oily
head and selecting the spot for his first blow the head came
round slowly and met his eyes. Razak kept his neutral
expression and stared back across the deck, dimly illumi-
nated by the light escaping from the open cabin door.
There was nothing, either, in Dahti's eyes – no suspicion,
no query: it was a look without a message.

But Razak felt that familiar fear, the electric tingling
between his legs. There was something about this man –
Razak was sure he knew what was about to happen. He
held up the packet of cigarettes invitingly and made his way
across the debris of netting, rope and tackle haphazardly
strewn around the narrow confines of the after deck and
joined Dahti at the stern. He selected two cigarettes, stuck
one between his teeth and handed the other to Dahti. He
produced the lighter from his trouser pocket with his left
hand, flicked it into life under his own cigarette then held it
out, chest high, allowing Dahti to cup his hands around it
and lower his cigarette against the flame.

Dahti's bowed head was the invitation.

Razak dropped his right hand to the butt of the Beretta at
his hip. With one movement it was out of his waistband.
He hammered with all his might against the back of Dahti's
bowed head. The cigarette shot out of his mouth like a
bullet and landed in a shower of sparks on the deck at his
feet; his hand came up in an instinctive defensive arm jab
and tried to grab Razak's rapidly moving hand. But Razak
was winding up for another blow and the first smash had
slowed Dahti's reflexes. The Beretta slammed into Dahti's

56

face and across his nose. Tears blinded him but still he tore at his friend's shadow. There was no noise. No shout, no grunt — just the sound of bone crunching as yet another blow smashed into his face out of the gloom. His knees buckled as Razak delivered his round-arm *coup de grâce*. Dahti slammed on to his knees, where he remained for a second before his face crashed into the deck.

Razak bent down, grabbed a handful of Dahti's hair, pulled his head and shoulders off the ground and with all the power of his stubby, muscular legs hammered his knee into Dahti's bloody face. Dahti gave a throaty bark, a series of muted liquid coughs and collapsed once more in an untidy, death-like heap at Razak's feet.

Razak gave a quick glance over his shoulder at the wheelhouse. There was no change. The old boat chugged its way through the calm water into the unrelieved blackness of the night. The air was crisp with a cold edge to it. Razak, covered in perspiration and breathless from his exertions, with an underlying mixture of fear and adrenalin-inspired triumph, shivered as, without taking his eyes off Dahti's recumbent body he thrust the Beretta back in his belt.

Dahti was a heavy man. Razak strained and gasped as he dragged him into a sitting position with his back against the stern bulwark. Half turning him, Razak put his hands under Dahti's armpits and heaved him upright so that he was hanging over the stern of the boat. After another quick glance showed him that no untoward sound had reached the wheelhouse he eased Dahti slowly forward, hanging grimly on to his legs as the body began to slide over the side. But the dead weight was too much for him. Instead of slipping Dahti gently into the water as he planned he lost control, let go, and Dahti's body hit the water with a resounding splash.

Razak didn't stay to watch the effect.

He threw himself into the darkest shadow and saw the boatman's head come up with a jerk. The man stared around him and then, half standing, gazed at the stern of the boat. Razak crouched low and remained still, confident that by the thin light thrown from the open cabin door there wasn't a great deal he could see. He was right. The boatman wasn't all that curious; the inspection of his boat lasted no more than a few seconds before his head returned to its former position and his toe took up the steering once again as he picked up his doze where he'd left it.

Razak gave him a few more minutes then clambered back over the deck rubble and slipped silently into the cabin. After cleaning Dahti's hair and blood from the metalwork of the Beretta he jammed it back into the side of the mattress, stretched himself full length, closed his eyes and drifted into an untroubled sleep.

It seemed that he had barely dropped off when he was suddenly wide awake.

Automatically he reached for the pistol and opened his eyes. A dim light filtered through the cabin porthole. He sat up and brought his feet on to the sticky, oily floor and listened. The overpowering noise of the engine that had lulled him into a deep sleep had diminished to the steady tick, tick of an idling motor. He padded across the floor in his bare feet and peered out of the door. The strange light that had woken him was the precursor of dawn – a thin strip of grey-blue nudging into the eastern horizon where, faintly, could be discerned the line that demarcated sea from sky. But Razak wasn't interested in the beauty of early dawn vistas. Adjusting his eyes to the light he stared around him and, as the boat's shape hardened against the tentative dawn a voice, almost in his ear, said, 'Where's your friend?'

He didn't answer immediately. After a few moments gazing into the distance he slowly turned his head and, peering through the gloom, looked up into the whiskered face of the boatman.

'Isn't he with you?'

The boatman stared back.

'Why should he be?'

Razak began to look around him, agitated. Acting, like lying and cheating, was a normal activity for him; he had no problem switching from one to the other.

'He couldn't relax down below – wanted some fresh air.' Razak stared back into the disbelieving, grizzled face. 'He said he was coming up to see you after he'd been for a walk round the boat . . . Maybe he's sleeping under the nets?'

The boatman shook his head, 'I've just been round the boat,' he said harshly. 'I thought you were both sleeping in the cabin – ' he stopped in mid-sentence and his eyes darted around again. 'I heard something'.

'When?' said Razak, sharply.

'In the night. A splash – a noise . . . I thought a fish – a tuna, something big.' The boatman began to wail and clutch his head, but Razak stopped him in mid-flight.

'My friend has fallen overboard?'

The boatman could only grasp his head and wail again. Razak grabbed the man's collar and shook him. 'When did you hear this noise?'

'Hours ago. Many hours ago . . .' the boatman brought himself under control 'It's too late; he would have drowned within minutes . . .'

'No!' screeched Razak. It was now his turn for hysterics. 'We must turn back and look for him – immediately!' He clasped his head in his hands and began to rock backwards and forwards. 'Quickly! Turn the boat . . .'

The boatman made no move.

'Come on! Come on!' urged Razak. 'We've no time to lose.'

'My friend!' The boatman studied Razak's distraught

features with sympathy and placed his hand on his shoulder. 'Look – ' he waved his free arm in an arc, encompassing a still, black infinity. 'That is water. It is not as if your brother had fallen out of a motor car driving across the *badw*. The current would carry him where God alone takes his children. If I turned the boat, where would I go?' He waggled his fingers around in a zigzag motion. 'Boats do not travel in a straight line.' He brought his face closer to Razak's. 'Your friend is dead.'

Razak shook his head, feigning disbelief. He allowed another few minutes' requiem as the two of them gazed at the distant beginnings of a new day. 'He is lost, but we must go on,' he said, breaking the silence. 'Why did you stop the boat!'

'It would look suspicious to go alone into an empty harbour,' responded the boatman. 'In a couple of hours the sardine boats will start filtering in. We will join them and become just another boat back from a night's fishing.' He jerked his chin at the engine room. 'How will you manage the Jew on your own?'

'You have a landing spot arranged?'

The boatman nodded. 'This is not the first trip I've made.'

Razak showed his teeth again. 'Good. How long can you stay?'

The boatman shrugged and allowed his mouth to droop. 'I shall have to leave tonight, at last light. You never know – ' He pulled his sceptical face again and jerked his thumb over his shoulder – '*Jahud* that way,' he pointed his thumb in the other direction, 'and our brothers the Syrians that way. Everybody wants to be our enemy today.'

But Razak wasn't interested in the views of a Shiite fisherman. His was a much bigger game – one that dealt in fact and result rather than philosophical observation.

'That'll give me enough time to arrange things. Who will give you your reward?'

The boatman sniffed, then brought something up from the back of his throat with a noisy hawk and fired it over the side of the boat. 'I don't need reward. A blow to our enemies and success to the arms of our martyrs is reward enough. Everything will be settled on the Day of Judgment and when the last Israeli is driven out of our land and into the sea — '

'The day is not far away, my brother,' said Razak. 'I will remember you.'

'That is sufficient.'

6

Beirut

The Hezbollah network in north Lebanon had brought hostage shifting down to a fine art. No additional organization was needed to remove Macauley's near-dead body from the fishing boat in an out of the way area of the harbour to a holding cell in a Hezbollah village on the Tabaja inlet. After a day there Macauley was stuffed into the recess behind the back seat of the inevitable ramshackle Mercedes and shifted inland. He spent another day of unspeakable horror entombed in the cellar of a derelict barn and then, supervised by Razak, he was packed into a metal coffin welded to the underside of an old Chevrolet pick-up truck for the trip to Beirut.

The truck entered Beirut from the east; an innocent load of vegetables that passed without comment through the militia check-point at Bourj Hammoud then crossed the river by the old disused railway yards. The road filtered them into the Corniche Pierre Gemayal. This allowed them to avoid the centre of the city and they zoomed past Police HQ on the corner of Rue de Damas and avenue Abdallah Yafi before cutting into the shell-devastated area of Borj Abi-Haidar in the south-west of Beirut. Here, with the pick-up concealed in the ruins of a once prosperous car sale room three of Razak's own team appeared out of the ruins, dragged Macauley from his coffin and whisked him deeper into the shell-battered district. Using a system of passages and tunnels under once elegant houses and buildings, they arrived at Razak's secret, well-concealed and untraceable dungeon in the bowels of a collapsed 1930 Paris-style apartment block.

Macauley was thrown on the floor and stripped of his bindings. Then he was half carried, half dragged into the lowest passage and dumped on the wet, slimy floor.

There was only one door leading off the passage, into a room no larger than a standard bathroom. But this had no bath. No lavatory, no amenities, nothing. In one corner was a scruffy, threadbare and wafer-thin mattress. No light, no window through which its solitary occupant could observe the passing of life; and he lived, or rather existed, in worse conditions than the prisoner in the Château d'If nearly two hundred years ago. He had no way of knowing it but he was the last of the political prisoners; the last Englishman in Beirut. It wouldn't have done him any good had he known it. He'd given up. Captivity had become a way of life; he had no thoughts of freedom.

Razak would have been happy now without him but it was not for him to set release dates and organize press conferences. He was stuck with him, even though this Englishman had lost his interest for his captors; they ignored him unless extreme boredom got the better of them and they took turns at venting their unhappiness on him. The prisoner knew when the mood was upon them and had perfected a method of rolling himself into a protective ball and presenting the less sensitive areas of his body for punishment, but his captors generally received little satisfaction from kicking and beating an inanimate, lifeless object. They wanted screams of pain. They were not ordinary people. They were Shiite Muslims with fanatical ideas and their brains were uncluttered with thoughts and reasons. Sadists of the worst kind, they thought they were inflicting pain and misery on behalf of God.

Macauley presented a much better subject for their frustrations.

'Get him in a mood to talk to me.' Razak stepped over Macauley's naked body, squatted on his heels with his back to the wall and lit a cigarette. He looked like a bored child sitting in a corner watching grown-ups arguing politics.

As he watched, the four members of the team set about Macauley with enthusiasm. They got the right sounds out of him and managed to keep him conscious for much longer periods than he and Dahti had been able to in Rome. He began to take an interest. Macauley's pain threshold must be increasing all the time.

When he'd finished his cigarette Razak joined in. He directed the force of his brutality at Macauley's head and face and when he'd reduced it almost to a pulp he waved the others to one side and lowered his face close to Macauley's.

'Can you hear me, Macauley?' he shouted.

A bubble of sound forced its way through the gap that had been the American's mouth. It made no sense. It was the sound of a hurt puppy.

'A wet cloth,' snapped Razak, without looking away from the mess in front of him. He wiped Macauley's face with it, cleaned his lips, then prised them apart and squeezed the dirty, bloody, liquid into his mouth.

'Talk to me, Macauley,' he whispered.

The others leaned forward.

Macauley's mouth began to work but only Razak could hear or make any sense of what was coming out of it. One of the watchers, impatient, said, 'Why are we wasting our time with this pig? Why don't we just kill him?' The man spoke in Arabic and the very sound brought Razak's head up.

'You — ' he hissed at the speaker. 'Go and get food. Bring

some for the Englishman as well.' He gestured with his thumb, 'The rest of you – out!'

After they'd left, Razak turned his attention back to the American.

'You are a dead man, Macauley. They want to kill you. I can save you . . .' There was no reaction from the tortured face. Razak stared hard at him. 'This time tomorrow, Macauley, you could be dying with nails thrust into your knees; you could have boiling oil poured into your ears . . . You don't want this . . .' his voice took on a wheedling tone, as if he couldn't understand why a man should put up with pain when there was an alternative. He'd proved it many times: that even the bravest of men give in eventually. He moved his face closer so that he was almost kissing the American. 'If you think you have tasted punishment what these men have in store for you is worse than your worst nightmare. There is no need for you to die; there is no need for you to suffer more. Talk to me, Macauley; talk to me about Kamel al-Majid's money . . .'

One of the Hezbollah, Mubin Harb had disobeyed Razak. He'd gone no further than the cellar entrance. He understood English and from his position at the foot of the stairs he watched and listened.

Thurston Macauley's voice, after the initial incoherent mumblings, gained strength. Not sufficient for Harb to hear or understand the details of the Majid money but enough for him to realize that this was no ordinary hostage; this was something special, something personal to Razak and had nothing to do with the great crusade against Israel and the West. The word 'money' was enough to grip his attention; and then the amount. It was something totally beyond his imagination – $150 million, American – he could buy a country with that! But where was this money? Whose was this money? He strained his ears. Geneva? Where was Geneva? In the West. And Razak, their trusted leader, was going to have all this money for himself. Not if Mubin Harb had anything to do with it. He retreated carefully and silently and rejoined his companions in the upper ruins of the apartment block.

He said nothing at first, but made himself comfortable squatting on a section of smashed concrete joist in the concealed watch-post. He savoured the smells on the night air and studied the stars in the clear sky above the ruins of the devastated city. People were moving about the streets and picking their way over the rubble but they seemed to have no purpose or destination. Traffic at the junction at the far end of the road was sparse but making enough noise for three times the number of cars. There must be more to life than living like a homeless rat in the cellars of a destroyed city. Had God just given him the opportunity to lead the sort of life he'd heard that other people took for granted; had God offered him this chance? He stared about him. There was no sense of life. The light had gone out. The struggle no longer had the purpose of the earlier days. The leaders had given the hostages back to their people, they had no more use for them; and what use had they been other than to make money for these selfsame dedicated leaders? And where was Mubin Harb's share? Whatever the answer, he knew that for all his dedication his only reward was that he would be sent back to his poverty-ridden village in the Jabal al Halzoun in the north. And now that the world had been given back its hostages it had lost interest in Beirut, in Lebanon, in the martyrs who had perished in the struggle, in the Israeli atrocities in the south – they'd lost interest in everything. So, Mubin Harb, go home and till the land until you're needed again, or go south and seek martyrdom and paradise at the end of an Israeli bayonet, for there is nothing more for you to do here in Beirut. He sighed deeply and lit a cigarette. God had shown him another way. Now he needed advice. He tugged a mouthful of smoke from the cigarette, shielding its red glow with his cupped hands and with a low whistle gestured for his companion to come closer.

'This pig that Razak calls a Jew is an American,' he said into the other man's ear.

'Jew or American it doesn't make sense,' responded the other man, taking his lead from the low, muted tones of Harb's voice. 'The word is that our mission is finished. All the other people, the English and the Americans, have gone back to their countries – ' he glanced cautiously over his shoulder – 'except our Englishman.'

'I hear he is going soon.'

'Then why do we now have an American among us?'

Harb waited a moment before replying. 'This one is different. He has access to money.'

'To buy his freedom?'

'To bribe an Iraqi general.'

'What has this to do with the Jihad?'

Harb shook his head slowly. 'Nothing. It's Razak's personal business. He is using us for his own means. The money, a great deal – more than can be counted – is to be given to him. The American told him where it can be found.'

'And then Razak told you?'

'No. He is keeping it for himself – all of it.'

The other Arab stared intently into Harb's face as if gauging whether this was a subtle trap or not, then made his decision. 'We must have a meeting,' he said, his voice even lower. 'This development must be fully discussed by all of us – ' he glanced around paying particular attention to the hole leading to the cellar steps – 'except Razak, of course. You speak the language well?'

'Sufficient.'

'Good. You must talk alone to the prisoner and persuade him to allow you to share the whereabouts of this money. I will talk to our brothers and you will be given the opportunity to spend time alone with him. Do you agree?'

Harb directed a thin stream of smoke towards the star-speckled sky. He didn't hesitate. 'Of course.'

Razak was nearly finished with Macauley. But the American had covered himself: he'd ensured that there would be no transfer of accounts without his countersigning the transfer documents. This was a problem, but not an insurmountable one. But there was something not quite right – Razak had a nagging feeling that in spite of his pain and torture and the threat of more the American was holding something back, something important, more important than money, more important, probably, than life itself. Razak's thinking process was a simple one: surely no man would bring more pain and suffering to his already abused body for money which he is never going to touch? There was no point. The American had already earned himself a stay of execution. There had to be something else. No country pays $150 million for the picture of one man standing outside the American White House in Washington.

Razak dragged himself to his feet, glanced over his shoulder at the cellar exit and gave a low, off-key whistle. After a short pause another whistle sounded and Harb's head appeared round the corner of the stairs.

'Have they come back with the food?' demanded Razak.

'They're on their way.'

'Tell the others to cover them until they are underground and join us here.'

'What are you going to do with this?' Harb aimed a kick at Macauley's head but caught him only a glancing blow. Macauley's eyes remained closed. He gave no indication of having felt it.

'You will see,' said Razak. 'Bring the others down here.'

When all four Arabs were gathered round, Razak said, 'We're going to bury this thing.'

'Kill?' grinned one of them.

Razak stared him down. 'I said bury. But I want him kept alive. He's going to be bartered. Only we five know of his presence here. The honour that comes from the capture of a Jew will be ours – ours alone . . .'

Harb caught the eye of his fellow conspirator and held it for a few moments. There was no exchange between the two men, no expression – just a meeting of eyes and an understanding.

'How do you propose to bury a man who is not dead and yet keep him alive?' asked one of the men who'd gone for the food.

'We will bury him in the wall,' replied Razak, coldly. He could have been referring to a new rose bush that he proposed planting in his garden. 'Standing up.' Razak got to his feet, walked a couple of metres along the passage and tapped the sodden wooden panelling. It gave a damp, hollow response. 'Bring a lever,' he ordered and continued tapping the wall in different places.

When he'd prised four of the planks away from the wall he began to poke at the soft, wet clay underneath. It came away quite easily. After several minutes hacking away he threw down the metal lever and turned to the four watching men.

'Make a place for a man to stand for several months – you!' his eyes settled on one of the men. 'Get a tool and cut a hole in the wood large enough for this pig's face – ' he indicated Macauley's body, lying curled up in a heap, with a jerk of his chin – 'to be seen. He will need to be fed through it.'

The Arabs liked the sound of this novel idea and set to with a will. When they'd finished they stood back and admired their work, an alcove in the wall just sufficient to take a man's body, standing, like an Egyptian mummy in its sarcophagus. The man who'd been designated carpenter propped his work up against the wall and this also received its share of admiration. He'd joined the four planks together with three nailed battens which protruded by half a metre on either side; a crude hole had been hacked so that Macauley's face could gaze out of his upright coffin at nothing except the dripping wall opposite. This was to be his horizon. But there was more to come.

'There's a possibility that he could dig his way out with his hands,' observed one of the men leaning against the wall and studying the texture of the clay.

'And go where?' asked another.

'Nevertheless . . .'

'Break his arms – '

'No,' interjected Razak. 'His hands are needed.' He didn't say what for. The others accepted that Razak had a reason, but they hadn't finished.

One of the men picked up the iron bar they'd been using to scrape out Macauley's tomb. 'His legs?'

Razak considered it for a few seconds. 'Yes.'

And they broke his legs, crudely and roughly. Macauley's horrendous screams echoed up and down the narrow passageway looking for an outlet and almost took the roof off the cellar. Razak and the other Arabs studied Macauley's anguish with little nods of approval but otherwise their faces remained totally devoid of feeling. They picked up the still conscious figure and crammed it, with its feet not quite touching the ground and its arms jammed against its sides, into the alcove. Then they hammered the boards back into place. He couldn't slip down, he couldn't move and there was nowhere he could go, and when he opened his eyes there was nowhere else to look except straight through the hole in front of his face.

For some time they stood around staring at Macauley's

face until they became bored. One blew a mouthful of smoke into the hole and watched it disperse around Macauley's head, but it had no effect. He was going to be unconscious for a long time.

One of the men detached himself and went to the foot of the stairs where he'd left the other hostage's food. He squeezed a handful of black bean stew on to an old wooden tray, balanced an unpeeled hard-boiled egg on top of it and added a lump of this morning's now stale pitta. He came back and kicked on the door in the passage and shouted, 'Cover head!' through the crack. It was the only English he knew. After a few seconds he threw the door open, studied the interior of the tiny room by the light from the passageway then, satisfied with what he saw, threw the wooden tray across the room at the figure with the dirty bag on his head squatting in the middle of the mattress. The figure didn't move. The Arab waited a few moments, staring at the unmoving man, as if daring him to uncover his head or go for the food before he was given permission, then walked backwards and slammed the door. He banged the door with his fist, put his mouth to the crack and shouted in Arabic, 'Eat!'

He then joined his comrades and they washed their hands and mouths, made their prayers and, with their consciences purified and clear, squatted at intervals with their backs against the wall along the passage and began, noisily, to eat their own meal.

7

Razak had forbidden any conversation with Macauley. But Razak was not always there and the rule of fear works only when the threat is hovering in the vicinity. Razak's sorties into the outside world left many opportunities for Mubin Harb. But he had to be careful and take his time and it was nearly three months later, when the English prisoner was taken away and Macauley, crippled and half blind, was removed from his upright coffin and placed in the newly vacated prison cell, that Harb was able to get to work on Macauley.

It still took time and persuasion but eventually it all came out. Macauley, in his pain-racked delirium, seemed prepared to talk to anyone. It was as if the seal had been broken and the contents were now there for the taking. Harb adopted the sympathetic approach and Macauley reacted. In a fever of garbled Arabic and English and unrelieved nightmares Macauley told him not only of the Majid money but what he'd learned of Razak's association with the Iraqi agent Abu Dahti and Razak's own affiliation to the Iraq GID; he spoke of Razak's treachery, of Razak's intentions, of Razak's determination to keep the money out of the hands of both Iraq and the Hezbollah Central Committee and put it all in his own pocket. Harb lapped it all up; he could see the way open to a living paradise rather than having to wait for the one God had prepared for martyrs who fell in the struggle. But he must not rush it, he had to bide his time and make sure there was nothing more he should know before the decision to slit the American's throat was made.

But, now that he was out of his coffin, Macauley's brain began to work again. The long hours in the dark, the unimaginable pleasure and luxury of being able to lie down, and turn over, and crawl from one side of the room to the other – the cell, for him, was like a de-luxe suite in an exclusive resort hotel. And, apart from the ministrations of his new friend, the ugly, nameless Arab with foul breath, whom he had managed to set against Razak, he had a great deal of time to think about the other part of the Majid deal.

According to Doerflinger it seemed more than likely that Majid had already paid with his life for disclosing details of Iraq's hidden nuclear potential. Macauley had no doubt that shortly he was going to pay with his. So was it all wasted? Two lives, so far; 150 million bucks and all this agony for Saddam Hussein's potential nuclear threat. He was a man mad enough to blow everything into ashes if things didn't go his way. Already he'd displayed his warped mind to the world in the Kuwait oilfields; he was quite likely, next time, to go down in a nuclear ball engulfing not only the oilfields but the Middle East and half the world with it. Paradise was the fanatical destination of his religion; it wouldn't concern him how many millions took the same trip. There was no doubt about it in Macauley's mind, Armageddon wasn't all that far away and the man screaming to start it was a bloody maniac. There was only one thing to do. Washington wanted the details of the nuclear components hidden in the desert kept secret; they didn't want to upset Jordan. Washington's idea was the ultimate Ranger operation: in, destroy, out, and 'What nuclear dumps?'

But, tough on Washington. Nobody was going to be able to tell them in what holes, in what desert Saddam Hussein's stock of plutonium-239 and the rest of the nightmare components were sitting waiting for the mad-man's big day. Not he — not Macauley, because poor fucking Macauley was going to be broken up in little pieces and fed to the fucking vultures. Macauley stared through his one good eye into the blackness above him. Somebody should know what he died for, and what Saddam had got in store for them. Correct, Macauley! So how the hell does he pass the word, to anyone, that the countdown to Armaged-don has already begun? Maybe Razak could help? Macauley dragged his broken body into a sitting position in the corner of the room. *Now that is not as silly as it sounds! Let's try it out on bad-breath.*

Over the next few weeks Macauley trickled out snippets of information to Harb. He made them sound like the ravings of delirium: mention of nuclear installations in the desert; of the real conspiracy behind the Kamel al-Majid/ US negotiations; that the money was only a small part of the eventual reward there for the taking . . . Harb told his three friends of the fortune that could be theirs. They pushed him back into Macauley's room to find out more. Their peasants' reasoning wouldn't allow them to imagine the enormity of what was within their grasp, but their natural greed made up for any deficiencies. Macauley played his cards as they were dealt.

'You must keep me alive,' he urged Harb. 'Otherwise there is no way your story can be verified. I am the only person who can do that . . .'

Harb was a peasant, but he wasn't a stupid peasant. 'No. I know where the sites are. Your knowledge is no longer of use. You can die now — '

'Who will listen to you?' Macauley struggled with the words. 'Who will give money to an insignificant member of a terrorist gang?'

Macauley's honest description of Harb's status earned him half an hour's punishment, but it was carried out not as a vindictive reprisal but more in the manner of a strict father chastising an errant son. Harb, when he'd exhausted himself, left the room to recover and to think over Macauley's admonition.

Two cigarettes later it began to make sense.

He returned to Macauley's cell with a bucket of water, a lump of soap and an old dhoti and cradling the injured man in one arm proceeded to wash his face of the blood that he had caused. As he gently dripped water into Macauley's bruised mouth, his bad breath wafted into the American's face and hung there like a woollen mask. And he couldn't brush it off.

'Many other countries would pay for this information,' Harb suggested when Macauley had stopped groaning. 'We could even do business with Israel. Maybe Iraq would pay not to have their secret made public?'

Macauley's one seeing eye focused on Harb's face. 'They'd more likely kill you than give you money to keep the secret. You can't trust Iraqis. Look at your friend Razak,' he said with difficulty.

Harb's face tightened. The picture was sufficiently vivid for him. He didn't trust, or like, Iraqis either. 'My own people – ' he began.

'They'd use the information and give you nothing – probably kill you as well . . .'

'You are trying to save your life, Macauley. You are not interested in whether I and my friends benefit from what you have told me. You just want to live . . .'

Absolutely! Macauley kept his eye on the Arab's face. Sincerity dripped from every angle of his broken features. 'There is no reason why we should not all benefit,' he said carefully. 'My country – ' he was careful not to pronounce the word America; he'd learnt to his cost that the very name was likely to send a rush of blood to the head of a true Hezbollah fanatic with the inevitable result. 'What my country,' he repeated, 'will pay you for this information will make you and your friends as rich as Kuwaiti sheikhs. The Majid money will be as the husks of corn that blow in the wind compared with what you and your friends will share. But – ' He had to blink several times to keep his eye focused on the bearded face above him. It broke the intimate contact he'd established. But only briefly.

Harb's eyes narrowed. 'How do you propose – '

Macauley re-established ascendancy. 'One of you will contact any of my country's embassies, anywhere in the world and tell them that not only am I alive but that I am guaranteeing the information you are ready to give them. You will be invited to discuss its value with a senior official from Washington and come to agreement on how payment is to be made. They will also guarantee you a safe haven anywhere in the world. When all this has been arranged to your satisfaction you will have to present my body – my *live* body – ' he stressed, 'as verification of your facts. Only when I am placed in my government's hands will agreement, and payment of the money, be honoured.'

Macauley paused to allow all this to sink into Harb's brain. He'd had enough dealings with the Arab community, especially those like Harb who hovered just below gutter level, to know that you don't push, you don't force, and you don't overplay your hand. You dribble the grains of sand slowly, carefully, on to the bare board and allow the other's finger to trace the pattern. Harb proceeded to do exactly that. Without a word he stared hard into the American's good eye and his battered face, then got up and, without looking round or saying a word, opened the door, went through it and locked it behind him.

With a silent whoosh Macauley let out the breath he'd been holding and allowed his head to drop back on to the dirty mattress. He stared blankly at the ceiling before dropping his eyes to his crippled legs. There was no feeling in them. The fractures had set together in unnatural angles: he offered up a brief thanksgiving that the skin hadn't been broken. He had them to thank for that at least. In these surroundings the sort of wounds fractures could make would have resulted in almost instant death by septicaemia. He could be further grateful that for nearly three months he'd been suspended in his upright coffin and that no weight had been placed on the fractures. Not much to be thankful for. He knew his legs were never going to be of any use to him again. But Macauley, if anything, was philosophical about it – life without the use of legs had to have some compensation over being dead in a Beirut cellar.

8

Baghdad

The President of the Revolutionary Command Council was always available to a member of the family, particularly when that member was Sabba'a al-Tikriti his half-brother and Controller of the Da'Irat al Mukhabarat al-Amah, the Iraq intelligence service.

'The intelligence that has just arrived here from my source in Damascus states that the treachery of Kamel al-Majid was purely money for defection,' al-Tikriti said.

'What source is that?' demanded Saddam Hussein.

Tikriti hesitated. Mentioning names meant sharing the credit. But he could afford it. 'Abu Dahti, a senior GID operative who was briefed to investigate the traitor's activities. A reliable man, conscientious and trustworthy.'

'You spoke to him personally?'

Tikriti considered very carefully before he committed himself. 'Dahti and I use the principle of no personal contact. We have a perfect cut-out system that keeps his cover intact. So you see, speaking to him personally is not necessary for his information to be totally reliable. The report came in his personal code through an intermediary; it was done outside Damascus official perimeters. Majid's actions remain a secret. I guarantee it.'

'Can we accept that defection was the only commodity for sale?' asked Saddam.

'Had he given the Americans anything else we would know by now. I have checked, personally, every item that

78

Majid had access to. There is nothing missing and there have been no copies made of any documents or maps. I would stake my life on this . . .'

Saddam Hussein gave a throaty chuckle. 'Careful, brother!'

Tikriti didn't return the chuckle. He was too busy controlling the cold shiver that sent his lower stomach into a turmoil. Saddam's jokes, like his paranoia, very often had two sides to them. 'The people involved in the initial uncovering of this traitor's activities must be highly praised. Will you consider that personally?'

Saddam didn't answer. 'Where did Majid put this money he sold himself for?'

'Abu Dahti reports that nothing was ever paid. Majid was to receive his bribe when he presented himself to the Western press in Washington. This makes sense and bears out the events. Had he received money he would not have come back to Baghdad.'

'So the matter is closed?'

'No harm has been done. The agent, Dahti, will remain incognito, and at large on commission to investigate any unusual American activities that might have resulted from Majid's treachery.'

'I don't want to hear any more about it, Sabba'a.'

'You won't, brother.'

9

Razak delivered the last of the Western captives, the British journalist Les Pritchard whom he had had in solitary confinement for the past two years, to the Hezbollah High Command who in turn handed him to the Syrian propaganda machine in Damascus. For a short time Pritchard held everybody's attention. Razak was nothing, just the postman, and he made sure it remained that way. As an anonymous figure it was no trouble for him to take the Syrian Airlines morning flight to Geneva and begin the overtures towards transferring the American money from Macauley's coded account. He hadn't expected it to be a walkover. It wasn't. Swiss banks took themselves very seriously. This was a great deal of money; it took more than the mere mention of the coded procedures Macauley had discussed with the bank for them to relinquish their hold of it. Razak realized that there was going to have to be a great deal of coming and going; some serious paperwork by Thurston Macauley. He thanked the God who'd persuaded him to keep the American alive; and gave more thanks that he'd kept Macauley's hands in good working order.

Razak returned to Damascus and by using Abu Dahti's procedures for contact with his GID Baghdad control silenced any fears in Baghdad concerning possible information leaks in the Kamel al-Majid/Macauley affair. They were happy. He was happy. As far as they were concerned Abu Dahti had succeeded in carrying out Sabba'a al-

Tikriti's instructions to the letter and now would remain active in the field running his own private little war against his country's enemies. For Baghdad's inner circle the Kamel al-Majid treachery was a closed book; there was no more interest in the Macauley affair. Things were back to normal. Dahti would eventually vanish from the scene. These things happen. Secret agents, particularly Iraqi ones working in foreign countries, were prone to mysterious disappearances. After a lengthy silence from Dahti he would be written off as a casualty of the continuance of the struggle against the Great Satan. Razak was a nonentity, his name had never risen in the initial Dahti briefing – he was free and running. It was now time for him to gather unto himself the riches that, in his opinion, he rightly deserved.

Razak shivered inadvertently in the crisp night air as he picked his away across the rubble leading to his cellar. He stopped and stared at the starry sky and the three-quarter moon that cast its shadowless glow across the jumbled outline of silent, deserted ruins of Beirut's battered skyline. In the distance, towards the centre of the old city a pink glow of restored street lights and shops and other signs of activity shimmered in the sky. Normality was on its way back; it was starting in the middle and working its way outwards. Razak stopped to recover his breath; he listened to the steady hum of civilization and stared without expression into the devastated distance. The Lebanese were beginning to live again, but it wasn't coming here, not to his part of Beirut – there was nothing left for it to come to, just holes in the ground and uncleared rubble of destroyed buildings. If it did ever come it wouldn't find Razak. He would be enjoying the fruits of American largesse. This he didn't doubt.

He cursed under his breath as he approached the concealed entrance to the cellar. No one had challenged him. From the corners of his eyes he studied the secret observation post. There was no outline of a sentry's head. But even this caused no feeling of misgiving. He knew his Hezbollah colleagues. A lazy lot. They wouldn't survive without the driving leadership of people like him, they would all be squatting in the basement eating, drinking, smoking, talking. He almost wished he was an enemy — what pickings he and his Iraqi brothers would have here with this idle lot. On tiptoe he crept through the entrance and halfway down the stairs. Total silence. He stopped and frowned, his ears pricked, his senses alert. The minutes crawled past.

Not a sound.

By now the 9mm Beretta was in his hand, the safety catch off, his finger lightly on the hair trigger. He pressed himself against the chilled, damp wall and waited in the dark. Then he made up his mind. Carefully he took the rest of the steps and peered round the buttress at the foot of the stairs. A dull bulb glowed with just sufficient light for him to inspect the underground cellar. A quick glance was enough to make out one man crouching at the far end of the cellar, an unwieldy Russian-made Kalashnikov tucked under his arm with the barrel rested precariously on his bended knee and pointed straight at Razak's face. He'd obviously heard him coming.

Razak brought his head back swiftly.

He'd recognized the man. Remaining out of sight at the foot of the stairs he called, softly, 'Badran?'

There was no reply.

He tried again. 'Badran, this is Razak. Point that gun somewhere else.' He waited a moment. 'I'm coming down.'

He waited again then moved carefully round, making sure he was completely visible to the man. His face was neutral but his brain was working overtime. The young man, the lower part of his face covered with wispy pubescent hair and a dirty *shamargh* on his head and round his neck, remained crouching with one hand resting on the butt of the machine pistol his finger still curled round the trigger. He watched Razak approach warily but made no move or sound. He hadn't spoken a word so far.

'The prisoner?' demanded Razak.

Badran jerked his chin in the direction of the wooden door. He appeared to be nervous. His eyes did not leave Razak.

'Still there?'

The young man nodded.

'Where are the others? What are you doing here on your own?'

'They've gone.'

'What do you mean, gone – gone where? When?'

Badran, the youngest member of the unit, had obviously drawn a very short straw. He gulped nervously. He was afraid; this was evident by the way his hand shook as he held on to the machine pistol and the way his eyes refused to meet Razak's, but while he had the Kalashnikov he knew he had the upper hand. Razak searched his face. There was no fear in the boy's eyes. But there was something else. This disturbed Razak. He was the leader – Badran should be cowering, and he wasn't. Razak waited. Badran cleared his throat nervously with a dry, rasping bark.

'I have been left to pass on the proposals – '

Razak's patience was nearing the point where he felt this conversation might better be carried on with a cocked automatic pressed against the youth's temple. He kept the lid on his temper for a few moments longer; he had an ominous feeling about what was coming next.

'Tell me first where they've gone and then you can talk to me about these proposals.' He tried a reassuring smile at Badran but it did not settle the youth. Razak's reassuring smiles were a rarity and usually had the opposite effect. He followed it up with the offer of a cigarette. It was refused, but he lit his own and raised his eyebrows.

Badran swallowed. 'They have gone where, they say, they cannot be reached. That is what I had to tell you.'

'So, you have told me. Now tell me why they have gone to this unreachable place – then tell me the other things.'

'It is to do with what the American told Harb.'

Razak felt a cold hand grasp his heart. 'American? What American?'

'The one you said was a Jew.'

Razak stared into the young man's eyes. He didn't wilt. 'He's an American Jew – and Harb had no permission to talk to him . . .' He paused. 'Do you know what Harb and the American talked about?'

Badran shrugged. 'We had a meeting.'

'Ah! Meetings! Very democratic! Talk to me about it.'

Razak's sarcasm went over Badran's head. 'The American talked of a great deal of money. The sum of 150 million American dollars was mentioned. The American told Harb you were keeping it all for yourself. We have decided that it should be shared equally amongst us all . . .'

Razak managed to fight the sickness in his stomach. He appeared calm and reasonable to the inexperienced Badran. 'Equal shares! Equal shares! You have decided! Is this what you do when I am away? Decide affairs; make decisions? This is what you do at your meetings?'

The young man shrugged again. His hand remained on the Kalashnikov, his finger unmoved from its trigger. 'There is also the question of the other money . . .'

'Other money?'

'The money to be negotiated with the Americans for the map references.'

Razak couldn't control his puzzlement. 'Map references?'

'The desert sites that the American had been empowered

to pay for,' replied Badran ingenuously. 'Harb said you knew all about it; you were going to make yourself very rich while we scrabbled for bread crusts in the street . . .'

This was what had been bugging Razak all along. The American *had* been keeping something back; but it hadn't taken long for the treacherous Harb to get it out of him. Why had the American told Harb and not he, Razak? And what sites? How much extra money? Razak's brain slowed down to thinking pace. There was much to be done here; the American had much pain coming to him; he had a lot of explaining to do.

'Harb was lying to you. Tell me exactly what the American told him,' he said with a false lightness.

Badran wasn't deceived. 'Harb left instructions of what I was to tell you.'

Razak gritted his teeth. 'Tell me.'

Badran reached into his pocket, his other hand still on the trigger and, watched closely by Razak, he drew out a folded sheet of paper. He met Razak's cold black eyes for a moment, then opened the paper and began to recite from it.

'The $150 million that the American mentions is to be obtained from the Switzerland bank by Razak – ' the youth glanced up into Razak's face and gave a nervous smile. It wasn't returned – 'if he hasn't already done it'.

'Continue.'

'And split into five equal amounts; these amounts to be credited to accounts opened in names which will be indicated to Razak at a later date.' The boy stopped again.

'Is that it?' Razak's face was expressionless. The young man's next words brought the black thunderclouds back again.

'There is more.'

Razak's face turned to stone. He jerked his chin in the air.

Badran dropped his eyes again to the sheet of paper. 'Razak is then to approach the Americans and negotiate the exchange of the map references, revealed by the American, Macauley, for money. This also is to be equally shared and deposited in a further five, different, secret accounts in Switzerland . . .'

'Did the American indicate to Harb how much these map references would be worth to his government?' Razak wanted to know what the map references referred to, what gave them a value to America, but he dared not expose his ignorance. He had to be careful. But Badran did it for him.

'It was suggested by the American that his people would pay as much again. They gave him the money to buy the information, but he got it without paying. Now they must pay again. Harb thought that the knowledge of these sites could allow us to auction the details to interested countries. Our riches from such an auction would be beyond belief, particularly as the American told Harb that his country would pay more than anyone else . . .'

Badran stopped talking. Razak had closed his eyes. A gentle continuous murmuring of foul, gutter obscenities dribbled from his lips, rising in volume with every other word until he was shouting at the top of his voice. The young man's hand tightened on the Kalashnikov but came away as if the weapon was red hot when Razak's eyes opened and stared him down. The swearing had stopped in the middle of a particularly foul piece of filth.

'I should read you the rest of this,' said Badran.

'So be it,' hissed Razak.

Badran lowered his eyes and continued reading. 'The American is to be kept alive until all the arrangements have been completed in case his information is faulty. You have three months in which to effect the first part and three months after this to make overtures to the Americans regarding the desert sites . . .' Badran stuck a dirty finger on the paper to keep his place and looked up again. 'Would you like to read the rest yourself?'

Razak had brought himself under control. They are typical Palestinian fools, he thought. Why should he do any of this? This idiotic youth could be killed like a rat in a cellar. As for the others, wherever they were, they could sit and wait until the sun rises in the west before he gave them one dinar to share between themselves. 'No,' he began, then, suspiciously, 'how can there be more?'

'Let me continue.'

'Quick, then.'

Badran lowered his eyes again, ran them along the line to where his finger rested and continued: 'Should Razak fail to carry out any of these arrangements Harb's team will (1) pass on details of his treachery to the Supreme Council of Hezbollah at Baalbek; (2) inform the controlling body of Hezbollah in Iran that, according to the American, Razak was involved with Iraqi intelligence in Rome where he and other Iraqis took him prisoner; (3) it would be suggested that he was involved in conspiracy with the American over Iraqi secret matters . . .'

Razak had gone white. The sound coming from his throat that had made Badran stop reading was like that of a man choking to death. Razak looked as if he was having a stroke. His rage, mixed with fear, had deprived him totally of speech and thought. He was blown, he was exposed – a group of Lebanese peasants had him by the hairs, there was no way out – he had to share and risk everything at the hands of these four ignorant creatures. He would have been better sharing the problem with his old friend Abu Dahti.

'There is more.'

Razak merely stared at the boy.

'Any attempt to harm any of the four of us will result in the Americans being informed that you, and you alone, were responsible for the capture, the kidnapping, the torture, beating and humiliation of the American, Macauley . . .'

Razak didn't need to know what that last simple clause meant. The Americans would believe them, they wouldn't rest until he'd paid the full price. As far as one of their own was concerned there was no limit to the extent of their retribution. They would hound him to all corners of the world. They had specialists for just such a mission. In that respect they were as bad, if not worse, than the dreaded Israeli Mossad. He'd got the message. He was well and truly cooked unless everything he'd worked for was to be shared with four Lebanese peasants − and any one of them was likely to blow the plot wide open at any moment. But he had no alternative.

'What are your instructions?' he asked Badran.

'To pass on your acceptance of the terms.'

'How?'

Badran made no acknowledgement.

'Do it,' said Razak finally. 'And what do you propose doing yourself?'

'I am to look after the American while you occupy yourself with the team's demands.'

Razak nodded. 'Do that. Has he eaten?'

'Not this evening.'

'Go and get his food. I will stay and guard him until you return.'

Razak controlled his anger until Badran had left the cellar. Then he gave it full rein.

He kicked open the door of the cell, slammed it shut behind him, locked it and stood with his back pressed against it. He was shaking like a man with the ague. White flecks of bubbly foam had built up in the corners of his mouth and as he stared at the American his eyes glazed. An uncontrolled furnace was building up inside him. Macauley,

88

from his crouching posture in the corner of the room, needed only a second's study of the Iraqi's face to know what was coming. And he knew what it was for.

He had just time to roll his body into a ball before Razak hurtled across the small room and allowed his anger its full expression. He was out of control even before he landed the first blow.

'I knew it! I knew it! I knew it!' he screamed, spitting froth and snot as he kicked and thumped Macauley's curled-up body. 'Why you not tell me what you told the other man? You pig! Why you tell others – not me?' Kick, kick, kick, kick, kick – his pointed leather Chelsea boot gouged into Macauley's back and side, but they were wild, undirected kicks that made little impact on Macauley's remaining vital parts. He screamed in time with each blow, and whimpered, and cried – he'd learnt how to behave with his torturers. As long as the screams came they paid no attention to the direction of the blows and this particular Arab was working himself up into such a frenzy that it would tire him out very quickly.

Razak was out of condition. He gave up after twenty minutes.

Once he had recovered his breath and composure he produced from his pocket the plastic-wrapped documents he'd negotiated with the bank officials at Geneva. 'For your life, Macauley, you will authorize this money to be transferred to an account or accounts of my choosing. No tricks, no silly mistakes, no codes other than the one in which the authorization is to be made. I repeat, your life depends on it.'

Macauley didn't hesitate. He did as he was ordered.

Razak studied the official document as best he could; its wording meant very little to him; he was at Macauley's mercy. But he had every confidence that Macauley had been well and truly softened up – and the signature and coded authorization, as far as he could tell, although a little shaky looked authentic enough. He refolded the document carefully and placed it back in his pocket. He turned back to Macauley. 'Now you will tell me,' he hissed as he stood over the American, 'everything you should have told me before, and what you have now told the other man . . . You must realize that they will now kill you and sell your information – you are a fool!' He couldn't help himself – he rushed back across the room and aimed two more wild kicks at Macauley's head. But there was no venom or power in the kicks. 'Talk! Talk!' he shouted.

Macauley lowered his arms from his face and raised his head cautiously. His one working eye was bruised and swollen where a couple of Razak's blows had found the target but he managed to point it in Razak's direction. He told him exactly what he had told Harb but with an added refinement at the end.

'My people will only pay for secrecy; they won't enter into an auction, it's just them or nothing . . .'

Razak nodded thoughtfully. His brain was working overtime: 150 million US dollars, plus an amount that must, at least, equal it! It was almost beyond the realms of comprehension.

Macauley ignored his captor's faraway look and continued mumbling. '. . . but already too many people know.'

'Who else?' Razak came back down to earth.

'Harb must have told his friends . . .'

'You shouldn't have told him of these map references. That was a very bad thing to do.'

Macauley didn't reply. He left it to Razak to work out the ramifications. And it didn't take many seconds. Macauley, after all his experience of Arab savagery, was taken by surprise at the sudden change of atmosphere. One moment they were quietly discussing untold riches for one of them and the next his face was being viciously slapped and pummelled by a raving lunatic. He had no time to protect himself and quickly passed out.

When he came to he was on his own. His eyes refused to open and his lips felt like two over-sized bananas. He touched his face gingerly. Every part of it was wet and sticky and when he ran his tongue carefully round the inside of his mouth he could feel, through its numbness, several gaps where teeth had been broken or dislodged. And the pain was mounting. There was nothing more he could do. Despair. Like a great black, all-enveloping mass it filled his head and drove out all logical thought. His brain collapsed, his mind cracked and in the peaceful suspension of a body and mind floating in a black limbo he curled up into a ball, draped the wet cloth round his face and head and cried like a lost child.

PART TWO

10

The solitary barman at the Occidental Grill on Pennsylvania
Avenue leaned with his elbows on the bar and studied
tomorrow's racing form. A hard drinker in a smart navy
blue suit sat opposite him on a tall stool and gazed intently
at the white onion in his slightly pink gin and soda water
rising and falling at the whim of the soda's bubbles. At the
far end of the long bar where it curved, two men sat close
together. In front of them were two snifters filled with an
expert casualness to within a cigarette paper's width of the
top with Jack Daniels and alongside them, cheek by jowl,
two long frosted glasses of ice-cold draught beer. None of
the glasses had been touched.

Joe Doerflinger stuck a heavy forefinger on the six-by-
four glossy print he'd placed on the bar between them and
studied the image. He gave the impression it was the first
time he'd seen it.

It was a photograph of a dishevelled, bearded scarecrow
of a man. Anyone who had seen pictures of British hostages
immediately after they'd been released would have known
he belonged to that group.

'D'you recognize him?'

The other man nodded. 'Les Cohen.'

The second man stared intently at the photograph. He
was taller than his companion, a fraction under six foot
three, and younger, in his early forties. His hair hadn't
changed from its youthful short cut and, as yet, hadn't

acquired any grey to go with its light brown colour. He was
clean shaven, his face normally hard set; it was the face of a
cynical man who'd seen the worst an unpleasant world
could offer. But it hadn't affected his eyes. Jack Cunningham had kind eyes, women were always telling him this,
but his eyes belied a hard and sometimes ruthless edge that
hovered just below the surface. Jack Cunningham could
have been an executive of almost any profession. To those
who made a study of men who used the side door at CIA
Central at Langley there was only one thing he could have
been – government agent – one of the Intelligence
groupings, probably a CIA accreditation; in fact a definite
CIA accreditation. And they could tell you by his manner
that he'd been doing it a long time. But Cunningham was
international. Wisconsin born, there was little trace in his
voice of his origins. His voice rarely betrayed his antece-
dents; if anything it had a European edge to it – British
European.

'Why the interest in Les Cohen?'

'He was the last hostage to be released from Beirut.
Hezbollah don't want any more of them. They got
everything they wanted out of it and they've given the
game up. They're all hanging around now scratching their
asses and trying to decide what their next trick's going to
be . . .'

'You're a cynical old bastard, Joe! Maybe they've turned
civilized?'

'No fuckin' way! The bastards now have American and
British money coming out of their ears. The French gave
them everything they asked for even before they asked for
it; they started opening the shop at the first sign of one of
their nationals being given the eye. Hezbollah got bored
with screwing the bastards – there was no fun in it, no
publicity. The Krauts were even more fuckin' abject . . .'

'You don't have to vent your spleen on me, Joe. I've

been there, done that. I know what side of the road they drive on in Beirut and I know what point of the compass their asses tilt to when they bang their heads on the mosque floor. What I'd like to know is where all this is leading to?'

'Well, first of all you've been reassigned, Jack.'

Cunningham turned and smiled. It made all the difference to his features: it knocked years off his age. But it wasn't a genuine smile. 'I haven't heard that expression for a few years, Joe.'

'Our Leader likes to watch old war films. He gets all his dialogue from the movies. It's infectious. I'm using it myself. For you, though, Jack, it means you've moved into my league. I've got a job for you and it's been designated by the President himself. He asked for you, personally.'

'You haven't answered my question, Joe. What's it all about?'

'It's about Thurston,' Doerflinger said quietly.

Jack Cunningham's face hardened as he stared into Doerflinger's eyes then, seeing nothing there, lowered his own to study the picture of Les Cohen. But he wasn't seeing Les Cohen; Cohen's features blurred and misted into those of Thurston Macauley, his dearest friend, a man who'd been quite prepared to put his life where his friendship was alongside his best friend who'd gone a ditch too far in the Vietnam débâcle.

The river reached brown and boiling, swollen above its banks with the October monsoon rains, surged round what was normally a gentle curve but was now a rushing torrent and vanished into the jungle. The five survivors of the Special Forces party turned their backs to it and faced the barrage of small arms fire that cut through the thin foliage of the overlapping jungle. They held their fire. The Vietcong could afford to take their time. This was the wind-up game; for once the VC had it their way and were making the most of their superiority. Their taunts in broken English interspersed with the clap, clap, clap of AK47s and told the Americans what was going to happen to them when they were captured. The patrol faced their unseen enemy and waited.

It was Cunningham who made the move.

Jake Force was made up of bits of everything – ex-Green Berets, like him and Macauley, Marine Corps misfits too individualistic for corps duty, regimental outcasts and local specialists from the Vietnamese Special Services. Three helicopters had dropped the twenty-man reconnaissance party into a clearing deep into VC country.

It was almost as if they were waiting for them.

One of the H34s was hit by a 60mm mortar as it hovered inches off the LZ and blew up, killing everybody in it. They should have aborted the mission there and then, but the other two helicopters discharged their human cargoes and whirled out of it, their 50mms firing at everything and everywhere. This allowed Cunningham, Macauley and the remaining fifteen men to throw themselves, ducking under the H34s' blades, through the sharp elephant grass and into the surrounding jungle where they regrouped, and fought off the first assault. As they moved deeper into the jungle the heavy monsoon rain crashing into the canopy of leaves above them concealed the sound of their movements. Well trained, fit, they were able to move quickly and after several hours lost their pursuers. But it was only the beginning. Unwittingly, they'd found what they'd been briefed to look for – they'd been dropped into the heart of the main VC force in front of Xuan Loc.

The unit's wireless and its two operators along with three of the rifle group had gone up with the helicopter; they could do nothing with the information except begin the long walk back. Cunningham briefed his team; it was imperative that at least one of them made it back to base with the information. But it was an unlikely possibility, and they knew it. They remained together for the rest of that night, and at first light split into two groups, one of five and one of ten. The smaller party headed off rapidly and the larger group of ten men, including Cunningham and Macauley, remained in position to cover their rear. The rain hadn't let up; if anything it had intensified. Where it had helped them yesterday now it turned sides. The VC had moved round them and were waiting in a well laid ambush. Five of Cunningham's party were killed or wounded in the first fusillade. Cunningham, Macauley, the two other Americans and a tough Vietnamese scout charged the ambush position, taking the VC by surprise and breaking through the cordon. They met up at a track junction and headed south. In the distance they could hear spasmodic shots as the VC dispatched the wounded Americans. Then there was silence. They knew they were being tracked again.

The following morning, in a quick instantaneous ambush they managed to kill two more VC. The Viets pushed on remorselessly, forcing Cunningham and his party back until they found themselves herded on to the bank of the swollen river.

'Looks like this is it, Mac.' Cunningham curled into the foot of a large Meranti tree and checked his last magazine of ammunition.

Macauley held Cunningham's eyes for a moment, then gave a wry smile. 'It's been fun knowing you, Jack.'

'Sure —'

Clap-clap-clap. One of the Americans standing behind a nearby tree gave a light cough, fell against the tree and slithered down it to rest on his knees. The carbine dropped out of his hands and he bowed his head as if in prayer. He was dead. Cunningham stretched low and retrieved the carbine. He removed the magazine and laid it beside him.

'Jack!' The Vietnamese scout had dropped to the river's edge and was standing in the water up to his knees. 'There's a crossing here, under the water. It's a fallen tree. The flood's covered it . . .'

Cunningham turned his head. The Vietnamese was treading his way delicately across the foaming river. It looked as if he was walking on water. Watched by Cunningham and Macauley he stopped three-quarters of the way across, balanced himself and signalled with his hand that he'd come to the end of the tree.

Cunningham, the remaining Marine and Macauley risked several bursts into the jungle around them to keep the Vietcong from seeing what was going on, then with Macauley and the Marine firing single shots Cunningham watched the Vietnamese scout jump for the bank, miss it and fall into the raging torrent. It picked him up and threw him against the curved bank where he grasped a hanging branch and pulled himself on to firm ground. He scrambled into the jungle, waved to Cunningham, and took up a hidden position opposite the fallen tree.

'Go on, Mac, your turn — ' Cunningham rested his hand on Macauley's shoulder. 'When you get over there don't wait, move off and get back to Company — '

'No.'

'This is no time to fuck around, Mac! That's an order. Move!'

'Let him go first.' Macauley pointed to the Marine, who was calmly firing single shots at anything that looked remotely human.

'I said you! Go!'

'OK. But fuck you, Jack!' Macauley rolled on to his belly and slithered down the bank. As he began the tortuous passage across the swirling water-covered log he glanced quickly over his shoulder. Cunningham had turned his back and had joined the Marine in firing the last of his ammunition into the encroaching jungle. Reaching the other side, and helped by the scout, he scrambled up the bank, took cover and watched the other side of the river as he waited for Cunningham and the Marine to make their break.

'Go on.' Cunningham tapped the Marine on the shoulder. He didn't argue.

Clap-clap-clap-clap . . . The AK47s continued their rattle from the depths of the jungle in front of Cunningham, but still they didn't charge. Why bother? They knew the river was behind the Americans — they knew it was uncrossable — the VC for once were enjoying themselves; no danger and the outcome a foregone conclusion. Clap-clap — Cunningham gathered himself to change position, to fool the enemy into thinking there were still several men in front of them, when he felt like he'd been slammed in the chest by a baseball bat. He fell, watched helplessly by the three men on the other side of the river.

Macauley never gave it a second thought. He rose quickly to his feet. 'OK, you two,' he snapped authoritatively. 'Get out of here. You know what to do . . .'

'What are you going to do, Lieutenant?' The Marine ignored the order as he scrambled to his feet and moved close to Macauley.

'Never mind what I'm going to do — you get back to base. I might see you there . . .'

'Like fuck you will! I'm staying with you — sir!'

'Do as you're told, Marine! That's an order! Move out — now!'

Macauley moved upriver a few metres, threw off his pack, loosened the sling of his M-14 and slipped it over his head and shoulders. Without hesitation he aimed at the submerged tree, threw himself into the water and allowed the onrush to carry him with it. He thumped hard into the tree and held on. With the force of the water threatening to carry him over the top of it and into the main part of the swirling river, he managed to hook himself on, then haul his legs over to straddle the tree bridge. Carefully he worked himself on to his knees, then to his feet, and scrambled back to the enemy bank where he threw himself down beside Cunningham's inert body. He slipped the M-14 carbine off his shoulders and fired half a magazine in a long

101

burst to show the VC that they were still in business then turned Cunningham over on to his back. He was still alive.

It was then that the VC decided something was wrong and charged for the kill.

Macauley hoisted Cunningham on to his shoulder just as the enemy patrol burst out of the cover of the jungle. Macauley swung his carbine round and, with a one-handed grip, emptied the magazine at the charging Cong. Two of them fell. The others hesitated for a brief second, just long enough for Macauley to throw down his carbine, grasp Cunningham with both hands and throw himself into the raging river.

He hung grimly on to Cunningham's unconscious body as the river bucketed and pulled, most of the time dragging them under the water; a quick mouthful of air as they surfaced, but Macauley had no way of helping Cunningham. It was just a question of hanging on; of drowning rather than being taken for humiliation, torture and caging in bamboo animal pens by the Vietcong. Several times Macauley passed out. But he never let go. He had no idea how long they'd been swept down the river when, with a tremendous thud that almost dislodged his grip on Cunningham, he was hurled against a huge boulder. He felt his numbed knees grate on rock and then his feet touched solid ground. Gasping, he dragged himself and his load through the shallow swirling water of a bank outcrop and on to muddy but firm land.

He lay on his face for several minutes heaving up water, then forced himself to his knees and dragged Cunningham further into the cover on the bank. He turned him on to his back. Miraculously, he was still alive. What's more, he opened his eyes.

Opening his eyes and finding himself in Macauley's arms being hugged back to warmth and life was something that would live with him as long as he had breath. Macauley had been prepared to give his own life for him. Cunningham

102

loved Macauley as only a soldier, who'd been to hell and back again with another and looked death in the eye together, could love another man. It was a realization not lightly accepted.

Cunningham's eyes came back from the past. He stared a little longer at the photograph of Cohen then rested his elbows on the bar and reached his hand out for the remains of his beer.

'What about him?' he said disguising the emotion in his voice. 'Thurston's dead – he disappeared nearly six months ago. Nothing's been heard since.' He turned his eyes and met those of Joe Doerflinger. 'Or has it, Joe?'

Doerflinger watched him. 'Thurston's alive. Beirut probably – no, Beirut definitely! His last mission was highly classified – ultra. He was on a presidential courier mission carrying stuff from Jordan. He changed flights at Rome and that's where he was last seen.'

'He had no back-up?' Cunningham stopped drinking in mid-swallow.

'None. It was a strictly confidential mission that only he, I and the President know about. He carried nothing; everything was memorized. He'd met a secret Iraqi emissary, you don't need me to spell out the delicacy of that – it was very much one of those "for your ears only" packages.'

'Why didn't they use a secure phone?'

Doerflinger shook his head. 'This was too big for phones of any description. It was stipulated before the mission got off the ground that information would only be passed, eye to eye, to me. The President wanted it that way; he didn't want to risk leakage of any of this information.' He glanced sideways at Cunningham. 'You don't need me to tell you that it's not everybody in the White House loves our President. One whisper of this lot and Christ knows what could happen – we're talking Iran/Contra proportions here,

Jack – so, no phones. Anyway, that's neither here nor there – you've been given a job to do. The whys and wherefores of what led up to it are of no consequence – not any more. But I'll give you a little hint: Macauley was shown something and his job was to come back to the President and tell him what he'd seen. Like I said, it was far too delicate for mortal ears.'

Cunningham stared at him. 'And you're not going to tell me what sort of hold Thurston Macauley had over the President – what it was that made him more trusted than the next man?'

'Nope. Read into it what you like. That's the background. Macauley was blown somehow, somewhere, and was rolled up in Rome – at the airport, would you believe! Nobody saw it happen. He got off a Royal Jordan Airways at Rome and that was the last anybody saw of him.'

Cunningham reached over and picked up the smaller of the pictures.

'Cohen. Jewish?'

'Gotta be.'

'What's he got to do with it?'

Doerflinger didn't look at the picture. 'Didn't I say? He was a hostage too.'

Cunningham looked askance. 'OK, I'll take your word for it. But why are we sitting here looking at pictures of British hostages?' He met Doerflinger's unblinking eyes. 'I see. You, and your friend the President, reckon Thurston Macauley ended up like them, chained to the cold water pipes in a bricked-up basement in Beirut?'

'Les Cohen spoke to one of our people in London. He reckons there was another guy around in his prison in Beirut but nobody seems to have mentioned him. He said the guy spoke English. None of the other hostages who've been approached corroborate his story.'

'So it's all down to Cohen?'

104

'S'rite.'

'How does a Jew walk away from a Palestinian hostage situation?'

'Ask him. He's living in London — where you're going tonight. He's got mates in the embassy there, they'll arrange a meet for you. You take it from there. Usual coverage. You're top man wherever you go; same codename; same White House phone number for clearance. Just pick up the ball and keep running with it until you find Thurston Macauley.'

'It'll be my pleasure.'

'Find him and bring him home. You'll find tickets and things at Dulles airport office . . . Any questions?'

Cunningham shook his head.

'Good. Any problems, come straight through to me. Have a nice trip, Jack!'

11

London

Jack Cunningham stood patiently in the sparsely occupied queue for foreign nationals at London's Heathrow and thanked God he was a foreigner. He watched the file of humanity waiting in an unending queue that vanished round the corner in the entrance channels for European passport holders. The immigration officer gave his passport a cursory glance, a brief 'good morning' and not even a nod to the Special Branch detail standing under the baggage sign.

It was raining outside. It had been raining the last time he'd left London. Maybe it was still the same rain; maybe it never stopped raining in London. But he loved it all the same. He'd chosen the same hotel; you can't improve on perfection – Cunningham's philosophy – and he paid the taxi off at the Connaught Hotel. He hung the DO NOT DISTURB sign on the outside doorknob, poured himself a large dose of Johnnie Walker Blue Label and got himself ready for bed. He didn't bother looking at his watch. For the time being he was working on Washington DC time and it was time for bed. He pulled the curtains, and in the dark sat up in the comfortable bed and sipped the whisky. When it was finished he slid under the sheets and slept like a baby.

It was still raining when he woke up at half-past six the next morning.

He gave it another half-hour and dialled a Chelsea

number. The phone was picked up immediately: no name, no greeting, no welcome; just 'Hello.' And then silence.

'Hi, Kerrie . . .'

'You bastard!'

'I didn't think you cared!'

The invective had given a hard edge to her voice; now it softened, husky and sleep-laden. There was an unspoken invitation somewhere in there.

'Where are you Jack?'

'Near enough to offer you breakfast. I'm at the Connaught. Slip something on that'll come off easily and come and join me . . .'

'You're a rotten bastard, Jack. You left me high and dry two months ago, vanished without saying a word. I'm not too fond of you at the moment.'

Cunningham grinned to himself. 'So no breakfast?'

She yawned. 'What's the time?'

He told her.

'For God's sake, Jack! It's the middle of the night!'

'Go back to sleep then. How about lunch?'

'I'll be with you in half an hour. Don't start without me.'

Cunningham put the phone back on its rest and rang room service. He knew Kerrie Sinclair – if she said half an hour that's what she meant. A rarity among women, she didn't make unpunctuality a feminine virtue; she'd be there all right, full of indignation for having been stood up two months ago. But that was part of the business; items were for young people who slipped out of their diapers and set up home together – Kerrie and Cunningham weren't an item. They were too old, to start with, and they were intelligent. Kerrie Sinclair and Jack Cunningham took what they could from each other; they took it when they could and if one of them started belly-aching about impermanence that would be the end of the affair. They'd been at it a long time – ever since as a twenty-two-year-old

Annapolis graduate she'd been persuaded to opt for Naval Intelligence and found herself attached to a two-man CIA team on a watching brief in Buenos Aires during the British Falklands campaign. Her present post suited them both. Assistant naval attaché at the US embassy, she doubled as a senior executive in the Defense Intelligence Agency. Cunningham could relax when he turned over and closed his eyes; he wasn't going to give any secrets away in his sleep – not to Lieutenant-Commander Kerrie Sinclair, USN.

She'd barely finished stirring her coffee when he started.
   'Tell me about Les Cohen.'
   She gave him a sad smile, 'And I thought it was my body you'd come all this way for! Are you making something out of him?'
   He didn't reply. She knew what he meant.
   'Officially?'
   He grunted. It could have been anything.
   'Why don't you come to my office and do it the proper way . . . ?' The smile wasn't reciprocated. It was business. She drank some of her coffee and replaced the cup in its saucer. 'Cohen, or rather Pritchard, which was the name he came out of Beirut with, is suspected of being a Mossad man, not just run of the mill but the real thing – a trained *katsa* – one of the few. We believe he was picked up by a Hezbollah team in the genuine belief that he was a British journalist. He'd have lasted about three minutes if they'd suspected he was a Jew; Christ knows what they'd have done to him if there'd been the remotest suspicion that he was anything to do with Mossad. I dread to think about it.'
   'Any proof?'
   'Nothing that you'd want to put your hand on and swear your life away. He was in Beirut legitimately as a freelance journalist and Reuters took him on in good faith. He was

actually calling himself Pritchard. That's the byline he used as well. But a Cohen, bearing all the hallmarks of Pritchard, according to our well-entrenched source, did the full set at Midrasha – the Mossad Academy north of Tel Aviv – and came out of it with a very high rating. Then, as is practice with the Mossad, he vanished from sight and this Pritchard surfaced in Beirut. Oh yes, he had all the background – passport, credentials, the lot. The fact that "Pritchard" had spent the last twenty years in the Far East freelancing here there and everywhere went totally unnoticed. Unnoticed that there was no pictorial evidence to support the background. The Mossad doesn't do things by half!'

'What about his relations? There was enough publicity when he was picked up and even more when he was released.'

'That was easy enough. You know what *sayanim* are?'

'Tell me.'

'They're voluntary Mossad helpers; pro-Israeli Jews, in this case long-term British citizens. We have 'em at home as well but you can multiply by ten! It wouldn't have been very difficult to raise a few relatives in England . . .'

'How d'you substantiate all this, Kerrie?' It was a superfluous question and Cunningham knew it. Kerrie wasn't the sort of person to accept, and pass on, a load of coffee morning conjecture. She'd have done her homework. She wouldn't necessarily tell him how she'd done it.

'Take it as read, Jack,' she fiddled with her coffee cup but didn't pick it up. 'Les Cohen, on one of the Mossad Academy's little exercises, and they do these things very seriously, got himself shot – three rounds of .22 in the lower chest. Our new friend Pritchard has three bits of plastic surgery on the skin of his lower chest . . .'

Cunningham searched her eyes. She stared back, eyes narrowed. 'Who had a close look at those?' he asked.

'A very reliable source,' she responded, without taking

her eyes away, 'who knows a covered-up bullet hole when she sees one.'

Cunningham's expression remained unchanged; what was going on inside was his business. He thrust it into the background; jealousy and other emotions were not compatible with the espionage game. But now he knew who Cohen told about Thurston Macauley. 'How can I get to know Les Cohen?' he asked.

She reached over and picked up his wristwatch from the side table. She peered at it for a moment before relaxing back in her chair. 'Give him a ring at eleven; ask him out to lunch.'

'He does that for anybody?'

'Uhuh – very cagey man is our Les. He'll be expecting you to call, and when you're sitting there all snug, tucking into the pepper steak don't ask him about his work with the Mossad!'

'As if I would!'

'I know you, Jack Cunningham! Watch your step with this one, he's as tough and as hard as you, and he knows which end of the gun goes into the ear! Do it gently, Jack!'

'Sure.' If Kerrie's advice had found a home it didn't show on Cunningham's face. 'You want it done gently?'

'I didn't mean that – but now that you mention it . . .'

'Come to bed.'

12

Les Cohen didn't look like everyone's idea of a Jew. Which was probably the reason he was now sitting in the Guinea in Bruton Place drinking a pint of Young's bitter and not rotting away in an old sack under a pile of bricks on a Beirut bomb site.

He had light, sandy-coloured hair, blue eyes to go with it and a beak-like nose which only at a pinch could have been described as Hebraic. His chin, firm, had a Cary Grant-like dimple which went with a ready smile. A good-looking man, erudite and intelligent but modest and self-effacing, who for most of his adult life had little problem finding feminine company. Twenty-eight months chained to a wall and forced into acts of degradation by Arab peasants acting in the name of Muslim fundamentalism had affected him more than he would admit; but he refused to allow it to dominate his thinking. Outwardly he remained the same. He only allowed the nightmare to envelop him when he closed his eyes at night. But there were faces. They were there all the time; faces that didn't want to be seen, but nevertheless had been and would one day pay the penalty. Les Cohen promised himself that.

One in particular.

He was without a name in the cellar but Cohen knew him as Razak. He was a nasty, fat, oily piece of work, an Arab from the lowest, dirty, phlegm-running gutter in the dirtiest quarter of

East Beirut; and all the time he was there, overseeing, leaning comfortably against the wall and watching the pain. 'All clothes off!' the order came from one of his minions. 'Too slow!' Kick, kick. 'Faster, faster!' Kick, kick. 'All clothes off – lie down on floor. Keep eyes closed – tie shirt round head . . . turn over on back . . . Why you got snipcock? You Jehudi? No talk! You Jehudi! You got snipcock' . . . Kick, kick, kick. 'You Jew . . . admit you Jew; admit you Israeli . . .'

'Get stuffed!'

'What mean?' Kick, kick, kick.

'Fuck off!'

'Understand, snipcock! Understand "fuck off"! Now you will understand punishment.'

And then it really started. When they got tired of kicking, Razak moved in. He would pick up a Kalashnikov and beat him senseless. He was still beating him even when he came round and he kept on until his arms would no longer carry out his desires. Then one of his people would move in and take over. They had a marvellous time – they kicked; they spat; they beat every part of his body with the butt of the weapon until the circumcision that had offended Razak disappeared into a swollen mass of black, bloody gore. And that was only the third day. For twenty-eight months Razak enjoyed himself at regular intervals; a masturbatory thrashing whenever his frustrations got the better of him. But he never got the better of Les Cohen.

Cohen swallowed two large mouthfuls of beer and watched as the tall American made his way towards him. Kerrie had told him nothing about Cunningham's background. All he wanted, she'd said, was a little chat about some of the people he might have met in Beirut. He might have fooled some, but not Les Cohen. For him there was no mistaking the profession of the man who stopped at the bar, ordered himself a pint and brought it to Cohen's table.

There was no exchange of names, no handshakes, just a simple introduction.

'We spoke on the telephone,' said Cunningham. Cohen nodded and Cunningham sat down and raised the glass to his lips. He came straight to the point. 'We have a mutual friend in Grosvenor Square, I believe?'

Cohen nodded. There was no need for the spy book rigmarole. 'Kerrie Sinclair? I haven't seen her for a few weeks. What's her problem?'

'No problem — ' Cunningham was happy that Cohen hadn't seen Kerrie Sinclair for a few weeks. He couldn't put his finger on it, he just didn't like the thought of this Cary Grant look-alike showing Kerrie his bullet holes. He thrust the vision aside. 'We've mislaid a package,' he smiled mirthlessly, 'or rather we've *lost* a package and Kerrie reckoned you might have spotted it during your, erm, holiday last year.' He could have been talking about an exotic African bird that had lost its way and found itself on the branch of a tree in Wigglesworth.

Cohen studied Cunningham's face for several seconds, then raised his glass to his lips and emptied it. He lowered the glass, inspected it, then said, 'Are you ready for another?'

Cunningham didn't look down. 'No thanks. I'll stick with this one for a minute. You going to have lunch with me?'

'Here?'

'You'd rather somewhere else?'

'Uhuh. This'll do fine. I won't be a minute.' He ordered another pint of Young's, paid for it and left it standing on the bar while he made his way to the lavatory. On his way he studied the back of Cunningham's head. Cunningham hadn't moved. Cohen ignored the lavatory and made for the phone. He dialled the American embassy and asked for

113

Lieutenant-Commander Sinclair. It didn't take long to find her.

'Kerrie, this guy you've sicked on to me – what does he look like?'

No hesitation. Kerrie roughed out a pen picture of the man sitting with his back to the bar in the Guinea. 'Why what's the problem?'

'I don't like him.'

'Do me a favour, Les – try.'

'Sure. He looks like a spook to me.'

'You've been reading too many spy thrillers. He's just a US government statistician, nothing glamorous. Try and help him. I shall be grateful . . .'

'That's encouraging. When?'

'Have a nice day, Les!'

Cohen pulled a wry face at the telephone and returned to the bar to collect his new pint. Kerrie Sinclair was one woman who'd got under his skin. But she wasn't playing hard to get – she just wasn't playing. It was only the once, a night to remember and he'd thought he was home and dry. But the beginning turned into the end; nothing came after that. Kerrie seemed to have taken him in her stride; there hadn't been a second time and he was beginning to doubt there ever would be. He couldn't make it out. She wasn't married. She entered into the spirit of things and kept nothing back. She liked it. He thought she'd liked his way, but there it was – the eternal enigma: somebody was having it saved for him. But why the once? He sat down opposite Cunningham, put his elbows on the table and lowered his voice. The pub was filling up; the lowering of the voice in a crowded area was automatic. It was also a dead giveaway.

'I was the last of the hostages to be turned loose,' he told Cunningham. 'But I suppose you already know that?'

Cunningham gave a slight nod. The Beirut hostages had been hovering on and off the front pages for several years.

114

The releases, drawn out for maximum coverage, had swamped the airwaves since the last gaunt-looking pawn had sat uncomfortably in a Damascus studio under the lights of a thousand media cameras. Everybody in the world knew who had been a hostage – and who'd been the last to leave. Cohen was no Terry Waite or John McCarthy, his coverage had been minimal. When his time came the novelty had started to wear off, but he was still a Name.

'I'd been kept in solitary for the whole length of my stay; I didn't see or hear or speak to any of the stars of the show. In fact the only bloke I spoke to during the two years plus was a malicious bastard by the name of Razak, and then our conversation was limited to the odd "fuck off" by me in reply to the odd insult from him. We took an instant dislike to each other but he was in a position to do something about his.'

'Was that his real name?'

'No. Secrecy was a fetish with those guys. I never saw his face, but I know every nuance of the bastard's voice. I've built up a picture. One day – '

Cunningham cut him off before he built up the dying embers of hate. Cunningham wasn't interested in Cohen's life and times with the Shiite Hezbollah. Cohen didn't take umbrage at the interruption. 'You told Kerrie you heard an American voice just before you were released?'

'He was screaming in an American accent.'

'I'm glad you can see something funny in it.' Cunningham's inclination was to ram his beer mug into the bastard's face. This could be Thurston Macauley he was talking about and the thought of anyone finding Macauley's screams of pain something to make light little quips about cut into him like a hot knife. He controlled himself. Strangely, since talking with Doerflinger about Thurston's disappearance it was only now, at this moment, that he'd

115

even considered the fact that Macauley might be under-going torture and pain, even though there was more than sufficient documentation that it was part of the hostages' everyday ordeal. Somehow he couldn't see Thurston Macauley lying on the floor screaming. It sent a cold ripple down his spine. And his thoughts must have shown on his face.

Cohen bridled. 'After two years in a fuckin' hellhole I reckon I'm entitled to see the funny side of anything.'

Cunningham back-pedalled rapidly. He needed this guy. Now was not the time to needle him. He smiled sadly and lifted his glass of beer. 'I agree. Tell me about it.'

Cohen stared at Cunningham across the table as if trying to make up his mind whether putting Kerrie Sinclair in his debt was worth sitting here talking to this unsympathetic bastard. He made up his mind. It had to be worth it. 'You understand I didn't know where I was; I didn't know a bloody thing other than the cupboard they kept me in. Every so often I was told to put a dirty bag over my head and they dragged me out for a cold shower somewhere in the bowels of the building where they were holding me. I never left that building from the day they dragged me out of my car, bashed me across the head and threw me into the back of another. OK – you're not interested in that; you want to know about the Yank. Right. I don't know what day it was; I don't know whether it was night or day but there was this bloody awful racket started up. It got closer and closer. There were about five different voices all shouting and cursing in Arabic and then there was this sound like a cook bashing the guts out of a bit of tough steak. They stopped outside my door. Now, over the months I'd managed to make a little gap at the hinge side of this ramshackle wooden door from floor level up. They never noticed. They wouldn't, would they?'

'You had a knife?' Cunningham tried to keep the disbelief out of his eyes – and voice.

'I used these – ' Cohen held up his fingernails. 'I took off matchstick-sized pieces, sliver by sliver. It took me months before I had a narrow gap and a mouse-eye view of the passage outside . . .' He paused and his eyes went blank as he took himself back to the nightmare. 'You can't just sit and cry and ask why the bloody hell it's you and not someone else being buried alive – man's not made that way, he'll keep fighting.'

'Some will,' agreed Cunningham, 'Others . . . ?' He shrugged and left it at that. 'What did you do with the bits of wood?'

'Ate 'em. Going back to the Yank . . . I threw myself on to the floor and looked through my gap. All I could see were feet. They were busy kicking something into a pulp. I knew the feeling.'

'Was your friend Razak there?'

'Yeh. He was running this particular rat hole. That bastard wouldn't have missed out on a beating-up. Sure he was there – I recognized his voice. When they'd worn themselves out they all squatted down, lit cigarettes and studied their handiwork. So did I.'

'Tell me about the man on the floor.'

'Not much to tell you. By this time he was flat on his back opposite my crack, at eye level – he'd been worked over by five bored Arabs who'd been fired up by a hatred of anything American; the fact that this one was in no position to defend himself had made it all the more entertaining so they'd really let themselves go. His face could have been anything; from my angle it looked like a pound and a half of raw liver. One eye was hanging out of its socket. There was blood everywhere, but he was still alive – there were great bubbles, as if he was working the guts out of a mouthful of bubblegum, bright red that kept reaching the size of golf

117

balls before bursting in little splattering explosions. One of the guards was fascinated. He leaned right over for a closer look and every so often poked a bubble with the point of a knife and giggled at the miniature shower it produced. Lovely little fellows! There was worse to come . . .' Cohen picked up his glass and took two hefty swallows. Cunningham, expressionless, waited patiently. He didn't push.

'They finished their cigarettes, recovered their energy, then broke both his legs.'

'Jesus Christ!' Cunningham went cold inside. *Oh God! Pray it's someone else. It's not you, Mac, it can't be!*

'He felt it.' Cohen wasn't enjoying his trip back. Tiny beads of sweat kept appearing just above his top lip and every so often he made an unconscious gesture with his forefinger to wipe it dry. Cunningham's jaw remained set, his eyes unflinching, his thoughts only of Thurston Macauley; a laughing Thurston Macauley telling him to fuck off when told to turn his back on his friend, Cong bullets, and certain death to escape across the river. What he was hearing had to be about someone else. Cohen didn't make it easy for him.

'His screams nearly brought the roof down. I thought I'd seen a lot of unpleasantness in my life but this was too much. I left my hole, curled up in the corner and shoved my hands over my ears, but it only deadened the noise. After a hell of a long time it stopped. I went back to the crack and steeled myself for another look. They'd dragged him about two metres further along the passage, I could just see his feet. Three of the Arabs were squatting against the passage wall watching the other two at work. I bloody near ruptured my eyeballs to get them round far enough to see what was going on. God – they must have hated this poor bastard! It's amazing what an evil mind can construct for making his enemies unhappy!' Cohen stopped again for another long drink. This time Cunningham joined him. He still said nothing. He just listened.

'They'd ripped off part of the wall panelling and, I don't know whether you know it but the walls in these basements are made of a type of soft baked clay . . .'

Cunningham shrugged.

'Anyway, they were gouging out a rough sort of alcove.' Cohen pulled a face. 'Alcove would be a flattering description. This, what I could see of it, was just a crude depression. They jammed the poor bugger into it . . .'

'He was dead by now?' asked Cunningham.

Cohen shook his head. 'He was conscious again, making noises. They rammed him into this depression. He just fitted. There was no room for movement of any description and when they picked up the wall panel I saw that they'd cut a hole in it, a hole about the size of a small dinner plate. I reckoned, from the height of it, that would be about where his face was. They hammered the panel back and banged a couple of extra battens to hold it in place – and there you go . . .'

Cohen's face had hardened to rock as he got to the end of the description – a sort of pale, chalk colour as he reminded himself of nearly two and half years of living like a caged animal. He had to glance around his surroundings for a moment to reassure himself that this wasn't just part of the nightmare and that shortly he'd awaken in the filth and grime and claustrophobic horror of a Beirut cellar. He finished his beer and thumped the glass back on to its mat with a little more force than he'd intended.

'D'you want another one?' said Cunningham.

'Make it a Scotch.'

When he returned to the table Cunningham waited until Cohen had helped himself to a large sip and said, 'Did any of that make any sense to you?'

Cohen shook his head. 'I don't think anything those

119

fuckin' madmen did made any sense; this no less than anything else . . .' He stopped and thought for a moment. 'Although as far as this guy's concerned there's a lot more than meets the eye. To start with, he hasn't surfaced even though Hezbollah's declared the game finished, and even stranger, no one's claimed him. If he's a Yank I'm surprised your people aren't raising all sorts of hell. Your lot are getting as nonchalant as the bloody British . . .' He waited to see if Cunningham was going to take umbrage; he would have liked something; some sort of reaction, some show of anger – but he'd tried to needle the wrong bloke. Cunningham merely tilted his head slightly and encouraged him to continue. He did.

'So no reaction from the Americans and nothing at all from any of the Shiite militias who were running these shows. He's a mystery man, he's like that Dumas character, "the man in the iron mask", except this poor bastard's the man in the upright coffin!'

'D'you think he's still alive?' asked Cunningham.

Cohen shook his head. 'Under any other circumstances I wouldn't have given him a cat's chance. But think about it – why go to the trouble of walling him up in a Beirut basement with a hole for his face? It looked like they intended feeding him through that hole to keep him alive – if you can call it that. They could have dumped him as they did with what's-his-name, Buckley, the CIA bigwig who got himself rolled, but no, they went to some trouble. They wanted him alive, but they didn't want anybody to know it. Hopefully, they might have moved him by now – there's a vacant slot in that particular hellhole that I left . . .' Cohen stared accusingly at Cunningham. 'So who was he?'

Cunningham didn't respond. 'If he's still alive what d'you think the chances of finding him are?'

'None.'

'Thanks!'

'D'you know Beirut?'

'I've been there.'

'Not for some time you haven't, I'll bet.' Cohen almost grinned but his face wasn't ready yet for that luxury. 'The last time I had the opportunity to gaze around it was like a bloody great beehive that had a giant boot thumped into it. There are cellars in cellars; rooms made out of shelled masonry; collapsed buildings with tunnels connecting underground compartments – imagine trying to find a one-eyed fly on a dung heap! That would be easier than trying to find an undeclared, unacknowledged hostage in Beirut today.'

Cunningham didn't flinch. 'Have you still got any contacts there?'

Cohen looked incredulous, then suspicious. 'What sort of contacts?'

'Islamic Jihad . . . Hezbollah . . .'

Cohen relaxed slightly. 'You're not thinking of going to look for him?'

'I'm not thinking of anything. I just asked if you'd got any contacts there.'

'You're fucking mad! Forget it!'

Cunningham drained his glass slowly. 'OK.'

'Is that it, then?' asked Cohen.

'Looks like it. You going to eat with me?'

Cohen shook his head. 'I've lost my appetite.' He stood up and studied the tall, grim-looking American, then turned on his heel and headed past the bar towards the pub entrance. No handshake, no thanks for the drinks, no goodbye. Cunningham picked up his empty glass and made his way to the bar as he watched Cohen's tall figure disappear through the door. Now that he was on his own he could behave the way he felt. Almost. What he really felt like doing was screaming at the top of his voice. Even if his victim wasn't Thurston Macauley – and Cunningham had no illusions that the man he'd just been hearing about, the man whose legs had been snapped like sticks of charcoal, was anyone but – this Razak was someone he'd very much like to meet in a dark alley. He ordered a double whisky, no water, no ice, and threw it to the back of his throat. Without waiting for his change he left the pub and began to walk.

He walked for over an hour, oblivious of his surroundings, but it did nothing at all for his state of mind. His anger would last until someone had paid for some poor bastard's broken legs.

13

Cunningham made himself comfortable with a large gin and tonic and a bowl of mixed nuts opposite the bar and settled down to read the price list. But he needn't have bothered. There was no one interested in him, and he knew it. But old habits took an awful long time to die. He left his drink virtually untouched and made his way to the private telephone behind the reception desk.

The number guaranteed a direct line to Joe Doerflinger in Washington.

Doerflinger slept above the shop. The time difference didn't matter. Cunningham didn't apologize. 'Joe, can you have a word with your friend at FBI and find out whether they've got any top Israelis in their sights this week?'

Doerflinger didn't waste time with chat. 'Can I ring you back?'

Cunningham glanced at the hotel brochure on the table in front of him and read out the Ritz phone number. 'I'll be in the bar.'

'Where else!'

'Shalom, Joe.'

Cunningham had finished his gin and tonic and ordered another when a discreet note was placed on his table. He went back to the phone booth and closed the door behind him.

'Jack,' said Doerflinger. 'Paul Schuster sends his regards and offers you the following: there's a Mossad heavyweight under the eye at the moment in Baltimore. They're letting him stew for the time being and waiting for him to show them some new faces. He's reckoned to be the third most senior Israeli intelligence item in the US. His name's Arthur Payne . . .'

'Real name?'

'Shlomo Halevy. He's documented. He's real. D'you know him?'

'No. Has Paul got enough to take him out?'

'Bound to have if they're keeping him on ice. Is that what you want, to have him taken out?'

Cunningham didn't hesitate. 'Yeah. Today – now. Can do?'

Doerflinger gave a deep bellylaugh. 'Sure. Schuster likes that sort of thing! Don't go into detail, Jack, but what d'you want him for?'

'A face card. The guy I'm playing with over here doesn't know the bluff game, he's likely to want to see me.'

'Have we already talked about this player?'

'Yup. I'm about to get a bit heavy on him. Can you tell Paul to hit Halevy now and give me a single word at this number – ' he read out the telephone number of the Connaught Hotel and his room number – 'the minute the guy's put on ice. OK?'

'There'll be a bit of noise, Jack.'

'I don't mind. I'll bargain his release. Play it with me, Joe. Tell Paul to go along with whatever I say if I have to deal with him direct. Will that be OK?'

'Take it as done.'

124

14

Kerrie Sinclair's mouth formed a moue as she dialled Les Cohen's home telephone number. The moue turned to a tight-lipped grimace of frustration when the metallic artificial tones of an answering machine told her to ring another number. Then she relaxed. A good thing in a way. If the Brits were bugging Cohen the chances were that he knew about it. He wasn't, after all, someone who'd just walked in off the factory shop floor. Cohen was a senior Mossad agent – he was one of the most highly trained intelligence operatives in the world. The British would have to get up very early indeed in the morning to catch him with his pants round his ankles. She dialled the number she'd been given. It was answered by a lady who said she was his sister. Could she take a message?

'Ask him to meet me in the Flask at Highgate – Kerrie Sinclair,' she said. 'Seven o'clock. Don't ring me from home – '

'I understand,' responded the voice

Cohen had barely got going on a large Johnnie Walker when Cunningham walked through the door. He studied the tall American over the rim of his glass for several moments but offered neither greeting nor an invitation to sit down. Cunningham's bland expression didn't change as he pulled out the chair on the opposite side of the table and sat down.

'Hi, Les,' he grunted amicably. 'Sorry to have to do things this way but I don't want my voice going into the tape box attached to your phone line.'

Cohen's eyes continued studying him. He looked cool and detached, but his eyes betrayed a hard awareness. He glanced sideways at the door through which Cunningham had entered and, confident that the American, like himself, had thrown any interested natives, returned his gaze across the narrow table and sipped the barely diluted whisky.

'I thought you and I had said goodbye.' He kept the drink in his hand ready for another swallow. 'Have you got Kerrie Sinclair on a string?'

Cunningham ignored the first part of the question and offered Cohen a brief smile. 'You know women. It's probably the other way round. Can I get you another one of those?'

Cohen didn't return the smile. 'I don't think I'm going to be here long enough. Is Kerrie coming or not?'

Cunningham shook his head. 'Nope. You sure you don't want another?'

'No thanks.'

Cunningham went to the bar and bought himself a large Chivas Regal – no ice, no water – and, standing sideways, kept his face to the entrance and one eye on Cohen. But he needn't have bothered. Cohen wasn't going anywhere. He looked relaxed, settled and unconcerned that an evening with a beautiful American woman had turned into a brief encounter with a six foot three American shadowman.

'OK, Les,' said Cunningham, when he rejoined Cohen, 'I'm going to be brutally frank . . .'

Cohen stared at him.

'I want you to go into a trance and try and remember everything about the place where you said you saw this American walled up – ' He paused to sniff the aroma of his Scotch – 'and everything about him that you haven't

126

already told me.' He stopped, pursed his lips and emptied half the Chivas Regal down his throat. He gave it time to do its stuff then nodded contentedly and held Cohen's unresponsive eyes.

'Is that it?' said Cohen. He too lifted his glass, but this time drained it.

'Not quite. I also want the names of all these people you said were giving the fellow the good news and the names and contact points of all your mates, Jew and Arab, who are still in Beirut and its environs – '

Cohen actually smiled.

'Piss off!'

Cunningham smiled back. Viewed from another part of the pub they looked like a couple of old chums sharing a pleasant reminiscence. But the eyes weren't smiling – neither man's. 'I thought something like that might be your reaction, Cohen, so I'll rephrase it – '

'Why d'you call me Cohen?'

'To show you that's the end of the foreplay. I'm a dirty player, Les, I want something from you and I've got two face cards here that I think will stand some heavy money. D'you want to see either of 'em?' By rights, and according to the rules of the game, Cunningham reckoned, Cohen should be on his feet at this stage, his middle finger jabbing at the ceiling with a curt 'Screw you!'

But Cohen was a serious player. He was curious. And it was more than curiosity about why the Yanks were throwing heavyweight intelligence people after a buried man. It couldn't be national pride – they'd given up that tired old banana when Reagan went back to the ranch. He didn't move. He didn't react. Not even a shrug of the shoulders. His face betrayed nothing.

Cunningham studied him for a moment, then continued.

'Les Cohen, senior member of *Ha Mossad, le Modiyn ve le Tafkidim Mayuhadim* which, in case you've forgotten, is the

Institute for Intelligence and Special Operations, known to us ordinary mortals as the dreaded Mossad!' He waited. Still no reaction. '. . .Les Cohen, pretending to be one unfortunate bloody Englishman, Les Pritchard, trained at the Midrasha which is just outside Tel Aviv on the Haifa road, who is now field officer and probably resident agent UK . . . Are you still with me, Les?' Cunningham didn't wait for a reply. He kept his voice very low, barely above a whisper – anyone wanting to overhear would have to be squatting on his heels in the middle of the table. Cohen listened as if it were someone else being described. 'This Les Cohen I'm talking about is, or was, a star turn. He graduated out of the Midrasha fairly near the top. Was made Far East desk man with the code name "Pritchard" and then senior resident *katsa*, Beirut . . . You don't want me to go into the rest do you, Les?'

Cohen still said nothing.

'OK, then. So when you're unhitched from the radiator pipes and they haul you out of the dungeon and ship you here you're still in play. The Brits don't go a bundle on undercover Mossad people taking their names in vain and setting up shop in London so it looks as though you're finished – blown. It's back to Tel Aviv, Les, because you're burnt if the rumours MI5 are nurturing about you in Thames House are confirmed by a US embassy tip-off. How'd you like it so far?'

'I couldn't give a bugger!'

'Very English. Looks like the stiff upper lip culture's rubbing off.' Cunningham studied his target for a long moment. His eyes had lost the slight mocking glint and were now ice cold. 'OK – so you don't give a bugger. But what about your people? D'you think they don't give a bugger too about losing their senior resident who's nicely dug in for ever more and is bomb-proof? It takes years to get a guy like you, a celebrity, one who's paid the entrance fee, set up and in position in a bubble like London. D'you want to have a word with the boys on the Europe desk back home before you cease giving a bugger?'

Expressionless, Cohen studied his empty glass, then, with one finger, flicked it across the table towards Cunningham's resting arms. 'I'll have that drink now,' he said tonelessly. 'Johnnie Walker, Black, large, little bit of water.'

Cunningham emptied his own, went to the bar and refilled them. He placed the two glasses of whisky in the middle of the table, sat down and leaned forward on his arms.

'Had any more thoughts?'

'Funny,' said Cohen as he took the first sip from his new drink, 'how you Yanks put your own salvation and personal security on such a high plane.' He sipped again, taking his time. 'And assume that everyone else feels the same way. Personally, I don't give a monkey's fuck whether I close up shop here or not. And as for, as you call them, my people, d'you think for one moment they'd consider running any sort of apparatus knowing that it could be compromised at any time by a loud-mouthed Yank.' Cohen narrowed his eyes and leaned forward, closer to Cunningham's head. 'Not that I'm admitting to any of this fantasy of yours, but if anything I've ever read about the Mossad is remotely factual, and if I am what you say I am, then your balls wouldn't be worth a couple of hard-boiled eggs.'

Cunningham smiled again. 'I rather assumed you'd raise such a hypothesis, Les. I did say I had *two* face cards.'

Cohen's apparent equanimity slipped for a fraction. But it was no longer than that.

Cunningham's expression didn't change. 'D'you want to see me on the other one?'

'Go on.'

'How's your memory?'

'Fuck my memory. Let's have a look at the card.'

'OK. Get hold of this name and stick it up there for the time being. Shlomo Halevy.'

'Who's he?'

'A little bit more senior than you, Les. He's head of an Israeli intelligence cadre operating out of Baltimore. He's very highly thought of in Tel Aviv and losing him'll cause a lot of unhappiness among your people. But that's only part of it. If he goes on trial for espionage it'll put Israeli/US relations back to those bad old days when Pollard went down for the same thing . . .' Cunningham paused to make sure it was going in. He studied Cohen's eyes. It was. 'Remember Pollard and your Avi Sella? It still rumbles. FBI were sick, CIA were sick and so was Shimon Peres who'd been peeing blood trying to get American cooperation on a new Gaza initiative. You remember all that, don't you, Les?'

'You said something about a card.'

'It's coming. I'd just like you to feel the importance of what I'm suggesting. If this Halevy is brought out into the open and shown to the American media it'll make such a bloody stink that Israel can kiss goodbye, or at least *au revoir*, to the $400 million aid packet that your Prime Minister has just winkled out of us for technical development and the like . . .' Cunningham raised his glass against the light, studied it, and then carried it to his mouth. Before he sipped he returned his eyes to Cohen's. The banter had gone. There was now a hard, interrogatory glint behind his expression. 'How are you reading me so far?'

Cohen returned Cunningham's inspection blandly. He was an old hand at this game; old enough at it to realize that Cunningham had a very serious advantage, and that that advantage was backed up by a solid lump of collateral. He wasn't bluffing. The card was a trump.

Cunningham read the admission in Cohen's eyes. He

didn't wait for his answer. 'Your handlers have to be Mossad's Meluckha Department. Europe or Tel Aviv?'

Cohen made no reply.

Cunningham didn't let it upset him. 'If you want to discuss this with Meluckha's Europe headshed in Brussels I'm prepared to look the other way. Personally, and if I were you, I'd go right to the top, Tel Aviv – save you having to tell the story three times over – and tell them to have the American desk confirm Halevy's problem . . .'

Cohen's survival instincts cringed at the casual manner in which the American reeled off his knowledge of the Mossad chain of command and base structure, but he realized that this was all part of the process; Cunningham was showing him that he was no ordinary field officer of an American intelligence agency, and he certainly wasn't from a government research and statistics department as Kerrie had described him. This man was special. There was a lot of weight here. And he wasn't finished yet.

'I can't put him back into his shadow,' continued Cunningham, 'but what I could do is have him quietly sent back to Tel Aviv with a nasty testimonial. That way there'd be no political repercussions. It would be a small price to pay, Les. Your Prime Minister will be very grateful to have a loophole arranged by you.'

Cohen's response was to lift his glass and empty it.

Cunningham raised his eyebrows. 'D'you want another one of those?'

'No thanks,' grunted Cohen.

'OK. Oh, one more thing,' added Cunningham, without rancour. 'You're under British security surveillance. You had a watcher yesterday.'

'I had one today as well,' said Cohen, standing up. 'They don't take themselves too seriously. They don't worry me.'

'Your phone – '

'I know. Simple stuff, but effective. Don't use it.' He

began to move away. 'I'll ring you. Will you be in after nine?'

Cunningham looked up at him blank-faced – *which would be quite nice for a knock on the bedroom door and a face full of .22s. No way, Les!* Cohen knew what was going on in Cunningham's brain; he'd have been surprised at any other reaction. But he wasn't troubled by the response. 'No – leave a message with a number I can ring. Can you get a decision this evening?'

Cohen didn't reply. He tilted his head slightly, turned on his heels and left the pub. Cunningham sat and sipped contentedly at his Chivas Regal while he waited for Kerrie to join him.

15

Within three hours Cohen's sketchily drawn report and assessment of his meeting with Cunningham was sitting in front of the Israeli Prime Minister in the cabinet office in Tel Aviv.

Confirmation of Halevy's situation was unavailable; his number two in the A1 – the highly secret unit of Israeli agents working under deep cover in the United States was incommunicado, and rightly so, but they had no doubts about Cohen's reliability and the veracity of his report and the A1 unit was quickly closed down and its members dispersed. The cabinet's interest was heightened by the lack of information available on Jack Cunningham. With all the *sayanim* apparatus in places that mattered in Washington they still failed to come up with any form of match to the name and profile. This in itself was enough to provoke a small crisis.

The Head of the Mossad, sitting at the Prime Minister's right, stared stolidly in front of him. He knew the business too well. If the Americans wanted anonymity for one of their agents they would get it. They were past masters at keeping shadows intact. Cunningham, whatever his real name might be, was covered. He would be impenetrable. But he would also be special – very special. He would have access to FBI strategy and inside knowledge of its activity, and, by the sound of it, before the activity took place. A man with international contacts; he'd blown Cohen's cover, which meant he was probably responsible for Halevy getting himself burnt.

'. . . so will you summarize, Shmuel?'

The Head of Mossad jerked himself out of his reverie. He'd decided long before the discussion had started what he was going to do. The PM was going through the motions. Everyone had their say. They'd be unanimous after they'd given their views an airing. Talking, having their say, made them feel important. Politicians! He looked at no one in particular as he summed up.

'Cohen must do exactly as the American wants.' He paused. 'For three reasons.' His voice was clear and decisive. There was no interruption, no nodding or shaking of heads, no objections; the collective eyes of the Israeli cabinet centred unblinkingly on his face. The deathly silence that had descended after the earlier babble of exchange and forced opinions was broken only by the scrape of a water bottle dragged from the centre of the table.

'The first – ' he emphasized with a raised finger – 'is to secure the release and return to Israel of Shlomo Halevy . . .'

'Unpublicized,' interjected the Prime Minister.

'Unpublicized,' repeated Shmuel Saguy with a trace of annoyance at the interruption. But it went over the head of the PM, who continued: 'And an abject apology without committing Israel to any admittance of abusing American hospitality and friendship by espionage rings – '

'Of course, Prime Minister,' responded Saguy acidly. 'May I continue?'

'You must, Shmuel. But try not to waste time. What's the second reason?'

'The second reason,' said Saguy, disguising his exasperation, 'is to prevent Cohen being exposed as having been an Israeli agent whilst in the hands of Hezbollah. This would raise a multitude of undesirable questions from the world's media. They would feel, and probably rightly, that Israel playing hostage cards could have caused untold harm to the American and British hostages. We could never even begin to explain how one of our senior intelligence agents masquerading as a British journalist was taken by the Shiite and held hostage. Hezbollah would make a meal of it. They'd be able to say they knew one of their hostages was an Israeli secret agent and that's why all the others were kept so long . . . A matter of Palestine/Arab security . . . It was Israel's fault, not theirs – '

'Rubbish!'

Saguy ignored the single exclamation. 'This American, Cunningham, according to Cohen's assessment, will keep the curtain in place if Cohen gives him a lead into West Beirut . . .'

'Cohen has only recently been released from being a hostage. Isn't he at risk going back?' asked a hitherto unheard voice.

Saguy wasted no time on him. 'Of course he is. But that's what he's paid for, to take risks – love of country, a deep sense of patriotism and a great big cheque paid into his account every month. That's what he, and all the others, take risks for.'

Another voice demanded to be heard. 'According to this,' the owner of the voice tapped a heavy fist on the sheets of paper in front of him, 'Cohen is already at risk, which means that the Mossad is too. In here he says MI5 has him under surveillance. How did that happen?'

Saguy stared at the speaker until he wilted. He managed to keep the contempt out of his eyes. 'It's a routine surveillance. London has nothing better to do with thousands of pairs of legs now that the Soviets have stopped making a nuisance of themselves. All the returned British hostages are given the same watch. It's not ominous as far as

Cohen is concerned. It won't reflect on him.' He paused to bring their minds back to the reason why they were all there. 'As soon as the Prime Minister nods in my direction I propose instructing Cohen to carry out Cunningham's wishes. Our people in position in the west of Beirut can cover them through to where Cunningham wants to go, or we can put another agent in specifically to look after Cohen.'

'I don't want too many of our people involved in this.' The Prime Minister had been quiet too long. It wasn't characteristic.

Saguy looked hard at him. There was nothing ulterior in the statement – and it wasn't advice. It was an order.

'. . . one "jumper", one *katsa*. I don't want our business in Beirut exposed to American curiosity.'

'I had in mind – ' began Saguy.

But the Prime Minister stopped him with a limp wave of the hand. 'One good man plus a cover agent to take care of Cohen. That's it. The American can look after himself and Washington can take care of any kickbacks – if kickbacks there are to be. No bargaining, Shmuel. That's my decision.' With cold eyes he studied the head of his country's Central Institute for Intelligence and Special Duties. The message was there for Saguy to read – no deviation. 'Are we all agreed, then?' he finished.

'Shmuel said there were three reasons why we should get involved in this,' said the earlier questioner. 'I've only heard two so far.'

A murmur went round the table.

The Prime Minister locked eyes with Shmuel Saguy again and raised his eyebrows.

Saguy acknowledged the question with the merest movement of his large head. 'The individual the American has been sent to find was a special envoy between the US

President and Hussein of Jordan. It was, by every indication, personal and private stuff between those two. But
Hezbollah got to hear about it and decided it was important
to them.' He stopped and drank half the glass of water in
front of him, then slowly placed it back on the table. There
were no interruptions. 'Anything that concerns Hezbollah
to this extent concerns Israel. If anybody is holding this
information, waiting for the crucial moment to divulge it,
then I shall want to know about it too. If Cohen is holding
the hand of the American, the American will have to share
his findings with him. This is our main interest. To this
interest individuals are expendable.' He waited another
moment. 'So are principles.'

16

The message waiting for Cunningham when he got back to the Connaught at half-past eleven was to ring a Hampstead number and ask for Rosie Perry. It turned out to be another of Cohen's 'sisters'. She told him Cohen would be at the same place they'd last met – tomorrow, midday.

It was an unusual start to the day for London: warm, the sun shining, clear sky overhead and the surging mass of people for once looking less than miserable. Cunningham easily threw off his watcher and sat outside the Flask at a wooden picnic table in a secluded corner of the front area. Cohen slid on to the uncomfortable ledge seat and the two men sat for a few minutes in silence while they ensured that one of their watchers hadn't been lucky and stuck.

'D'you want a drink?' asked Cohen eventually. He appeared much more relaxed than in their previous meetings; it was as if a weight had been taken off his shoulders. His instructions from Tel Aviv had been clear. There was no longer a need to shadow-box with the American. He stood up.

'Pint of bitter,' responded Cunningham. He continued his surreptitious survey of the pub and its surroundings while he waited for Cohen's return. It was too early for the lunch mob. The people sharing the morning sun and enjoying their unemployment benefits were the serious drinkers, the locals, and there were few enough of them for Cunningham and Cohen to sit in comparative isolation. But it didn't go to their heads; they continued speaking in undertones – it was a professional habit.

Cohen opened the batting. 'My people are not sure whether to take you seriously . . .' It was a normal opening gambit. They both knew the moves by heart. 'You're not a known factor so there's no way they can weigh this thing up. It seems we have no business to discuss.'

Cunningham let Cohen's words hang in the air for a moment while he sampled his beer.

'Has anyone tried to talk to Halevy?' he said at length.

'They think he could be out of town.'

Cunningham swallowed another mouthful of beer. That meant all the stops had been pulled out to verify Cunningham's story. Halevy had disappeared. It was a serious proposition.

'He's not,' said Cunningham.

'How can we be sure it's your people who have him and not our neighbours?'

'You'll have to take my word for it.'

'And if I don't?'

'Tough on Shlomo. What do you want, Les? Or rather, what do the people want?'

Cohen took his time. 'OK, Cunningham. First, they want a top name to talk to in the States, and secondly, if you have got Halevy, permission for one of our embassy people to have a face-to-face with him.'

Cunningham was ready with the answer.

'OK the first. Director FBI Intelligence Group suit you?'

'Adequate. And the second?'

'Negative, Les. Halevy stays under cover until our little bit of business is concluded.'

It was Cohen's turn to think. He didn't take long. His orders from Tel Aviv had been quite specific. 'OK. I'll pass the name and number on. They'll want to check it out . . .'

'Naturally.'

'. . . and assuming you and your people are all on the level with this, I'm authorized to offer any help I can give you.' Cohen paused and studied Cunningham's face. It was always worth a try – not with a great deal of expectation. 'D'you want to tell who's running you on this Beirut chase?'

'Don't be silly, Les.'

' – or what your status is?'

'Even sillier.' Cunningham finished his beer. 'Come on, drink that up and we'll go and get something to eat. When we've done that I'll give you that name and number to pass on and then I'll explain exactly how we're going to play this little expedition. OK?'

Cohen didn't reply. His mind was busy mulling over how little Cunningham had given away. Yesterday it had been cut and dried. Tel Aviv had said go ahead. Tel Aviv already knew the Director of FBI Intelligence; they also knew his telephone numbers – business, personal, private and everything else; they even knew his girlfriend's phone number, so Cunningham's offer amounted to nothing before they'd even started. And there was not a lot Cunningham could offer on Halevy. They knew the FBI had him; the only thing they didn't know was where they had him. Cohen was only stalling for his own benefit; he was the one losing out, he was the bloke who was going to have to have a second go at the Beirut bungee jump – and the elastic was beginning to look decidedly frayed and dodgy.

Cunningham swirled the last of the wine around in its thin glass and swallowed it over a mouthful of ripe Stilton. 'How d'you fancy Paris as a jumping-off point?'

'It's all the same to me,' said Cohen.

'Monday – any time Monday,' said Cunningham. 'US

140

embassy. Ask for extension 2116 and leave the name of your hotel. I'll ring you and arrange a meet.'

'What name?'

'Cunningham. Here are a couple of ground rules for you to enter into your memory bank. Don't touch British airports on this ride. You're still a face for the newspapers and likely to attract attention. I don't want that – for you or me. Plus there's this little Brit team that's looking after your back. You'll have to lose them. My recommendation is that you go by one of the ferry ports as a foot passenger. You shouldn't have any trouble there.'

Cohen smiled. It was almost as if being active again had given him a new lease and a new outlook. 'I'm not worried about them – or airports . . .'

'But I am,' said Cunningham. 'Take the ferry. I'll expect you in Paris Monday p.m.' He loosened up as he raised his finger for the waiter. 'And then it'll be your turn to pay a bill.'

17

Cunningham and Cohen spent two days in Paris, during which time they convinced themselves they had lost any interest from the British and picked up none from the French. Cohen had been covered by people from Mossad's Meluckha 'C' Branch in Paris and moved around quite openly. His progress was reported directly to Shmuel Saguy in Tel Aviv.

A Canadian passport for Cunningham and a New Zealand one for Cohen were cobbled together by the CIA's Paris station within the US embassy in Avenue Gabriel and documents prepared to establish them as freelance journalists. A cover was prepared to identify them as being on a CNN assignment covering the post-Gulf-War Middle East domestic scene from an Arab point of view. On this basis visas were legitimately applied for, and granted, and the two men left Paris together on the daily Air France flight for Beirut.

Accommodation had never been a problem in Beirut. It was even less of a problem now and the Commodore Hotel in West Beirut's Hamra district welcomed them with open arms. A once grand edifice on the newly named Rue de Baalbek, it had been the unofficial HQ of the foreign press corps in the days when the only danger to pressmen was getting killed. John McCarthy being kidnapped convinced foreign correspondents that there wasn't something special about their calling and that in Hezbollah eyes they too, like anybody else, were more than fair game in the hostage business. This had a marked effect on the once over-crowded accommodation and well patronized bars of the Commodore. When Cunningham and Cohen booked in it had all the ambience of a working men's club in Sunning-dale.

But the hotel's telephone system hadn't changed; it was still just as suspect. The pause when the receiver was picked up, the undisguised click, the whirring of an old-fashioned bugging system and the hollow bounced-back sound as if talking into an empty baked beans tin made an outside call a risky business. Cancel a lunch appointment, no problem – but anything else and the whirring of the tape recorder beside the hotel switchboard worked itself up into an almost deafening crescendo. It was common practice to stroll down the Rue Sadat to the Backstreet Club, off the Rue Bliss, to make a telephone call in comparative peace of mind, and the gin wasn't bad either. The phones were probably tapped as well but more efficiently; there were no backsounds to upset the caller's complacency.

But it wasn't good enough for Les Cohen. He had a better system.

Without telling Cunningham he left the hotel and caught a cruising taxi in the Rue Emile Edde. He instructed the driver to take him to Port Crossing and the taxi took off into the traffic with the driver's thumb glued to the horn. Cohen spent the next two kilometres sitting at an angle watching the traffic through the rear window. When he turned to his front he caught the driver's eyes in the rear-view mirror. They were waiting for the confrontation and Cohen's un-Mediterranean features came under close scrutiny.

'You want Arab girl?' asked the driver in broken French. Beirut taxi drivers didn't see many, openly, Western men heading towards the red light district these days. 'Pretty ones, very young . . .' He grinned to show that he too was a man of the world and could probably guarantee Cohen, for a large fee, one of the more common transmittable diseases.

Cohen looked at him blankly for another half-kilometre then answered in equally execrable French, 'That sort of thing – but I'll choose my own', and by his tone and expression cut out any further conversation. The possibility of the driver reporting the collecting and dropping-off point of a well-built Westerner was unlikely, but a garrulous Westerner would always be a subject if the question ever came up.

'Drop me over there –' Cohen leaned forward and rested his arm on the driver's scrawny shoulder while keeping his finger pointing straight ahead.

'Other side of the Etoile – OK?' The driver took his eyes off the road and his thumb off the horn to turn his head and study Cohen's eyes. The silence after the continual din was as refreshing as the switching off of a dentist's drill.

'OK,' responded Cohen quickly. 'Anywhere beyond those lights.' He sat back abruptly so that the driver could concentrate on where his taxi was taking him. But it didn't matter. Everybody's horn was ringing as if Lebanon had won the World Cup and they raced round the large roundabout as if they were the only car on the move. The driver screeched his tyres against the kerb, turned round again before he'd fully stopped and offered another lewd remark in his broken French, then a bit of gratuitous filth in Arabic as a matter of habit. Cohen could have talked the Arab driver under the table in his own language, filth and all, but he gave no reaction as he paid up and got out. He moved back from the edge of the road. The taxi squealed into a tight U-turn and sped off, horn screaming, back into the Etoile.

Cohen waited until the taxi had been ensnared by the noisy traffic going up Rue El Maarad before moving off in

144

the opposite direction. He studied his surroundings like a stranger to the district and walked casually along the open boulevard, taking side roads and then returning like a lost tourist until, satisfied, he returned to the main boulevard and took one of the smaller roads running into the mean backwaters behind the glitter. He stopped by the first entrance after the corner and lit a cigarette. His elbow twice pressed the bell on the solid wooden door and once more as he replaced the packet of cigarettes in his pocket. Then he continued, walking without haste, studying each of the lower-class cafés that proliferated in the gloomy street. He seemed to find one he liked. The Café Voltaire's door was open and the aromatic smells of *kibbah* and lamb roasting in olive oil for the inevitable *shwarma*, mingled with the tingling smell of smoky charcoal, coffee and Turkish cigarettes, poured out into the street. He kept his expression of neutral curiosity in place as he took a seat at a small table just round the corner from the open door and ordered a large pastis and a glass of weak lemon tea.

He took his time sipping the lukewarm concoction, leaving the pastis to gather strength after its heavy dosing of water, and gazed about him with mild interest. The Lebanese barman didn't disturb him but watched surreptitiously. He had a good idea what Cohen was waiting for.

The first girl who poked her head round the corner of the door didn't linger; a quick experienced look, a meeting of eyes and acknowledgement and she pulled her head back and disappeared into the street. The second girl lasted a few minutes longer before she went the same way and the third girl went about the same distance. Cohen moved on to his pastis just as the first girl returned, raised her eyebrows and after a brief nod over the lip of his glass from Cohen pulled out a chair and sat down.

She was more attractive close up if one could read features under a heavy coating of thick red lipstick, purple eyeshadow and heavy black-coated eyelashes. She was still in her prime, for her profession – about twenty-four years old – but her amateur make-up managed to detract rather than attract. She wasn't Arab. Probably Lebanese – her lighter skin looked as if it might have been diluted by a French connection some time in the past. Perhaps her mother had enjoyed the same profession and made the ultimate mistake. Her dark brown eyes were intelligent, but sharp and suspicious as she sized up her potential customer. She didn't smile, her lips could have been glued together by the dark red, almost black lipstick, but she entered into noisy negotiation with Cohen with the attitude of someone who didn't give a damn whether he wanted it or not.

The waiter leaned on his counter and watched and listened with interest.

She opened the bidding in French, saw very quickly that she was getting nowhere and tried Arabic. The waiter smiled to himself. He could see she was wasting her time. She progressed tentatively to stilted English, and Cohen responded. Neither he nor she looked too happy at the outcome and she pulled a face at the waiter over Cohen's shoulder when he stood up to pay for his drinks. The waiter shrugged significantly as he banged the till drawer and dropped Cohen's coins noisily into the tray.

Neither of them spoke as she led him back down the street towards the corner of the boulevard and he followed her through the door where he'd stopped to light his cigarette. She led the way up the stairs to a banistered landing and then turned off, up a narrow flight of stairs that ended on a small landing with two doors leading off. Cohen ignored the shapely bottom under the tight leather miniskirt and the smooth, olive-skinned legs, long and finely tapered, that hovered just in front of his eyes. He concentrated on his surroundings.

Cohen's woman opened her door, glanced at him over

her shoulder and he slid into the room behind her. He waited while she locked, and double-locked, the door. He wasn't surprised, or worried, by her precautions as he leaned against the wall and watched. She turned and smiled nervously: the cracking of her lipstick was almost audible. Cohen smiled back thinly and without further ado she kicked off her shoes and threw herself on to the bed.

'There's whisky and cognac in the cupboard.' She waved her hand in the direction of a rickety, modern, plywood sideboard. It had a tarnished mirror on a swivel with a heavy crack across one corner as if a dissatisfied customer had taken his frustration out on it. Another lump was missing from the other top corner, but there was still sufficient for Cohen to catch sight of his haggard features as he reached down to open the fragile, ill-fitting doors. He straightened up and took another quick glance at himself as he placed the bottle of indifferent grape brandy on the tray alongside two thick glasses, a bottle of Vittel water and a half-bottle of yellow-coloured liquid with a large Arabic pattern on a green background. It could have been anything. Cohen nudged it to one side, poured an inch of brandy into each of the glasses, doubled the volume with warm Vittel and handed one to the girl.

'My God, you've changed, Les,' she whispered after a first sip and a grimace. 'I hardly recognized you. What did they do to you?'

He smiled indifferently. 'I've improved a hundred per cent since they let me go. You should see some of the others!' He searched her face. 'How long ago was it, Ruti?'

She thought for a moment. 'Four, five years – best not think about it, Les.' She'd abandoned the broken English she had used earlier and now, in the safety of her room, spoke Hebrew. Her eyes softened at the recollection of their last meeting. But Cohen didn't want any elaboration

147

of long-term memories – re-establishment of the association was enough. He shrugged her searching glance to one side.

'How long have you been on station here?' He glanced around the dingy room and pulled a face. 'You deserve better.'

Ruti didn't smile. It didn't matter to her what she deserved; she was doing a job, she was a trained agent. In this business everything went and this particular post was one of the drawbacks, but she knew how to handle herself. She wasn't a whore – she only looked like one. 'I've been here about a year,' she said at length. 'I'm not complaining.' She became businesslike. 'I've been told to put myself at your disposal. Apparently you're being covered by Baruch Lev who's just moved back into position here. He's looking after your back. D'you know him?'

'Only by sight.'

'He's all right – a bit loud, but safe. As far as I can gather he stays out of sight. His major responsibility is to act as guide dog, and Rottweiler if you meet with unpleasantness. He'll be good at both. He was part of the Submarine project on the east border before it closed down so he knows more than most of our contacts here. My little bit is just that – a little bit. I have to put you and Lev together and act as postmistress.'

'Does Lev have any locals on his payroll?'

'Only he would know that.'

Cohen sipped his brandy and water meditatively. 'OK. Arrange a meeting,' he said as he put his glass down. 'Say tomorrow morning . . .'

'Where?'

'Make a suggestion.'

Ruti frowned, then nodded her head. 'Better use this place. I can cover the entrance from the café over the road. Nothing unusual about that.' She smiled deprecatingly, 'Just a local whore hanging around to earn the rent money. Safe enough. Here's a key to the front door, I'll leave this one on the latch.'

Cohen ignored the slight touch of bitterness. He glanced at his watch. 'That's about long enough for a short time. See you tomorrow morning, then, eleven o'clock.'

It was probably one chance in several million that Razak should raise his eyes and glance across the road at the moment the prostitute and her customer entered the building on the corner of the Rue Felix Ebouć.

Sitting at a pavement table of the café that occupied the corner of Ruti's mean street and the glitzy boulevard, toying with his glass of sweet thick coffee, Razak for a moment stopped teasing the teenage Lebanese prostitute sitting with him and glanced over her shoulder. He was just in time to see Ruti's tight, slim, leather-clad bottom, the miniskirt revealing most of her long shapely legs, disappear through the door. This was more like it! Then he saw the man. His lip curled. A Westerner. He studied him during the brief moment that he paused before he followed the girl through the door, first with curiosity, then with interest, and finally the slow dawning of recognition.

He turned his chair ninety degrees so that he was face on to the door where the two people had entered, and renewed his conversation with the young prostitute. But there was no depth to it; as young as she was she'd already learnt the signs that she had someone on the hook. This one wasn't. And he looked mean and cheap. She got up to go.

'Just a minute.' Razak had finished thinking. He slid £10 under the saucer of her coffee cup and put his hand on hers as she reached out for it.

She sat down again. 'Not enough,' she lisped.

'I'm not paying for that,' he showed her his nice white teeth in a hiss of contempt. It didn't put her off.

'Whatever it is it's still not enough,' she said.

'Is this your regular beat?'

'What's it to you?'

'D'you want a broken leg?'

It was the expression on his face when he said it. She knew he meant it. A broken leg in Beirut in 1994 wasn't a big deal, and a lot of them didn't know how to stop once they started. The promise of a broken leg could lead to all sorts of additional problems.

'No, thank you,' she whispered.

'Then answer the question.'

'Yes.'

'Good. Listen carefully. On the other side of the road, just behind your shoulder – don't turn round! About two doors down. Who works from there?'

She couldn't help it, she needed more than that to orientate herself. She turned her head quickly, then back again. 'It's a big place. I think there's twelve rooms – twelve flats, I mean – '

'I know what you mean! I asked how many girls – '

'About fifteen. Some share.'

'D'you know any of them?'

She shrugged her shoulders and pouted her thin, inadequate lips. I work here. I know most people . . .'

'Good. Take that money,' invited Razak, 'and go over there and find out what girl has just taken a man in.'

Her eyebrows arched. 'Why?'

'Just do as you're told.' His lips tightened. 'I'll give you another ten when you come back and tell me.' As she got up from her chair, he clicked his tongue. She hesitated.

'What?'

'Find out if there's any other way out of the building.'

'There isn't – I know.'

This was easy money. She tripped across the road, stood on her tiptoes to press a button and speak into a grille and the door clicked open. She vanished from Razak's sight. She rejoined him in less than ten minutes.

'I had to give the concierge £2.'

'Take it out of that.' He pushed another £10 under the saucer but kept his hand on top of it. 'Talk.'

Razak never forgot a face. He needed a much closer look at the face he'd seen briefly across the road, but he was fairly certain he wasn't going to be disappointed. Even at that distance; even so briefly; even without its straggly beard, unkept hair and a bent, dog-like stance from lack of exercise he was sure that he'd just seen Les Pritchard. Razak closed his eyes and brought the memory picture closer. You don't look deeply at a man's tortured eyes several times a day for two years for a shave and a haircut to make him invisible. That was Les Pritchard in the heart of Beirut. Why would Les Pritchard risk coming back to Beirut? Would any man be that stupid? But Les Pritchard was for many months within a few yards of one Thurston Macauley, who represented all the money in the world. Razak's mind never took the simple option: Pritchard was here and Pritchard was a danger to Razak's future. These coincidences showed the hand of God. It was God who had invited Razak to sit down at the corner café and talk to a teenage whore; it was God who had made Pritchard walk past on the other side of the road with another whore. And that was all wrong. Why would a man who, from the curiosity value of his own misfortune, could have almost any woman he chose, come to Port Crossing in Beirut to fuck one of the cheapest whores in the world?

'Does she accept business at the door?' Razak asked the girl when she'd told him where Ruti's apartment was.

'What's wrong with me?' asked the skinny whore plaintively.

'Answer my question.'

'No, she does the streets.'

'These streets?' Razak pointed his chin along both directions of the boulevard and then the narrow streets running off. 'Every day – all the time?'

The teenager nodded. 'But she doesn't do much business,' she said cattily. 'Not as much as me.'

Razak nodded absently. The bells were ringing. Thirty years of ducking and weaving in the dirty game had given him a special way of looking at choosy whores; and he knew what prostitutes needed to do to earn a living. If Pritchard's whore wasn't lying with her legs open and arching her back at least six times a day, every day, something was wrong.

'D'you have a pimp?'

'Of course.' She looked over her shoulder to make sure he was loitering there in case this one starting throwing his fists about. 'We all do.'

'What about her?' He pointed his chin again at the door on the other side of the road.

'I don't know. Why don't you ask her?' She glanced at him coyly. 'You sure I can't offer you a little relief or something?'

Razak didn't answer. He was still thinking.

She stood up. 'I have to go now. Can I have my money, please?'

He barely noticed her as he lifted his hand and allowed her to collect her winnings then sat back in his chair, called for a newspaper and waited for a confirmatory look at Les Pritchard.

18

Razak was ready when the door across the road opened and the man he knew as Les Pritchard came out.

Cohen glanced once up and down the street, then strode briskly in the direction of the Place Etoile where he was soon in the midst of the crowd. Razak followed. It was only then, when he was among people, that Cohen seemed to relax. He took no evasive action but stared around him as if he were just a tourist. It worked. Nobody gave him more than a second glance.

Razak watched him hail a passing cab, moved in closer to get its number and then carried on walking round the Etoile to return to his starting point at the café. The telephone was downstairs, mixed up with the lavatories and miscellaneous boxes, crates and cases. Razak didn't notice the smell or the disorder: it was all very normal to a man who spent most of his waking life under the rubble of south Beirut. But he hadn't lost all his friends; least of all those of the Hezbollah underground movement within the Beirut establishment.

The Commissaire in charge of Beirut's police and traffic administration was only too pleased to help his friend Razak. 'A taxi driver's details? Absolutely no problem, my dear brother. Anything else?'

'Not yet, brother – but do you have a complete list of authorized whores?'

'We do. Have you caught some clap – ha, ha, ha? Give me her address. Do you have her name?'

'I'll come back to you. Thank you, brother.' Ruti's fate was sealed with lewd chuckles all round.

Razak was taken by the taxi driver's infant son, bare-footed and clad only in a dirty stained *sabaya*, to a food stall, erected incongruously on the hard concrete of what used to be a Citroën concessionaire's showroom floor before a couple of Israeli tanks, during the 1982 siege, following up on half a dozen rounds of 120mm, took a short cut through to the next street. The boy's father was squatting in a group drinking Turkish-style coffee and munching hot pitta bread, every so often filling his mouth from a bowl of *fool* – warm black bean stew. Not a pretty sight. But it affected Razak. He slapped the child round the head and flicked a twenty-piastre coin into the dust at his feet. The child picked it up and ran. It was worth precisely nothing.

The child's father came a little more expensive. He wanted money for his interview. He wanted real money – American money. For $5 he remembered picking up a Westerner; for another $5 he remembered dropping him at the Commodore Hotel and for $5 more he'd be prepared to go to the Commodore and see his friend who was on the door and would remember the Westerner's name, and anything else he might want to know at $5 US a throw.

'Let's go,' said Razak.

That wasn't the intention, muttered the driver to himself, but with ten American dollars in his pocket and the possibility of more to come this wasn't the time to make waves.

Razak waited impatiently as the taxi steamed in the hot sun on the other side of the road while its driver leaned against the Hotel Commodore's front wall in the shade and smoked cigarettes with his friend the main hall bell-boy.

'He's a journalist from New Zealand,' said the driver as he climbed back into his taxi and started the engine. As he pulled away he stuck his hand over his shoulder and, when he studied its harvest, turned fully and regarded Razak's face. 'D'you want to know something else?'

Razak wiped the running sweat from the unbearded part of his face with a grubby cloth and stuffed it in his side pocket. He was wondering whether he should kill this insolent fellow when he'd exhausted the man's information. He was in the mood for violence; his face stared back aggressively at the mean features in front of him. 'Turn to your front,' he growled. 'Look where you're going. I don't want to die in a road smash in the middle of Beirut.'

'It would be God's will.' The face vanished and Razak addressed the back of the man's head.

'What other things have you to tell?'

The hand came over the shoulder again, closed over yet another $5 note and went back to the wheel

'This New Zealand journalist booked in with a Canadian journalist named Cunningham.' He stopped talking and waited. When nothing came from the back of the taxi he said, tentatively, 'Is that worth more dollars?'

'No.'

The driver shrugged his shoulders, then offered a bonus as goodwill. 'This Canadian journalist spoke to the American embassy this morning.'

'So?'

'The American embassy – not the Canadian embassy.'

'It doesn't mean anything. None of it does. Drop me over there, by that café . . .'

The driver did as he was told. He leaned across the front seat and stuck his face out of the window. 'That'll be £4,' he said.

'What for?'

'The fare.'

Razak stared at him for a moment. He turned over his left hand, studied it and made as if to empty whatever he saw there into his right hand. Then, spitting on the ground, he hurled the non-existent handful into the driver's face. 'Eat that!' he snarled and walked away.

Baruch Lev did the same as Cohen had done the day before but chose a different café. This one was no less dirty than the other, no less smelly, but the sort of place a man in his mid-twenties with Armenian features and colouring would find something to work his frustration out on. He did.

Ruti went through the same charade as she'd done with Cohen, but this time every move she made was made under the eye of Razak.

He'd had his homework done for him. His friend the Commissaire had given Ruti the treatment. Not only was she not a registered prostitute, she was not a registered anything. There were no records of Ruti; she had no identity. If she carried any documents they would not have been issued from Lebanese Central Registry. In the words of the Commissaire she qualified for 'an in-depth examination of some severity . . .'

'But you have business with this whore, my friend?'

'I think so.'

'Hezbollah business?'

'Of course.'

'You want some assistance?'

'I might.'

'I will put a very good man at your disposal. One of the best. He will be awaiting your call. Please use him. And when you have finished this business, my brother, I would like to talk to this whore – ' he laughed jovially. 'She is beginning to interest me.'

And, to Razak's surprise, she was walking across the road towards him in her working kit – black leather miniskirt, heavy make-up, ponytailed hair flouncing up and down – having left her newly acquired customer alone in her rooms to work out his own entertainment. Razak lowered his head over his newspaper and watched her from the corner of his eye. She sat down at a table sideways on to her apartment, ordered coffee and casually lit a cigarette. But Razak wasn't deceived. He could see she was wound up like a clock spring.

He lifted his newspaper and moved slightly in his seat to be able to study her without turning his head. She'd taken no notice of him; he was just another bearded, swarthy Arab in a cheap suit, but as he looked again, casually, she stiffened. He followed her glance.

Walking briskly on the other side of the road was the man he'd seen leaving her apartment yesterday, the New Zealand journalist who bore an unmistakable likeness to the former hostage, Les Pritchard.

Razak watched him slow his pace as he approached the prostitute's door, glance at it, then carry on past. Before reaching the first café he turned abruptly and retraced his steps and, without hesitation, stuck a key in the lock, opened the door and disappeared. After the door closed Razak left his table and moved into the interior of the café. With a wink at the solitary waiter, he picked up the private telephone near the cash register. Razak was well known. He was at home here. He rang his friend the Commissaire at Police HQ on Avenue Abdallah Yafi and after a brief exchange went back to his table on the pavement. He studied the girl again, this time more openly. She'd relaxed; some of the tension had gone when Pritchard entered the building. But she wasn't happy with Razak's attention and turned her eyes rapidly towards the waiter and ordered another coffee.

It took about ten minutes from the time he'd telephoned. Razak was impressed. He watched the unmarked car manoeuvre into a space on a bombed site on the other side of the main road and waited until the casually dressed man got out of the car, crossed the road and sat down at an empty table. As he lit a cigarette he made brief eye contact with Razak. It was enough. A fractional nod of the head and Razak stood up, picked up his unfinished drink and moved into the gloomy interior of the café.

From where he stood at the bar he still had the apartment entrance and the back of Ruti's head well in sight. He remained standing there finishing his coffee until a few minutes later he was joined by the man from the police commissariat.

19

Cohen tapped gently on Ruti's door before pushing it open.

Baruch Lev was standing with the window behind him and the bright sun turning his thin shape into an outline. His face, in deep shadow, was pointed towards the door and his right hand rested on a small table behind a plastic vanity mirror. When he saw who it was he took his hand away. In it, held easily and competently, was a small .22 Beretta which he tucked, unselfconsciously, inside his trousers on his hip. He moved away from the window and sat down on the edge of the bed. They didn't shake hands. Cohen pulled up a dining chair, turned it round and, sitting down, rested his arms on the back as he studied the young man.

He was far too pretty. And he knew it. But his eyes, dark brown to match his tight, curled hair, were sharp and intelligent and his clean-shaven jaw showed more determination than he was entitled to have. Cohen didn't like him. He was too good-looking – too good-looking by half – and he had too much confidence as well.

'Have you been told anything?' Cohen asked him.

Lev shook his head. 'They said if there was anything you wanted me to know you'd tell me. But one thing . . .' he cocked his head to one side. 'I was told to keep my ears open for rumours of unpublicized Western hostages still being held in Beirut.'

'Where'd you hear that?'

The young man's casual and flippant attitude hardened. He stared coolly into Cohen's face. 'It doesn't matter where I heard it – the fact that I did is sufficient. Now, can we get down to business?'

Cohen stared at the Israeli agent for several seconds. Lev didn't wilt. The job didn't faze him; looking after an old worn-out *katsa* was well below his capabilities. He bore the older man's scrutiny with equanimity. 'So – have you heard any?' Cohen said.

'Any what?'

'Rumours.'

Lev relaxed and smiled. 'Not yet: I've got a black – a local guy – in my pocket. He's good. He's been with me before and he's not known as one of us. His mouth doesn't run away with him.'

'You sound as though you're in love with him.'

'He's not the shape I like.' Lev grinned. 'Ruti's got the things I like to play with. Anyway – tell me what the game is and what you expect of me.'

'Nothing dramatic,' said Cohen. 'There's a Yank tucked away somewhere in the city. I don't think they moved him out – the hole they'd got him in was too good, very secure, well hidden. I want to find that Yank.'

'Is that all?' Lev poured himself a solid shot of the thick liqueur from the yellow-labelled bottle. 'Where was this American last seen?'

'In a hole in the ground. Could have been somewhere in Borj Abi-Haidar – ' he pointed at the window with his chin – 'south.'

Lev sipped his drink and nodded. The nod could have been satisfaction with the taste or agreement that south was the obvious area. 'I'll get my man on it . . .'

'Discretion's paramount, Lev. The fewer people who know about this deal the better.'

'I hadn't thought of putting an advert in the paper, Les.

My boy can move in all sorts of places, he doesn't have to mention specifics, just a hint here and a hint there and a good pair of listening ears is all you need for this game.' He sipped again and pulled a face. This time it was the liqueur that forced the grimace. 'What's this Yank's name; what does he look like?'

'Macauley.'

'Macauley what?'

'I don't think you need bother with anything more than that. First of all I doubt whether at the moment there's a single American on the loose in Beirut, and as far as statistics are concerned there's none still in captivity – not any more. This one's a mystery man and he's gotta stay that way – orders from the top.'

'Our top?'

'You'd better believe it.'

'So, what makes you or anybody else think this guy's in Beirut? Has anybody made a definite sighting?'

'Yes.'

'You gonna tell me who?'

'Me.'

The younger man studied Cohen's blank features. He knew vaguely Cohen's history. He didn't believe half of it but you had to admire the man. He softened his interrogatory tone. 'And you think he's still here?'

'That's the big question. But this is where he was last seen and this is where the search starts. He could, of course, be boxed by now, but I somehow doubt it. Personally I think he's still alive.'

That was nearly enough for Lev. He knew when to stop. But there was just one more question. 'What did he look like?' The past tense was deliberate. He knew his Arabs, he knew better the fanatics of Hezbollah; the past tense, in Baruch Lev's experience, was a fairly logical tense when it came to an unpublicized American hostage.

161

Cohen let it ride. 'Like his name I don't think it matters, but, for interest's sake, when I last saw him he looked like a goat that had been skinned alive and had an overripe melon for a face. He might have improved since then.'

'Or got worse. OK, that all figures. I'll get Robin to start moving around.'

'Robin?'

'He's my man, the one I mentioned. Christian. I recruited him in the south. Bit of a smart-arse. Fancies himself but knows what it's all about. He'd been a captain in the South Lebanese Army and got bored with soldier work. He's got an apartment here and knows Beirut like the back of his hand; got contacts all over the place. He'll dig your Yank out if anybody's going to.'

'Is Robin his real name?'

'As far as you're concerned – '

'Fair enough. What's the rest of it?'

'Robin'll be sufficient,' said Lev, guardedly, and emptied the glass of yellow liquid into Ruti's sink. He turned the tap on to swill it away then came back to Cohen. 'Now it's my turn.'

Cohen raised his eyebrows.

'Who's this American at the Commodore?'

'His name's Cunningham. He's an archivist, a statistician, something like that – '

'Oh yeah!'

'The American State Department want to put this Macauley to rest so that he just becomes another statistic. Simple as that.'

'OK, I believe you,' said Lev without conviction, 'so let's lay down a couple of ground rules – OK?'

'Go on.'

'No direct contact with you or Cunningham at the Commodore.'

'Right.'

'Robin stays out of the group. He's my boy, which means my orders and my direction. Until I say so you don't meet him; you have no contact and nothing to say to him. OK?'

'I'm not arguing. Here's one of mine. Ruti will work the telephone exchange between you and me. If it goes out of order leave a message at the Commodore; say "Matthew's had to leave early. He'll be in touch." I'll then come and check out what's gone wrong. If there's a total panic, and as a last resort, leave a phone number for me to ring at the Backstreet – number's in the book. OK?'

'Got it. Anything else?'

Cohen shook his head. 'Not for the moment.' He stood up. 'Unless your man turns something over quickly I'll meet you here, same conditions, in three days' time. We can then reassess. Is that all right with you?'

'Sure. Three days, then. Shall I go first?'

'Yeah. I'll wait ten minutes and allow you to clear the area. Ruti'll be out on the street somewhere covering the entrance. Don't acknowledge her if you see her . . .'

'You didn't need to say that.' Lev obviously wasn't a man to take advice freely. Cohen took note. This was a prickly young bastard who knew it all. He was going to have to be handled. Lev stopped at the door and studied Cohen for a few seconds. 'Have you got a weapon?'

'No,' said Cohen.

'Is that wise?'

Cohen studied the young man. There appeared to be genuine concern in his face. Baruch Lev was of the age where the comforting bulk of a piece of hot iron stuck in his trouser band was like having a second, more potent penis. He was the type who wouldn't be seen dead without either. 'I'm supposed to be a New Zealand journalist,' said Cohen patiently. 'How would I explain a gun in my belt?'

Lev didn't reply. If anybody wanted to know why he was

163

carrying one they would get the first two rounds in their face and by the time they'd wished they hadn't asked he'd be legging it over the hill. But Cohen was a different generation. Different methods; different thoughts.

'I can talk my way out of trouble much easier with a cover and without having to explain a gun. You look after yourself and I'll look after me.'

'OK. I'll see you then.'

'Sure.' Cohen was glad to be left on his own.

Razak inclined his head towards the other man and said, 'That whore's playing a funny game.'

The man from Police HQ studied the back of Ruti's head. 'How?'

'She picked up a guy in the café down the road there, took him up to her rooms – ' he jerked his chin in the direction of Ruti's apartment – 'over there, and left the guy steaming while she came to the café to drink coffee. Wouldn't you think that's a funny game?'

'Is that what you had me brought here for?' The Commissaire's man didn't find any of this funny. Whores were funny people, they did funny things, but none of these things were funny enough to be laughed at, and none warranted a member of the Special Branch of Internal Security leaving his cool office to stand at an indifferent bar with someone who could well be the boss's bum boy. 'Is that the only funny thing she's done?' he said with a stony face.

'She's not touting for work.'

'Maybe she's getting over a dose . . . Maybe she's having a period, maybe she's just bloody fed up.' *Like me*, he almost added.

Razak shook his head. 'I don't think any of those – ' he broke off abruptly as the door across the road opened. Ruti's head turned slowly. Razak jabbed the policeman in the side. 'Look!' he hissed. But it wasn't Cohen, it was the man she'd picked up in the café. He made a quick decision. He knew where Cohen was staying; he didn't need to follow him again. But this was different. This one had been closeted for half an hour with Cohen; it meant something. The man had to be followed and talked to. 'There's another man upstairs in that girl's room,' he hissed again. 'If she joins him keep a watch until he leaves but don't bother following. I can get him any time. When he's gone move in and put her out of the game. I'll join you when I've run down that guy over there . . . OK?'

The policeman didn't argue. This was more like it. Rough-handling a whore was well within his province. He nodded briefly and, with half an eye on Ruti, watched Razak cross to the pavement opposite along which the young man was walking and blend, magically, with the few people using the sidewalk. The policeman didn't realize it but he was watching a master of the art of tailing at work. Razak could make himself inconspicuous in an empty telephone booth.

The policeman ordered a watered down ouzo and moved out again to a table on the pavement. He lit a cigarette and watched and waited. It wasn't a long wait. He was only halfway down his drink when the second man left the apartment. The girl hadn't moved. He was beginning to agree with Razak – something very funny was going on.

He watched Cohen out of sight and emptied his glass just as the girl signalled the waiter. She paid her bill and after another few minutes searching through her voluminous bag stood up and walked casually in the opposite direction to the man who'd left her flat. But she didn't go far. She stopped abruptly, turned as if she'd forgotten something, then crossed the road and made her way to the apartment entrance. The policeman hadn't moved. Like Razak, he knew the watching game very well, but as she stopped at the door he stood up, crossed the road and joined her as she searched for her key.

'Hello,' he said.

She started. Stiffened. Then raised her head from the open bag and turned slowly.

'I'm sorry,' she said, slightly out of breath. 'I'm not working.'

'That's all right.' He smiled genially and showed her the card in the palm of his hand. Grasping the wrist holding the bag with his other hand, he said, 'I'm not interested in that part of your business. Shall we go upstairs?'

Ruti wasn't unduly worried. She'd seen the card; she knew what he was. It was not uncommon for these people when the weekend or holiday time was approaching to supplement their income with a bit of strong-arm extortion. She had funds. She studied him. This one wasn't going to cost much. 'I've done nothing wrong.' She allowed her voice to tremble and looked frightened. This was what they expected; this was what he would understand. But he didn't relax. He kept a tight hold of her wrist as he upended her bag on to the doorstep and invited her to pick out the key.

He watched her closely as she scuffled the rest of her stuff back in the bag and stayed closely behind her as she moved towards the stairs. He remained polite and understanding all the way up the stairs, with just the odd placatory sound until they reached her room. She left the door open for safety, but as soon as he was in the room he elbowed her to one side, kicked the door shut and turned the locks. Then he turned round. She ducked but she was a fraction too slow. As she lost her balance he grabbed her outstretched arm and, with a vicious jerk that nearly pulled it out of its socket, threw her across the room, where, taken unawares, she crashed against the wall below the window.

Without allowing her to recover he followed up and kicked her hard in the side. This time she screamed. He pulled her up by the hair, slapped her twice across the face and let go of her hair. The impetus of the blows carried her in the other direction. Collapsing on her knees, she shook her head, but before she could move he was above her again and swung his fist hard against the side of her face. He was breathing hard, but not unduly concerned. He was fit enough for this sort of work. He hit her again, hard, and her head crashed on to the worn carpet.

She hadn't had time to think, she had no idea what it was about and, just as her head began to clear she felt herself picked up bodily, thrown through to the other room and then picked up again and tossed like a rag doll on to the bed. Rape? Surely not! She couldn't believe it. Who would want to rape a whore? A policeman? God! He could have it for nothing, with anyone – and pick up a bonus when he'd finished. This wasn't right. She knew what had happened. She was blown. They were going to kill her. But before she had time to develop this theory another heavy blow to the head sent her swimming into a black vortex and she lost consciousness.

20

Unlike Les Cohen, Baruch Lev played the evasion game by instinct. He assumed, automatically, that he'd have a follower no matter where he was, no matter where he went. But he'd never been followed by a man of Razak's genius.

After a tour of different parts of the city it became obvious to Razak that Lev not only knew Beirut and its back streets as well as he did but that they were heading for the Green Line and the Christian East. After that it was simple.

Lev finally went to ground in a shoddy apartment block alongside the old railway line in Qobaiyat, on the extreme east of the city. It was easy to watch, and it wasn't long before Razak saw Lev reappear with another man, an Arab, not Palestinian but almost certainly Lebanese, in good Western clothes and a smart Saddam Hussein moustache. He looked military.

Razak followed them the short distance to the crowded commercial centre on the other side of the railway track and watched them huddle together over minuscule cups of coffee and what looked like glasses of brandy standing in saucers, French style, in a café on the edge of the road. It was easy to watch from the other side of the road where food stalls gave him the ideal cover. As he picked and chewed lumps from a plate of savoury-filled hot pitta bread he burned the Arab's features into his memory. He seemed to have unravelled a very interesting little group of people but, as yet, hadn't worked out how all this should concern him. There was no doubt in his mind that his former prisoner Les Pritchard was wandering around Beirut; a more foolish act he couldn't believe would be possible. But somehow, at the back of his animal mind he knew it was all connected with the wreck lying in a damp, dark hole in the cellar of a ruined building in the devastated area of Borj Abi-Haidar.

When the two men split up Razak chose to follow the Arab. It was a simple decision. He knew where he could find Pritchard and, after a few simple enquiries, he established where Pritchard's friend lived. He knew the common denominator – the whore. She was, he raised his eyes to the sky for a brief religious moment, safe and sound in her flat with the heavy hand of the security service holding her face down in a bucket. And now he'd got a fourth.

Razak studied the building where the Arab had gone to ground. He'd got more style than the prostitute's early guest. No scruffy hovel on the railway track for this one; he liked his comfort – and presumably his status which made him, unlike Razak, a connoisseur of the female sex. Razak smirked, unusually. With a fine apartment like this one he'd have no embarrassment about entertainment. But it didn't make it any the less fishy for Razak.

He watched his new target's home for another hour and then followed him to the Al-Ajami restaurant on Rue du Caire in Hamra. This man, he decided, was his mark. He left him tucking into his *mezze* in the company of a very attractive and elegant *métisse* and had a good idea where the moustache would be operating for most of the hot afternoon. He took a final long hard look at his target and set off back to the Najmeh district and the apartment on the corner of the Rue Felix Eboué.

169

21

Cohen and Cunningham sat on the veranda of the St George's restaurant in the burnt-out shell of the Summerland Hotel on the coast at Jnaha. Cunningham turned his head back from studying the magnificent natural bay below them, its crystal clear waters reflecting the perfection of the cloudless sky. They had reached the cheese and the bottom quarter of a bottle of one of the better Lebanese vintages.

The restaurant still had a minimal Western clientele, but it was getting smaller by the week. Rumblings of renewed Hezbollah dissatisfaction with some of the deals negotiated on their behalf had drawn back into their protective shells the diplomatic community and the others who thought the bad old days of kidnapping Westerners were a thing of the past. It was a question of 'none but the brave' even for lunch on a beautiful warm, idyllic clifftop.

Cohen reckoned it was safe – still – but only just. 'Your instincts,' his voice returned to a normal, just above the whisper, level when he'd regained Cunningham's attention, 'are just about spot on. The chatter in the marketplace is that there is a stranger still in the box in Beirut – '

'Anything definite?'

'Chatter, Jack. Just market chatter. But that's all it takes. D'you know this guy personally?'

Cunningham made no response.

Cohen didn't pursue it. 'Suit yourself, chum! I think your brother Yank is still in place. It's a question now of

patience. A bit of digging here, a bit of digging there . . .'
He searched Cunningham's face. He didn't find much. 'Is there a time limit on this project?'

Cunningham continued picking away at the cheese, following it up with the red wine. He cleared his mouth and touched it with a heavy damask napkin. 'There is if he's still alive; if he's dead he's dead. I'll want the body and that'll be the finish.' He paused and stared into Cohen's face. 'And we'll have all the time in the world to round up the cowboys who did the damage.'

Cohen finished his wine, lit a cigarette and leaned forward with his elbows on the table. 'Our team's just doubled its size. We've got a home-based boy who knows his way around this shit heap and he's already putting out feelers. He's had a nibble or two but nothing for us to get excited about.'

'What's his name?'

'I'm not sure you need to know.'

'Great. So if I've got some guy up against the wall with my piece stuck in his ear and he says his name is Sammy X and he's a friend of yours I turn my back and walk away, do I?'

'His name's Baruch.'

'Baruch what, for Christ's sake?'

'Lev.'

'Thanks. What does he look like?'

Cohen gave him a fair description of Baruch Lev with the minimum of background and none of his own assessment of Lev's character. He waited for the next one.

'And the other guy?'

'His name's Robin.' Cohen met Cunningham's eyes and held them. 'Robin nothing. That's all I know about him. He's local, Lebanese, a former South Lebanese Army officer who's joined our side. He's Lev's man, and Lev ain't sharing. And I don't blame him.'

'And how will I know Robin nothing if the occasion arises?' asked Cunningham. 'What's going to stop me barging him over the edge if he gets in my way?'

Cohen shrugged. 'You'll just have to play that one when you come to it. You know his name's Robin, there are not many Arabs with a name like that and you know he's a former SLA officer. There's your scene, Jack – an Arab named Robin who used to be a pro-Israeli soldier. But, for God's sake don't try looking for him.'

'Baruch Lev and Robin nothing!' Cunningham winced.

'What's next on your agenda?' Cohen asked.

'Oh, that's up to you, Les – and your funny team. But I'm having a drink tonight with an Australian photographer who met Brian Keenan. He reckons that makes him an expert on the hostage situation! He might have something to say.'

'It's one way of wasting your time. I'll see you some time tomorrow and let you know whether anything's happened. You never know – I'm due for a bit of luck.' He stood up. 'Right, now I'm going to the Backstreet – unless you've got something else in mind?'

Cunningham stopped him.

'You asked me about Macauley – '

'What about him?'

'Thurston Macauley and I were at the Point together. We were also a couple of the early ones into Vietnam and we stayed there together right through to the end.' Cunningham rocked back in his chair and lit a cigarette. Cohen didn't move. 'You could say we became quite good friends . . .'

Cohen shrugged.

'In fact he was, and is my best friend . . .' He fixed Cohen with a stare: 'Find him, Les!'

22

The policeman studied Ruti's unconscious body from the other side of the room then walked over and stood above her. After a second or two he kicked her to make sure she wasn't faking then, satisfied, he picked her up and threw her on her back on to the scruffy bed. She didn't make a sound, not a whimper, nor did she move; the mist was clearing and her brain was coming back to life. But slowly.

The policeman made a note of the time. Then, starting with the chest of drawers near the window, he began to go through the flat with his version of a fine toothcomb. Every so often he stopped what he was doing and moved back to the bed to study Ruti's state of unconsciousness. He didn't seem surprised that she was still out and even when he pulled her head up by her hair and let it drop he didn't notice the instinctive tightening of the neck muscles. Her eyes remained loosely closed, like a person drugged or dead. But she was listening – waiting.

In the deep drawer at the bottom of the chest the policeman struck his first nugget of gold – tucked under nylon underwear and slinky black stockings his hand touched metal. He allowed his hand to rest on it for a moment, as if testing its capabilities, before brushing aside the clothes and taking out a small DES .32 self-loading pistol. He studied it with interest. It was of French manufacture and the magazine fully loaded. His lip curled – a handbag gun, it was too small to stop an angry man if he was really determined but there was enough there to defend what little she had worth defending. He unloaded it and stuck the weapon in his pocket. It was his now, and she had nothing. There was no longer a need for him to continually look over his shoulder. But there was one more thing; something more important than a lady's little target pistol to look for. Money. All whores had ready money. They hid it from their pimp – it was here somewhere. He turned to stare at the woman on the bed. It'll be under the mattress. The stupid *putains* had no imagination. He walked over to Ruti's side and slapped her face.

She swallowed and groaned but kept her eyes closed.

'Where do you keep the *fric, putain*?'

'No – ' she moaned through bleeding lips.

'No? No what?'

'No money . . .'

'Stupid whore!' He slapped her face several times and ended with a full-blooded punch. She passed out again.

He spent the next fifteen minutes testing the floorboards with his weight. They all creaked, and were all loose but it didn't improve his state of mind. Whatever he was going to find he wanted to do it before the Commissaire's friend came back for his share. He rolled the threadbare carpet up and studied the uneven floorboards. He tested them again with his weight. Nothing happened. None of the boards flew up and revealed a chest of dollars, francs and pounds. He put everything back the way he'd found it and looked at his watch again. He'd been messing around for two hours. He rang Police HQ and asked if there were any messages for him. Nothing, they told him. So where is the man called Razak? And how much longer was he going to have to wait in this flat? He poured himself a half-glass of the liquid from the yellow-labelled bottle, lit a flat Turkish cigarette and sat down in the one armchair in the room. He sipped the drink. It pleased him far more than it had Baruch

174

Lev. He drew smoke into his lungs, sipped again from the glass and turned his head to look at the woman on the bed again.

Ruti's tight little leather miniskirt had risen above her thighs. A trace of white lace caught his eye. He sat, legs outstretched, sipping the yellow liquid, smoking, and staring at the rise of Ruti's thighs. He felt a definite stirring in his loins. He glanced at his watch for the umpteenth time and then at the telephone; but his groin's demands had taken over his thinking. And why not? he debated. What's the point in being a senior officer in the security service if the perks of the job are denied? She's only a whore — she won't even notice it.

He emptied his glass and set it on the floor beside his chair as he stood up and stretched. He checked the door. It was double-locked. There were going to be no surprises here. He walked over to the bed, took off his jacket and removed the heavy Makarov automatic from his hip and placed it on the side table. He removed his belt and allowed his trousers and underpants to drop around his ankles as he reached out, placed his hand on Ruti's bare thigh and pushed so that she lay flat on her back.

Ruti kept herself limp. She made no sound or movement; feigning unconsciousness, she prepared herself for a rough and brutal assault. But it wasn't like that. This one was an exception. Perhaps he had necrophiliac tendencies. He didn't try to slap her awake. Instead she felt his hands move smoothly up her thighs, undo the zip of her skirt and ease it down over her ankles. With the minimum disturbance it was followed by her briefs and then her legs were gently parted. His fingers probed. Instinctively she stiffened, but he was too involved now to notice. She forced herself to lie still as he climbed on to the bed and knelt between her legs. His fingers searched deeper, and then his hand and

175

she stifled a cry as he brought his other hand into play then entered her with a rush.

After a moment she allowed her eyelashes to flutter fractionally and she could see the outline of his head as he pumped slowly up and down. A little wider and she could see his face. His eyes were tightly closed. She moaned, softly, deliberately, as if still only half-conscious; then, slowly as if becoming aware of what was happening to her, she moved her body languidly, thrust her breasts upwards and, with her eyes still closed and moaning ecstatically stretched her arms above her head and grasped the side of the headboard.

He liked it. He grunted and groaned and growled obscenities in Arabic as he moved into higher gear. There was nothing on his mind except total ecstasy as he approached a magnificent climax. But he never got there.

Still gently moaning, Ruti's searching fingers ran slowly down the back of the headboard until they brushed against the butt of the .22 Mossad-issue Beretta hanging from a cup hook by its trigger guard. She grasped the butt. Cocked, the hammer full back, she held her position for a few seconds as the policeman began his final frenetic burst. Timing her moment she brought her hand, with the small pistol firmly in its grasp, round the side of his heaving body and held the muzzle to the side and under his jawbone. She let it ride with the movement of his head for a few seconds, then squeezed the trigger.

For a moment she thought it was a misfire.

Then it happened.

His eyes shot open as the lower part of his body continued surging into her and then he seemed to frown as, in the middle of the final thrust, his body stiffened and his eyes glazed over as his erection died and he collapsed on top of her.

She pushed him out and wriggled from under him. His

body, flaccid and empty, crashed to the floor by the edge of the bed but she followed it out, held the muzzle a couple of centimetres from his left eye and squeezed the trigger again. Out of breath, she fell to her knees beside him and gulped in great lungfuls of air. She shut her eyes tight and shook her head, forcing the tears back and clenching her teeth. She wished she hadn't. The violent movement reawakened the searing pain in her brutalized face; but it brought her quickly to her senses. Without getting up she crawled across the floor to the sink and filled it with water. Dragging herself up by the rim of the basin she washed, first her face and then, standing up, the part of her body that had just been violated. She didn't feel any better. She wouldn't, ever.

She threw the miniskirt and briefs into a corner and dressed in a sombre ankle length smock-like dress. She slipped on simple flat-soled sandals, picked up a large floppy shoulder bag and padded into the washroom.

They'd never look there: it was far too dirty for the true Muslim. On her knees by the squat lavatory, she thrust her hand into the hole and felt around underneath the thick concrete slab. The flat plastic-covered bag was resting safely on its ledge. She took it to the sink and turned the tap on it before stripping the plastic and opening the packet. She dropped into her shoulder bag the money: over 2,000 US dollars and a huge wad of Lebanese pounds. The code book went too, and finally her own personal address and procedure book. She threw the plastic covering down the lavatory, then, with a shake of the head for carelessness went back to the dead man's coat and retrieved the decoy, the small French-made DES .32 automatic, from the pocket. It had served its purpose; having found it had made him comfortable and relaxed enough to think of other things.

She took one last look around the room. She'd never

liked it. The safe house she was going to in Snoubra was a more fitting home. She'd been blown as a prostitute; she couldn't use that one again – thank God! Now she could start a new cover. But she had to get there first and put out the alarm. Cohen and Lev first, then Tel Aviv. With luck they'd call her home.

She slipped the first of the double locks and glanced again, quickly, round the room. She hadn't forgotten anything – she just had to get away, now, and quick. She turned her back on the room without regret and stepped out into a new life.

Razak glanced at his watch as he turned into the Rue Felix Eboué. He'd been away for the best part of two hours – long enough for all sorts of things to have happened. But, first of all, had Pritchard left the girl's flat? He ran his eyes over the now crowded pavement by the café. He couldn't spot his new friend. He moved across the road to be able to see the bomb site where'd he'd parked his car. It was still there, shimmering under a full, midday sun that blasted mercilessly out of a pale blue, cloudless sky.

He crossed the road again. The apartment door was ajar. He studied it before pushing it open. Convenient? Too convenient. He pushed it shut behind him and withdrew the solid Beretta from his waistband. He flicked up the safety and eased back the hammer. Razak had survived thirty years in the killing business because he'd never been shy about pulling a gun when his instincts dictated. Something was dictating now.

Slowly and carefully he moved up the stairs, stopping at each door and pressing his ear against the panelling. Midday in a Beirut whorehouse. There would be more noise in an undertaker's chapel of rest. But Razak took his time. He was in no hurry. He'd reached the last door on the first landing when he heard the muted crack from behind the right-hand door on the small landing above. He stopped, held his breath and listened. A thud almost above his head, then another crack, louder, one that he was able to identify.

It was the light, crisp explosion of a .22.

Razak's face hardened. The policeman's standard weapon would have been a self-loading 9mm: .38 or 7.65. What it wouldn't have been was a .22.

He went lightly up the narrow stairs and stood with his head pressed against the thinnest part of the door. There was movement: a scuffling of feet, and drawers opening. He tested the door with his finger. There was no give. It was locked. He moved to one side and with his back resting against the neighbouring door drew back the slide on the Beretta by a fraction of a centimetre and inspected the rim of the round in the breech. He let it close silently and tapped the bottom of the magazine in the butt before turning sideways to Ruti's door. Resting the automatic in the crook of his left arm he waited silently, his breathing steady, his face a mask.

Ruti stepped out of the door and froze.

Razak didn't move. He looked relaxed and at ease as his eyes covered Ruti from head to toe. 'Put the bag on the floor.' He spoke in Arabic. 'Then move over there and stand with your face against the wall.'

'Wh-who are you?' She tried to brazen it out, but she knew it was a forlorn hope. This man she knew. She'd seen him this morning sitting in the café opposite. Another policeman? He didn't look police — but who did? State Security — or Secret Police? Worse. She offered a tentative smile. It was rejected. Razak's face, mostly the eyes, were cold, cruel and unyielding.

'Get over there with your face against the wall.'

He waited until she had moved before stooping down and picking up the bag by its strap. He slipped it over his other shoulder then took the two paces towards her. 'Turn your head to one side.' His voice remained without inflection; no excitement, no anger – nothing. She did as she was told. 'Close your eyes.' She was glad to. He pressed the Beretta's muzzle against the junction of her eye and nose and let the barrel rest against her cheekbone while his other hand went over her shoulders, down her back and between her legs. There was nothing lascivious in his probing; it was purely business, sex had nothing to do with it. He stepped back half a pace but kept his arm outstretched and the automatic still against her face.

'Arms against the wall . . . Move your feet back . . .'

'Wh-who – wha—?'

'No talk. Do as you're told.' His voice was still unemotional. It offered no chance; no mercy. It was worse than a shouting, screaming fanatic; worse than being beaten against the wall. This voice offered nothing but death. She pushed her body away from the wall and waited.

His hand came round the front, felt between her breasts, under her armpits and down the front where it went between her legs again. The gun was removed from her face and she felt it grind into the soft spot at the base of her spine. It touched a nerve and she hissed in pain. 'Don't move,' he warned, as his hand went down her thigh to her ankle and then the other leg. The pressure was removed from her spine and his voice came from his original position.

'Walk backwards to the door, open it wide and go through and stand in the middle of the room.'

She did exactly as he said.

She heard the door close and the lock thrown.

'Lie with your face on the floor.'

Razak studied the body of his erstwhile drinking partner and curled his nose. There was no pity, only contempt. A glance at his bare arse told him what had happened. Death was the perfect dancing partner for fools. He went to the table and emptied Ruti's bag, spreading its contents about with his hand. He picked up the French .32, slipped the magazine out and tested it with his thumb. It was fully loaded. 'Where's the .22?' he asked.

She made no reply.

He walked round to the blind side of her body and, without warning kicked with all his strength just above her hip. She hadn't yet prepared herself for more violence, and for a second absorbed the pain. Then it reached her brain and brought a scream of anguish all the way from the pit of her stomach. Razak, from experience, knew exactly where the pointed steel-capped toe of his shoe would cause the most hurt. The scream kept coming until he turned her over on to her back with his foot and placed the sole of his shoe over her mouth. The scream died to a gurgling warble as she fought for breath. He removed his foot and gave her a few seconds to recover, then, in the same dispassionate voice, repeated, 'Where's the .22?'

Ruti turned her head sideways and dribbled out the contents of her stomach that had retched its way into her throat behind the pain. She was no longer interested in what happened to the carpet. Neither was Razak. He touched her side with his foot again as a reminder.

'In – in . . . the l-lavatory,' she managed, and was sick again. This time it was mostly blood. She cleaned her mouth on the carpet and tried again. 'I – I th-threw . . . it away. No more use . . .'

But Razak was no longer interested in the .22. He believed what she said. She'd killed a policeman with a pistol; she had no need to keep it. In fact she'd be totally stupid not to have got rid of it. That the policeman had got himself killed was of no concern to Razak. What did concern him was the fact that a whore would go to those lengths. A very peculiar whore, this. But it all made sense as he turned the leaves of the small elastic-banded notebook he picked up from the table. Code. He thumbed through it. Page after page of handwritten five-letter groups. Very interesting. He picked up the other pad and flipped it open. Notes, notes and more notes. He glanced down at the girl on the floor. She was doubled up with both hands clutching her side; blood dribbled from the corner of her mouth and her eyes were tightly closed as she savoured her pain.

His eyes widened. 'You're a Jew?' The surprise in his voice caused a raised inflection on the word 'Jew'.

She didn't reply. It didn't matter at this juncture. He knew what he'd got. All her notes were in Hebrew with, here and there, a word, and sometimes a sentence, in English. It could almost be called indiscretion but – Razak looked at her again and allowed his lips to droop, he knew the form, he'd been there himself – there usually wasn't the time to sit down with a decoding book and unravel every insignificant detail. She must have been at it a long time. She'd developed a little complacency. He gave the money a cursory glance. Useful stuff, but not worth getting killed for; not for a man who was dealing in hundreds of millions!

He pulled the chair round so that it was alongside Ruti's curled-up body and sat down with the notebook in one hand and both arms resting on his knees. He reached out with his foot and touched her hip.

'Straighten up, hands above your head – open your eyes.'

She was slow to react. His foot went up and his heel came down into the tender spot he'd already created. It was only a gentle touch, a warning to show he didn't want to hurt her again. That they were going to be friends now and discuss their problems. She hissed as she straightened up and, painfully, turned on her back. She clutched her hands above her head and looked into Razak's eyes.

'All right?' he asked commiseratively, and, without waiting for the reply which he knew he wasn't going to get,

went straight into the next part of the act. 'You're a Jew –
you're a Jewish spy, a Mossad . . . Don't bother denying it,
it's all here.' He flapped the notebook up and down. 'You
realize you're going to die, don't you?'

She kept her eyes on his face but said nothing and gave
no sign that she understood. She knew what the Lebanese
Secret Police would do to a Jewish spy. She knew even
better what they'd do to a female Jewish spy. The
instructors had gone at this one at great length at Midrasha;
they'd even revelled in their lewdness. But this was real.
Her stomach ran to liquid.

'Answer.' Razak still didn't raise his voice. That in itself
was frightening.

She shook her head as much as her clasped hands would
allow but didn't trust herself to speak. He nodded to himself
as if he understood, then said, 'I am not of the police. I am
not of anything official. I do not intend handing you over
to the authorities. All I want is a little information on some
people I think you might know. Nothing more than that. I
do not want to hurt you.'

A trick? Ruti studied his eyes. Typical Arab eyes –
sincerity dripped from them; it could be turned on and off
like a light switch. It didn't mean a thing. But it was an
interesting approach.

'When you have told me this little bit of information I
will leave this room; leave your stuff here on the table and
you can go where you like . . .' He jerked his chin at the
dead policeman: 'I don't want to know anything of him.
You can make that your business. But –' he paused
significantly and narrowed his sincere eyes into hers. 'But –
if you do not want to help me without pain I can also
accommodate you there . . . Do you want to help me?'

She swallowed the stuff that had collected in her throat.
It made her retch again. When she'd recovered she said,
with difficulty, 'What do you want to know?'

'I want to know what the man named Pritchard is doing in Beirut; who his friends and contacts are and what part you and your Mossad people are playing in his affairs. Also, who is the man you picked up in the café this morning and left in your flat while you drank coffee across the road. Who is he, what is he, and what is his connection with Pritchard?' Razak sat back in the chair, crossed his legs and aimed the Beretta at the side of her head. It was a notional, and fanciful gesture. It didn't mean he was going to shoot her – not unless things got out of hand. 'Talk,' he said softly.

'Can I sit up?'

'No.' He rested the automatic on his knee. 'Just talk.'

'I don't know – '

'Tsk! Tsk!' He clicked his tongue admonishingly. 'You *must* answer the questions if you want to live. I can hurt you very much. I can break each of your fingers, one at a time; I can break your hands and your feet, and I can shoot you in the knees – I can give you very, very much pain. But what I can do is nothing to what that man's people –' he waved the pistol in the direction of the dead policeman – 'will do to you if I pick up that telephone and call my friend at the Avenue Abdallah Yafi. They will crucify you seven times over before asking you what your name is. You can walk out of this apartment and start a new life or you can spend the rest of your days waiting for your mind and body to recover. Answer my questions.'

She turned her eye as far as it would go to look into his face. There was nothing there to guide her. *But the longer it's drawn out the less likely they are to inflict serious damage. Chat him up . . .* 'I don't know the name Prit—' It was as far as she got. Midrasha's philosophy was wrong; their teaching was out of date. Before she could draw breath Razak had moved smoothly out of the armchair, parted her hands above her head and clamped his foot on one of her wrists.

184

She tried to struggle but the Beretta's muzzle suddenly gouged into the corner of her eye and she dropped back to her original position. But only for a second. She felt her middle finger taken gently in his hand and then, with a quick jerk backwards it cracked and was torn out of its socket. She had no time to absorb the shock; no time to scream. The pain was so startling her back and shoulders leapt off the floor and she fainted before she realized what had happened.

The pain had diminished to a dull, nerve-tearing throb when she came to.

'You stupid whore!' Razak's voice came from his original position but she didn't want to look. She kept her eyes firmly closed to contain her tears and her teeth clenched against her lower lip to prevent the groan of pain that had built up inside her. What's the point? She didn't know. How much pain must she absorb before she finally had to concede? Not much. She had no high opinion of her pain threshold. It had never been properly put to the test; but she'd been near the brink on just bruising. She'd never yet had fingers broken as easily and as painfully as if they were pieces of buttered matzos; and she knew she'd never be able to stand another one.

She'd taken too long to think about it. Razak was back at her side and had her wrist in his hand again.

'NO!' she screamed. 'No, no – I'll . . .' But Razak had already got another finger in his hand and with a crisp twist of his wrist that too snapped. But this time she'd fainted before the noise of the crack echoed round the scruffy room. Razak was neither pleased nor disappointed. Inflicting pain was a means to an end. He had no fetish in that respect. This he knew would bring the result. No one could put up with a systematic process of pain infliction; the promise of ten equal nerve-shredding items of unbelievable agony unless there was a high ideal at stake. But this philosophy was beyond his horizon; no one should accept pain either for money or for the sake of ideals.

Razak was right.

'His n-name is not P-Pritchard,' she gasped when she returned to the nightmare. 'It's C-Cohen – '

'Cohen? Cohen! You're wrong: his name is Pritch-ard . . .' A little shadow of doubt crept into Razak's voice.

'Cohen,' she repeated.

He sat up in the chair and stared at her for several seconds. That might explain many things. 'All right, Cohen . . . What is this Cohen doing here in Beirut?'

This was the hard bit. The very thought ground against her principles; it made a mockery of her training – but the throbbing and shrieking agony of the mutilated fingers on her right hand allowed her brain to override her misgivings. 'He is here on a Mossad mission . . .'

'A Jew! Pritchard is a Jew?' For the first time Razak's set expression showed animation. Angry animation. 'You're lying, you whore!' He stood up and touched her damaged hand. She tried to pull it away as he waggled one of the broken fingers.

'N-no!' she shrieked. 'It's the truth . . . Please – '

It had to be. He'd had an Israeli Mossad agent in captivity for two years and made no gain from it! How could that happen? What if it came out that he, Razak, had freed an Israeli secret agent without even knowing that he'd got one! He would be a figure of absolute ridicule; he would be laughed at throughout the Arab world. He set his expres-sion again.

'What is this mission?'

Ruti began to cry. She knew what reaction her response would have. She could feel the increased pain in her hand already.

'I, I – d-don't know . . . Please,' she cried, 'I don't know, I don't know –' She cringed in anticipation. But nothing happened. She opened her eyes: Razak was still sitting staring at her.

Pritchard – he couldn't bring himself to call the man Cohen. Pritchard he'd been for two years; Pritchard he'd stay until he, Razak, could wipe his face off the records. He could be here for only one thing. Nobody would send a former hostage back into the furnace for an ordinary operation – not even the Mossad could be that heartless. Oh, yes! Pritchard could be here for only one thing. Macauley. It had to be. It all fitted in. The Americans wanted their man back; they wanted him back with all his secrets. They'd sent an American pretending to be a Canadian, a Jew from the Mossad who'd lain in the same cellar, another Jew, a young and fit one, to cover Pritchard's back while he looked for his old dungeon, and a local, a Mossad-trained dog to sniff out the entrance to that dungeon. A four-man team. It was as simple as that. This whore was just the letterbox – the go-between, the cut-out. She'd know nothing except how to put one and one together so that one and one could make four. It was the usual system, a safe system provided someone like him didn't break into the chain. Razak knew all four of the team, plus the connector. None of the team had that advantage. Many purposes were waiting here to be exploited. His mind raced . . . Now he had it – the plan, and what he was going to do. He was going to help the Americans find Thurston Macauley.

The girl on the floor was staring hard at him. She was waiting for more punishment – or another question . . .

'And the other man?'

She'd broken her trust. It didn't matter now. 'Also of Mossad. H-he's here to look after Cohen.'

'Name?'

'Lev – '

'Go on.'

'Baruch Lev.'

'And you don't know the reason of the mission? What these men are here for? Neither of them has said anything to you?'

'I just bring them together.'

'When are you bringing them together again?'

'I have done my part. Now they make their own rules.'

'And if Tel Aviv wants you to pass on information to one or the other?'

She closed her eyes in thought. And prayer. 'I have a number and a code . . .'

It was enough. 'Ring the number,' ordered Razak. 'Make the code. Tell Pritch— Cohen you have urgent information from Tel Aviv for his ear only. He's to come to this apartment for your briefing.' He leaned forward on the edge of the chair and caressed her arm. He ran his fingers down to her wrist and tapped the back of her hand with his forefinger. No words. The gesture said everything. 'If you send the wrong word and he doesn't come I shall first of all finish what I started with this, then, to satisfy my anger I shall attend to the other hand and then your feet. Do you understand?'

She closed her eyes and said nothing. She understood perfectly; she anticipated the agony as he spoke, and she knew he meant it. But it wasn't enough for Razak. He bent one of the broken fingers back so that it touched the top of her wrist. She rose off the ground and twisted her body with a shriek. But he released it before she fainted.

'I asked you if you understood.'

She nodded her head furiously in spite of the pain it brought with it. But she couldn't speak. He was satisfied.

'Let us go to the phone while you still remember what awaits you if you decide not to be serious.'

Les Cohen collected his message from the Backstreet Club and rang back immediately.

'What time?' he asked without preliminaries.

'It's urgent,' was all she said.

'Are you all right? Nothing wrong, is there?'

Ruti gripped the receiver tightly with her left hand. If anything was to be done, now was the time. Just three words. That was all that was required to send Cohen and Lev far underground. But she couldn't do it. Razak would sense she was giving a warning. 'I'm all right': that was all that was required, that would be the last he'd see of Mr Les Pritchard. He knew the form; it was almost too obvious. He held her eyes then lowered them to her hand dangling at her side. He frowned. She knew he knew.

'Yes,' she replied. Razak nodded in approval. 'I've got a headache.'

'See you shortly.'

She hung up the phone and allowed Razak to lead her across the room. He'd replaced his own gun in his waistband when he'd picked up the policeman's Makarov from the table by the bed, and, with this weapon cocked he indicated with it for her to sit down in the chair he'd vacated. She did so without thought. Her mind was a blank; she couldn't force it to start anticipating, or working out what was going to happen next. It was just as well.

'Lie on the bed.'

She stared. *Oh, my God! Not again!* But she needn't have worried, not with Razak – for him she was the wrong shape; wrong sex. She moved slowly and painfully across the room and lowered herself on the bed.

'On your face.' She felt sick.

Razak whipped the top sheet off the bed, bit one end of it and tore it in half. He wound it up into a binding and tied her legs tightly together, then, ignoring the shrieks of agony that tore into the pillow under her face, dragged her injured

189

hand towards the other, tied them both together and, forcing her backwards, tied them again to the bindings round her feet. He turned her on her side. The shrieks had been absorbed by the pillow and all that came out of her bruised mouth were moans in short gasps and broken sobs as she struggled to overcome the pain.

'Shut up!' said Razak menacingly. 'When Cohen knocks on the door you call out "Come in!" in a good voice.' He raised her closed eyelid with his thumb and frowned into her eye, 'Nothing else. Do you understand?'

She tried to nod.

'Speak.'

'Y-ye-ss.'

'Then stay still – no noise.' He bent down and grabbed the dead policeman's legs and, without effort, dragged the body round the end of the bed and propped it against the wall by the washroom. He went to the door and stood surveying the room. The bed was out of sight; he could just see the feet of the dead policeman. He went back and kicked them out of sight, causing the body to judder down on to its side. Razak sneered into the corpse's face, shook his head in disgust and went back to the entrance. He slipped both catches on the lock, left the door fractionally ajar, and, checking the breech of the Makarov, made himself comfortable in the corner behind the door.

23

Razak heard the front door bell ring and began counting as he mentally paced the distance Cohen would be walking to the café along the road. A few minutes later the door downstairs closed quietly. He didn't hear the steps as Cohen came lightly up the stairs but he was ready for him. With the gentle scrape of Cohen's knuckles on the door Razak pointed the gun at Ruti

'It's open. Come in,' she said obediently.

She closed her eyes and turned her face into the pillow. One thing she didn't want to see was the accusation in Les Cohen's eyes when he saw what she'd led him into. The door squeaked as Cohen eased it open just sufficient for his body to pass through.

He froze when he saw Ruti lying curled up on the bed and took an instinctive half-step backwards through the door.

But it was too late.

The pistol shaved down the side of his face and came to rest just below his cheekbone, pointing slightly upwards.

'How nice of you to come back to see us, Les.' Razak's whispered voice brought back every detail of his worst nightmare. It was a voice he'd never forget. 'Keep on walking, my friend,' breathed the voice, 'and stop by the chair. Say hello to your friend, the whore.'

Cohen's clenched jaw refused to slacken as he stopped at the side of the chair and stared across the room at the figure on the bed. But there was no pity in Cohen's eyes. This was the game; this was the final move – she'd lost and had ensured that he went down with her. He kept his hands at his side, but open and splayed out, and waited for the instructions.

'Turn round, please, Les. Goodness me!' Razak smiled broadly when Cohen turned to face him. 'I had forgotten what a handsome man you are without your beard and all that dirty long hair; but your eyes are the same, your nose – that fine beautifully shaped Jewish nose . . .' He spat the word 'Jewish'. He was enjoying himself. 'But of course, my friend, as you now recognize me I couldn't possibly forget you, could I? I was so pleased to see you yesterday and to realize that your little holiday with us hadn't imperilled your sexual powers! But such a good-looking man – why a whore, Les?'

'What d'you want, Razak?'

'What do I want?' The bantering tone in Razak's voice vanished as if cut by a guillotine and his thick lips tightened into a white line. Razak had made himself angry. 'What do I want? What do I want? I want to know what Jewish agents are doing in Beirut; I want to know what it is that brings Les Pritchard back; what it is that brings American agents masquerading as journalists to the backstreets of Beirut; I want to know all that and more – and you're going to tell me . . .' He stopped. His voice changed. It became almost wheedling: 'If only I'd known, Les, that you were a Jew all along – a filthy Israeli spy. Why, Les?'

Cohen kept his mouth closed. He now knew what the end of the road looked like and it wasn't going to be Damascus. If anything was going to be handed over to anyone this time it was a heap of broken bones with a neat bullet hole in the middle of its head. This had always been on the cards; he should have run like a scared rabbit the minute Cunningham had mentioned Beirut. He tried to work some moisture into his mouth and throat: parched, dry as a bone. Perhaps this was a good sign; maybe it was all a nightmare and in a moment he'd wake up in London covered in sweat as he surfaced, shaking, from another dream encounter with Razak. But he wasn't going to wake up.

He watched the gun come up in Razak's hand as if in slow motion. His thought was almost one of elation. The stupid bastard was going to kill him. He was going to miss out on the torture. Come on! Come on! Razak – pull the fucking trigger!

BANG!

The explosion deafened him. His eardrums puffed out, then closed; his eyes filled with red as a giant hand smacked into his groin, thumped him hard against the wall and his legs collapsed from under him. *Ha! Ha! Typical bloody Arab – bloody bad shot! Can't even find the bloody killing spot!*

Cohen forced the mist from his eyes and refocused them. His face was ground into the dirty, sticky carpet and he could taste the dust, brought in by a hundred years of customers' shoes, seeping into his open mouth. And now, into his distorted view came Razak's down-at-heel, scruffy, pointed black Chelsea boots. They shimmered in front of his eyes as the waves of pain came over him. One of the boots worked itself under his shoulder and he was flipped on to his back. Now the pain was unbearable. He tried to concentrate on what Razak was telling him but gave it up. Then –

BANG!

Oh, God! Oh, God!

The explosion almost picked him up off the floor.

The force of the bullet into his other hip hit him like a hammer, but his brain wouldn't wait for the pain to catch up with the other. Eyes tightly closed, the deeper blackness

193

from inside his head closed in on him and he prayed that this was death.

But it wasn't going to be that easy.

His death lasted only twenty minutes.

When he came back to life he was sitting in a pool of blood, his back propped against the old armchair. His eyelids were heavy as he tried to open them. Heavy and sticky. Looking down into his lap he was able to watch the thick, gooey red liquid gently oozing out of the little pools at the top of either thigh. It held a sort of horrible fascination for a moment. And then the pain hit him. There was no way he could suppress the scream of agony as the broken parts of his left thigh bone ground together with the slight movement he made to adjust his back against the chair.

It brought Razak to his side again.

'Welcome back, Les.' The infliction of pain had dissipated his anger. He was calm and collected once again; he was almost friendly; nearly apologetic. 'I hope you had a nice sleep? Please don't reply, I can see you are in great pain. Please, sit quietly, let me do all the work . . .' His eyes searched Cohen's lap and tut-tutted at the amount of blood. 'My poor friend,' he said, considerately, 'I suppose you are wondering why I had to do that?'

Cohen kept his head bowed. He didn't want to know; he didn't care. But Razak was unstoppable. A bowed head wasn't going to get in the way. Kneeling down beside him he grasped a handful of hair and raised Cohen's head. Once upright he kept it in place by jamming the barrel of the Makarov under Cohen's chin and pointing with his other hand at the bed.

'That's the reason, Les.'

His face was close enough for Cohen to smell the powerful meaty flavour of his breath; Razak's last meal was still there among his teeth. Cohen focused his eyes on

194

where Razak was indicating, and he knew too what was coming next; he knew why Razak had crippled him. He was going to use Ruti against him. It brought the game of questions and answers down to a very simple equation.

Razak walked across the room, dragged Ruti's bound body off the bed and dumped her in the middle of the room. She met Cohen's eyes and looked away quickly. There was no message. They both knew what was coming next.

Razak squatted down on his heels beside her and untied her mutilated hand. She made no attempt to hold back the cries of anguish as he roughly dragged the hand out and held it to Cohen like an offering of a bunch of flowers. 'Two broken, Les, very painful. There's another six of those and two thumbs.' He bared his large teeth in his version of a smile; it wasn't very pretty, but that didn't worry him. 'Those are the simple things. But as you know, my friend, there are many other things men can do to women; unpleasant things; very cruel things . . .' He studied Cohen's face then allowed the smile to fade. 'So, do we understand now? Are you going to answer my questions?'

For Cohen there was no dilemma. He knew Razak's capabilities when it came to dishing out physical pain. He knew that the first test of the girl's pain threshold, the first probe into her vulnerable body, and he wouldn't have a single scruple to call up to justify not letting this evil bastard into Cunningham's objectives. But all the same it was a pity. He studied the girl's pain-racked face, her closed, over-made-up eyes; the black and blue liners smudged and running and overlapping the heavy bruising already evident on her tender skin; the thick pasted lipstick spread across her face like a bloody razor cut where two sets of Arab hands had been to work, and he wondered whether he'd be willing to betray his trust if it had been another man.

195

'What do you want, Razak?'

'Ah – ' Razak smiled again. 'A different tune. The Western mentality. Your concern for the female body makes life so easy for your less principled friends. I would be more concerned about the welfare of my goat than one of these – ' he flapped Ruti's hand again and got the scream he'd invited. 'Is she worth it, Les?'

'Ask your questions.'

As a reply Razak, with Ruti's hand still held lightly in his, grasped one of the unbroken fingers and pressed his thumb down hard on its knuckle. With an upward jerk on the finger and downward pressure on the knuckle the crack was as loud as a breaking bottle. Ruti's startled mouth opened to its full extent in front of Cohen's horrified eyes but nothing came out. The scream was blocked somewhere at the back of her throat as she mercifully fainted.

Cohen tried to move forward, but turned green as his shattered hip and groin took the strain. He sank back gasping, the shrieks of agony in his brain being allowed only a series of heaving groans into the smiling Arab's face. 'Why – ?' he managed, but got no further.

Razak touched Cohen's foot with the barrel of the Makarov. 'Because, my dear Les, I don't want to have to keep prompting you to tell the truth. You can now see what will happen if you lead me the little dance; I shall not query your lies if you wish to tell them, I will not invite you to consider a false answer. I shall merely break another of the whore's fingers. Any pain she might suffer will be entirely at your discretion. Does that explain your query?'

'Leave her alone,' Cohen managed to gasp again. 'I don't want her hurt again.'

'And neither will she be – if you tell the truth.'

And Cohen did exactly that. In half an hour the whole of Cunningham's mission was laid bare in front of Razak: the origin of the mission dating back to Cohen's sighting of

Macauley and its progress from there; of Cunningham's strength, as dictated by his ability to influence Israel's attitude in Cohen's enforced participation, and the added involvement of Mossad in the shape of Baruch Lev. As he filtered the questions Razak's mind was already working on how this good fortune was going to be put to his advantage. The germ of invention had already taken root.

Ruti began to stir at Razak's side. It began with an unconscious St-Vitus-type dance of the whole hand, the subconscious instinct raising the damaged fingers so that they didn't tap the carpet. Then came the agonizing moan. Razak, blank-faced, watched the dancing hand for a minute or so then dismissed it, and its owner, from his mind.

'Do you know why Cunningham wishes to find Macauley?'

'They are old friends. He wishes the body to be properly interred in America.'

'No other reason?'

'Not that I know of.'

'Baruch Lev?'

'What about him?'

'How much does he know of the American's business?'

'He's here to help me, not the American. He has no contact with Cunningham, and vice versa; he knows less than you about it,' muttered Cohen bitterly.

'And Lev's back-up?'

Cohen hesitated. Is there anything about the set-up this bastard doesn't know? Even Ruti didn't know definitely that Lev had local help. The hesitation was a fraction too long. Ruti's drawn-out scream as Razak picked up her hand by its newest broken finger seared into Cohen's brain like a red-hot poker. But Razak went no further. It seemed he accepted that the gesture, the threat, was enough to jerk Cohen out of his indecision.

'Leave her alone, Razak! You're getting everything you want – just leave her alone!'

'Go on, then,' said Razak.

'Lev has a local help. His name is Robin . . .'

'Jew?'

'Lebanese.'

'No other name?'

Cohen shook his head.

'Background?'

'He's personal to Lev. You know the system; there's no background,' lied Cohen. 'I've never seen him, I've been given only the name.'

'OK,' said Razak, surprisingly. 'I think that's about it, unless . . .' he paused and showed his teeth again, 'unless there's anything you'd like to add.'

Cohen didn't reply and for several minutes the two men sat and looked into each other's soul. Cohen knew where he stood – at the edge of the precipice. There would be no continuation to this story. But then, he'd always known that the end wasn't going to be tucked up in a soft bed in a darkened room with care and consideration to help him on his way. This was the end in the intelligence game, the field agent's requiem – a bullet in the head and, hopefully, oblivion. Much better, he convinced himself, wryly, than dropping away bit by bit of old age or cancer. But it didn't help to know that his oblivion was coming in a few minutes. Let's get it over with . . . He broke the silent communion.

'Can you let the girl go?'

Razak shook his head.

Cohen nodded sadly and closed his eyes.

The two explosions with a few seconds' delay between the first and the second caused no interruption to the busy life in the streets below. This was Beirut 1994: a couple of pistol shots, no matter where, was normal background music to the disturbed city centre. Nobody took any notice; even less notice than of the earlier two from the same building. It just didn't matter.

Razak placed one thousand of Ruti's US dollars plus all the Lebanese pounds on his friend the Commissaire's desk.

'I didn't think I should leave this behind for the investigation team,' he said seriously. 'You never know . . .'

The Commissaire understood. He swept the pile of currency from the desk into its open drawer in one experienced movement. 'I will hand it to the team myself when they make their preliminary report. Let me get this quite straight, brother. You left the inspector watching the whore's front door while you went about your business – '

'Exactly, and – '

The Commissaire smiled gently and held up his hand. 'Thank you, brother, but it is for I to be sure of the facts for later examination. Have patience with me . . . When you returned, the inspector had disappeared so you approached the whore's apartment. You had, you mentioned, seen a customer enter this building before you left?'

Razak nodded. Both the Commissaire and he were taking the charade seriously. But he kept his mouth closed. The Commissaire's version was a good one – and interesting.

'So you telephoned me that a suspected Israeli agent had been seen watching this building and you feared that the gallant inspector might have bravely tried to capture the man by himself. I joined you and entered the building by myself and I heard a shot ring out. Just as I reached the door another shot was fired and when I went in I was confronted by this man, who later turned out to be the Israeli agent, standing in the room aiming a gun at me. I shot him dead . . .'

'Exactly as it happened – '

The Commissaire smiled deprecatingly. He was a very good actor. He had the looks for it too. 'It seems that the Jew was depraved. He had beaten up and then raped the whore and had been taken by surprise by the inspector, who tried to save the girl. The Jew shot him dead. A second wild shot hit the girl in the face, killing her instantly.' He held Razak's eyes for several moments. 'Does that accord with your recollection of the events?' He paused. 'In the very unlikely event that you are asked to make a statement concerning your actions in this affair, do you agree that the only part you played was to recognize the Israeli agent going into the flat while you took morning coffee in the café opposite . . .'

Razak's eyes didn't waver. 'That is, indeed, all I did.'

'. . . with your friend an inspector of the Special Security Unit of the police?'

'I hope you receive the just rewards and commendation for your bravery, Commissaire.'

'Thank you. Is your work likely to involve any more such activities?'

'I don't think so, brother, but if it should . . .?' He left the question open-ended, and waited.

'You have all my resources at your disposal.'

'Thank you, brother. Erm . . .'

The Commissaire kept his face blank. The bill was about to be presented.

'Can you withhold the announcement of the death of the Jew, Cohen, for two or three days?'

The Commissaire smiled condescendingly, and with relief – the bill was a small one. 'For you, my friend? A difficult request, but this will be done. You have my word.'

24

Robin pressed his top lip against his teeth and ran the sharp little scissors against the lower edge of the dead straight line of his black moustache. He relaxed the lip, smiled in admiration at the reflection in the mirror then turned away to commence the difficult task of choosing shirt, tie and today's suit. Robin was full of admiration for himself; it was necessary that others took the same view. The decision made, he presented himself for further admiration in front of one of the full-length mirrors in the main room of the apartment.

Satisfied, he opened the slightly over-long navy blue jacket and slipped the massive Israeli-made Desert Eagle self-loading pistol into the special leather bracket on his belt. The weapon was his pride and joy — and with reason. Nobody had ever stood up to continue an argument after being hit by one of its .11 Magnum bullets. It was too much gun for the sort of trouble he was likely to encounter, but he lived with it — it went with the image. He closed his jacket on it but didn't worry about the way it dragged the lower half of the coat out of shape. Bulky lumps under jackets was all the rage; it was part of the macho sartorial image in sophisticated Beirut this decade.

He met up with Baruch Lev at the same scruffy café they'd used the day before. Robin, the Lebanese, looked wildly out of place; Lev, the Israeli, looked as though he'd been born there; but nobody gave either of them a second glance.

Across the street Razak was watching again from one of the food stalls, drinking his tea and eating *shwarma*. His reward came after fifteen minutes.

He saw a third man join Lev and Robin. The newcomer had the shifty air of one who'd been in the ducking and diving business for a long time. He couldn't keep his head still, and even as he sat and accepted the small cup of coffee Robin ordered for him his bottom was continually rising off the chair as he covered the area behind him. But he was paying attention to what was being said, Razak could see that from his stool at the roadside stall. His replies were acknowledged by the curly-haired Jew with emphatic nods. Robin looked slightly superciliously at his scruffy fellow Arab and left most of the talking to Lev. His contribution was to play with his moustache and send his thick, sensuous lips into approving or disapproving pouts. From Razak's vantage point it looked as if every so often he was offering a kiss to the nervous newcomer.

The whole situation was highly agreeable to Razak, and a sugar-coated *crêpe* added to the rapidly sweetening of his disposition. It appeared that Razak's luck was on a very long roll, for the longer he studied Lev and Robin's friend the happier he became. He knew him. Abu Qalaq was a Lebanese renegade, a turncoat who had embraced Hezbollah and been a member of one of Razak's earlier teams; he was one of the hard men who had brought the movement of hostages from one safe house to another under the eyes of the Syrian Army and local militia down to a fine art. Now no longer useful, they were a liability to their former master, the reformed, and holier than thou, Supreme Shura Council. No wonder this Lebanese looked worried and ill at ease above ground and out in the unaccustomed open. He'd have been marked for take-out. His removal from the scene of his former triumphs would have a very high priority with the Council's unofficial executioners. The taking of American and British hostages had proved a political failure, and to cover this failure the taking of Western hostages had been declared irreligious and a crime against Islam by the very people who had begun it and ordered it to be carried out. They had been allowed to purge themselves by disowning the men who'd obeyed their commands. Those who had carried out their wishes were offered no such opportunity to atone. They had become pariahs.

After two more cups of coffee each the three men split up and went their separate ways. Razak, after a short interval, went with the former Hezbollah hard man and cornered him in a dingy cellar in the basement of a former office block in the Mazraa district in south Beirut. It was a meeting of promises conducted with Razak's Beretta pointed at the fugitive's jugular. Qalaq got the message and accepted it. In return for his help Razak offered immunity from further persecution. The man could come out into the open and live the life of a rabbit like the rest of his pardoned friends.

'They're looking for an American,' he told Razak. 'One who disappeared during the good days and did not return. They're looking for the site of his grave so that they can take his bones back to the land of the Great Satan.'

'Is that all?'

Abu Qalaq hesitated and studied Razak through narrowed eyes. He was trying to work out how the next little gem would be received, knowing that if any Americans were still unaccounted for, this man, if any, would know where their bones were rotting. Also knowing this man, there was the possibility that he'd got the American somewhere in a hole of his own. You could never tell with men like Razak.

'They are also looking for the people who took him in the first place.'

He needn't have worried. Razak took it all in his stride. 'Have these people said where they're from?'

'Not directly. They led me to believe they are private investigators acting on behalf of the Great Satan's government. They mentioned money for information – any information.'

'Why you?'

Qalaq shrugged his shoulders. 'It happened. God willed it.'

Razak wasn't impressed. 'When do you meet them again?'

'I go to the Café Suleiman and take coffee any morning at eleven. One of them will pass by and check whether I am there and receive my information . . .'

'If you have any.'

The Lebanese looked smug. 'I won't be there if I have no information.'

'Don't become smart, my friend. You haven't yet earned equality; you can still be punished.' Razak stared Qalaq back into his earlier servility. 'Enough of this. Tomorrow morning you make your rendezvous. You will tell your contact that you have discovered a man who knows of an imprisoned foreigner. You will tell that this man is prepared to sell his information; the price will be high, but the information genuine. Do you understand that?'

'Do you know of such a foreign prisoner?'

'That is not your business. Do you understand what you are to tell the people?'

'Yes. And if they ask to meet you?'

'You tell them you will have to discuss meeting places with me and report back. You will do this tomorrow.'

'What about my own position?'

'We will discuss that when you have made the introductions. If everything goes in accordance with my wishes I will see to it that you are able to walk the streets like any other man – if, due to your stupidity, it doesn't succeed then I will hunt you down and kill you myself. Does that satisfy you?'

'I will do my best.'

'No you won't. You will do exactly as I have indicated. Pray that you succeed.'

At noon the following day Abu Qalaq turned up at the rendezvous he'd arranged with Razak. The contact had been made, he told him, he'd done exactly as ordered and they asked that an approach be made for a meeting.

'Did you see them both?' asked Razak.

'Only one,' replied Qalaq. 'He said he would make the arrangements direct with you if I arranged the meeting.'

'Which one was that?'

'He calls himself Robin.' The former hostage-taker looked Razak up and down then pursed his lips like a tailor assessing a client. 'He is one of us; he is of Lebanon. What do I tell him?'

'Tell him to come at half-past five to Rue Moussaitbe – you know it?'

'Of course.'

'Sit at a table in one of the cafés opposite the Turkish hospital; sit where you can be seen from the road. I will join you when I decide it is safe to do so. Tell your powerfully built friend to come alone but to have his master waiting at the end of a telephone to be told where to go when I am satisfied with the arrangements. Is that perfectly clear?'

Abu Qalaq nodded miserably. 'Half-past five this evening, Moussaitbe. Café opposite Turks' hospital. Anything else?'

'You will leave immediately after you have made the

205

introductions. You will leave the area and not try to contact me . . .'

'Will there be payment for me?'

Razak regarded him with disdain. 'Not from me. You will get what you can from these people. What they pay you is their business. I don't want to see you again.'

'Your promise?'

'Will be kept.'

Razak spent the next half-hour in his underground HQ with the man guarding Macauley. During that time he managed to put the fear of God into him with hints that the Israeli Mossad were on the track of Macauley and that there was a possibility that they might find him. Razak offered Badran a graphic account of what would happen to him should the Israelis enter the dungeon. But, assured Razak, with his help the two of them would frustrate these people. Badran listened, if not with conviction with hope, to the details of Razak's plan and agreed to the part that Razak had allotted him. Razak left him less happy than when he'd arrived but with the knowledge that he'd carry out his part. If he didn't, Razak had assured him, the enormous sum of money that he, Razak, was arranging for him would go up in a puff of smoke.

Razak studied the Israeli-trained agent for some time before moving from his position. He took it for granted that Robin would come alone; he wouldn't want to prejudice the operation by having Lev carry out back-up – not at this stage. Razak was a professional, he expected other professionals to behave as he would. The beginning of a friendship was not the time to sow distrust. That came later when there was more to be gained. He nodded at Qalaq, who muttered a few brief words to Robin then got up and, without looking round, vanished into the traffic in Rue Moussaitbe.

Razak sat down in his vacated chair and ordered a thimble-sized cup of thick Turkish coffee and waited while Robin sized him up. He was very similar in build to Razak, but that was where the similarity ended. Robin's smooth, moustachioed, Arab matinée idol looks were in direct contrast to Razak's shaggy beard, collar-length hair, and a jacket that looked as though it had spent a considerable part of its life under the bricks and debris of its tailor's shop before ending up on Razak's back. Robin's highly polished shoes branded him as a man of good taste; Razak's old Chelsea boots told a story of their own. Altogether Robin wasn't impressed with his contact, but, nevertheless, he opened the bidding.

25

'I don't like the man,' Robin told Lev when he telephoned him half an hour later from the public phone box in the Turkish hospital across the road.

'You're not expected to like him; you're not going to go to bed with him,' growled Lev, without a trace of humour. 'You're supposed to be negotiating some sort of bloody deal with the man. How far did you get?'

'I don't trust him either.'

'What's the deal? Does he know anything, or is he just trying to squeeze a few baksheesh out of a couple of gullible guys?'

'I think he's got something,' said Robin reluctantly. 'I think you'd better come and watch the way his mouth and eyes work. Bring some cash.'

'How much?'

'He's asking $25,000 US for the information and $75,000 for the body –'

'Body?'

'Sorry! The American according to this guy, is still breathing. He says he can take us to him.'

'He'll accept $10,000 for the whole bloody lot or I'll give him a dose of nine milli –'

'He's no dummy, Baruch. You're going to have to play this one with a little more finesse than that otherwise he'll take off as fast as his little boots'll carry him.'

'Did he offer any history?'

'No. Listen. Here's the programme. It's his — I just agreed. No offer, no promise. OK? Here's what you do. Get a cab to Borj Abi-Haidar. Have him drop you off about halfway down Rue Abdel-Ghani Arayassi. Turn into Rue Osman, then Rue Abdullah Shaffie. Halfway down this he says you'll find a former Peugeot showroom; that's about all that can be seen of it — the old Peugeot sign's hanging from a bent lamp-post. The rest's a pile of rubble. OK?'

'So far.'

'You'll find it. Be there at half-past seven; he wants to give you the once-over before committing himself.'

'Will you be there?'

'Too right, my friend! And there'll be a large bit of cocked Desert Eagle hovering a few centimetres from his backbone — if he's got one!'

'See you at half-past seven, then.'

'On the dot!'

Lev replaced the receiver and rang Ruti's number. No reply. He let it ring for some time then gave it up. He wrinkled his nose; she must be working. How urgent was this? Could be just a bloody con. A chum of Robin's shifty-eyed cellar rat working the deposit game — half now and half when he produced the body, and that would be the last he ever saw of the bastard . . . Did Les Cohen want to know any of this? He'd leave a message at the Commodore. He changed the .22 Beretta for something a little bigger, a well tried and reliable Glock 17. He stuck that inside his waistband and dropped a spare seventeen-round magazine in his coat pocket. He felt somewhat overloaded but, as they said, better safe than sorry; and there's nothing more sorry than a gun without bullets.

Lev found the bomb-blasted Peugeot showroom without difficulty. He stood in the shadow and cover of a similarly derelict shop on the opposite side of the road and waited.

At twenty-five past seven he saw movement at the back

of the Peugeot building. The street was deserted, there was no traffic, no shops operating; this was one bit of Beirut that had really been given the works by the Israeli airforce, and then Ariel Sharon's picked Commandos. They'd left nothing to be going on with; there was no business to be done in piles of bricks and dust and burnt, broken timber. In this derelict, deserted street movement was something that caught the eye. It caught, and held, Lev's.

The first person he saw moving through the rubble was Robin. There was someone else behind, in the shadows, but he stayed there as Robin picked his way across the debris and stood at the back of the former showroom. There was no gun in his hand so Lev checked his own Glock and made sure it was cocked. He still didn't move. Somewhere behind him a tinny clock went through its routine. Half-past seven. Lev moved from his doorway and waited. Robin met his eyes across the road and rubble and nodded. He had probably seen him before he moved but Robin knew all about discretion. He waited until Lev was on his side of the road then held up a finger, its movement protected by his body; he then turned, made eye contact with Razak, lurking behind him, and nodded. Razak waited a few moments then came out into the open.

The three men stood for some time, Robin in the middle, Razak and Lev on either side of the street studying each other. Finally, as if synchronized, the two men on the outside joined Robin.

There were no introductions, no handshakes, just a keen appraisal of Razak by Lev and a searching glance by Razak at the dark grey Glock hanging casually in Lev's hand at his side. Razak showed him his own empty hands. 'You can put that away,' he said. 'I am here for business – not trouble. You have brought some money?'

Lev kept the pistol in his hand. He didn't answer the question. 'Tell me about the man you say is still held here.'

Razak held Lev's eyes, then glanced sideways at Robin. 'You said you had arranged everything. Do I now have to repeat everything I told you?'

Robin said nothing.

Razak shrugged his shoulders. He turned his back on the two men and began picking his way through the scattered bricks that covered the once shiny, tiled showroom floor. Lev waited until he reached his entrance point and said in a low voice, 'OK. Let's assume you know what you are talking about. Can you take us to this person?'

'I repeat my earlier question. Have you brought money?'

Lev reached into the inside pocket of his jacket with his free hand and brought out a thick bundle of notes.

Razak made his eyes gleam greedily. 'Twenty-five thousand dollars US?'

'Ten thousand dollars US,' responded Lev. 'Half when I meet the man who is being held, the other half when I establish he is the man we are looking for.'

'That wasn't the agreement.'

Lev flipped the bundle with his thumb so that Razak could see that each note was a hundred dollars. He waited for the gesture to sink in. 'It's all I'm prepared to offer at the moment. If there is such a person, and it's the person I'm looking for, the rest of the money you ask for will be paid by the people employing me – ' he forestalled Razak's objection with a wave of the Glock. 'I'm not prepared to argue beyond that. You want to do business? Do it. If you don't, too bad. You'll be at least $5,000 out of pocket whether the prisoner is the one we want or not . . You following me?'

'The money's not enough.' Razak had to play the game properly. He could see what he was dealing with – he *knew* what he was dealing with. 'This prisoner is American. I can take you to him. He must be worth more than $5,000 . . .' he allowed a wheedling note to creep into his voice. A Jew

211

dealing with an Arab would expect it. And Razak could see he'd hit a button; the flash of interest in the Israeli's eye, even though it was as momentary as a blink, was noted. Razak had done his business; he knew he'd sold his produce.

Lev dragged it out for a few more moments. 'OK – if the prisoner's American you get $10,000 for the location and $10,000 for his being the man we want.'

'It is hardly worth my while . . .'

'OK. Goodbye!' Now it was Lev who began to turn away. But Razak gave in. With a shrug of his shoulders, a drooping of his lips and a sideways twist of his hands Razak acknowledged that he had been bested in the bargaining. 'How will I receive the balance of the payment?'

'We will discuss that when we establish the identity of the prisoner.'

'It is the man you are seeking.'

'How do you know that?' said Lev sharply.

'There are no American captives in Beirut except this one.'

'You know his name?'

Razak shook his head. 'You will discover that in a moment.'

'Then you accept the deal?'

'I accept.'

'Lead the way.'

It took twenty minutes for Razak to lead the two Israeli agents down a myriad of narrow destroyed streets, small crumbling alleys and untouched mountains of brick rubble before arriving at the corner of what had been a grand middle-class street on which stood the ruined apartment block, the cellar of which Razak had made his impenetrable dungeon.

Razak drew the two men into the cover of the wall of a half-destroyed building, and with a gentle pushing motion of his hand indicated for them to wait there. Lev's gun was once more in his hand and Robin's jacket was open, allowing easy access to the big Desert Eagle. Their eyes met; they were both as cool as if they were sitting in a street café in Tel Aviv's Dizengoff Street studying the local skirt. This barely warranted the minute bubbles of sweat on Lev's upper lip; it was just a tiny warning. Imprudently he brushed it aside from his brain. Razak returned within a couple of minutes.

'It's all clear,' he said in a stage whisper. 'There's no guard outside.' He bared his teeth, but it wasn't a smile; his eyes were flat and cold. 'Very lax. Times have changed – '

Lev wasn't interested in the changing times. 'Lead the way.' He brought the Glock up where Razak could get a good close look and rested it in the crook of his arm. 'Just a minute – '

Razak stepped back into the cover of the wall.

'How far?'

Razak pointed with his chin. 'Across the road, one of the gaps in that row of big buildings.'

'You sure there's no outside guard?'

'Absolutely. There's probably one or more below with the body, but even then – ' he gazed up and down the deserted, bombed-out road then glanced down at his watch – 'it could be empty. Like I said . . .'

'Let's go and find out.'

'One thing, though . . .' Razak hesitated and gazed around him again, 'One of us must guard the entrance against their return.'

'Robin – ' Lev jerked his head at the big man leaning casually against the wall. No words were necessary. He drew the heavy, already cocked, Desert Eagle from the toggle on his belt, flipped off the safety catch and tucked it under his folded arm. Razak studied Robin's attitude for a

213

moment and gave him a little nod of approval. He got nothing back.

Razak crossed the road and with Lev in close attendance moved down the road for about fifty metres. He stopped, made a mute gesture with his finger at the derelict building then placed the same finger across his lips. He glanced over Lev's shoulder. Robin hadn't moved.

'Get on with it,' hissed Lev.

'Through that entrance,' whispered Razak, pointing at a gap in the debris, 'down the stairs – there are about fifteen steps – to a corridor. A few metres in there's a wooden door to the right. Your person is in there . . . D'you want to go in front?'

Lev's lips tightened. 'Don't be bloody silly!' He tapped Razak's arm with the Glock. 'You lead. Don't make any sudden movement – nothing clever. Got it? This has a very delicate trigger – goes off by itself if anything worries me. Go carefully . . .'

Razak merely nodded into Lev's cold, untrusting eyes and proceeded through the hole in the bombed building. He could feel Lev close behind him. At the foot of the stairs he stopped and put his hand just above his shoulder. It was unnecessary. Lev was balanced on his toes, every sense alert, matching Razak's movements perfectly.

They waited like two statues, listening, Razak peering into the gloomy corridor lighted only by a bare, low-wattage bulb suspended from the ceiling, and Lev watching the muscles at the back of Razak's neck for the first sign of sudden movement. The Glock, steady in his hand pointed unwaveringly at the base of Razak's spine; Razak was within a fraction of a millimetre's movement of Lev's finger of being a cripple for the rest of his life – if he was unlucky. If he was lucky, death by a mushrooming STX expanding bullet would be instantaneous. Lev wasn't concerned about either option. Razak lowered his hand and moved cautiously along the corridor. His hand went up again and without taking his eyes off the length of the passageway he leaned his head backwards and placed his hand over the side of his mouth to direct his barely audible words over his shoulder.

'No one here.'

'Is that the door?'

'Yes. I'll keep guard here while you go in and inspect the body.'

'No way! Go and bring him out.'

Razak turned his head fully. 'You have to go in. He'll be chained by his legs; he can't be moved . . .'

'Lead the way, then.'

Razak ran his hands up the side of the door and found the lock. He fiddled with the key. It squeaked and grated and he gave another theatrical glance at Lev.

'Open it,' mouthed Lev, then placed his lips close to Razak's ear and hissed, 'Is there any light in there?'

'No,' whispered back Razak, 'but you can see inside from that — ' he pointed at the hanging bulb. 'There's not much to see.'

'OK. Go in, stay in front of me, go to the far wall and stand still. One wrong move — ' he didn't finish the warning but stepped back half a pace and urged Razak on with a poke of his finger.

Razak opened the door fully and did exactly as Lev had instructed.

Lev waited at the door, adjusting to the half-shadows caused by the light from over his shoulder. His eyes searched the room, settled for a moment on Razak standing very still, his back against the dirty damp wall and following every movement of his eyes. Something wrong! Nothing concrete; nothing substantial; nothing he could put his finger on. But there was definitely something wrong, his

215

instincts told him so. He allowed his eyes to leave Razak and study the apparition on the mattress in the other corner.

The figure, squatting or kneeling, was covered in a dark blanket that draped over it like a small Red Indian wigwam. It swayed gently backwards and forwards, soundlessly, metronomically and as his eyes became accustomed to the faint light he could make out the shape of the head. It was bowed as if in prayer. Lev stared for a moment then raised his eyes and studied Razak. Razak hadn't moved and, like Lev, he was staring at the figure on the mattress.

Lev took a sideways step forward, ran his free hand over the shape of the head and, with one eye still on Razak, grabbed a handful of the blanket and lifted it.

'Macaul . . . ?'

He got no further.

His left arm, raised above his head in the motion of lifting the blanket, offered the perfect target. The needle-point of the eight-inch thin stiletto in Badran's hand slid upwards, through Lev's ribs and into his heart in one smooth movement. He kept it there for a brief second, shifted his balance slightly then twisted his wrist. The widened blade at the tip tore his heart almost in half. Lev was dead even though he remained like a statue with the blanket in one hand, the Glock in a useless, unfeeling hand. His mouth was still shaped for the question he was never going to finish and his eyes, with the same puzzled expression, remained staring and bulging for almost three seconds. It was enough time for a blank-faced Razak to take the two steps across the room and gently remove the automatic from Baruch Lev's dead hands.

He nodded to Badran, who withdrew the stiletto and admired the almost bloodless blade before wiping it on the mattress and replacing it in its thin sheath that was lying between his knees. With the prop of the stiletto removed,

216

Lev's knees gave way and he folded up in a heap on the floor.

Without waiting for the twitching to stop the two Arabs lifted the body on to the mattress, arranged it to look like a sleeping figure and covered it with the blanket.

'Go and hide yourself,' hissed Razak. 'I'm bringing in the other one. Come when I call you.'

26

Robin's eyes, apart from the intermittent and casual inspection of his immediate surroundings, hadn't left the spot where Lev and Razak had disappeared into the ground. He saw Razak's head appear out of the rubble and stare around him. Then the rest of his body appeared. Robin's hand tightened on the butt of the Israeli automatic when Razak began walking briskly towards his position. No Baruch Lev. He studied the area behind the approaching Razak and flicked up the safety catch. Absently he ran his thumb over the cocked hammer and kept his hand in position there when Razak, his teeth gleaming in a smile, stopped in front of him. He held his hands out in a gesture of prayer; it was supposed to convey good news and, at the same time, reassure Robin that he had no concealed weapon. Robin didn't trust him. He kept the heavy automatic in position.

'It is the man you are looking for,' said Razak, breathlessly. 'Your partner sent me to ask that you join him.'

Robin didn't move. 'Why?' he asked laconically.

'He didn't confide in me,' replied Razak humbly. 'He just said to come and get you.'

Robin studied Razak with disdain. 'Who's to guard the entrance?'

Razak spread his hands again. 'I'm just the messenger.'

Robin shook his head. He didn't like this; he didn't like

218

it at all, and he still didn't trust this evil-looking bastard — not one little bit. But Lev wouldn't have sent for him if it wasn't necessary. He'd heard no gunfire, and even if he had he knew the one man sure to climb out of that hole in the ground if there'd been trouble would be Baruch Lev. He kept his feelings off his face and, with a jerk of his head, indicated for Razak to lead the way. The Desert Eagle dropped discreetly to his side but remained ready to cause havoc at the twitch of a finger.

Razak dived into the hole in the rubble without hesitation. Robin delayed fractionally and stared about him before following him down. There was no sound. Dead silence as he descended the stairs and joined Razak in the passageway.

'In there. He's looking after the American — he's badly damaged . . .' Razak stood under the light bulb and indicated the open door of the cell. 'He doesn't need me in there. I shall go to the top of the stairs just in case.'

Robin dismissed him with an unfriendly glance and peered round the corner of the door. 'Baruch?' he hissed. It was his first mistake. He had turned his back.

Razak moved like a striking snake. From the back of his waistband the heavy 92F Beretta appeared in his hand and he slammed it with all his strength just above Robin's right ear. In shock Robin's finger tightened on the trigger of the Desert Eagle and the explosion of the first round boomed like a battleship's broadside in the confines of the narrow passage. Robin staggered and tried to turn, but Razak was on his way with the next blow. This came sideways and smacked solidly into the side of his fleshy neck. Another round from the Eagle thundered and another bullet thudded into the ground. Razak moved back slightly and balanced on the balls of his feet. With Robin staggering forward and trying to bring the Desert Eagle round Razak had more time to pick his spot. This time it was perfect. A

219

round arm swing with precise timing thwacked the mass of
the Beretta between the corner of Robin's eye and his ear.
The bone of the eye socket cracked with the sound of
another exploding round and the huge automatic dropped
from Robin's numb fingers and crashed to the floor.
Robin's unconscious body followed it.

But it wasn't enough for Razak.

Moving beside the Israeli agent's head he reached down
and grasped a handful of expensively oiled hair and pulled
the head upwards, about two feet off the ground. Taking a
firmer grip on the slightly sweaty and blood-coated Beretta,
he tapped the side of Robin's head with two light, ranging
blows then swung his arm back and gave it all his strength.
There was another nasty crack as something broke and the
oily hair slipped from Razak's grasp and thudded to the
ground.

'Have you killed him?' Badran appeared in the doorway.
He stared at Robin's unconscious figure, his fingers
trembling with excitement as he lit a cigarette. As promised,
Razak had dealt with the Mossad agents. Badran raised his
face to Razak's: he almost felt he owed this man his life and
he let his expression show his gratitude. 'Would you like a
cigarette, Razak?' he asked nervously.

Razak's bulging eyes focused on the Shiite's face as he
dragged air into his lungs. He shook his head and after a few
minutes he was able to speak.

'He's not dead. Not yet. *You* can do that later. Strip
him – '

'Why?'

'You will see. Do as I say. Get everything off him.'

Badran did as he was ordered. By the time he'd finished,
Razak had recovered sufficiently from his exertions to
accept Badran's cigarette. He stood over the naked body of
Robin and studied it. He seemed satisfied.

'What are you looking for?' asked a puzzled Badran.

'Nothing in particular.' Razak wasn't going to confide in this idiot that he was looking for distinguishing marks: wounds, cuts, other features that might have someone look at such a body and say, 'Yes, that's Robin what's-his-name because I remember *that* scar.' Everything had a reason. Razak had already worked out his future.

'Tie his hands and arms behind his back . . .' He stared around then, cigarette dangling from his lips, wandered slowly down the passageway. He stopped in front of the blunt end of a joist jutting about five inches out of the damp bulge of the wall and tested it by hanging from it with one hand. It was as solid as any part of the bomb-damaged building. '. . . and we'll hang him up here.'

'Why?'

'Don't keep asking questions. Just do what I say . . .'

'But?'

'But, nothing! Lift him.'

Robin was not an easy man to hang by his hands and arms from a jutting buttress six feet from the ground, but the two Arabs managed to heave the dead weight into position before collapsing, their mouths open gasping for breath and their chests heaving with the exertion, at the feet of the Christ-like figure hanging from the wall.

The strain on Robin's shoulderblades was horrendous. It was sufficient to bring him out, with a blood-curdling scream, from the comparative comfort of deep unconsciousness. As he became aware, the agony of his head and face wounds faded into insignificance and the screams, from the pit of his stomach, reverberated up and down the narrow passage as the hideous noise sought an exit from the chamber of horrors.

Razak dragged himself to his feet after a few minutes, balanced his half-smoked cigarette carefully on a ledge near the ground and stood up in front of the suspended man. He studied Robin's face; his own was without pity. Robin saw

221

nothing. He heard nothing except the fearful noise coming from his own mouth. After a second or two Razak bent down and retrieved Robin's underpants. Without taking his eyes from Robin's face he rolled the pants into a ball and rammed them into his open mouth. The screams muffled, Razak watched his victim's head droop as he slipped into a faint, then turned his back, squatted once again on his heels with his back supported by the wall and retrieved his smouldering cigarette. The silence as the two men sat and smoked and studied the hanging figure was as eerie as the noise had been grotesque.

Razak stubbed out his cigarette and entered the cell. Grabbing the dead Baruch Lev by his coat collar he dragged him out through the door and propped him against the wall opposite the hanging man. When Robin opened his eyes again the first thing he would see was his friend's bulging, dead eyes. Razak knew all about the psychology of shock – and if that didn't work he knew even more about the physical application of pain.

'A wet cloth, Badran,' he said, studying the barely visible rising and falling of Robin's thick, black hair covered chest. 'And then get the American back into his place. Chain him, as before.'

'Are you going to help me to get him out of the wall?'

'You didn't need me to help you put him back. I'm going to be busy with this Jew-lover. Give me the towel.'

He dragged Robin's blood-soaked underpants from his torn mouth and bared his teeth with satisfaction at the faint groan that came out with them. He stood back at arm's length then commenced slapping the helpless man's face, viciously, with the wet towel.

It had the right effect.

Robin's eyes opened but focused on nothing. His shoulders had locked into an agonizing, searing cramp, his right eye, with its smashed socket, would never see again

222

and his head felt as if six-inch nails had been driven forcibly into his skull. The towel whipped again across his face and drove some of the blood from his one seeing eye. He blinked several times and tried to wipe it with his shoulder, but it wouldn't reach. He closed it on the red mist.

But it wasn't good enough for Razak.

He grabbed a handful of Robin's bloody, oily hair, raised his face and pushed it as far back into the wall as it would go. He then held a fistful of the towel in a tight grip and squeezed the remaining liquid into Robin's upheld face. Blood and dirty water trickled into his eyes, down his cheeks and ran into the corner of his mouth. The squeezed-out cloth was run across his face and an open hand hit him cruelly and with strength across his damp face. He forced his good eye open and stared blearily into Razak's bearded, unyielding face. Nothing was said. Razak, without letting go of his hair, moved to one side and directed his head downwards and across the passage.

Baruch Lev's dead face grinned up at him.

Robin clenched his eye tight to dispel the vision. Baruch Lev propped against the wall in a darkened, gloomy damp passage, dead – his bulging eyes staring at him reproachfully, his teeth bared as the muscles of his face tightened in rigor and dragged his lips apart. A thumb pushed the closed eyelid upwards. He blinked the pain away and stared again. No illusion. His stomach contracted and tried to eject its contents, but all he managed was a mouthful of foul-tasting bile retched upwards to mix with the blood and dirty water and saliva already there. He tried to spit but nothing happened. Then the bearded face came close to his and the voice spoke.

'Tell me all about yourself, Robin.'

There was nowhere to go. He was going to die. Let's get it over with quickly. In reply he managed to spit out the mouthful of muck, but without the strength to reach its intended target, the bearded face; it trickled down his chin and hung suspended until it built up sufficient volume to drop on to his chest. But the message was clear.

'You want more pain?'

Robin tried another spit but fear had left nothing in his mouth to work on. His throat was as dry as dust. He closed his good eye again when Razak said calmly, 'So be it. More pain you shall have.'

Razak clicked his fingers at Badran, who had returned from his chore of replacing Thurston Macauley in his cell and was now squatting on a ledge watching the proceedings with an anticipatory grin on his swarthy features. He raised his eyebrows at Razak's signal.

'Give me your knife.'

'You going to kill him?'

'Give me your knife.'

Badran stuck the handle of the thin blade into Razak's outstretched hand and admired the needle-like point, the slight widening above it before it resumed its elegant rapier-like slimness; at any other time a thing of crafted beauty – eight inches of bright lethal beauty. But Razak was not interested in its beauty. He touched the point to Robin's Adam's apple, which automatically swallowed itself out of danger. Razak followed it until the point of the blade entered Robin's neck by half a centimetre and he watched a trickle of blood form round the point and course erratically down Robin's neck. Robin hissed and opened his eye.

'If you close your eyes again,' Razak advised him, 'I'll slice off your eyelids. Keep looking at me and talk to me about your life.'

'I have had no life,' croaked Robin, with difficulty. 'I have nothing to say to a creature that crawled out of the afterbirth of a whore's womb. Go back into its dirt and meet your brothers . . .'

Badran grinned with delight. Razak took it in his stride;

224

he couldn't have done better in similar circumstances. He held the thin blade up to Robin's good eye and said, 'Join me there!' He stuck the stiletto back into the hole he'd made in Robin's neck and drew it downwards, between his breasts and over his bulging stomach; the stiletto did a neat circle round his navel and stopped when it ground against his pelvic bone.

Robin gritted his teeth and tried not to let the scream escape. It came out as a high-pitched whistle, gaining intensity as the knife reached lower down his torso. He tried not to look but his eye refused to obey him. The flesh of his body lay back in a ridge as far down as his eye could see; at the top, just reaching the middle of his chest a channel had filled with blood that was moving downwards into the white and pink where the flesh slowly erupted with little bubbles of blood and awaited the main flow. Robin finally let go and bellowed at the top of his voice.

Razak was unaffected. He studied the point of the dagger and wiped it on the mass of hair, rapidly absorbing some of the overflow of blood, on Robin's chest. After a moment the bellows from Robin's mouth became sobs, then long moans and imprecations on Razak's head.

'Tell me about your life, Robin,' urged Razak, monotonously.

Robin tried to speak, but nothing came. He focused his eye, now hooded in pain, on Razak's cold, unfeeling eyes and tried to nod. He'd had enough. Razak wasn't going to give him the quick death he prayed for. 'W-water . . .' he managed to gasp.

'Some water for our honoured guest, Badran,' said Razak over his shoulder and Badran trotted off chuckling to himself. Despite the situation with his friends, Razak was good fun to be with.

Razak tilted the chipped mug into Robin's lips and let him drink. Some water went into his mouth, most dribbled out of the corners on to his chest and found its way into the trickling blood. But he'd had enough to moisten his mouth. He was able to speak through the searing pain that kept knifing its way into his brain.

'W-what is it you w-want?'

'Start with your father's name; then your mother's, your brothers, sisters, cousins, and tell me everything you've done since the unfortunate day the hyena that was your father watched your she-goat of a mother give birth to the mongrel that turned out to be you. Start with the names – I will remind you if you lose your way . . .'

It took half an hour's probing by Razak before Robin reached the time of his recruitment by the Mossad agent Baruch Lev. Nearer dead than alive, he decided that was as far as he went; there was nothing more Razak could do to hurt him more than he'd already done. There was no part of his body that did not scream; his brain refused to accept any more and was operating a form of anaesthetization on his pain ducts. But he'd underestimated Razak – and overestimated the effect of anaesthetization.

'You met up with the Jew, Lev. You became a creature of Israel, of the Mossad; you left the traitors' army and doubled your treachery by working against your own people . . . Tell me everything about that.'

'There's nothing more to tell.'

Razak looked into Robin's bleary, pain-racked eye and raised his eyebrows in surprise. 'Robin, you have gone so far, why stop now? You owe nothing to nobody, you are a free man now, you can talk as much as you like. This creature is dead – ' He turned and kicked Lev's unresponsive body. 'You owe him nothing. He can tell nothing, he can bring nothing on to your head. Talk to me, Robin. Finish the story.'

'Nothing more,' groaned Robin. 'Finish me. Please – kill me . . .'

'No — not yet. Do you need a little something to encourage you?'

'Please kill me.'

Razak studied the wreck hanging in front of him while he thought over what Robin had told him. He now knew more about Robin Gouda than Robin Gouda's brother. Razak was Robin's alter ego — he was a shave and a haircut away from being Robin Gouda. But there was this little bit more . . .

'Listen to me, Robin. Wake up, Robin!' He slapped Robin's face lightly several times to bring him back into the nightmare. 'Open your eye, Robin. Come on, Robin — '

Robin's eye opened.

Razak held it locked to his own as he ran the point of the stiletto lightly across Robin's lower stomach until he found the soft point of his groin, a spot where his thigh joined his torso. Still with his eyes on Robin's he felt down with his other hand, like a lover seeking with his fingers the entrance to his woman's body, not wanting to relinquish the pleasure of drinking the beauty of her face, and found the spot he wanted. He touched the needle-point of the stiletto against his finger then, lowering his shoulder, put his weight against it.

The stiletto slid into Robin's groin as easily as if it had been made of butter. There was a puzzled look in Robin's eye. But only for a second. Then horror. Then pain; then pain again and his eye bulged and tried to force its way out of its socket as at the same time his mouth opened. Even Badran lowered his head in horror: he'd begun to have enough. He rapidly scrabbled for a cigarette to calm his nerve.

But not Razak.

He placed his hand over Robin's mouth and watched the eye contort. It was the only means left to Robin to seek relief. It finally turned upwards into his head, leaving only the yellow-tinged white for Razak to stare at, and he passed out once again. Razak half turned to his sick-looking companion, pointed to the handle of the stiletto, still sticking obscenely out of Robin's heavy, hair-covered groin and for once he grinned. 'Our friend thought he knew what pain was all about; he didn't realize that he has barely touched the fringe of real pain.' He continued, showing his teeth through his beard, 'I am in love with this dagger, Badran – in fact I am very attached to it. Perhaps you would like to offer it to me as a gift?'

Badran waved his hand. 'Please. What is a simple dagger between friends?'

'Thank you, brother.'

Razak gazed down with pleasure at his gift and caressed its plain silver wired haft. But he didn't remove it from Robin's groin; instead he gave it a little twist. The new surge of pain sliced into Robin's subconscious and with an agonizing scream brought him back to the chamber of horrors. He tried to raise his head. Nothing happened. His eye, unseeing, bulged at nothing, and all the time the terrible noise that came from his open mouth bounced off the walls and echoed into his brain. He couldn't stop. And Razak let him get on with it until out of breath his chest heaved and the awful noise lessened and was replaced by gasping, choking sobs.

Eventually he managed to make his tongue work. 'Kill me,' he pleaded. 'F-fini – '

'That will be your reward, Robin – ' murmured Razak solicitously, his face close, drinking in the aroma of fear and agony from Robin's breath – 'after you have finished talking to me. Shall I remind you of where you stopped?' He leaned back and lifted Robin's head by his hair. Studying the one eye he reached down with the other hand, found the handle of the stiletto and gently withdrew it.

'Aghhhhh!'

He held it up and showed it to the eye. 'There are many other places this little friend of mine would like to explore. Let us see if we can curb his impatience, Robin; let us talk about the Mossad, the Jews and the interesting work you did for their money . . . Go on.'

Haltingly and with long pauses Robin brought his life story up to date. Razak, who had tired of standing in front of the suspended man, squatted on his heels with his back to the wall and chain-smoked cigarettes as he listened and prompted. He was totally satisfied with what he had heard. There was nothing about Robin's life he did not know. A few more questions and the man could have his wish and die. Razak was no longer in a hurry. Everything was ready for the final move.

'When did you last see the Israeli agent, Cohen?'

'I've never seen him.'

Razak had no reason to doubt this. It would be a very silly and stupid move to lie at this stage of the journey to the great Paradise. 'And the American, Cunningham, who is staying at the Commodore Hotel?'

'N-no.'

'No what?'

'I don't know this man. I have never seen him – or heard his name.'

Razak relaxed, lit another cigarette from the end of the one between his lips and crushed the used stub into the floor. He sat back and thought over what he had heard. There were no flaws. He was sure the Lebanese turncoat, Robin, had bared his soul. Everything was there, the scene was set and all he had to do was play the part that had befallen him – befallen him by God's good will, he told himself, and all the riches in the world and the rewards he so richly deserved were within his grasp. He glanced out of the corner of his eye at Badran, who was gazing with morbid fascination at the agony of the man hanging on the wall. Something must be done about this creature too. But first –

'Can you hear me, Robin?' Razak studied the big Arab for a moment with a quizzical expression. Robin appeared to be sleeping – or dead.

'Robin!' He raised his voice.

Through the blood-smeared face, streaked like a Red Indian warrior's warpaint by the passage of tears and sweat the solitary eyelid lifted and Razak was able to see into the man's tormented, tortured soul. It was like lifting a curtain into the back door to hell. Razak stared, for a moment shaken by the horror he'd seen revealed, then recovered. He dragged deeply on his cigarette, exhaled with a whoosh, and said unemotionally. 'The time has come for you to begin the long journey, Robin. How do you choose to begin it?'

Robin made no reply. He closed his eye and allowed his head to fall on to his blood-soaked chest. He looked as if he'd been crucified. He could well have been praying.

'You promised I could finish him . . .' With his shirt sleeve Badran wiped the spittle that had dribbled out of the corners of his mouth as he gazed at Robin's bowed head. Anticipation brought a sparkle to his lacklustre black eyes and he'd recovered his courage after the earlier period of feeling sick. This was his reward; his voice took on an entreating whine. 'You promised – '

Razak dragged his eyes away from Robin's naked body and looked disdainfully at the youth. 'Are you man enough for such a task?'

'Watch me!'

Razak continued to stare into the young man's face. 'Go on, then.'

Badran stood up. He raised his chin at Razak and spread his hands. 'How do I do it?'

'Huh!'

'Give me my knife.'

'What would you do with it – stick him like a pig?'

'If necessary.'

Razak returned his gaze to Robin. 'Go and find a proper tool. A sharp blade. Cut his throat – it's the quickest . . .'

'*He* didn't complain at the way I sent him –' Badran turned sideways and kicked Baruch Lev's body. 'He went quick enough.'

Razak shook his head. 'Do as I say. Go and get a proper knife.'

The youth's mouth tightened as he prepared to stand his ground but when his eyes met those of Razak his resolve melted. There was something in the depths of Razak's eyes that he had seen before. It frightened him.

He returned after a few minutes with a black-handled butcher's knife. Its twelve-inch blade was honed down to a narrow strip but it was a long time since it had been used on a goat's carcass. Badran ran his thumb along its edge then moved in front of Robin. He glanced over his shoulder. 'OK?'

'If you think so,' responded Razak. He studied the youth's face curiously. Killing a man in the heat of action, or in a sudden flurry of fear and anger, was within the capability of almost any man; to kill a man hanging naked from a wall as if he were a skinned, but living animal took a different mentality altogether. He lowered his gaze and looked at the boy's hand holding the knife. It was shaking. The boy was terrified under his veneer of bravado. 'Do it,' he said calmly. 'Cut his throat.'

Badran stood in front of Robin. He reached out and gingerly took a handful of hair and raised his face. Robin had been listening. His eye was open; he stared straight into the boy's soul.

'Go on,' insisted Razak.

231

Dragging his eyes from the one tormented eye staring accusingly at him the youth gripped the knife until the knuckles of his hand threatened to burst and placed the blade at an angle just above Robin's Adam's apple. He drew it sharply away from him. A gap like a second mouth appeared on Robin's neck and thick red blood spattered out like a miniature fountain, but it wasn't deep enough – the knife ground up against the windpipe, but there was not enough strength behind the slash for the blade to penetrate. Robin made no sound other than a guttural choking that bubbled out of his mouth and made no sense. His eye remained fixed on the face of his assailant.

'Again,' urged Razak. He hadn't moved. The cigarette between his lips smouldered and a perfectly straight, undisturbed funnel rose towards the ceiling of the cellar until he spoke and sent it into a frenetic squiggle.

Badran tried again. It still didn't succeed, then in a rage he closed his eyes and began hacking hysterically at the naked, bleeding body. Slowly Razak crushed out his cigarette and got to his feet. He moved across the passage, grasped the youth's shoulder and worked his hand down his arm until he reached the boy's wrist. 'Enough,' he said. 'Go and wash yourself. Give me the knife.' Tears of frustration and shame coursed down the young man's face as Razak carefully ungripped his rigid fingers from the bloody sticky haft and, after wiping it, took it in his own hand and elbowed the youth out of the way. 'Go!' he hissed.

When Badran had left the passageway he raised Robin's head carefully and placed the sharp edge of the blade against the exposed windpipe. He looked into Robin's eye. 'Go to Paradise, Robin.' A quick jerk of his wrist and Robin was dead.

By the time Badran had washed himself and recovered some of his battered confidence and returned Razak had cut down the dead man. He lay in a heap half propped against the wall opposite Baruch Lev.

'Pull his feet,' instructed Razak. 'Level him out and spread his arms.'

'Why?'

Razak still held the butcher's knife in his hand and as he spoke he tapped it gently on the palm of his other hand. The youth was going to need an explanation.

'This one's got to be hidden; he must never be found again. If, by chance some idiot falls over his body and runs up and down the street screaming of his discovery everyone will know that Robin Gouda is dead . . .'

'So Robin Gouda is dead! So what?'

'I don't want anybody to know that he is dead. Robin Gouda will have many friends; he has brothers. I don't want those friends and brothers to come here looking for the place where he met his end. I wouldn't like them to find you squatting here smoking your cigarettes.' He gazed deeply at the youth's attentive expression and pointed his chin at Robin's bloody corpse. 'Would you like to go through what he's just gone through?'

Enlightenment came slowly to Mufid Badran. He blanched. 'We must find a very deep hole for him. What about the other one?'

'Let us dispose of this one first.' He studied Robin's body for a moment; it was unnecessary, he'd already decided what was to happen but he made it appear that it was an off the cuff decision. 'We shall make it impossible for him to be traced back to you. We shall bury the identifiable parts of him in different places – just in case,' he added, 'somebody does turn him over and traces the body back to the former army officer, Robin Gouda.'

'How will you do that?'

'His head will be removed – ' Razak ignored the beginnings of a retching noise in Badran's throat, and continued in a cold analytical tone: 'you can find a home for that – and his hands. Fingerprints,' he pointed out, 'can be easily disposed of. A headless, handless corpse will bring no brother or friend to avenge it. You will be perfectly safe from retribution, my young friend.'

'Will you do the cutting?'

'Of course.'

Badran concealed a sigh of relief. 'What about the other one?'

Razak followed his glance. 'That? That's just the body of a Jew, an Israeli spy. That can be dumped anywhere and its discovery will be greeted with much rejoicing. But that's not for us to worry about. This one is.' He touched Robin's fleshy side with the point of his boot. 'Let us get to work.'

A faint green tinge was working its way into Badran's sallow complexion. 'P-perhaps I should go and find suitable b-burial places while you are doing the, er, the work?'

Razak was already on his knees. His lip curled as he studied Robin's dead face and mutilated neck; 'Perhaps you'd better. A good idea – bring bags with you when you come back – ' but he was talking to himself. Badran had already gone.

27

Razak, on his return from his second visit to Geneva, the possessor of more money than he'd had a right to even dream of, decided it was time that Razak should die. He removed his beard. It was the first time he had seen his face since he was seventeen and it had taken him some considerable time to realize that here was a completely different individual; one he himself didn't recognize. The pleasure grew on him as he carefully, but amateurishly shaped the moustache that he considered emulated that of the late Robin.

Robin's apartment on the Rue Mounemriad in the smart Snoubra district was like a miniature Aladdin's cave of good living. Everything was of exquisite quality; everything hand made; everything with the name Robin Gouda in, or on, it. The perfect disguise. And the pleasure . . . For the first time in his life Razak felt silk against his skin and the beautiful heavy cotton of the finest London-made shirts. Settling into Robin's opulent lifestyle offered him the choice of a boulevardier and he made the most of it. Sadly, but not critically, Robin had been that little bit bigger in every department, but Razak, who had never had a suit made in his life, shrugged this aside as of no consequence. It was probably the correct conclusion – and not only in Beirut. Looking in the cheval glass in the bedroom he saw only what he considered to be a well-dressed man with an unkempt mop of hair and a slightly crooked version of a

David Niven moustache. Both of these he had corrected in the Vendôme salon; the moustache now fitted over his thick upper lip like a mink glove and his military haircut gave him the appearance of a lieutenant-colonel in town on advertising duties.

He felt pleased and comfortable in his new role of Robin Gouda, former major in the South Lebanese Army and lately aide to the recently deceased Mossad *katsa*, Baruch Lev. Here was a totally different person and the more he studied himself in the salon's multiple mirrors the less likely he considered it that anyone, even his father if he managed to drag his bleached bones out of his grave, would recognize in this clean and distinguished-looking man the one-time Iraqi intelligence agent and Hezbollah hostage organizer, Razak. He was reborn. Razak was dead and buried without head or hands. Robin Gouda was alive and well.

Jack Cunningham glanced at the hook under Les Cohen's room number. The key was still hanging there. Encouraging, he decided. Cohen must have struck that seam of luck he was speculating on and dived off into the wilderness. Cunningham wasn't worried. He hadn't seen or heard of Cohen since they'd had lunch together out at the Summerland Hotel two days ago, but Cohen wasn't the sort of person people worried about. Nevertheless, news of some sort would be most welcome. His Australian photographer friend had come up with nothing new – which was to be expected. The factions in Lebanon seemed to have come to an eerie and unusual understanding. They weren't killing each other – at least not to the extent, as the Australian had put it yesterday, of making Beirut the interesting location for freelance opportunity it had been in the past. Violent death, if not a rarity, was becoming difficult to turn into news. He walked slowly up the stairs to his room, past

236

Cohen's locked door, and undressed and threw himself under a warm shower. Which is usually the moment when somebody knocks on the door or the phone rings.

It didn't fail.

The phone rang insistently.

'There's a Mr Gouda to see you,' the receptionist told him. 'He said you're not expecting him but wonders whether you're free to see him?'

'Did he say where he's from?'

'No. He came before but you were out. He said he doesn't mind waiting.'

'OK, ask him to meet me in the bar in – what's the time now?'

'A quarter to six, sir.'

' – in about fifteen minutes.'

'I'll see he gets the message. Sorry to have troubled you.'

'No trouble.'

The bar wasn't crowded. From the description given him by the reception desk Cunningham had no difficulty picking out Mr Gouda. He was already standing at the bar, sipping from a long glass. Deliberately he kept his eyes away from the approaching Cunningham.

A heavily built, fit-looking man with a lighter than normal Middle East complexion, he could well have passed as a sun-loving European. Cunningham bracketed him as he walked towards him across the wide expanse of the bar area; good clothes – very good clothes, but ill-fitting probably because the coat had been cut to accommodate a fairly heavy holster under the right arm. And the length was also slightly out of proportion. But it didn't spoil the effect. This was a man who paid for his appearance. His tailor was probably a crook: he'd even made the trousers a fraction too long. But the shoes – these were of top quality, and clean. They looked London, good enough to be a pair of

237

Wildsmiths Oxford's, or Church's. Cunningham was intrigued.

'You were asking for me at the desk?'

The man still had a half-filled glass of lemon juice in his hand – a *citron pressé* – which he hurriedly replaced on the table as he extended his hand to the American.

'Mr Cunningham?' he responded.

Cunningham nodded.

'Mr Jack Cunningham?'

'You've got it right on both counts,' said Cunningham drily. 'How can I help you?'

'Will you sit down? Can I get you a drink?'

'Sure. Whisky and water, no ice.'

'Any special brand of whisky?'

'Uhuh. As it comes.' Cunningham wasn't interested in the whisky, he was more concerned about a stranger strolling into the Commodore Hotel and asking for him by name. He certainly wasn't a policeman and, by the way he was dressed he wasn't official – unless he was an official very much on the make. And who wasn't on the make in Beirut this year – or any year! Which left, considering the fairly large bulge under the oversized jacket, only the obvious, and least desirable – one of the hundred and one intelligence groupings operating in this part of the world. He gave his visitor a sideways glance – but whose intelligence organization?

The two men sat and sized each other up while they waited for Cunningham's drink to arrive. Razak continued playing with his *citron pressé* until the waiter had placed the whisky, a small sealed bottle of chilled Vittel water and a small ashtray-sized bowl of cashew nuts on the table and slithered back to his place at the side of the bar.

'It's bad news,' said Razak after glancing around the almost empty bar lounge. Nobody was listening, nobody was interested but he kept his voice at a pitch that reached

238

no further than the other side of the low table. He waited for a comment from Cunningham, but all he got was a slight movement of the eyebrows as Cunningham emptied the bottle of water into his whisky and sipped it. It told Razak nothing, except, perhaps, that the whisky was not to the American's liking. He continued, 'Lev and Cohen are both dead.'

Cunningham managed to keep his face devoid of expression. He studied Razak coolly for several seconds over the rim of his glass then lowered it. 'Who are these people?'

Razak glanced round the room again, then locked his eyes on to Cunningham's. 'Two Israeli agents.' He paused while he brought out a packet of cigarettes, opened it, and offered them across the table. Cunningham shook his head. 'D'you mind?' whispered Razak.

'Doesn't worry me. Why are you telling me about two Israeli agents?'

Razak put a match to the end of his cigarette. 'Mr Cunningham, we're all on the same side; same team, same object. I was working with Baruch Lev – ' he cocked his head to one side and waited. He got nothing from Cunningham – 'who was working under the direction of Les Cohen.'

Cunningham picked up his glass again and took a good mouthful. He tasted nothing. This guy seemed to have got all the words and names right – but Cohen and his mate? Two Israeli Mossad top-notchers put down in the same breath? There had to be something wrong. 'What did you say your name was?' he asked noncommittally.

'Gouda,' replied Razak. 'My operative name is Robin.'

'Tell me about yourself.'

Razak knew what Cunningham wanted. It was identification – not his picture on a card to say what he was and where he lived, but something that was only passed by word of mouth by people of untrusting disposition. 'I am Baruch Lev's local contact – ' His eyes hooded slightly and unconsciously he touched his fingers to his new moustache. Cunningham detected a slight nervousness. 'I *was* Baruch Lev's local contact,' he corrected. 'We had worked together for several years, since I left the South Lebanese Army . . .'

Cohen's Robin nothing. It couldn't be anybody else. But was this enough to take him on face? As Cohen had remarked, how many people named Robin had served in the South Lebanese Army? How many would admit to it – both the 'Robin' and the SLA – to a stranger in a Beirut hotel?

'How do you know my name?' asked Cunningham, still noncommittally.

'Cohen told me to come and see you if something happened.'

It seemed that without admitting the connection Cunningham had signified he was prepared to listen. Razak chewed the end of his cigarette before crushing it out. He frowned into Cunningham's face and waited.

'And you say both these men are dead?' Cunningham asked.

'Yes.'

'Tell me how they died.'

Razak sipped his *citron pressé* and sucked the dryness from his mouth. 'We were looking for an American – which, of course, you know.' He didn't wait for Cunningham's acknowledgement. There wasn't one anyway. Cunningham appeared almost uninterested. 'And Lev had discovered a former Hezbollah gangster who reckoned he knew of someone who might know someone . . .'

'Can we get down to the meat of the thing?' interrupted Cunningham.

Razak shrugged. 'I was meeting another informer nearby so I kept in the background. He hadn't yet appeared and

240

the next thing I heard was a tremendous amount of gunfire round the corner. I moved into position very quickly and found three men standing over Lev emptying their pistols into him as he lay on the ground . . .'

'Who were these people?'

'Oh, didn't I say? I recognized two members of the Special Security Section from the Avenue Abdallah Yafi HQ. The so-called Hezbollah informer was an undercover member of the SSS. There was more gunfire coming from round the corner so I ducked out of sight and crawled towards the shooting. Cohen had been badly wounded but had crawled under cover and was keeping the rest of the ambush party from showing their faces. I think, in fact,' said Razak through tight lips, 'they were waiting for him to finish his ammunition so that they could take him alive. They must have known from the informer that these were two Israeli agents. A captured Israeli in Lebanon has enormous barter potential,' added Razak knowledgeably. 'I managed to crawl round the ambush and attracted Cohen's attention. He was in a very bad way. Emptying my magazine at them – ' he tapped his left armpit to indicate to Cunningham what magazine he meant – 'I was able to make them keep their heads down while I carried Cohen to a safer position. I wrapped Cohen in my coat and managed to hide us both until the sounds of the hunt disappeared. He was shivering and losing a lot of blood and when I told him I would get him to a doctor he told me it was no use. He was probably right. He'd been hit four times by automatic fire, one of them in the throat making it very difficult for him to speak. Eventually he managed to get out enough words to tell me to come to you and explain what had happened . . .'

'Where did you leave him?'

Razak lit another cigarette. 'The SSS brought in more people and began combing the area. It was only a matter of

241

time before they discovered us. Cohen knew this. He was dying, he hadn't long to go and he knew I couldn't carry him through the ring of searchers. He told me to make a break for it and leave him. Of course . . .' He hesitated. Cunningham's face was as blank now as it had been at the beginning. 'I had no intention of leaving a comrade, but he insisted. He said that you must know exactly what had happened. That was of the utmost importance; he would make sure he wasn't captured. There were still more rounds of nine-millimetre in his magazine. A few minutes after I left I heard a single shot from where I had left him.'

'He killed himself?'

'He was dead all right. I had worked myself round to where a crowd had gathered round Baruch Lev's body. A short time later another group arrived with Les Cohen's body. The back of his head was blown out. He must have stuck the muzzle of the automatic in his mouth and pulled the trigger. The SSS men threw him down beside Lev and congratulated each other on the death of two Israeli spies.' Razak sat back in his chair with a sombre expression and reached for the remains of his cold drink as he waited for Cunningham's reaction.

'Why are they keeping it quiet?' Cunningham asked after a moment's reflection.

Razak smiled grimly. 'They always do. First they allow the rumour of a capture to trickle its way to Tel Aviv, then they sound out the going rate for prisoner exchange.' Razak had done his homework. 'A Mossad agent would rate very high – about 600 Amal or Hezbollah prisoners in Israeli camps would be the going rate for Baruch Lev if he was still alive. Dead, a bit less. The Jews like their dead back. They pay well.'

Razak tightened his lips. He was settling well into the role of local Mossad 'black' agent. But there again it wasn't all that difficult for Razak, who was already doubling, if not

242

trebling his triple-agent status from Iraq's GID to Iran's SAVAK and then Hezbollah. The Mossad was just another small step. 'So no publicity – not yet.'

Cunningham kept his eyes blank. The fact that Les Cohen was dead was one hell of a setback, but it wasn't critical. Cohen's original mandate had been only to lead him to contacts, after which he would make the running himself. So, Cohen's contact had turned sour in a very nasty way, but it didn't mean that all was lost ... He studied Razak absently, then asked, 'Did Cohen tell you anything else?'

'About what?'

'Other than that I was staying here at the Commodore and that his death would be of interest to me.' It was difficult to keep a sardonic tone out of his voice. There was something about this man that grated on his nerves, but he couldn't quite put his finger on it. But at the moment he was all he'd got and he'd have to make the most of it – provided, of course, Mr Robin Gouda was prepared to be made the most of. He adjusted his tone to something a little more accommodating. 'Did he tell you whether he'd made any progress towards finding this American he was looking for?'

'I knew from Lev that the American Cohen was looking for was supposed to be an unknown – a mystery hostage who'd got left behind after everybody else had been sent home. Cohen insisted that the man was still alive and in Beirut and that bears out what my own personal contact told me ...'

Cunningham pricked up his ears. This was the first time personal contacts had been mentioned. He looked hard at Razak.

'Personal contact?'

'The guy I was supposed to meet when Lev and Cohen were being shot down. I didn't wait to make contact. As I explained, my one interest was to see what was happening to those two; I put everything else in the background . . .'

'Can you still raise this guy?'

'Certainly – unless he was put off by the SSS activity in the vicinity. But he may not have connected me with that. My role with Lev and Cohen was very much the shadow bit; I didn't mix, I was just to make the contact and pull them all together. He wouldn't connect me with two Jewish guys getting themselves the business in the next street. Why?'

'Would you re-establish contact with your man?'

Razak drank some more and reached again for his cigarettes. He studied Cunningham's face at length as he lit it, then, removing a minute speck of tobacco from his tongue, narrowed his eyes and said, 'Under what conditions?'

'What do you mean?'

'I was employed by Baruch Lev to do work for the Mossad. He paid me from special funds. I have an obligation – '

'Baruch Lev is dead. I'd have thought your obligations, along with your special funds, are now terminated.'

'Very true. So, I repeat, under what conditions do you want me to re-establish contact with my informer?'

Cunningham gave it very little thought. He hadn't a great deal of choice. 'I'd like to take over those obligations, and, of course, pick up the option on those special fund payments.'

Razak smiled; it was a strange sensation with his new moustache, but not unpleasant. 'You're inviting me to join the CIA?'

Cunningham shook his head. 'I said nothing about the CIA. That organization is nothing to do with me. I'm a private limited corporation – just me – and anybody I care to offer membership to. You can forget about government

244

organizations, CIA or anything else. If you want to come along as my friend you're very welcome.'

'Your paid friend?'

'My paid friend. How about it?'

Razak went through the motions of thinking about the offer then showed his teeth in a smile of acceptance. 'How much?'

'Negotiable.'

'Then let's negotiate.'

Cunningham smiled back, cautiously. The man had character. He wasn't totally won over but there was a lot the man had going for him. Almost as much as he had going against him.

It was a very contented Razak who, that evening, sank into a perfumed bath in Robin's flat; who, dressed in one of Robin's fine silk oriental dressing gowns relaxed in the splendour that was now his by acquisition and, he considered, would eventually be his by right. Mr Robin Gouda's death, and Mr Jack Cunningham's proposition had brought him to the brink of his aspirations. His problems were about to be solved by the resources of the country he was intent on defrauding. The irony was not lost on him as he slipped luxuriously between the silk sheets of the late Robin Gouda's bed and closed his eyes on a very satisfactory day's work. And, even better, with a conscience as clean and pure as an East Beirut convent's mother superior he slept solidly and untroubled for the next twelve hours.

The sun was high in a pale blue sky when he made his way across the city to Borj Abi-Haidar.

He picked his way across the uncleared rubble of a once thriving market area and cut down one of its little back streets that had somehow survived the final Israeli onslaught. Three or four of Beirut's original slum dwellings

245

huddled together like old women discussing the events of the last hundred years and waited for their blast-damaged foundations to give way once and for all. One of the old houses had no front door. But this was nothing to do with the Israeli ground and air attacks. It hadn't had a door for sixty years. A passageway of worn stone slabs led through the building to a yard at the back, on two sides of which were open sheds from which came the heavy aroma of grilling lamb for the *shwarma* and stewing beans and *falafil* for the less exotic *fool*. This incongruous and impossible to find setting had been the main cooking depot for at least three of the Hezbollah units that had hostage-holding facilities in this area. It had been the most secure café in West Beirut. It still was, but now cooked food only for those who knew of its existence from the 'good days' and who came, out of nothing better to do, to talk of the time when there was almost a queue of the men most reviled by the Western world.

Razak's new appearance was regarded with suspicion by the two men sitting and smoking in one corner of the yard and even by the cook who had exchanged pleasantries with Razak for the past three years.

This was highly satisfying for Razak. If these people didn't recognize him, who could? He ordered himself a couple of *shwarma* and a glass of milky coffee and ignored the two men who had lapsed into a silent communion as they studied their empty plates. He glanced at his watch. Ten past twelve. Badran should be here any time now. He needed to feed himself and the American captive.

Razak pushed the half-finished *shwarma* away, lit a cigarette and sat back in his chair as Badran entered the yard. He studied the back of the young man's head. Badran, after a cursory uninterested glance in his direction, leaned on the greasy counter and whispered his usual order into the unresponsive face of the old Lebanese cook. Picking his plate of food up he slouched into the other corner of the yard, bent his head over the plate and began shovelling stewed beans and cubes of fat mutton into his mouth. With every mouthful his eyes moved sideways and from under his half-closed eyelids he studied the well dressed stranger. Nothing to worry about. He wouldn't be here if he wasn't one of the selected; nobody came here by chance. If he knew where the place was he was secure. But who was he?

He finished his meal quickly and picked up his prisoner's newspaper-wrapped rations. No questions, no surprised expressions, it was a twice daily occurrence. Nobody wanted to know why a hostage's portions were still being collected when everybody in Beirut – in the world – knew that there was no such thing as a Western hostage in Beirut. Badran gave Razak another sidelong glance and shuffled along the passage and out into the alley. Razak let him have a few minutes start and took after him. He knew the way Badran would go back; no security, that was one of Badran's problems – he never took evasive action, never changed his route and only occasionally glanced behind him. Razak curled his lip in despair as he cut round the back of some deserted buildings, came out just opposite the spot where the original Robin had waited for his friend the Jew and, with a grim smile at the recollection, took up position just inside one of the battered buildings. He removed the large Israeli automatic from its holster and waited for Badran to appear at the top of the road.

The first thing Badran knew of his ambush was the feel of warm metal against the back of his neck. He dropped Macauley's dinner and reached for the weapon in his belt. It had gone. Razak had lifted it out and now held it casually in his left hand. He made no attempt to unload it.

'Come in here.' The voice hissing into Badran's ear sounded familiar, but his brain had seized with fear – he couldn't place it. He wanted to turn round but the hard metal against his neck dug deeper as it urged him forward. He moved, shakily, over a pile of rubble and allowed himself to be placed up against the remains of a plastered inside wall. He was going to be killed. He wasn't a brave man. He wet himself and began to cry.

'Shut up!'

'Don't kill me – p'please . . .'

'Don't make me ill!'

Badran stiffened. Now he recognized the voice.

'Razak?'

'Turn round,' invited the voice.

Badran was very conscious of the dampness around his groin as he made a half-turn and stared into the face of the smart stranger he'd seen in the food shop. It sounded like Razak but looked like someone he'd never met in his life. He felt again the swelling and pressure on his bladder.

'Wh-who are y-you?'

'You don't recognize me?'

Play safe, Badran! 'Forgive me – no. Your voice is familiar . . .'

'It's me, Badran. Razak.'

'Oh, dear blessed God!' Badran stared into Razak's face. He studied his eyes, the moustache, the cruel mouth under it, and looked down at the smart clothes and polished, but dusty shoes. 'How can it be?'

Razak put away the Desert Eagle with a flourish but kept Badran's lightweight, old-fashioned MAB automatic loosely in his hand. 'Accept that it is. Go and pick up the American's food that you extravagantly threw on to the ground and then I'll tell you what has happened – and what is going to happen . . .'

They sat and watched as Macauley, huddled in the corner of his cell, stared at his food and picked over what little there was of it like a baby in its high chair trying to make

248

sense out of the mush it had been given. The change had occurred in the past few weeks: the American's mind had finally snapped and he was capable only of unintelligible grunts used with the basic actions of feeding and sleeping. Every so often he made little cooing noises and picked out a morsel, held it up to his eyes and rubbed it across his mouth with the flat of his hand. The two Arabs watched the performance with only half their attention. It was like a sideshow in the circus, an attraction to the main events, and repetition had caused it to lose its novelty. Badran kept staring into Razak's face; the transformation, now that he accepted that a transformation it was, fascinated him. He was as a child within touching distance of a magician performing his tricks. His eyes bubbled and every so often he shook his head and giggled, 'I can't believe it – '

Razak didn't stop him. This was what he wanted. He'd passed the test with flying colours. Razak the Iraqi agent, Razak the Hezbollah hostage-taker was dead – he no longer existed.

'Badran,' he said earnestly. 'This is the plan. This is how we're going to get all that money to buy your fields, your orange groves, and when the weather gets too hot for you in the south, your spacious house in the mountains in the north overlooking the sea . . .'

Badran stared, and giggled. 'I shall have all that? And the girls . . . ?'

'And the girls. Anything you want. Now listen.'

'I'm listening.'

'I am going to arrange for you to meet an American.'

Badran's eyes almost burst out of his head. 'An Amer—'

'Don't interrupt,' said Razak patiently. 'Listen. Just listen. You will meet this American. Don't worry, I shall be there too but you will not know me as a friend. I am Robin – understand? Robin.'

'Like – ?'

249

'Like nothing! Just Robin. Have you got that?'

Badran hadn't. But he nodded his head. He was still counting the hectares of his orange groves in the south on the Palestine border. 'What do I say to this American?'

'You will say that you have heard about an American being held prisoner in Beirut.' Razak turned and pointed his chin at Macauley. 'That American.'

'In the name of God!'

Razak ignored Badran's explosion. 'And you will be persuaded by the offer of money to reveal where he's held so that the other American can come and free him and take him home.'

'Have you lost control of your senses, Razak? Did you flush away your brain with your beard? This American belongs to all of us, not just you and me. There's Harb, Qadir, Rashidi. They will not agree to this American being given away. He is our money, our future . . .'

Razak studied the youth for several minutes. He didn't seem nearly as menacing as the former Razak, the Razak with the fierce beard, the long steely hair, the real Razak. In outer appearance this one was like a smooth city broker – but the eyes told a different story: there was the old Razak. The eyes turned Badran's stomach to water.

'It is not your three friends who guarantee your money, boy,' hissed Razak. 'It is I, Razak. Not your friends, or him – ' he pointed to the American, still rummaging among the bits and pieces of his meal – 'not you – ' he jabbed his thumb at the slack-jawed youth, then brought his hand back and laid it flat across his chest. 'It is I!'

The final emphasis made Badran jump. 'What will I say to the American?' he mumbled.

'I shall teach you. Listen carefully.'

28

Jack Cunningham tore the embassy note into small pieces and flushed them down the lavatory. It was no more than he'd expected: Robin Gouda didn't exist, there was no such person. At least that was Washington's conclusion. But then that was the conclusion that made Robin Gouda authentic. No one would admit his existence – least of all anyone who'd made use of his dubious talents. He watched the bits and pieces of paper swirl down the waste carried by the inadequate flush and absently pumped the handle again to make sure there was no delayed upsurge to bring the message back into life. Robin Gouda had produced his own testimonials. He'd run the course with certified professionals; he'd named them; it showed that he both knew, and was trusted in, the business. The only trouble was there was nobody left alive to confirm those testimonials.

Cunningham left the bathroom and slipped a navy blue blazer over his open-necked white shirt. He was in two minds about Mr Robin Gouda, and being in two minds was one mind too many. Robin fitted exactly the part he'd reluctantly, or so it appeared, agreed to fill. That was part of the second mind – he was too perfect for the job; he could have been reading for the part since the job was first mooted in the President's private office in the White House. Cunningham pulled a face at his image as he brushed his hair in the hall mirror. *And the trouble with you, Cunningham*, he told the reflection, *is that you've been so long*

*in this goddam game that you've forgotten how to look at the cards
as they come up in your hand – you're too bloody busy watching
the dealer's hands looking for the double shuffle – that's your
problem, Cunningham!*

He took his problems to the Backstreet Club off Rue
Bliss and sank them into a glass of Chivas Regal topped up
with a spoonful of chilled bottled water. He wasn't alone
for long. The Australian photographer who'd once been in
the same bar as Brian Keenan, and who reckoned he never
missed a trick or a new face, cut short his head to head
conversation with a heavily tanned but beautifully made up
Paris Match stringer wearing a short skirt and showing an
extremely nice pair of safely crossed legs, to join Cunningham at his table against the far wall.

He didn't wait to be asked. He sat down, pulled his chair
close and in as low a voice as he could said, 'There's a
whisper afoot that a couple of Israeli spooks have bought it
in a shoot-out with the police.' He raised his bottle of cold
beer without lifting his elbow off the table and lowered his
head to meet it halfway. He took a couple of swallows and
tilted his head again towards Cunningham's. 'Have you
heard anything along those lines?'

Cunningham shook his head. 'Where, when and why?'

'Dunno, but the whisper's genuine. The real story'll
come out when the cloth-heads decide there's capital to be
made or a bit of barter to be carried out. But – ' the
Australian glanced over his shoulder from his leaning
forward position to make sure no one had moved into a
position to overhear them; he had some very definite self-
preservation techniques for a simple Australian photographer – 'the word is the two snipcocks went down in a hail
of gunfire in a whorehouse over in the Majidiye district.
Apparently one of the girls got in the way and went down
with 'em . . .'

Cunningham's expression didn't change. 'Sounds like quite a bloodbath. Anybody walk away?'

The Australian gave him a sharp, knowing look. 'Don't take that lot as gospel, mate. By next week the story could be a street battle; an invasion foiled by one of the top dickheads in the security shed — all on his own! Or — ' he stopped and grinned. 'Or any story you care to make out of it. Anything'll go, but you can bet your Y-fronts the guy who takes the credit for front-line action'll be someone with egg on the peak of his baseball cap.'

'Has anyone seen any bodies?'

'Har! Har!' The Australian gave an artificial laugh.

'What does that mean?'

'It means no one has seen fuck-all. It means that some *jundie* who cleans out the shithouse in a certain building on Avenue Abdallah Yafi has been briefed to drop the hint around town so that people like you and me — ' he glanced over his shoulder again and gave his chin a little jerk in the direction of the bar — 'and her can start the thing moving in the direction of Tel Aviv — in her case, via Paris to add a little substance to it. Then, as it gathers speed they'll shoot out a little more, and then a little more, and at the end we'll have about a thousand different versions of how a senior shithead in the Security Service did it all on his own. But one thing's for sure. When they start these things running they've got something and you can bet your arse there'll be a couple of bodies hanging on hooks in the freezer room in that certain building I mentioned.'

'Israeli agents?'

'Something to do with 'em. Not necessarily top-liners but something to get the lads in Tel Aviv probing and going through the holding camps for the least likely lads to prepare for an exchange. They'll want the bodies, if they're definitely Jews. The cloth-heads'll want their strays in exchange. That's how the game's played.'

253

'Thanks.' Cunningham flicked the Australian's beer bottle with his finger. 'D'you want another one of those?'

'Some other time.' He glanced over his shoulder at the girl he'd left at the bar, still sitting alone, still nursing the same drink. 'I've got as far as her knee. I think a couple more gins and tonics and I'll get to the golden doughnut. Beats takin' pictures!'

Cunningham watched him slope across the floor to the girl and stick his hand back on her knee. She didn't move the knee, or his hand, and to confirm that he was on to a good thing slid her empty glass in front of him for a refill. It looked as though the Aussie was in line for some sort of doughnut.

Cunningham turned his mind back to the serious side of the business. The Australian's news, bitsy as it was, contained all the elements of his new friend's introductory scenario. Robin's version sounded more authentic. And so it should if Robin was straight – after all, he was supposed to have been there when the bullets were flying. So, how far could he trust Robin Gouda? It wasn't a question of trust – it was a question of whether Gouda could lead him to Thurston Macauley, dead or alive, and then bow out of the picture. Unless, of course, he could help in finding the man or men who put Macauley in the position he was going to find him in. Cunningham stared blankly at his half-empty glass of whisky and water and then, abruptly, picked it up, drained it and walked out of the club and back to the hotel.

Razak had changed his suit. This one fitted him no better but he enjoyed the sensation of almost unlimited choice. The navy blue silk shirt gave him that added feeling of success and good will. Cunningham sat in the far corner of the hotel foyer and watched him approach. The note Razak had left at reception had been a model of brevity. Which was no bad thing, thought Cunningham. God preserve us from loquacious Arabs — written or oral. And that, so far, was a big plus in Robin Gouda's continued association. He didn't chatter; he didn't over-elaborate, and he didn't put his thoughts on to paper. So far, so good.

Razak dropped into the chair beside him and propped his elbow on the armrest, allowing his hand to rest naturally on his chin and his finger to cover the movement of his lips.

'I have a lead,' he said without preamble.

Cunningham studied him for a moment. 'D'you want a drink of anything?'

'No.' Razak seemed impatient to get on with it. 'The person I mentioned I was meeting when Lev was killed — I have re-established contact with him. He has heard of an American . . .'

'Does he know where?'

'He thinks he knows someone who knows someone who has heard from someone . . .' Razak wasn't smiling; he was letting the bait out very slowly so that it drifted inch by inch past Cunningham's nose.

'In other words, a dead loss?'

'Oh no,' said Razak quickly. 'This is to increase the price we are going to have to pay for the information. All these people are going to have to be made happy by contributions to their provident funds! This man knows something, of that I am definite . . .' He stopped and gazed around the sparsely populated hotel foyer then rubbed his mouth with the knuckle of his right hand. 'How well do you speak Arabic, Mr Cunningham?'

'Call me Jack. *Ishma tulla hene . . .*'

'What does that mean?'

'Exactly!' Cunningham smiled crookedly, 'It's supposed to mean, hey you! Come here.'

This time Razak smiled. 'Then I think you had better let me do the bargaining with this individual. I have arranged for us to meet after lunch. Would you be interested in lunching with me?'

Cunningham gave it a few seconds' thought. Why not? It would be the first time since he left the States that someone had offered to pay for a meal. But that apart, a closer look at Mr Robin Gouda, particularly Mr Robin Gouda at play, might open up a few insights into his character.

'Do you carry some sort of weapon, Jack?' Razak's experienced eyes had already done their work. Cunningham carried nothing that was going to do anyone any harm. Unusual for this part of the world, but Razak had already encountered this strange trait earlier in his encounter with Les Cohen.

Cunningham shook his head. 'I don't think it's necessary.' He glanced pointedly at the heavy drag on the left side of Razak's jacket. 'I'll leave it up to you to make all the noise.'

Razak shook his head. 'Please, be advised. This is not a nice place. Trust no one, don't turn your back and always have a last line of defence. It's the only thing the sort of people we are going to deal with understand.' He reached down and brought up a plastic bag from between his feet. 'I insist you carry this at all times. It is a gift of friendship from me.' He handed it over to Cunningham and sat back in his chair with an expectant look. Cunningham let the bag rest on his knees until, meeting Razak's eyes and receiving a gently encouraging smile, he opened it and glanced in.

Baruch Lev's loaded Glock nestled in the bottom of the bag along with a spare magazine and a suede belt holster. Cunningham didn't touch it. He didn't need to, he knew all about the Glock 17.

'Nice gun.'

'I want you to have it.'

'Thanks. Where shall I meet you?'

Razak glanced at his watch. 'It's nearly time for lunch

256

now. Why don't you go upstairs and put that somewhere on your person and then I will take you to a favourite little place of mine. Do you have any objection to local food?'

'None,' said Cunningham comfortably, 'I'm a Christian carnivore. Like the Chinese, I eat anything that runs, swims or flies, provided it's cooked. Same for you, is it?' Razak was momentarily taken by surprise. He'd almost forgotten he was supposed to be a Christian. He'd been many things in his lifetime; a lifetime of lying, cheating, of double and treble standards, but he'd never been a Christian or a Jew. This was breaking new ground. It took a little bit of thinking about, and the thinking started now. He pulled himself up. He was going to have to be very careful when it came to showing his feelings about the unbelievers' eating and drinking habits. Could he eat pork? He'd eaten worse in the desolate Al-Anbar Mounds when he and Dahti were rounding up the British SAS soldiers — much worse. He'd even drunk their spirits, the British soldiers' scorching, throat-burning rum — but that had been of necessity, for survival. What he was contemplating now was immersion in the Christian culture, breaking all the tenets of his religion — and doing it for pleasure.

'Naturally!' he replied. Then after a moment, 'I'll wait here for you.' Razak was now a Christian and a lover of pork and alcohol. 'There is no hurry.'

Badran turned up as if on cue.

Cunningham had enjoyed his lunch and was now ready for business. The meeting place his new friend Robin had arranged was a simple café in one of the medium-sized roads that led off the main road into the city, Rue Ahmad Beyhum. It was clean and had no tables on the sidewalk. In this indoors-only café the tall American and his overdressed Arab companion did not look out of place. They drank their coffee and spoke quietly until the scruffy Badran slid

257

through the door. He ignored Cunningham and went through the greetings ritual with Razak. When he sat down he merely touched Cunningham's outstretched hand with the tips of his fingers then immediately transferred them to his breast and thereafter totally ignored the American. It was exactly as he had been rehearsed by Razak.

'He speaks no English,' advised Razak, 'and his French is from the gutter.' He paused and transferred his gaze from Cunningham to Badran, for a moment looking down his nose at the unconcerned youth. He turned back. 'Shall I interpret what you say, or would you like me to do the business?'

'You know what we want,' responded Cunningham and, like Razak, he stared hard at Badran. From the moment he'd walked into the café the young Palestinian had done nothing to cure Cunningham's scepticism about the Beirut underground faction. This guy fitted everything his experience told him to doubt. But he was all they'd got and a hundred per cent advance on the situation as at this time yesterday. He looked back at Razak and allowed his doubt to show. 'Take him as far as you can. But by the look of the guy I'd say put a few dollars in his pocket and you won't see his butt for dust. Don't commit me to any payment without some fairly solid collateral.'

Razak grinned. Cunningham seemed to be reading the same script as he'd presented to Badran. He ordered another coffee for himself and Cunningham, none for Badran – he was only the extra. Without waiting for it to come, he went into his act with the youth. They talked softly; they raised their voices to theatrical whispers; Razak played an intricate piano solo on the table with the fingers of his right hand and Badran slapped his forehead and snarled and half rose from his seat to leave. It was good Middle East theatre. Cunningham quietly drank his coffee and watched.

And then he was dragged on to the stage. Both men suddenly stopped and stared at Cunningham.

'He said, before he commits himself any further he wants to know how much money there is in it for him. He also wants assurance that he will not be held responsible in any way at all for anything that has happened to the American. He wants you to agree that he has had nothing to do with the American's imprisonment, he is just a watcher, a bystander who saw certain things happen.'

Cunningham looked Badran in the eye and nodded.

Badran's eyes remained somewhere between Razak's and Cunningham's head. They refused absolutely to meet Cunningham's. But the message had been passed.

Razak waited a moment then raised his eyebrows. 'He wants to know how much money you are going to pay?'

'And I want to know where the American is – and many other things before we come to that. Tell him.'

Razak told him.

'He asks for some money to be mentioned before he says anything more.'

'How much does he want?'

Razak relayed this to Badran. Badran quoted a figure. Razak roared with laughter. But it didn't last. It cut off in mid-pitch and turned into a hawking at the back of his throat. He went through the motions and offered an imaginary but noisy spit to the floor. Then his lips tightened and he turned his head to Cunningham.

'He asks for $50,000 US.'

'Tell him to go to hell!'

'I have told him to go to a worse place. May I make a suggestion?'

'Go on.'

'We make him an offer of $5,000 in his hand now, to lead us to the place where he last saw your friend –'

Cunningham shook his head. 'I'll give him $1,000 after

he's produced Macauley, dead or alive. Not a cent before . . . That's the offer, he can take it or leave it.'

'He won't take it.'

'Try him.'

Razak lowered his dark-tinted glasses and studied Cunningham's eyes before flipping them up again and swinging his head back to Badran.

The conversation started softly and gained momentum. At one point Badran rose from his chair, glared at Cunningham and moved towards the door before allowing himself to be recalled by Razak. The exchange then became conciliatory on Razak's part. Finally the conversation levelled out and both men fell silent and sat looking at each other.

'What's going on?' asked Cunningham. His expression remained one of total indifference, almost boredom. But then Cunningham was the only person at the table who was not acting. His reactions were not encouraging and Razak decided the farce should now enter its closing stages.

'He says he's not prepared to endanger his life for such a paltry sum and wishes you goodbye and suggests you look for someone else to help you with your search.'

Cunningham's expression didn't change. 'Tell him goodbye from me and thank him for the help he's given us – ' he smiled icily into Badran's eyes – 'and I'll take his advice and look for someone else, and, Robin?'

'Yes?'

'Say exactly that, and nothing else.'

Razak stared at him for a moment then nodded approval with his eyes. He turned back to Badran. After a few more words their right hands reached across the table and the tips of their fingers touched.

'He agrees to $1,500. Do you have such a sum?'

'Tell him he can have it when I've seen the American.'

'He asks what is to stop you going back to America once

he's done his share of the deal and leaving him with nothing.'

'Tell him to trust me.'

'I've told him.'

'What did he say?'

'He laughed.'

'OK,' said Cunningham at length, 'let's get on with it.'

It took twenty minutes for Razak and Badran to complete their act. It was almost a relief to both of them when Cunningham clanked his cup back into its saucer and said, 'OK, Robin, I reckon that's enough talk. You sure we can trust this guy?'

'No.' Razak smiled mirthlessly as he stood up and tapped the untidy bulge under his left armpit. 'But I never trust Palestinians anyway — they're a dirty underhand race of people. If this creature wishes to test our patience by leading us around Beirut on a wild goose chase he will feel the weight of this up his backside. Leave everything to me.'

'Sounds like a good start,' said Cunningham. 'Come on, let's go.'

It could have been a replay of Razak's earlier visit with Baruch Lev and Robin. The three men grouped together on the opposite side of the road and studied the derelict, bomb-battered building that housed Macauley's prison. Cunningham broke the silence. 'Tell this guy to get me closer so that I can have a good look at the entrance and exit he mentioned. Don't argue,' he snapped at Razak, who made a tentative effort to interrupt. 'Just tell him what I say — and don't put any of your own suggestions into his head. I want him to do exactly what I say. Got it, Robin?'

Razak nodded and indicated to Badran to move across the road.

Cunningham continued, 'We'll wait a bit to see if there's

261

any activity then I'll go down on my own. You cover this guy. Stick that damn gun in his side to keep him cooperative and keep a good look out. If there's any gunplay in the cellar don't come barging in until either you hear my voice or somebody else comes clambering out. OK?'

'I could come down with you,' murmured Razak. 'Look after your back . . .'

'Don't complicate matters. Just keep your eyes on this cloth-head and make sure he doesn't bolt. There are still a few answers I need from him . . .'

'He won't bolt,' said Razak grimly. 'He wants his money. And if I don't like the way he looks I'll give him a bit of this – ' With a sidelong glance at Badran he removed the Desert Eagle from its home under his arm, flicked up the safety catch and held it openly by his side. Badran tried to remember it was all very serious and managed to keep the grin off his immature features. Instead, he nodded several times, caught Cunningham's hard expression, and pointed to the entrance to the underground prison.

Cunningham went through the same motions with the Glock. He buttoned his jacket and closed it at the neck to cover his white shirt. 'OK?' he whispered to Razak.

'OK,' whispered back Razak. 'You've got the outline of the cellar in your head?'

Cunningham leaned back and stared at Badran. 'You sure there are no guards?' He glanced around the ruins.

Razak spoke quickly in a low urgent voice to Badran, nodded as the youth replied and tapped several times on his wristwatch, then turned back to Cunningham's ear. 'He said, in the old days there were people all round but now there's no need. Nobody's interested because nobody knows about a foreign prisoner . . . They'll only come up for food – if there's anybody there.'

'What'd he say about the time?'

'The time?'

'Yeah, he tapped his watch.'

'Ah!' Razak smiled, his teeth gleamed. 'He said it was after midday. They would have eaten and then gone to sleep. If there's anybody there at all he'll be sleeping off his lunch.'

Cunningham wasn't happy. It all seemed too easy. An American prisoner that nobody knew about and his guards, if he's got any, all fast asleep after knocking back a big meal in the local hostelry! He tapped his pocket and felt the reassuring weight of the spare eighteen-round magazine before moving across the mountain of rubble to the entrance to the underground passage. Without looking over his shoulder at the two Arabs he pressed himself against the wall and listened before moving delicately on to the first step.

It was deadly quiet and an atmosphere of damp and decay hit his querying nostrils. It felt and smelt like the interior of a long neglected mausoleum and as he waited, listening, his nostrils were assailed with a new smell – the smell of human habitation; an overpowering mixture of stale urine, faeces, unwashed bodies and rotted food. He tilted his head back, took a large lungful of fresh air and began to descend the concrete stairs. At the beginning of the passageway he stopped and peered into the gloom.

There was no one there. Everything was as the Palestinian had described. The light switch on the wall at the left at the foot of the stairs. He didn't touch it. The wooden door on the right hand side of the passage. Locked. He ignored it and walked the length of the passage. Nothing and no one. He returned and took the narrow opening on the left. Daylight filtered through a grille-covered opening high on the wall and by this light he could see a wash-basin and a tap with a short rubber hose attached that led to a small drain on a hardly discernible slope. The

263

shithouse. For how many people? He didn't pursue it – the whole place was a shithouse. Returning to the main passage, he mounted the steps again. Very carefully he pressed himself against the wall and, showing only a fraction of his head, covered the area where he'd left the two Arabs. They hadn't moved and they weren't talking. Robin looked tense, but he was doing his job: his head was continually moving. It gave Cunningham some small measure of comfort, and security. The Palestinian youth looked half asleep: his back against the wall he lounged like an out of work pimp and looked intently at the ground by his feet. And why not? Cunningham tightened his lips and turned back down the stairs. Money was the youth's only motivation; Cunningham would have been very worried if it wasn't.

He studied closely the bare electric bulb hanging at the foot of the stairs, and then ran his fingers lightly round the primitive switch. He found nothing to disturb him. He closed his eyes, his muscles tensed instinctively, and he flicked the switch down. No bang. No red blinding flash. Just a dim, low-wattage glow from the dirty bulb. He shook his head at his own nervousness and stood in front of the wooden door. He placed his ear against the damp panelling and listened. Nothing. His searching fingers found the key and he turned it slowly, soundlessly. He stood back, his finger on the trigger of the Glock tightened against the safety sear as he pushed the door with his foot. It creaked open. He put the gun in first then slid his body through the opening.

He waited.

Quickly his eyes adjusted to the semi-darkness as they scanned the interior of the room.

There was a strange humming sound coming from the far corner. It was low and unmelodious. He'd been too busy listening for danger sounds to hear it or recognize it.

It was human – just.

He pointed the Glock at the corner and moved cautiously towards the sound.

'Oh, Jesus Christ! Oh, God!' He stared down at the remains of his friend Thurston Macauley.

Macauley was kneeling. His head was bowed low and resting on his knees and from somewhere behind the mass of dank, greasy, dirty hair came that unbroken single note. The smell that assailed Cunningham's nose was horrendous. Macauley was naked and round his waist a raw wire tow-rope held him in place, like a dog, against the wall. Plastered on to his body was several months' excrement: the will and instinct to behave like a human had deserted him and he'd defecated where and when the need occurred. The wafer-thin mattress was similarly fouled and sopping with urine. The breaks in his legs showed as large obscene swellings and the brutal fractures were now rejoined in two totally useless appendages. The noise told him that Macauley's brain had gone. He'd withdrawn into himself; he had no sense of what had happened to him; he had no feelings, no ability to think or reason. Cunningham, kneeling close to him, ignoring the dreadful smell, wept openly.

'Mac, for God's sake!' It was all he could summon up. As the tears coursed down his rugged features he repeated it over and over again until sheer mindless anger took over from pity and, with the Glock still gripped tightly in his hand, he stood up and left the dreadful cell.

Wiping his face he stood at the top of the stairs gulping in air, and began to swear, at first softly to himself and then, as the vision of Macauley took over from the red screen of rage before his eyes, louder and louder, until he was shouting at the top of his voice.

It brought Razak across the bomb site at a run. In one hand he held, very steadily, the lethal Desert Eagle and in the other, by the sleeve of his scruffy jacket, the startled-looking Palestinian. Razak prepared his face for the encounter with Cunningham. He knew what Cunningham had seen; he had a vague idea what Cunningham was going through. But it had no effect on him; he had to make it appear that it had. But the fact that Cunningham was screaming his rage to the afternoon streets of bomb-blasted Beirut showed that the game was going in his favour. An angry and upset Cunningham meant a man on a mission of revenge; in a few hours, when Cunningham's brain started taking over from his heart he would want the heads of the men who had reduced Macauley to an animal. He, Razak, would be his instrument. He would find them, he would kill them and he would have all the resources of the American government to help him do it. Mubin Harb's days were numbered. While he sat hidden with his two jackals congratulating himself on having outwitted a man of his, Razak's, stature that same man was about to wipe him off the face of the earth. Razak was, indeed, highly satisfied with the state of events.

With Robin covering his movements and Badran playing his role to perfection by sulking and demanding his money, Cunningham released Macauley from his shackles and carefully carried him into the primitive washroom. There he cleaned him up as best he could. Macauley took no interest in what was going on. He was no longer in pain, he'd banished everything from his mind in a form of self-protection and the only sound that came from him was the continual nonsense crooning of an idiot. Cunningham hugged him like a baby. This was his best friend, he loved this man, but there was no more pity; it was cold, calculated anger. His face was set. Shortly the young Palestinian would have things to tell him, whether he wanted to or not. If this was the way these people wanted to play this particular game they had found someone to play it with; someone more ruthless and equally cruel. But first –

'Robin, have you got a car?'

Razak nodded. No problem, there were cars all over the place. Nobody seemed to care whether they were bought, hired or stolen. 'No problem, Jack . . .' He stood at the door with an expressionless face. 'Is this the man you were looking for?'

Cunningham draped his coat over Macauley's body. He didn't reply.

'What have they done to him?'

Still no reply.

'Islamic Jihad,' said Razak.

'What about them?'

'They will be the people to do such things. They have gone against their principles. This filthy business was stopped when McCarthy and Waite were released. The people who did this will be outcasts . . .'

'Go and get that car.'

'Shall we pay off the Palestinian?'

'Just get the goddam car, will you! We'll sort out the rest of the fucking business afterwards. First I want to get this man into civilized hands, then we'll think about other things.'

'I'll take the Palestinian with me — just in case . . .'

'Do what the fucking hell you like, but be quick about it.' Cunningham's patience was nearing exhaustion point. Anger, rage, pity and sadness had drained him; he needed quiet, a dark room, a very large bottle of Chivas Regal and no interruption or interference — most of all that — while he got down to some very cold and deliberate thought.

29

The medical staff at the American embassy in Beirut shook their heads in horror at the sight of Thurston Macaulay's body, but very quickly and without fuss turned him back into something resembling a human being. But there was nothing they could do with his mind: that had gone for ever, or so the Chief Medical Officer pronounced, and his legs were never going to be used again, not even with the most modern medical techniques. To compound this, Thurston Macauley's sight had gone; the MO thought one eye might be saved but the other one was totally finished. There wasn't an awful lot left of the Thurston Macauley who'd pulled Cunningham into the river at Xuan Loc and carried him to safety. Cunningham reckoned he had reason to get blind drunk.

A total embargo was pronounced on any details of Macauley's return; the Beirut embassy staff who'd come into contact with him were sworn to secrecy and within twelve hours of Cunningham delivering him into the hands of the ambassador Macauley was on a special US military flight to Washington.

Cunningham went with him and as soon as the aircraft had taxied to its isolated bay at Andrews airforce base Macauley was transferred to an unmarked ambulance.

Cunningham was steered in another direction; with his head bowed against the weather, he walked briskly with another agent to the waiting helicopter. Twelve minutes later they landed on the White House helicopter pad and five minutes after that Cunningham was sitting in a heavy leather armchair in Joe Doerflinger's office. There was nobody else there.

Doerflinger, his face set, listened without interrupting as Cunningham led him through the events in Beirut. He showed no regret or compassion when Cunningham told him of his nephew's physical state when he'd found him. But then that was Joe Doerflinger's way. It didn't mean he didn't care.

'His mind's gone too,' added Cunningham.

'You know all about psychodynamics, now, do you, Jack?' said the stony-faced Doerflinger.

Cunningham faced him down. 'I know when someone's brain's been reduced to a fucking omelette, Joe.'

'Don't get uptight on me, Jack. Mac's in good hands, they'll sort his body out and then somebody can poke around in his brain. You and I have got other things to worry about now than Macauley's problems. Did he say anything to you at all?'

'Like I said –'

'OK. Let's forget Mac for the time being and go back to Beirut. Have you got anything left there?'

'Yeah. The guy who turned him up . . .'

'Robin Gouda.'

Cunningham nodded. 'And if we want to break a few bones by way of retribution – that's if we're into that sort of business – he's all we've got.' He stared hard at Doerflinger's unresponsive face. 'We are interested in retribution, I presume?'

'It's more than that, Jack. Since you rang me from Beirut I've had a chat with the President. He wants me to be open and frank with you . . .'

'And you haven't been so far, Joe? Tell me something

269

new. You've never been open and frank with anybody in the whole of your bloody life – why start now?'

Doerflinger almost smiled, but didn't quite make it. 'Like I said, the President said I've got to. Now, sit back and listen and I'll tell you what Thurston Macauley was doing in the Middle East and why it was so important that you found out what happened to him.'

Cunningham did as he was told. There was no reason for him to interrupt, he just listened to the story of Macauley's abortive mission from A to Z and back again. 'So you see,' concluded Doerflinger, 'retribution's not the first word that comes to mind in relation to the shits that worked Macauley over. It's more than that. The bastards have got to be found and their bones ground into dust *after*, and I can't emphasize that more, *after* they've been sucked dry of anything they worked out of Macauley.'

'You're convinced he told them everything?'

'He had to, Jack. You've seen him, I haven't, but just before you arrived I had a word with DCI over at Langley. They've got Macauley isolated; his people say at first glance they've never seen anything like it – '

'I hadn't either.'

Doerflinger went on as if he hadn't heard Cunningham's interruption: ' – so my first instinct was to presume Saddam's people had been set loose on him. That would have sealed Mac's fate if they'd caught up with him. They would have wanted to know exactly what had passed. Nobody does what they did to Thurston for fun – '

'Not even Iraqis?'

'Not even those assholes. They'd be just wasting their time. No, Jack, this is a different fuckin' agency we're dealing with here; this is a bunch of opportunists who somehow got into the act. The extent of Thurston's torture indicates that they knew he had something of value – they might have picked up the smell from Iraq's GID people who must have wanted a look at Majid's contacts. They certainly picked something up from someone and I reckon they'll be out on the market fairly soon. We don't want that. No marketplaces; this information is ours, exclusively ours – we've paid for it in money and blood. So that's where you come in, Jack.'

'You mentioned 150 million bucks.'

'Sure. That was Mac's entrance fee. It should have gone to Majid.'

'It's still in the bank?'

'Like fuck it is! Mac knew how the game's played. Once he'd been blown he'd have tried to buy himself out. With that sort of money Christ could have bought himself down off the Cross and that's just about what I reckon Mac did, but then some bright bastard twisted the screw a little more and realized that 150 million bucks was just spending money compared with what else he had tucked away.'

'If they'd got everything, Joe, why the hell did they keep him alive – if you can call it that?'

'You've got me there, Jack. I've no idea. The money was originally placed in a secret account in Geneva in Mac's name. We have contacts. We managed to peek into the system there and found that it was withdrawn . . .'

'All of it?'

'The lot, in one go, and the withdrawal was covered by Macauley's signature of authorization. That's one reason why they kept him going. They had no reason after that, except – as we've just discussed – they must have found out about the Iraqi nuclear components dumps and have decided that with that information they could double the ante.'

Doerflinger snorted. 'Let's hope they're fuckin' peasants who think another 150 million for the location of the Iraqi dumps'll just about do the business. Go and find them, Jack,

271

and when you've got the information, kill them – any way you like.'

Cunningham continued staring at Doerflinger. He nodded slowly, but it was a reflexive action; his thoughts were on a journey starting nowhere, and going nowhere. 'Maybe the information could still be extracted from Thurston? Maybe this wild goose chase is not necessary.'

Doerflinger shook his head. 'Too early to contemplate. DCI had spoken to his deputy director for administration who said there's not a lot to work on. And we haven't got the time to sit around Macauley's bedside waiting for him to recover. No way out there, Jack – it's gotta be done the hard way.'

'OK. I don't know where I start on this one but – '

Doerflinger did. 'Why not start back in Beirut with Robin Gouda. He did well in finding Thurston; he did better than Les Cohen.'

Cunningham had already thought about it and rejected the idea – he didn't trust Robin, he was a bit too pat. But Doerflinger had no qualms. Coming from someone else gave the notion a little more credibility. He ran the thought back and forwards for a moment watched by an expressionless Joe Doerflinger. It had its points. Gouda seemed to know his way around. Even better, with the chances that the people he was looking for were Arab – Hezbollah, Islamic Jihad, or whatever – an Arab would be useful when the problems started.

'What can I offer him?'

'Nothing less than the bloody world, Jack! Offer anything that comes to mind. Money? As much as you think prudent. Most of those guys would give you their balls in exchange for residential status in the US – offer that as an inducement to a successful conclusion. Gotta be successful, though, Jack. We're not paying a fuckin' dime for anything but the goods.'

272

'I'll sign him up as an official CIA stringer. I want a US passport for him. We can rescind it when we've had our money's worth out of him, but a genuine one, issued here in Washington so that he can go anywhere I go. OK with you, Joe?

'Anything, Jack. They won't mind – it won't be the first time. There are more official CIA stringers with bullets in their head in forgotten holes in fields and cities around the world than there are desk-bound heroes in the Pentagon. If he becomes a nuisance kill the bastard.'

30

Razak stared at himself in front of the mirror in Robin's apartment and wondered where he'd gone wrong. It had all been wrapped up. Cunningham was going to lead a crusade to find the people who'd destroyed the American, Macauley, but after all his scheming he found himself in Beirut, with no American captive to use as a lever and no Cunningham to supply the resources to bring his, Razak's, plans to fruition. His eyes stared gloomily back at him. Americans weren't to be trusted.

So where now? It was two days since he and Cunningham had carried Macauley's shattered body out of the underground cellar, into the battered Mercedes he'd acquired and delivered him to the American embassy on the Avenue de Paris at Jamia. Cunningham had no time for him and he'd been summarily dismissed from the compound by the Marines security guard. Cunningham hadn't even said thank you. He hadn't even said goodbye. So much for all the plans and anger. He'd left the Commodore Hotel, his contact told him, and there was no forwarding address and no little packet of money to be collected by his new friend and colleague Robin Gouda. Razak's thoughts got blacker and blacker. But it didn't help. Badran had ducked out of sight now he'd got no one to guard but it wouldn't be difficult to get him back – the grapevine was still in place. Anyway, he wouldn't have gone far; he wanted his promised money. Whether it came from Americans or his

274

boss Razak didn't worry him, as long as it came from one or the other.

Razak worked Badran out of his system with some gentle invective. He was building himself up into a pleasant crescendo when suddenly he stopped. He smiled at his reflection. Badran is lucky. He has two ways of dying — quickly and neatly, a smooth gentle passage to the Paradise Mohammed has promised him as a believer, or, a slow, cruel and painful trip as the locations of Mubin Harb and the other two are clawed out of his soft body . . . The smile vanished. It was a risk that might panic the others; but it was a risk that had to be taken.

The message was a simple one. It had to be. Badran was a simple youth, anything else would be wasted on him. The message was unambiguous: 'The cellar. Half-past four. Today, Wednesday — payday. Razak.' There was no question that he wouldn't get it and wouldn't turn up. The word 'payday' ensured that.

Razak sat and basked in the afternoon sun, concealed from curious eyes but in a position where he could cover all approaches to the entrance of his former HQ. He was quietly smoking his third cigarette when Badran appeared at the far end of the devastated road and made his way across the ruins.

Badran approached the cellar entrance with the caution developed during the years he'd spent among Beirut's ruined streets. Nothing was taken for granted. It never would be. Badran, like most Palestinians of his age and generation, was scarred for life. He'd reached maturity knowing that no one was to be trusted. The gun was law and Islamic Jihad and Hezbollah were the arbiters of the system and Beirut would forever be a wilderness of ruins and devastation. Badran stared around him. The thought of all the riches must have dulled his razor-sharp senses. He sat at the entrance to the cellar and lit a cigarette.

As he placed his fisted hand to his lips and took a deep drag from the cigarette his ears just caught the faint scraping of a foot behind him. He had no time to turn but he felt the sudden displacement of air before an almighty crack against the side of his head sent him hurtling forward on his knees into the rubble. There was nothing for him to see, just a series of searing white flashes of a blade cutting into his eyes, and then another crack, this on the back of his neck, and then a black, red-tinted nothing. He lay unmoving, the cigarette, strangely, still clasped in his fist, its smoke winding in a corkscrew motion to nowhere and his head, split open at one side, resting at a dangerously obtuse angle to his shoulders on a piece of jagged masonry.

Razak threw down the four-foot length of two-by-four and reached forward to remove the smouldering cigarette from the youth's hand. He flicked it with his fingers and watched it arc through the air and disappear in a shower of sparks at the bottom of the pile of rubble, then jabbed the same fingers against the side of Badran's throat. The pulse was faint but regular. He studied the angle of Badran's head. It looked as if his neck was broken. He decided to leave him as he lay until he woke up.

The first sign that Badran was coming back was a loose, rasping growl from somewhere deep in his throat. Razak placed himself in a position where Badran would see him when he opened his eyes, made himself comfortable and went through the motions of cleaning his fingernails with the stiletto Badran had given him.

The afternoon sun glinting on the blade was the first thing Badran saw. The next thing he saw was Razak's bulk and his cold, cruel face studying the handiwork he'd carried out on the fingers of his left hand. Razak's eyebrows rose fractionally when he saw Badran staring at him, but he continued with his manicure.

'Raz-Razak?' Badran had difficulty speaking.

'Your neck is broken. You are dying,' said Razak without looking up from his curled fingers.

'Help me!' rasped Badran.

'What do you want? A doctor? An ambulance? Hospital?'

'Please.'

Razak stubbed his cigarette out and crouched down beside the youth. 'What value do you place on your life, Badran? What is it worth to you that you could be lying in hospital receiving the best possible treatment. That you would not die? Is it worth millions of American dollars?'

Badran closed his eyes. The pain in his head and neck was intense. Razak pricked his chin with the point of the stiletto and Badran's eyes shot open again. He started to scream but the cold blade laid across his open mouth brought instead a strangled, 'I-I-I don't u-understand . . .'

Razak put his face close to the youth's. He could smell the fear on his breath. 'Then I will explain to you. Left here you will die, because one move of your head and your spine will part; if I call an ambulance you will live. It is that simple.'

'Please do it.'

'Of course – after you have told me where Mubin Harb is.'

Badran shuddered. Harb had said he would be safe, that Razak wouldn't dare harm him because there was too much at stake. That Razak, by threat of disclosure, had been made harmless. Badran closed his eyes to hide from the black cruelty in Razak's face. *Where are you now, Harb? How are you going to help me now?* But Badran's communion was cut short again by the point of the stiletto.

'Where is Harb?'

Bargain, Badran, bargain! 'The ambulance first . . .'

'Where is Harb, pig?'

Badran didn't feel the stiletto's point enter under his chin until it touched the back of his tongue and his mouth filled with blood. He gagged. His tongue was skewered on the point of the blade. He tried to scream. The blood in his mouth choked it into a bubbling cough. After a moment of horror Razak withdrew the blade. This hurt even more and brought another smothered scream. Razak's expression was almost one of boredom.

'Where is Harb?' he said in the same tone.

Badran, without moving his head, tried to empty his mouth of blood. As he spat it out it reached no further than his chin. He tried again. The same thing, and even as he spat his mouth filled again.

'I don't know,' he gurgled, and watched with terror the stiletto approach his eyes. 'I don't know.' He cried. Razak stopped the movement of the blade. His eyes, for the first time, showed doubt. Something was wrong. Badran would not suffer pain out of bravery.

'What do you mean, you don't know?'

Badran continued spitting blood. 'There is no address . . . Please help me!'

'Continue talking . . .'

'. . . there is only a number.'

'What sort of number?'

'Telephone – '

'If you lie to me, scum – ' Razak touched the point of the blade to Badran's eyelid. It wasn't necessary. Badran wasn't going to lie – not any more. 'Tell me about this number.' Razak's face was close enough to Badran's to kiss him. Badran felt the bristles of Razak's new moustache rasp against his cheek as Razak ensured that not a single word went astray from his ear.

Badran emptied his mouth and summoned his strength. He wanted to save his life. That came before money. It came before dubious friends who'd hidden themselves out of harm's way and left him to face death on his own. He held no loyalty to Mubin Harb.

'Every Friday, after morning mosque I telephone this number . . .'

'What number? Where?'

'I don't know where.'

'What number then,' hissed Razak urgently.

'I have it written down . . .'

'Try to remember . . .' Razak brought the stiletto up to Badran's eyes again. 'Do you want this to help you remember?'

Badran shot his eyes back into his brain again. '00,' he began haltingly, then, in a rush, '3-3-1-0-8-6-053 – ' he stopped again for breath, let his eyes down, stared fixedly at Razak. After a longer pause, he swallowed something to moisten the back of his throat and gulped out, '9-7 – '

'Who do you speak to?'

'No one.'

Razak glanced up from the back of his hand where he'd scrawled down the numbers and scowled into the youth's face.

'How is that?'

Badran's voice, along with his reasoning, was fading. ' – a machine,' he managed after a long pause, 'I leave a message . . .'

'What message?'

Badran's eyes were closed. He looked dead. It took a long time before his dry lips parted and he had several goes at it. Eventually he got it out – and signed his death warrant. 'I say: Badran – Friday – the date – '

'Just that – no special words, no code?'

'Just that . . .' he coughed drily, a death rattle, but there were words in amongst it, 'that is . . . the . . . code . . .'

Razak got up. Then, standing astride the youth, he reached down and grasped his shirt collar. Badran's eyes opened, startled, but there was no time to say anything. Razak lifted and shook the boy's head from side to side.

Something grated, something snapped but Badran's eyes remained focused on Razak's. They weren't dead. Not yet. Razak let go of the shirt and allowed Badran's head to drop back. A gurgling at the back of the throat – it sounded like a frightened dog growling at an approaching shadow as Badran continued to stare accusingly at Razak. Razak wasn't disturbed by the youth's eyes; he was more concerned that he might still live. Standing upright he placed his foot on the side of Badran's head, moved it fractionally and when he found resistance, braced himself and pushed with all the strength of his thick, powerful legs. The crack of Badran's cervical vertebrae disintegrating sounded like the discharge of Razak's Desert Eagle but it didn't concern Badran. He felt nothing and heard nothing; he was on the way to the true life he had been promised.

31

Tel Aviv

The news of the deaths of two of its most senior operatives sent a shock wave of disbelief through the whole structure of the Israeli intelligence community. The Mossad, in particular, ranked it as a major disaster when one of their senior agents was murdered. Two was unthinkable.

He, or she, didn't have to be a high-profile operative within any of the Israeli intelligence organizations or one with the reputation that made Les Cohen's name such a byword among his fellow *katsa* in the Institute. Every member of the Mossad earned the right to unequivocal revenge should he fall in the field. In a perpetual state of war, retribution was a matter of principle; the Mossad's arm was the longest in the world, its memory everlasting and it had brought retribution down to a ruthless art.

Within the Mossad is a very special and highly secret unit called Komemiute. Inside this Komemiute is a select group of highly trained Mossad operators who are known as Kidon — bayonet — and are used exclusively as assassins and executioners. When a Kidon details its target, that target would be well advised to start reviewing his insurance portfolio and choosing his burial site. Kidon never fail. They are almost as infallible a force as the blade of a guillotine. Lou Mullins was one of this select group.

The thing about Mullins was that he didn't look like a professional killer. Professional killers rarely do. Mullins was a stocky man, no more than five feet six with dark hair and,

281

strangely, mid-blue deep-set eyes. His chin was also blue. It was always blue. It looked as if his chin was ready for another shave even as he washed away the lather of the present one. Women liked him. His friends reckoned it must be the hair that turned them on because there was not much else; his chest was a tangled black mat, his shoulders and lower back covered with tight hair and his pubic region extended to his navel – naked he looked like a human gorilla. He'd never bothered marrying because, as he often said, why keep on reading the same book over and over again when you can go to the library and get a different one each day? But outside womanizing he was a ruthless and tireless killer. When Lou Mullins packed his overnight bag somebody, somewhere was going to die.

He sat in the sparse office of the Head of Coordination at Mossad HQ on King Saul Boulevard in Tel Aviv and listened. There was no formality; there was equality between the Director and a senior Kidon operator. Nobody stood on ceremony and the two men treated each other with a form of respect that only they understood.

'Did Cohen leave anything behind?' asked Mullins. 'Did he have a drop or a safe house?'

'Nothing like that,' frowned the Coordinator. 'He wasn't on a scheduled case. This one was authorized by the PM and Cohen got the go-ahead personally from Shmuel Saguy.'

'The "go-ahead"?'

'Cohen originated the business from London. He'd been approached to go back to Beirut by an American with contacts . . .'

'What does that mean?'

'The American got the FBI to pick up one of the Al people in Baltimore and play on the PM's sensitivities about our special relationship with America. Cohen's Yank had muscle . . .'

'Hmmm. So Cohen goes back to Beirut and gets himself blown away. Was he on his own?'

'He had *katsa* cover – Baruch Lev. He went down too. Also a girl – a Resident – they killed her as well.'

Mullins knew what it was like. There was no time for tears, no time for recrimination. This was their war – secret, vicious, dirty, unrelenting. It didn't leave time for feeling sorry for anyone – or trying to come to terms with the fact that two of the world's highest trained and the most efficient operators of the dirty game should be killed without, apparently, a whimper.

'Who're we looking for?'

The Coordinator shrugged. 'Try this – CIA Washington are asking for information on a Lebanese named Robin Gouda. According to the story this guy was recruited by Baruch Lev when he was attached to the Beirut station.'

'*Robin* Gouda?'

'Robin's the in name with the Christian element; they pick these names off the wall. It makes it bloody difficult to put a file together on 'em.'

'I know of a Robin who's a lieutenant-colonel with the South Lebanese Army.'

'Robin Gouda?'

'Nah. Robin Aboud . . . Is there any trace on Washington's mystery boy?'

'You nearly hit the button there. He too was in the SLA – a major, but I think he found the sand was spoiling the taste of his champagne and getting into the caviare. They say he was a bit of a playboy . . .'

'Who says?'

The Coordinator tapped the side of his nose but said nothing.

Mullins wasn't disturbed. 'OK, then. *Was?*'

'Gave up soldiering some time ago and then vanished into the blue. Never been heard of since.'

'Photographs?'

'His file somehow found its way into the shredder.'

'Fishy?'

The Coordinator nodded. 'And convenient. He could have taken up other service; he could even have taken up with us. But there you go!'

'Has all this been passed on to Washington?'

'You've gotta be joking, Lou! I tell Washington fuck-all. No, this particular Robin Gouda is non-existent as far as anybody else is concerned. I doubt whether it's any use to you either.'

'We'll see. Are there any notes of him as being a "local" for Mossad?'

'There wouldn't be. If Lev was employing him seriously in the Beirut districts he would have kept him under his hat in case he needed to go back again. I've tried the coded local recruit files but I can't make an impression.'

'How about payment?'

'Nothing doing. If he was working him under cover Lev would have paid him from local funds and put it down as bread and fish.'

'So nobody's got any idea who or what Robin Gouda is – other than he was once in the SLA – which merits a question mark before we start, or how his name comes to be burning up the wires between here and Washington? What's he doing in Washington?'

'Ah! That's something else – we don't know that he is. Basically we've got two problems. We never divulge information on names – even Arab ones; we never give information without getting something more valuable in return; and we can't profit from this because we don't know who he is.'

'You reckon he's still in Beirut?'

The Coordinator nodded. 'I know he is.'

Mullins let his feet drop on to the floor and stood up in

the same motion. 'Good. Then I think I'll go and find this Yank and have a look at what he's picked up. I'll come and see you when I get back, if I may?'

'Are you likely to muddy any waters?'

'Not this time. I'm just looking.'

32

Sitting in Robin's favourite rocking chair, clad only in his
silk underpants and revelling in the efficient air condition-
ing that Robin had been considerate enough to have
installed, Razak very quickly worked out where Badran's
messages were going every Friday morning. 0033 was the
code for France. That was the easy bit. Paris, no problem
with the code there: number 1. But this is where the
trouble started. There are nearly nine million people in the
city . . . Razak sat back in his chair and stared at the ceiling.
Nine million people and probably every one of them has a
telephone and every telephone has a different number! He
offered a dry spit at the inconsideration of people. So, 0860
must mean something, but what about 5397? Keep ringing
until a machine answered? He spat again. Why hadn't Harb
chosen somewhere simple — like Outer Mongolia! He
continued staring at the figures and running through his
mind the simple code message that indicated everything was
going according to plan. That was no problem. A long-
distance call, an answering machine, an imitation of
Badran's voice once a week would give him all the time in
the world to find where this answering machine was. And
where that was he'd find Mubin Harb. Harb thought he'd
been clever: he had, but too clever. Three months to get
Macauley's money had been his ultimatum. Razak had a
right to look smug — he'd removed the American money to
where only he could touch it, and he'd done it in weeks,

286

rather than months. Harb would never see one dollar of this money; about that, Razak was quite determined. Apart from the minor blemish in the shape of Mubin Harb and the fact that he'd been, fortuitously as it turned out, prevented from killing Macauley on his final return from Geneva things appeared to be running distinctly in his favour.

He dragged himself out of the rocking chair and padded, barefoot, across the room to the kitchen. Robin drank beer. Cold beer. By the look of the quantity in the fridge there was no possibility that he was going to suffer a drought. Razak took the first one that came to hand and began pouring into the tube-like glass. The phone rang.

It was the first time the phone had rung since he'd moved in.

He stared at the instrument on the kitchen wall, bottle in one hand, half-filled, over-chilled, headless glass of beer in the other. The unmelodious clatter of the ringing tone filled the kitchen and met up halfway with the same racket from the phone in the other room.

And all Razak could do was stare at it.

Eventually it stopped. Razak's face relaxed. And then it started again. *Robin's girlfriend? One of Robin's many girlfriends? Mossad? His brother, his cousin?* But Robin had told him that no one knew about this place. His neighbours minded their own business, they were incurious about Robin's comings and goings; they wouldn't have known who he was if he'd been sitting on the end of the bed. So it wouldn't be a neighbour ringing. Razak put down the bottle and the glass and stood in front of the phone on the wall. It wasn't going to stop. He picked it up and held it to his ear.

'Robin?'

He frowned and held his breath and strained his ear.

'Robin, is that you?'

287

An American voice. He'd never heard this one through a phone before.

'Yes.'

'It's Jack. Come to the Commodore. I want to talk to you.'

The phone went dead but he kept hold of it, still pressed against his ear while he worked out the implications of Cunningham's return. He picked up his beer and drank the other half of it on his way back to the cool sitting room. The beer was fine. He reckoned he could get to like it. He poured the rest and sipped. This could only be good news. Cunningham was back in Beirut less than forty-eight hours after dragging his fellow countryman on to the plane. So he wanted revenge – or maybe he'd heard about the money and wanted his share? Not likely. American government people didn't need extra money, they had more than they could handle. No, it couldn't be that. Just revenge. That would do. It suited Razak perfectly – he was back on the high roller. The American was going to find Harb and the others and Razak was going to send them on their way. The day was turning out quite well after all.

Cunningham was waiting in the bar. He looked no different when Razak joined him. He'd changed his suit to one of light fawn and looked cool and relaxed with a blue shirt, unbuttoned, no tie. He was still drinking Chivas Regal with a touch of water. No ice.

'I've got a proposition for you,' he told Razak when he'd ordered him a cold beer. 'But before I say anything more I want you to know that I owe you one. You found Macauley, you probably saved his life.'

Razak shrugged deprecatingly. 'You don't owe me anything, Jack. You offered me a commercial partnership, I just did my part of it. I was lucky . . .' He offered Cunningham a sincere, 'it was nothing' expression, lifted his glass off the table and tilted it gently in Cunningham's direction before carrying it to his mouth. 'If there's anything else . . .'

Cunningham acknowledged him with his own glass, and said, 'There is. Like I said, I've got a proposition – but, first, how would you like to work officially for the CIA?'

Razak pretended to think about it. He drank more beer, lit a cigarette, blew the smoke up towards the high ceiling then brought his eyes down and met those of Cunningham. 'To what purpose, Jack?'

'You'd be on official salary; you'd have the backing of the US State Department, and you'd be an official agent of the Central Intelligence Agency.'

Razak played the game to its limit. He wasn't going to jump in like some *bedu* well-watcher looking for a job with status and the chance to wear a shirt with a tie when clocking on for the office every morning. He played hard to get.

'What difference would that make to our current set-up?'

'I'm not CIA, Robin. I'm empowered to offer you this on their behalf, following my recommendation. For my part I can't offer you protection and back-up. All you'd get out of me is payment on result with a retainer. When I go looking for the people who snatched Macauley I'm not going to have time to wait around while the guy who's supposed to be helping me out is running up against other people's bureaucracy. You're Lebanese, Robin. All Lebanese in some countries' eyes are Palestinians, and all Palestinians are bad news. Restrictions, Robin, there'd be so many restrictions on having you around I wouldn't be able to move. Taking all that on board, you'd just be a liability to me.'

Razak conjured up a hurt expression. 'And how would being an official member of the CIA prevent me from being an Arab and a Lebanese, Jack?'

'You'd be an American citizen.'

289

Razak lifted his beer again and moved his eyes away from Cunningham's in case he saw the look of triumph that was impossible to conceal. This was the realization of what he'd planned. It was hard to believe that it was all dropping, inexorably and without effort, into his lap.

'Would I have an American passport?'

Cunningham tapped his coat pocket. 'I have it here. I want a photo and a few details from you and the embassy here will push it through. All the other documentation will be done in Washington when I give the word. And that's all I want from you now – the word.'

'You have it,' said Razak sincerely. 'And our arrangement – yours and mine?'

'You take your orders from me until this assignment is finished. Now we've got things to do. We've got to find these bastards, find them quickly, and I haven't got a goddam clue where to start. I don't know whether they're here in Beirut, in the Lebanon, or even if they're in the Middle East itself.' Cunningham picked up his glass of Chivas Regal and drained it. There was frustration in his whole manner. He ordered another drink. 'Got any ideas?'

Razak did his thoughtful act again. He sat back in his chair, drew his eyebrows together and sucked delicately on the wet end of his cigarette. After a moment he blew out a long stream of smoke and glanced across at Cunningham. 'Have you told me everything, Jack?'

'What d'you mean?'

'Let me put it another way. Why does this particular hostage's treatment merit a large-scale manhunt for the people who mistreated him? None of the others got it. Your Colonel Higgins was kidnapped in 1988 and murdered – hanged – in 1989. Nobody came rushing out from America to revenge him. Then there was Bill Buckley taken by Islamic Jihad in 1984. He got worse treatment than Macauley – eighteen months of torture of the worst kind and, unlike Macauley, was brutally murdered. Again, Jack, no retribution, no hunt for the killers.' Razak studied Cunningham's face and allowed a concerned look to cross his own. 'You don't mind my asking this?'

'Go on,' Cunningham said evenly.

'What is so special about finding the people who ill-treated Mr Macauley?'

Cunningham thought for a moment then nodded. 'OK. Macauley was carrying some top secret information when he was picked up . . .'

'What sort of information?'

'Let's leave it at that for the time being, Robin – top secret information. The leader of the team that worked on him, we understand, is a guy named Razak – ' Razak's face showed studied interest – 'and we suspect this Razak now has control of this information. We don't give a fuck about the others, because as far as intelligence goes Razak is the only one who would understand the value of what Macauley was carrying. So, it's not the team we're after, they can all go into the bucket as far as we're concerned; everyone's prepared to look the other way and put it down to an eye for an eye and all that sort of thing, when four Arabs go down. But we want Razak. He's got to be found, squeezed and then taken back to the States. We want the bastard to suffer.'

'Fair enough,' said Razak, immediately. 'It's the only thing these people understand.' He frowned again. 'What does he look like, this Razak?'

'Our information is dated. We have a description going back about two years, but you know as well I do that it doesn't take much to change a face. No, Robin, I don't think two year-old descriptions are going to serve any purpose at all. We're starting from scratch. All we've really got to go on are the other four whose names we've got . . .'

'How did you get those?'

Cunningham considered for a moment, and then decided that if 'Robin' was going to be useful, he'd need more information.

'Les Cohen.'

Razak evinced surprise. 'Cohen? How come?'

'He was a prisoner of this Razak. While he was incarcerated he watched Macauley arrive and receive some of his initial treatment. He had a secret crack in his prison door or something, and was able to pick up everything that went on. He made a record of the names that were mentioned – Mubin Harb, Abu Rashidi, Husam Qadir and Mufid Badran . . .' Cunningham stared into the distance. 'Pity Les got himself put away. He was just about the only guy, other than Razak's four bully boys, who could have pointed the finger at him . . .'

'And the dead can't testify,' added Razak philosophically.

'You're goddam right about that.'

'Jack, let me take this away and think about it. It might be worth my having another word with our earlier friend – if he can be found.'

'Could be a start. What makes it difficult for him to be got at?'

'You paid him all that money, Jack . . .'

'He earned it.'

'Sure he did. But what do you think these guys do when they've got a bit of cash in their pocket? They take off, Jack. They get out of the way before anyone knows about it. He's probably bought himself a villa in Cyprus or Libya by now and picked up a new identity. They don't hang around.'

'See what you can do.'

'Sure. And, Jack – '

'What is it?'

'Thanks for your trust.'

292

The short, dark-haired man in a well cut English light-weight suit sitting on a stool at the top end of the L-shaped bar finished his drink, stubbed his cigarette into the overflowing ashtray and left just as Razak stood up and said his goodbyes to Cunningham. He walked straight across the foyer without looking left or right and out of the main door. For a second he waited at the top of the steps as if deciding on a taxi or not and when he heard Razak's steps behind him made up his mind. Turning left, he walked down Rue Commodore. He crossed the road, stopped in front of an electrical appliance shop and glanced casually back the way he'd just come. Satisfied, he walked another ten metres and opened the door of an old Peugeot badly parked between two other nondescript vehicles and climbed in.

'D'you get a good look?'

The man in the passenger seat didn't turn his head. 'Yeah. He doesn't mean a thing. Smooth, smart and rich – he must be an operator.'

'OK, we'll sit and see whether his mate comes out. You'll like him.' The short man turned his head and grinned. 'He's a Yank.'

There was no answering grin from the man in the passenger seat. His definite Arabic features were badly scarred and his mouth, which appeared to have been widened on one side, had a lopsided slant. It looked as though the doctor who'd done the stitching had run out of face and dragged extra skin in from somewhere near the corner of his eye. It gave him a permanent scowl. A heavy moustache did nothing to alleviate the ugliness of the man and the cruel, calculating diamond black eyes. He would never smile. He hadn't got the face for it. He hadn't had it before his accident, and even if he wanted he would never be able to smile now. His companion's Western features, in contrast, mixed interestingly with his Levantine complexion and short crewcut-like crinkly hair and his face had the lines of a man who would always see the amusing side of things. They made an incongruous couple.

'You take the American,' said the short man, 'and I'll make the smart-arse my business. Your man's name is Cunningham. Although he's American he's carrying himself around as a Canadian journalist. Don't interfere with him, just mark him for future reference and make notes of anything he does.' He punched his companion on the arm to make sure everything was going in. 'By that I don't mean I want to know everything he eats or what time he goes to bed. I want to know any time he visits embassies or any strange people he meets . . . OK?'

Abu Dahti grunted and got out of the car. He stamped his scuffed shoes on the rough pavement to allow his trousers to fall into place and walked briskly towards the Commodore Hotel. He fitted in. Not the scruffiest man in the street; not as smart as 'Robin'; not as noticeable, he looked like almost every other middle of the road Arab who could afford to drink lemonade in the Commodore's cool lounge.

Lou Mullins watched him disappear and grinned quietly to himself as he lit a cigarette and switched on the car's engine. But behind the grin there was a steely glint and a determination not to go the same way as his two Mossad colleagues, Les Cohen and Baruch Lev.

Lou Mullins's business was assassination. It was more than instinct that told him he'd just marked his next client.

33

Tel Aviv

'The man who killed Cohen and Lev,' said the Coordinator when Mullins returned to his office two days later, 'is reckoned to be a front-line Hezbollah hard nut named Razak.'

'Real name?' queried Mullins.

'Not known.'

Mullins debated with himself silently for a moment, then said, 'You in the mood for a funny story?'

'No I'm not,' snapped the Coordinator. 'Let's stick with the unfunny. Cohen and Lev's deaths don't exactly touch my funnybone.'

'I meant funny peculiar.'

'Go on then – but don't try to make me laugh.'

'About six months ago,' said Mullins, 'one of our patrol boats sneaking about at night around the waters off Jounié, north of Beirut, fished a guy out of the water – '

'I've already heard this story.'

'Not this part of it you haven't. The sailor boys thought it was a corpse.'

'Like I said . . .'

'Let me tell it, though. But he was still alive – which if he'd been one of ours would have been a miracle, but in this case he was one of theirs, so he was just a lucky son of a bitch. Nothing more than that. Apparently he was wearing a coat which kept him alive. It had trapped the air and acted like a life jacket – '

'And you found this funny?'

'I haven't got to the funny bit yet. Be patient, my friend, we'll come to that in a minute.'

The Coordinator looked pointedly at the watch on his wrist, looked back at Mullins, then nodded, 'Go on, then. But try and make it a quick minute.'

But Mullins wasn't going to be hurried. 'He'd been given the works, a real going-over; by the look of the back of his head a going-over with heavy metal. Anyway, they kept him alive and brought him here. D'you know what he was?'

'Tell me.'

'He was a senior operative of Da'Irat al Mukhabarat al-Amah − GID − Iraq secret intelligence.'

'He admitted that?'

'He talked in his sleep,' Mullins replied without change of expression. 'He's genuine. We checked his clothes. Made in Baghdad. We put him through the wringer. He's known. His name's Abu Dahti − real, and he's a bastard, a top bastard, highly respected in Iraq senior intelligence circles.'

'And now you're going to get to the funny bit?'

'Sure. Thank you for your patience, Coordinator,' said Mullins, drily. But it streamed over the top of the Coordinator's bald head. 'He's decided to join our community. He's turned. He's now one of us.'

'Very funny! And all this out of gratitude for our fishing him out of the drink?'

'And the fact that he had no alternative. We've boiled him alive; he's given us everything − and more! He can't go back − unless we ask him to.'

'What are you waiting for? We've always wanted someone in with Baghdad's top thinkers. Hand him over, Lou, and let's get him in place before he begins to melt.'

'Not this one. He's on a roving commission. Makes his

own schedules. He can go back when his present commitment's done and I've finished with him.'

'What commitment's that?'

'It's where we started this conversation, Coordinator – Cohen and Lev being dropped. The guy who put our new brother into the water with a headache was named Razak!'

'Shit!'

'Exactly. And according to Abu Dahti this Razak is also Iraqi. He penetrated SAVAK on behalf of GID who in turn shipped him across the border to run a Hezbollah hostage-holding cadre. He's a bastard too.'

'I grade him worse than that, Lou: he's killed two of ours. But there you go — you going to take this Dahti with you to point the finger?'

'Already did. He's the only person on our side who can give the nod. I wouldn't know this Razak if he was standing against the wall with a placard round his neck. I showed him Cunningham and his mate Robin Gouda but it didn't do anything for him. I'll probably take him with me again — you never know . . .

'Rather you than me.'

'No risk. Dahti wants Razak's balls on a string to hang round his neck; he wants him just as badly as we do. He has this deep psychological motive for pulling him apart. I might just let him do that and sit in a corner and applaud.'

'You sure it's nothing deeper than that, Lou – just a need to repay a severe bashing round the head and a long swim in warm water?'

'It'd be enough for me. Wouldn't it you?'

'OK. I wish you luck, but don't turn your back on this bastard; people like him can keep turning like a kid's spinning top. Half the time I don't think they know who their real master is. Make sure he's issued with a return ticket!'

'Is that it?'

'No. I've been asked to remind you of the details of Cohen's original mandate – as sanctioned by Shmuel Saguy and authorized by the Prime Minister . . .'

'You taping this?' queried Mullins.

'Only that bit. Just in case . . .'

'Just in case of what?'

The Coordinator ostentatiously reached into his left-hand drawer and clicked a switch. Only then did he reply. 'Just in case you end up in a hole like Les Cohen and they ask me whether I'd passed on to you the poisoned chalice. I have. It's done – it's in there. Now a little word of warning, my friend, not that you need it. Outside there in the jungle things haven't changed. Forget all this political stuff, the conferences, the kissing and shaking hands of smug, self-opinionated politicians on the White House lawn and the hugging and cheek-rubbing in Gaza – we're still at war; we're always going to be at war. It's always going to be us against everybody else . . .' He looked hard at Mullins's black round jaw and then into his cool blue eyes. 'Don't let anybody tell you anything different. One other thing – '

Mullins smiled.

'What're you grinning at?'

'There's always one other thing.'

'It's smart-arses like you, Mullins, that make this job so satisfying – ' the Coordinator allowed his face to relax slightly; not enough to call it a smile, just a loosening of the muscles around his tight, thin lips – 'but so fucking complicated! Give some thought to this American who got Cohen stuck on the hillside. He obviously hasn't yet found what he was looking for in Beirut so, while you're running for this Razak character see if you can do what Cohen was unable to do, find out what it was that made the Americans go to the lengths they did to secure Cohen's services. Have a good hard look at this American and the Arab he's taken on board and find out what was so important that Cohen

298

and Lev had to be buried for. Everything's connected. I think if you run along in this American and his new-found buddy's wake you'll find your lead into Cohen's killers. That's my advice – take it or leave it!'

'Any limit when I get there?' asked Mullins casually.

'None. Just drop this Razak into the nearest hole when you've finished with him.'

'What about the American?'

'Like I said, go along with him until you've established what's motivating him and then, if he gets in your way, push him over the edge.'

34

Razak gave Cunningham the best part of a day and a half to
think about it then returned to the Commodore and took
up his usual place in the bar. He was getting quite used to
cold beer; it was much better than lemonade or crushed
lime. He shovelled a fistful of cashew nuts into his mouth
and, catching the barman's eye, pointed to the phone and
gave him a limp underhand wave.

'I have made progress,' he told Cunningham when the
phone was answered, 'but I am not sure that the news
is good.'

'I'll be right down.'

Ten minutes was all that was needed to drag himself off
the bed, under the shower and throw on a clean shirt and
trousers. Razak was having his second beer when he got to
the bar.

'I managed to find the Palestinian who helped us with
Macauley,' said Razak through the last of the nuts. 'He
wasn't very cooperative.' Razak washed down the nuts
with a swig of cold beer then went on: 'But with a little
persuasion he remembered one or two interesting facts . . .'

Cunningham kept his face free of expression. He could
well imagine what form Gouda's 'little persuasion' must
have taken.

'The name of this man you mentioned, Razak, came up
again. It seems he was a very important man in the
Hezbollah field committee – '

300

'What's that?'

Razak touched his moustache with a paper napkin, screwed the napkin up and bounced it into the ashtray. He turned on his stool and looked Cunningham in the eye. 'The Hezbollah field committee was the organization that ran the hostage situation. Razak, my informant told me, was one of its chief organizers. He said, but he couldn't substantiate it, that he came from Iran – he was an Iranian . . .'

Cunningham wasn't unduly impressed. 'It takes all sorts.'

'The word is that this Razak disbanded his organization while he still had Macauley in chains. Macauley wasn't reported as a captive to Baalbek, you know – ' he glanced sideways at Cunningham – 'which bears out the theory that he had a private arrangement with Macauley and that, having extracted information from the poor man, he cleared his gang away so that news wouldn't reach the Supreme Council. This all agrees with your thoughts on what happened to Macauley while he was captive.'

'I thought you said you had some progress to report. All you've told me so far is what I told you the day before yesterday.'

'Patience, Jack! You know how we Arabs are with the dispensation of good news.' He bared his white teeth under the black moustache. 'Dribble, dribble – a little bit here, a little bit there . . .'

But Cunningham wasn't in the mood. 'Then stop the dribble, dribble and turn the tap on. Tell me something that I haven't already told you.'

Razak's lips closed like a rat trap. 'OK. My informant reckons there might have been a deal made between Razak and his men. It is a possibility that they learned something of what Macauley had in his head and persuaded Razak to pay for them to leave Beirut and go to different countries until the deal was finalized.'

'That makes sense.'

'Sure. Apparently they left one man behind to guard and feed Macauley.' Razak raised his glass to his lips and studied Cunningham's expression again from the corner of his eyes. It was going down well. Encouraged, he replaced the glass on the bar, called for more nuts, and continued: 'Only one man. Which explains how we were able to penetrate Macauley's prison and release him without opposition. The one man, it seems, when he found his prisoner gone wanted to hang himself. Such was the effect of the wrath of this evil man Razak.'

'And did he?'

Razak was getting carried away with the story. 'Did he what?'

'Hang himself.'

'Oh, no. But he's a very frightened man. He's dug himself a hole and refused to come out. He will die of fear,' pronounced Razak, contemptuously. 'A sick and gutless creature . . .'

'So how does this help us?'

'That's what I was coming to. My informant had discovered, by accident, where this individual was skulking his life away. I went to see him. He was easily persuaded to talk about his problem, particularly as I offered him safety and immunity from Razak's retribution . . .'

'How were you able to offer him that?'

Razak shook his head sadly at the American's lack of imagination but didn't reply to the question. 'He said the other three men of the team have gone to Europe. Razak has also left the Lebanon. He might be with them in Europe, he might be elsewhere. The man didn't know. What he did know was that every week he was to phone a number that had been given him and leave a simple message. By this means the criminals would know that whatever the plan was it was still going on . . .'

'What if this character missed out on the call?'

'He didn't know.'

'Any guesses?'

Razak shook his head. 'I've got the telephone number.' He took a piece of paper from his pocket and smoothed it out in front of Cunningham. It didn't take Cunningham a second. One glance was enough.

'That's France – Paris to be exact. You reckon this Razak and the rest of his mob are all sitting pretty in Paris. Is that what your contact implied?'

'One of them, at least, is. I wouldn't know about the rest – neither did he . . .'

'What name?'

Razak shook his head impatiently. 'He didn't know. What do you think – we ring this number and see who answers it?'

'Christ no!' Which is exactly what Razak wanted to hear. 'We pack up here and make for France right away, first thing in the morning. I'll get some tickets booked. That'll give us time to have a deeper conversation with this friend of yours – '

Razak stared into the bottom of his glass of beer. 'That will be a problem . . .'

'Why?'

'He wasn't too happy about giving me the number. I had to convince him it was for his good. Sadly he took the thing badly – '

'You killed him?'

'Put it another way, Jack. I made him safe from Razak's retribution! Sorry, it couldn't be helped – sometimes the knife slips . . .'

There wasn't a great deal Cunningham could say about that.

Lou Mullins watched Razak stroll down the Rue Mounemriad and turn into the wider, more pedestrianized Avenue Madame Curie.

He seemed without a care in the world. And at that stage, until the entry into his life of Lou Mullins that was probably a fair assessment of Razak's state of affairs. He made no pretence of evasion, there were no surreptitious glances over his shoulder. He was relaxed in his new anonymity, a cosy little, impregnable world of his own. And why shouldn't he be? There was no one around Beirut now who could pose any threat to him. He'd cleaned the board; he'd got a new face, a new identity and a new friend – an American one, at that – what had he got to worry about? While he kept Cunningham on hold he did the things a man of leisure would do in Beirut. He ate at the good restaurants, he met the nice boys, and flirted with the women – he did the Robin Gouda act and got away with it.

And along came Mullins.

Mullins was one of those people who had an uncanny gift of appearing invisible. He could wander an empty street and not be noticed. It wasn't quite a gift: it was the result of serious application and years of practice. Mullins was a born secret agent; he'd taken up killing when ordinary intelligence work no longer posed a challenge and, for him, killing had now become a very ordinary profession. But he fancied Robin Gouda. There was something about this Arab that twitched at Mullins's deeper instincts. He couldn't quite put his finger on it – not yet – but Mullins placed great store on his twitches; they'd never let him down, which is why he was the Mossad's first-choice agent of retribution.

Mullins watched Razak happily ensconce himself in his favourite morning coffee house and within a short time he was joined by a good-looking, well formed young Arab with a sulky mouth but a bored expression. Mullins, who'd made a study of such things, left them in an earnest negotiating stance. Whether it was for love or adventure, only they knew. Mullins kept his own experienced counsel. The young Arab was either a high-class whore or somebody else's expensively kept partner on the loose.

He turned his back on the coffee house, satisfied that the negotiations were going to take enough time for him to have a look round Gouda's apartment.

He returned by the quickest route and made very short work of the security arrangements at the flat. He closed the door behind him and stood immobile gazing around the luxury apartment, now bathed in diffused light from the broken rays of the sun that had managed to slip past the drawn heavy damask curtains. He had no idea what he was looking for; and even less idea what it was about Robin Gouda that disturbed him. He was none the wiser after half an hour's diligent search. Razak had done his own homework. There was nothing out of place, nothing untoward. Mullins wasn't disappointed, it was all part of the business. The fact that there was nothing wrong didn't make a right — Robin Gouda, friend of Les Cohen's American blackmailer friend was no cleaner, or dirtier, than before. But Mullins's suspicion hadn't eased one iota.

He stared carefully around the apartment. Nothing amiss. Nothing looked different. He'd done his job properly; there was nothing for Mr Gouda to get wet under the armpits about. He slipped round the door and pulled it shut and slipped the lock.

There was one more thing.

He went back to his car and studied it from a distance. Old habits. He'd forgotten what it was like to stroll straight up to a car and climb in the front seat and turn on the ignition. This time he opened the boot first and shifted the spare wheel. The cheap-looking Polaroid was wrapped in polythene under a dirty oil cloth. It would have to be a very hungry, or dedicated, thief to go to that extent to find a cheap camera. But this camera was not cheap. Its simple housing concealed a highly professional 25×2 modified telephoto lens that would separate the individual hairs of Robin Gouda's moustache at fifty metres. The film was the fastest the Israeli technicians in Mossad's laboratories in the Hadar Dafnar Building in Tel Aviv could come up with.

Mullins drove down Avenue Madame Curie and turned into the Hotel Bristol. The extreme end of its car park, he'd noticed earlier, was almost opposite the turn-off to the Rue Mounemriad. It suited his purpose exactly. He was ready and waiting and had no difficulty spotting Gouda in the back seat of the taxi that turned into the road opposite.

Mullins slipped discreetly out of the car and, shielded by the Bristol's sentry-like date palms, rested the Polaroid on the concrete wall. It was more solid than an expensive tripod.

On maximum zoom he began clicking as Razak and the young man got out of the taxi, and continued until they disappeared into the apartment entrance. One after the other, six good colour photographs appeared, each of which featured a differently angled close-up of the former Major Robin Gouda. Mullins waited until the prints were biscuit dry then wrapped them in a prepared envelope and addressed it to M. Alain Rapasse, MEP, Brussels.

When they arrived the next day Rapasse, without opening the envelope, passed it on to the Benelux desk of the Mossad Europe organization and they, again without opening it and taking note of the innocuous but special mark Mullins had made on the envelope, had it dispatched by special messenger to the Coordinations Director via Head of Special Operations. A long way round, but a guaranteed secure delivery.

It arrived at its destination much quicker than had

Mullins been naïve enough to send it direct to Tel Aviv from Beirut. Along with it, by a different route, was a short note in special code from Mullins. When it reached the Coordinator's desk it was brief and terse –

> *Meet Robin Gouda. He's the man; the youth is of no significance but could be worth a dividend after identification; he looks embassy-friendly, could be a boyfriend running loose or an operator. Gouda appears clean and honest, probably homosexual, possibly both. Does this fit in with the army officer? His home and its contents contain nothing to dispute this. But! Suggest one of these prints be shown to the man who came out of the water. No reason. But! again. Fingerprint pad attached.*

M

While the package had circled Europe and back Mullins was staying at the Commodore Hotel. Booked in as Lou Mullins, Australian Broadcasting Commission, he kept a quiet and unobtrusive watch on Cunningham. He made no attempt to approach him. Although Cunningham had been designated clean and pure and friendly by the Tel Aviv faction he still hadn't passed the Mullins litmus test; for Mullins, Cunningham was still a man for watching, not handling. But watching someone do nothing paid few dividends. Mullins was about to get bored until, in the middle of the second day of inactivity, both his interests sat down together at one of the corner tables in the Commodore bar and stuck their heads together in deep conversation. It wasn't lost on him that nearly all the talking was being done by the American.

'OK, Robin,' said Cunningham, 'we're on the half-past two Air France flight to Paris.' He was pleased at Razak's reaction. He hadn't turned a hair. Neither had his expression changed. 'What do you need – ' he gave Razak

307

an up and down inspection – 'apart from a suitcase full of clothes?'

'Nothing like that,' replied Razak and touched his hand to the area just below his armpit. 'This is all I need.' He grinned lopsidedly. 'And a clean shirt.' The grin vanished as quickly as it came. 'Have you found something out about the phone number?'

Cunningham nodded but didn't elaborate. 'That gun won't travel on an airplane,' he said instead. 'Why don't you leave it here and I'll arrange something else for you in Paris.'

'No thanks,' said Razak emphatically. 'He is like my elder brother. Where I go, he goes. I will make arrangements . . .'

'Not travelling with me you won't.' Cunningham studied Razak's determined face for a few seconds then relented. 'Stick it in a bag, lock it, and give it to me. I'll have the embassy rush it through the diplomatic bag . . .' He thought for a moment. 'They can take mine as well.'

'The Glock? Then I'm happy!'

'I'm glad you're happy,' responded Cunningham, sardonically, 'Let's get going.'

PART THREE

35

Beirut airport was the last place Mullins expected his two targets to make for. He'd settled in for a long stay in the deserted city, he'd made his plans, everything was going to happen in Beirut. And then this happened.

He was taken completely by surprise when Cunningham and Razak strolled out of the Commodore and caught a taxi. He followed them through the airport into the departure lounge. But it was quickly rectified. A phone call to the joint Israeli Military Intelligence (AMAN)/Mossad control centre hidden in the East Beirut border suburb of Furn el-Hayak and he was connected, via Tel Aviv, direct to the Meluckha 'C' Branch in Paris. It was a marvel of clandestine organization. And it worked.

Cunningham and Razak were logged on their arrival at Orly and followed across Paris to their destination by a team of Mossad agents. Two of them stayed to watch; the rest dispersed. Mullins was able to take his time leaving Beirut for Tel Aviv and catching El Al to London. Supplied with a car by one of the resident British *sayanim* he made a leisurely crossing of the Channel in his British-registered car and nicely cobbled British passport. He disappeared into the heart of Paris until he was ready to take on Cunningham and Razak again. As yet, Mullins hadn't even broken into a light sweat.

Cunningham's contact in IBM's Paris Office, an ex-CIA

official, had no trouble interpreting the telephone number Razak had extracted from Badran. It turned out to be, not surprisingly, the unregistered branch office of an unregistered Lebanese map manufacture and distribution, *et Cie*.

'Five bucks gets you six and a half,' said Cunningham's friend drily, 'that it's a phone-booth-sized office, maybe a table, possibly a fold-up chair, but even that's not an essential because nobody's going to be there; no carpet on the floor and no pictures on the wall, not even a torn page of a worn-out fanny magazine to make it homely. But I'll tell you something it will have, you can count on it, and that's a solid, brand new shiny mortice lock and probably a counter-dropper installed to see whether anyone's managed to slip through it. What are you expecting, Jack?'

'Nothing more than that, thanks, Frank.' Cunningham was well satisfied. After what Razak had told him it sounded like a stroke of good luck. An answering machine, sitting on its own in a dusty office with a visitor once a week to make sure the thing had ticked over. He checked the date on his watch. Thursday. Tomorrow was mosque day; tomorrow someone was going to open his office and collect his recorded messages and then he was going home to decide what to do with them. He and Robin would go too. Better make sure the courier had something to listen to.

They left it until Friday morning. Razak wrote the telephone number on a piece of paper and propped it up in front of him. He dialled, cleared his throat and, disguising his voice to match that of Badran, read the coded message into the mouthpiece. He held the phone at his ear for another few seconds then placed it back on its rest and drooped his mouth as he glanced at Cunningham. 'It will be another cut-out. Harb wouldn't be so silly as to have this lead direct to him. Someone else will listen to the message and pass it on to someone else . . .'

'That's what you'd do?' said Cunningham, glancing suspiciously at Razak.

'Any intelligent agent would.'

'Let's go and see.'

It was a narrow street at the back of a smelly market area. Rotting fruit filled the gutters, and cars parked nose to tail reduced the street to a single lane. The address Cunningham had been given was a single door leading up a narrow flight of uncarpeted stairs. The door opened directly on to the busy street. The stairs led through a waiting room and up another, even narrower flight.

Cunningham went up quietly on his toes and inspected the single door on the minuscule landing. It was exactly as Frank, his IBM contact, had described. He touched nothing and returned to the waiting room below and stared around him. The chipped sign painted into the glazed section of the door read:

ANDRE BELLANGER

Traducteur qualifié
L'allemand–Espagnol–Anglais
*
Spécialiste dans la traduction
de documents civils et légals

A scrap of paper taped beneath the logo informed any would-be clients that the office was closed for a week due to a death in the family. Cunningham removed it, screwed it up and stuck it in his pocket. The translation business didn't appear to be a robust one. The door looked as though it hadn't been opened for the past six months, notwithstanding its expensive livery. Perhaps, like the tiny office above him, it was nothing more than a blind, a tax

313

dodge. Cunningham didn't dwell on it. It was sufficient that M. Bellanger wouldn't be disturbing them today.

Cunningham sat on one of the rickety chairs. He picked up the least dog-eared of the magazines on the table and made himself look as though he had some urgent translation problems for M. Bellanger.

The footsteps that came up the stairs were as light as a feather. Cunningham, as was expected, glanced up casually into the girl's face and went straight back to his magazine. This was not according to plan. Neither he nor Razak had considered women. Perhaps she wanted a *traduction?* No chance. She knew what she wanted; she knew exactly where she was going and Cunningham's offhand look didn't interest her. Her return inspection was less than cursory. The fact that for the first time there was someone waiting to do business with M. Bellanger didn't put her off either.

She squeezed through the half-open door beyond Cunningham's shoulder and continued her climb to the next floor. Cunningham leaned forward and heard the heavy click of the lock upstairs.

The door upstairs slammed shut.

Then there was a pause, just long enough to play the tape, wait for it to reset and then leave.

Cunningham hadn't moved.

He raised his eyes as she passed. She was even less to look at from the back. Skinny; the strands of hair sticking out of the bottom of the scruffy red baseball cap were lank and stuck together in dirt as if they'd been run through with a glue-covered comb – a long time ago. Her thin cotton skirt hung heavy and shapeless over ugly black, thick rubber-soled boots and the man's woollen pullover did nothing for a non-existent body. But she wasn't silly. Or a novice.

He gave her a couple of minutes then flicked the magazine on to the table and followed her down.

She was waiting just to the right of the entrance but he didn't hesitate. He slapped the envelope he was carrying two or three times into his other hand, as if in exasperation at the failure of M. Bellanger to appear, and turned to the left. Stepping off the pavement he walked briskly, avoiding the rotting cabbages and squashed peaches, without a backward glance.

The eye contact he'd made with Razak, studying the boxes of Breton artichokes stacked outside a shuttered warehouse, had been sufficient. Razak's surprise at having the girl pointed out as the target was less disguised than Cunningham's but he let her wait, watching as she studied Cunningham's progress. When he'd disappeared round the corner she moved off. Razak was too full of his own ability, too sure of himself to realize that he in turn was being followed. Mullins stopped buying fruit from an unloading lorry and joined the party.

The girl was in no hurry. If this was her only job she made the most of it. She led her two followers through a medium to large *supermarché* and an empty café where she played away the day's profits on a pinball machine. Finally, after a stone-throwing spell at the Canal St-Martin, she decided enough was enough and made her way back to the street behind the one where they'd started.

Razak had begun enjoying mentally torturing the girl while she was playing her pinball. Now he touched delicately the thin, leather-cased stiletto strapped to the thickness of his upper arm and relished the thought of helping it find its way through her fragile body. He studied the entrance of the grim-looking apartment block from the corner of his eye as he walked past.

It was nothing more than he'd expect from Mubin Harb: a step up from the gutter. The man wasn't worthy of anything better; the American's money would be wasted on him. Razak set his features as he continued to the end of the

315

street. This was going to be the easy bit. Harb was a lazy pig. He'd always been a lazy pig and he always would be a lazy pig. He'd be up there now, lying in a stinking bed, in a stinking room while he'd sent his little Algerian whore to check that his future was still intact. Razak loosened the blade with his left hand. *Your future, my friend, Mubin al-Harb, is about to be written.* His features blank, he turned at the top of the street and retraced his steps to where the girl had disappeared.

He pushed open the door of the apartment block and, without going in, looked around the small lobby. It was dark, dank and squalid. He leaned forward and searched the four walls. There was nothing but graffiti – ugly, dirty, crude graffiti going back to before the time of *Algérie Française!* and *F.L.N.* – and the stench of sour wine, stale urine and above it all the overbearing odour of boiling fish. What there wasn't was a board with the names of the apartment's inhabitants, just a battered box screwed to the wall where the postman could throw any mail addressed to the building and run for his sanity.

Razak cast aside his new-found sensitivities and walked across the entrance towards the stairs. He gazed up into the stairwell and counted six floors. Six times how many rooms?

On his toes he crept to the first floor and studied the three doors. Six times three. She could be in any one; any one of eighteen. He spat silently on to the dirty floor, waited a moment and listened. A baby squawked. A baby always squawked, and from behind the third door on the first floor came the sound of a man's voice raised briefly in a fierce curse. Razak moved up to that floor. The curse must have done its stuff – the squawking died as if something had been jammed into the baby's mouth. The curse wasn't repeated. He moved on to the next landing. Dead silent. A child's pram with a buckled rear wheel leaned drunkenly against the wall, but no sound came from within. Razak descended to the ground floor and looked forlornly for a door with CONCIERGE emblazoned on it. There wasn't one, not surprisingly. Nobody in his right mind would want unauthorized access to this roadside lavatory of a place – except, of course, Razak. With his lips tightly pressed together, he left the building and made his way diagonally across the road.

It was a run-down place, like everything else in this back street, but it was the only *boulangerie* in sight. He stared through the grubby window and received a flat stare back from a gnarled old woman behind the counter. The shop was uninviting and the smell only slightly less obnoxious than the apartment building across the road. But she'd know what was what: old women *boulangères* always knew what was what within several kilometres of their bread basket. Razak leaned forward to study the unappetizing and meagre selection in the glass case and waited for the shop's one other customer to stop talking and go. He smiled cheerfully at the old woman and received only a grunt. He pointed to a half-dead *kadayif* thickly coated with burnt syrup.

'I'll have that one,' he said in throaty Arabic.

She wasn't surprised – just suspicious. She shrugged her shoulders when he picked up the little paper packet and handed her a 50-franc note. He raised his hand and stepped back a pace.

'Perhaps you could help me?'

She stared down at the note, then watched him from under hooded eyes to see what it was going to cost her.

'There's a girl lives over the road,' he half-turned his head and jerked his chin in the direction of the door he'd just left. 'She's about twenty-two, wears a red American thing on her head. Dark hair – ' He wasn't allowed to finish.

'I don't know anyone like that.'

Razak smiled broadly, and for a fraction of a second she dropped her guard. The smile still intact, his hand shot out like a hungry snake and removed the note from her twisted, arthritic fist. He replaced the dead cake on the counter and without another word turned on his heel. He got only as far as the door.

'Just a minute.'

Razak came back.

The less afflicted of the hag's bony hands opened on top of the glass counter and the thumb and two fingers attempted to rub themselves together. They didn't succeed but the gesture was understood; her eyes took on the apathetic, hungry look that usually accompanies such a gesture.

Razak folded the note lengthwise. He tapped her open hand with it, but withdrew it before the fingers could close. Her eyes followed the note.

'That's not enough,' she hawked. 'Perhaps a little more?'

'Perhaps a little less,' snapped Razak. 'Perhaps nothing – perhaps I'll go next door – '

'She's a whore.'

'Name?'

'She calls herself Sylvie. Her mother was a *putain* too, it runs in the family, so was her grandmother . . . Are you *flic*?'

Razak shook his head. 'When were you last offered money by the police to answer a simple question? What's the number of her room? What floor?'

She told him.

He held out the 50-franc note but before her fingers could close round it he took it back and tore it in half. One of the bits fell on the floor and as she scrabbled for it she looked up and bared a row of dark brown stumps at him. The gob of spit she hurled at him just missed his shiny black

318

shoe. Razak thought this very funny. 'You're the girl's grandmother, are you?'

She got to her feet and shoved the two pieces of note out of sight somewhere amongst her greasy clothes. 'I hope you get syphilis,' she said by way of farewell.

Razak stopped at the door and turned. 'And that, mother, would make two of us – you with yours from long back and me with mine – ' Before she could respond he'd left the shop and walked openly across the road to Sylvie's apartment.

The number 12 was drawn roughly in pink chalk on Sylvie's door. The colour had no significance, it was probably the only coloured chalk she had and by the look of it the number was ready for renewal. Razak scraped his fingers on the panelling and stepped back a pace so that his face was at its most appealing angle to the fish-eye which in its normal position would centre just below his chest.

'What do you want?' came Sylvie's muffled voice.

'A word,' responded Razak. 'Business?' he smiled into the blank eye and stepped back another pace as the bolts on the door were shot.

'Do I know you?'

'May I come in?'

She stood aside reluctantly and allowed him to enter the tiny one-room studio. It was like an oasis in a community rubbish tip. Everything was spotless, which seemed at variance with her appearance, but even that, without the ugly baseball cap, showed a marked improvement. Close up she had very good skin, and with a little make-up judiciously applied she could have been a very pretty woman. As it was, she was attractive, if a little vague of expression. She looked hard at Razak. 'Who sent you?'

Razak gave her his best look – gleaming teeth, shining eyes, the lot. 'I don't know. It was the only way I could think of to get you to open the door. Actually – ' he glanced round the room again. The front door was still open. She wasn't that silly, she was poised like a spring. One wrong move from him and she'd be out of that door and down the stairs like a rabbit. He kept the smile in place; nobody ever got hurt by a smiling psychopath, or so they said at the GID psychological warfare school in Baghdad's Tahrir Square. ' – a friend asked me to get in touch with you.'

'What friend?'

'You probably wouldn't know him by the same name – it's Harb, Mubin Harb.'

She frowned suspiciously.

Razak broadened his smile. 'There, I told you you wouldn't know that name. Let me describe him . . .' Which he knew was going to be futile. He, Razak, wasn't the only man who could change appearance. But the fact that he described *someone* was gaining her confidence.

'Doesn't mean a thing to me,' she said when Razak had finished. 'But what's it all about anyway? Why would your friend, whatever his name is, want you to come and see me?'

Razak slapped his forehead with his open hand. 'Oh, that's stupid of me! Didn't I say? Of course I didn't! It's about the phone calls – the message, the thing you collect and pass on every Friday – that's what it's about . . .'

She watched his face for several moments.

'May I sit down?'

Still watching closely she nodded, absently, then reached behind her and pushed the door shut. Razak was home and dry. 'He said nobody else was to know about it,' she said. 'It was just me and him – an arrangement, like . . . I wasn't to talk to anybody about it . . .'

'I'm almost his brother. He didn't mean me. He meant anybody else – anybody French. You see he and I are of the same village, that makes us brothers . . .'

320

'How come you couldn't describe him?'

'I described him as he is at home. We all change when we leave there.' Razak smoothed his hands over his face and chin, 'See – no beard.' He rubbed his hand on the back of his head: 'short hair.' The smile was all-embracing, the sincerity oozed. 'I couldn't describe myself if I was asked . . .'

Her sulky features relaxed a little. Her mind operated on the basic elements: some you like, some you don't, but as long as the money's right . . . 'Do you want . . . ?' she gestured to the bed with her hand. 'You know?'

'Perhaps later,' responded Razak. It was time for business. 'But let me give you some money.' He smiled deprecatingly and brought out a large wad of rolled-up currency notes. She tried not to stare. 'After all, I have wasted a good bit of your time. A thousand all right?'

Her eyes bulged, but she took the note and rammed it into the depths of the cheap imitation leather shoulder bag. 'Why are you giving me all this? I've done nothing.'

Razak smiled. 'There is perhaps a small thing you can do.'

She was willing now. Anything.

'You haven't passed on today's phone message to my brother?'

She stared at him. Her earlier misgivings reappeared. 'You don't even know his name, do you?'

'He will have changed it.'

She allowed herself to be persuaded. After a moment's indecision she tucked her legs under her, allowing the shoddy skirt to ride up over her knees. But any female was on a loser with Razak. 'He calls himself Gilles,' she said.

'Gilles? Gilles what?'

'That would be telling.'

Razak's hand went unconsciously to the slim sheath on his right arm, but he managed to fight the impulse to draw the lethal blade and ram it into her face. His hand stiffened and returned to its reassuring place in his lap. He played down the importance of the name. 'Have you called him yet?'

'Nope.'

'I tell you what, if I give you another *mille* note will you let me do it? It'll be a marvellous surprise for him to hear my voice. It's all right – ' he rapidly assured her as he peeled another note from the roll and leaned forward to place it carefully on her bare knee – 'he won't be angry . . . How would I know about the telephone messages if I wasn't part of Gilles's family?' He smiled genuinely at the absurdity of a scruffy unwashed nomad like Mubin Harb giving himself a name like Gilles. 'You understand?' If she didn't, Sylvie, the prostitute daughter of a long line of prostitutes, was about to experience the sort of pain that is inflicted on a rare few. He gave her a few seconds to think about it.

She nearly lost it.

'There is no number.'

'What!'

'There is no number.'

Razak's thick eyebrows joined together over his nose, shielding his eyes like a pair of flip-up sunglasses. He lowered his right shoulder and allowed the fingers of his left hand to caress the plain hilt of the stiletto. He didn't move his stance; his eyes remained glued to hers. 'So, how do you pass on this information?'

'There is no information – it's always the same thing. I just say what it is. It's always the date and – '

'Never mind that. How do you pass this message on?'

'Over the phone.'

Razak stood up abruptly. He'd had enough. It was time to go to work. But she forestalled him. 'He rings me.'

Razak gazed around the one room. 'I don't see a telephone.'

'Not here, silly! I go to the Gare de l'Est at six o'clock every Friday and wait at one of the phone booths. Gilles rings and I pass the message. Simple, *hein?*'

Perfect! Razak's mind was in overdrive. This was the perfect cut-out; there was no way Harb, if it was Harb, could be caught out in the open. A phone number could be traced; that had already been done but he'd covered himself for just such an eventuality. Harb was taking this thing very seriously. It showed that he didn't trust Badran to keep his mouth shut when a sharp knife was being plied between his buttocks. Quite right! And it also showed that if he, Razak, got this far then he would get no further. Sylvie was watching very closely. There was more money on offer – she could sense it. Razak gave up thinking and glanced down at his watch.

'What time did you say you had to wait for the call?'

'Six o'clock.'

'Would you like to have some lunch with me?'

'I have to work. I have to earn my living.'

'Is Gilles your pimp?'

'No, I never see him, not since he asked me to do the messages.'

'He pays you well?'

'He sends me money to pay the rent of the office and the bills. He pays a hundred for every time I deliver the message.'

'That's not very much.'

'It's regular – once a week, and it's no trouble.'

'When I meet him I shall insist you are paid much more. Now, about this lunch? I have paid you for your time. Consider it work. You can tell your pimp I paid you 200 and you can put the rest in your mattress.' He resurrected another of his Omar Sharif smiles and stood up. 'How about that?'

'But I can't help you find Gilles. You must understand

that. If you try to talk when the phone rings he will hang up and that will be the end of my pension.' Her eyes widened. 'It might be the end of me.'

'Trust me.'

36

Just before he reached the last row of his artichoke leaves Razak rose abruptly and made his way to the telephone at the entrance to the restaurant. From there he could keep his eye on Sylvie. But it wasn't necessary, she was enjoying herself with a huge steaming bowl of *moules marinière*; she wasn't going anywhere, not until the last empty shell had been cast aside and the sauce mopped up.

'Jack, we've got a little problem . . .'

Cunningham listened in silence. There were always little problems; nothing in this business ever went smoothly. 'Can you buy her?'

'Yes, but I don't see to what point. She's got nothing to sell. The call comes in, Jack, not out.'

Cunningham was running out of patience. 'Where are you now?'

Razak told him.

'OK. Don't push her. Go through the motions, fill her up, make her happy, make her love you. I'll join you in about half an hour, we'll have coffee together. And, Robin, don't get her excited until I get there – don't start anything, don't make any suggestions. OK?'

'OK, Jack, I'll see you shortly.'

By the time Cunningham joined them Razak had done his stuff. Sylvie was as well fed as she'd been for a long time; Razak, if nothing else, was a convivial companion. For a man who preferred the smooth, round and slightly hairy masculine bottom he was well at home with the other side. There was a lot of giggling – much of it fine Armagnac inspired.

Without a word Cunningham handed him a plastic bag. Razak glanced into it and nodded with satisfaction when he saw the Desert Eagle snug in its pouch. He met Cunningham's eyes but said nothing, then turned to the girl.

'This is my friend, Jack.'

Sylvie studied Cunningham professionally, then gave a little hiccup. 'American – ' It wasn't a question. She'd stuck a pin in Cunningham with the expertise of a twenty-year-old hooker. She probably knew exactly how much he'd got in his wallet. 'I have American blood,' she said through a mouthful of Armagnac-soaked sugar lump.

Cunningham smiled condescendingly. 'Don't get carried away with it. Everybody under the age of fifty in France has American blood – it dates from 1944. I don't think they'll give you a passport on that!'

'I wouldn't want a passport.'

'What would you want?'

Razak had pulled his chair back and moved out of the picture. He lit a brown-paper Gitane and trickled smoke out of the side of his mouth as he watched Cunningham at work. It might have helped if Cunningham had warned him what he intended doing. After a moment he got up and indicated the washroom. Cunningham barely acknowledged him as he left the table and walked away.

Sylvie cupped her small glass in both hands and held it close to her bottom lip. She stared into Cunningham's slightly mocking eyes. 'What would I want? What would anybody in my position want? Money, Mister American, that's what I would like – money. Lots of money!'

Cunningham's expression didn't change. 'What would you consider lots of money?'

She hadn't thought it out. She lowered the little balloon

glass and unwrapped another lump of sugar. Playing money she liked. It was a good game. She was enjoying herself. She popped the soaked lump of sugar into her pursed lips and sucked. She was still thinking. 'I'm sorry,' she said suddenly and held her glass out to Cunningham. 'Would you like a sugar lump?'

'Thanks,' said Cunningham. He held the sugar gingerly, barely touching the level of Armagnac. He bit the wet part and allowed it to dissolve in his mouth. 'You haven't answered my question.'

'Was it a serious one?'

'Yes,' he said sincerely.

'OK,' she said at length, then closed her eyes. 'I think lots of money is 100,000 francs.'

'What would you do with it?'

She opened her eyes. They had a mischievous glint in them. 'I would buy nice clothes; I would leave my prison cell; I would go where there are many Americans and take all their money from them . . .'

'What would you do to earn 100,000 fancs?'

The glint in her eyes was replaced by suspicion. The game had finished. This was serious. She looked at the bait hanging on the end of the hook and thought it might be worth a tiny nibble. 'There's not much I wouldn't do – but it depends, doesn't it?'

Cunningham nodded. 'Would you betray a friend for 100,000 dollars?'

'You mean francs?'

'No. I mean dollars. American dollars.'

Sylvie stopped breathing for several seconds then, with a hand shaking so violently she almost dropped it, stuck the rim of the glass on her bottom lip and upended it. Her breath came back in short spurts. '*One hundred thousand American dollars,*' she whispered, then locked her eyes on Cunningham's. 'I would betray my daughter for that much money . . .' She hiccupped as the Armagnac reached its destination. 'If I had a daughter.'

'Would you betray Gilles?'

'For 100,000 dollars?'

Cunningham nodded.

'I can't.'

Cunningham glanced across the room. Just as well Robin wasn't listening to all this. He had a good idea what would be going on in the Arab's mind. Money was wasted on this creature. A few jabs with a sharp needle would be Robin's way; the subject of money would never have been raised.

'Why's that, Sylvie? Do you owe him that much loyalty?'

She laughed out loud. It took Cunningham by surprise. 'It's nothing to do with loyalty, my American friend,' she said after a moment. 'When I say I can't betray him I mean I have no way of doing it. I don't know where he lives, what he does, where he goes . . . Your friend – ' she turned her head to where Razak had been sitting – 'he knows all that.' She wrinkled her nose and gave a little hiccup. The Armagnac was doing its stuff. 'Actually, I told him a lie.'

Cunningham raised his eyebrows slightly then smiled encouragement. 'It wouldn't have worried him.'

She wasn't listening. 'I told him I didn't know Gilles's real name . . .'

'And you do?'

'Mmmm. It's Salih – Hisham Salih.'

Cunningham's expression remained even. A new name; not one of the four. Where the hell had he come from?

Sylvie studied him for a moment. 'Your friend thought his name was Harb. But the man he described looked nothing like Salih. Was it important that I didn't give the real name?'

Out of the corner of his eye Cunningham saw Razak coming out of the washroom. 'It doesn't matter. It's not important . . .'

'But I don't even have a phone number.' She glanced up at Razak as he sat down, showed him her empty glass and raised her eyebrows before turning back to Cunningham. 'Goodbye 100,000 dollars!'

Razak called the waiter.

'I'll have one of those, too,' said Cunningham. 'A large one. And a cup of coffee – large as well.' He leaned forward and rested his arms on the table. He lowered his voice. 'There is still a way for you to earn that money.'

She joined him in the middle of the table. 'Tell me.'

Cunningham waited until their drinks had been placed in front of them then said, 'When Gilles rings you at the Gare de l'Est you tell him that you could not make out the message because it was garbled. You say it was longer than usual but the machine does not play it back properly. Have you got that?'

She frowned. 'Yes, but I don't understand . . .'

Razak pulled his chair close to the table and stubbed out his cigarette; his brain was running parallel with Cunningham's – the light was shining quite brightly.

'You don't have to,' continued Cunningham after a quick sideways glance at Razak. 'Tell Gilles exactly what I have said. While he's thinking about it you say you tried to rewind it but something happened. Maybe the tape's broken; maybe the machine needs looking at . . .'

Her eyes sparkled with understanding. 'And I say, come and look at the machine . . .'

Cunningham gripped her wrist. 'No,' he hissed. 'You make no suggestions. You do exactly as I've said and let him make the suggestions. Is that clear?'

She tightened her lips contritely and nodded half-heartedly. 'What if – '

'Nothing. You just do as I say. We will come with you and watch from a distance.'

'But you must stand near me in case I forget . . .'

329

'You won't forget. We will be near, but you won't see us. You have nothing to fear from a telephone. If he has anybody watching the phone we will take care of them. Now, let's go over this again . . .'

Cunningham made her repeat three times what she had to say until she was word perfect. No suggestions, he drummed into her, just the facts and let him decide what he wants to do about it. Go along with everything he suggests. The fact that the message was longer than usual was certain to bring him out of his cage; he couldn't afford to leave it unchecked.

The Gare de l'Est is one of the scruffier Paris terminals. At ten to six on a Friday evening it was a mass of humanity: the French long weekend assault on the country added to the normal rush to get at the *boudin* and pastis after a hard day at the office. Razak, sipping coffee from the drinks dispenser, was closest to Sylvie. She tried to look as though she had a purpose. It failed. She just looked like a woman waiting for a telephone call. Cunningham found a bench seat near one of the restaurants, crossed his legs and held open the pages of the early morning edition of *Le Monde* that someone in a hurry had left on the seat. From a distance he saw Razak stiffen, drop the plastic cup into a bin then begin walking casually towards the telephone booths. He swung his eyes.

Sylvie had disappeared.

He stood up, folded the newspaper and walked slowly across the concourse, stopping only to drop the paper in one of the unused bins scattered around the rubbish-strewn station. Razak had stopped and was gazing at the arrival/departure board and as Cunningham watched he lowered his head and glanced towards the booths. Cunningham did the same. Sylvie's shoulders were hunched over the phone, her left hand gesticulating. Then, nervously, she removed her baseball cap and rubbed the back of her head. From

330

Cunningham's observation point things weren't going all that smoothly. But he needn't have worried.

After a while she replaced the telephone and turned round, standing at the booth's entrance searching the crowd for a familiar face. She spotted Razak and headed towards him, a broad smile on her face. For a moment he looked startled, then, with a warning shake of the head, turned on his heel and headed for the station exit. She got the message. She slowed down, studied the indicator board, glanced at her watch, shrugged and then, as if she had all the time in the world, wandered slowly in the direction Razak had taken.

Cunningham allowed her a good head start. She'd attracted no attention; she had no interested olive-skinned watcher. She was a woman all alone. Cunningham formed third in line until the three met in the car park.

'He's coming over right away,' Sylvie said breathlessly. 'I'm meeting him at the office.'

'Why?' asked Cunningham, urgently.

'He said he's in his car and has no key.'

'What time?' snapped Razak. His wrist was in front of his face, his eyes centred on his watch.

'He said he's coming now.'

'It's twenty past six,' interjected Cunningham. 'Where's he coming from?'

Sylvie shrugged. She was disappointed. Her new friends didn't seem very pleased with all the hard work she'd put in on the phone. 'I don't know. I told you that before. He said he'll go straight to the office and he wants me to meet him there . . .'

'We'll get a taxi, it's quicker,' snapped Cunningham. 'Did he say anything else?'

'He went on, and on, and on.' She pouted then smiled broadly, showing good even white teeth. 'He's very suspicious. Asked whether anybody had been asking about

331

him, what did the message on the answer phone sound like. Was it male or female – all that sort of thing. What was wrong with the machine? Why couldn't I fix it . . .'

They clambered into a taxi: she and Cunningham on the back seat, Razak in the front with the driver. 'And why couldn't you fix it?' said Razak over his shoulder.

'What do you mean?'

'What answer did you give him?'

'Ah! I said it played for several minutes but everything was garbled and when I lifted the cover the tape spilled out.'

'Did he believe it? Did he answer immediately?' asked Cunningham.

She leaned back and rested her head on the top of the seat. 'I'm not sure. He seemed to take a long time thinking about it. Then he said, don't touch anything. Leave things exactly as they are and that he was in his car and would come right away.'

Razak turned fully in his seat and studied Cunningham's eyes. Cunningham stared back. He made no sign, no indication. If he was pleased with the outcome he wasn't sharing it. Razak had other thoughts. Somehow he was going to have to talk to Harb alone.

Before the taxi turned into the road Cunningham leaned forward and tapped the driver on his shoulder. 'Stop here! Take my friend to the other end of the street.' He got out, pulling Sylvie after him, and stood in the doorway of a closed shop. Holding her by the arm, he peered round the doorway and inspected the narrow street. Rubbish was still lying around but most of the cars that had been parked there earlier had gone. The street looked cheap, dirty and miserable.

'Cross over the road, Sylvie,' said Cunningham, 'and walk down the other side. Don't look round, don't look scared. Look natural . . .'

'I'm afraid!'

'Don't be. Just do what we said. Go up the stairs, open the office and wait there. You have nothing to be afraid of, I shall be there to look after you. I promise, you won't be hurt.' He gave her a little push. 'Go on – don't look round.'

He withdrew into the recess of the shop front and pressed himself against its side so that he could follow her progress. There was no other activity in the mean little street. Hers was the only movement. As she reached the roadside door to the office she hesitated, stopped and, with Cunningham watching every movement, dived into her shoulder bag and brought out the key. She looked up the street once, then down, and for a brief second stared into the shop doorway where she'd left Cunningham. Then she opened the door and vanished.

37

The car came from Razak's end of the street.

It wasn't quite what he expected one of his former cellar rats to be driving around in Paris and he gave it only a cursory glance as it glided over the rotting vegetables. It was when the heavy black 750i BMW with opaque, smoked-glass windows parked with two wheels on the narrow pavement outside the door where Sylvie had just entered that Razak moved out of his hiding place.

The driver stepped out of the car and studied his surroundings. Short and slim, he wore a dark navy suit, black shoes and a white open-necked shirt revealing a chunky gold halter dangling across his collarbone. He was clean shaven but obviously an Arab. Razak looked hard. This wasn't Harb. He'd never seen the man before in his life. He kept his eyes glued to the man's figure.

A quick glance up and down the street and the new arrival vanished through the door. Razak gave him three minutes to mount the stairs to the first floor then abandoned his cover and walked briskly along the side of the wall.

Cunningham approached from the other direction. With Razak close on his heels he moved silently up the stairs.

They could hear Sylvie's frightened, high-pitched voice long before they arrived at M. Bellanger's waiting room. The door to the upper landing was open so the sound carried clearly. The Arab was very unhappy. He was also cross and suspicious. As the two men tiptoed to the foot of the next flight of stairs a loud slap followed by a startled scream came over the sound of the answer phone: even from Cunningham's side of the door the words of the message were crystal clear.

The man didn't wait for it to finish. With a piercing snarl at Sylvie, who'd taken refuge in the corner, he threw himself at the door. In his hand, dull and matt black, was a solid Smith & Wesson .38. Its two-inch barrel, extended by six inches of suppressor, waved in all directions as he crashed through into the waiting room. Cursing, he skidded across the floor and hurtled for the stairs.

A brief glimpse of Cunningham flattening himself against the wall brought an instinctive jerk on the trigger and the hollow-nosed bullet thudded into the wall an inch from Cunningham's ear. Six inches lower and he'd have blown the top of Cunningham's shoulder away.

He fired again, this time with an even wilder panic inspired pull of the trigger and the bullet crashed into the ceiling. Cunningham threw himself into a ball and fell backwards down the stairs. The Arab, wasting no time on him, leapt athletically over Cunningham's falling body and landed, balanced on both feet, at the foot of the stairs. He slithered across M. Bellanger's waiting room. And then he ran into Razak's Desert Eagle.

Standing to one side of the door, feet apart, Razak studied the man's startled face for the briefest of seconds, then smashed the barrel of the heavy weapon across the bridge of his nose. The crunch was audible. A gush of blood shot out of the smashed face and turned his white shirt bright red. The startled look remained but it was wiped away by the next, almost casual, blow of the heavy automatic which thudded just behind his right ear.

He went down on his hands and knees coughing and spitting and shaking his head, the silenced revolver still clutched in his right hand. Razak, unmoved, his expression one of total boredom, placed the heel of his shoe on the Arab's hand, transferred his weight to it and turned a half-circle. The small bones cracked like Chinese firecrackers and the revolver, helped by the toe of the same foot, skidded across the carpetless floor and came to rest against the wainscoting. Razak transferred the foot to the back of the man's neck and pressed hard. The noise coming from the smashed face sounded like a pig in labour.

Cunningham took one look. Satisfied that Razak was in control, he dashed back and rushed a shocked and shaken Sylvie down the stairs. 'Be back in a minute,' he hissed to Razak.

'No problem,' replied Razak coolly.

As soon as the sound of Cunningham's feet on the stairs vanished he sprang the lock on M. André Bellanger's office and dragged the half-conscious body through the door. He'd used his belt to bind the Arab's hands behind his back and dragged his trousers down to his ankles. Even if he managed to pull himself to his feet there was nowhere he could run to.

Razak kicked the door shut and turned the Arab on to his back. His face was a mess. Razak's initial blow across the top of the nose had been a carefully calculated precision stroke and the evidence was there in the puffed-up eyes behind which two glazed dots couldn't tell whether it was night or day. The Arab tried to focus on Razak, but nothing appeared: all he saw was a blurred face behind a film of red sticky pain.

Razak kicked him behind the ear, not enough to put him out, but just sufficient to loosen his tongue.

The Arab's mouth opened and a stream of blood-flecked bubbles surged out and ran down his chin. Razak studied the flow for a moment then put his face close and said in a hushed voice, 'What's your name, camel shit?' The bubbles

336

frothed but there were no words. Razak formed his fingers into a V and pressed down on the man's eyelids. 'Answer me if you want to live.'

'Who are you?' He struggled with the words through the blood and torn mouth and tried once again to focus on the face above him. 'What d'you want?'

'Your name?' repeated Razak.

'Gilles.' It came out with a mouthful of blood and bubbles. 'What – '

'Whore's son! Your *real* name.'

There was a pause. It was too long for Razak. His knee ground into the prostrate man's groin. 'Agh!' It did the trick. 'H-Hisham S-Salih,' he gurgled.

Razak eased the pressure of his knee. 'Quick, pig! If you want to live tell me – where is Mubin Harb? Quick, quick, quick!'

Salih tried to force his eyes open, but Razak's fingers were still pressing down painfully on the upper lids. He gave up. 'Go and eat rat shit!' he gurgled, and lay back to receive his punishment. Salih was no coward. He followed the words up with an almighty spit that landed on Razak's mouth.

With a bellow of rage Razak jumped to his feet, wiping his face with the sleeve of his coat. He was still rubbing when the office door opened.

'What the hell was all that noise about?' said Cunningham. But he wasn't really interested. He studied the man on the floor blankly. 'Is this one of them?'

Razak shook his head. 'Just a minute, Jack.' He took out his handkerchief and finished wiping away Salih's blood-flecked spit. Then, without warning, he kicked the helpless man hard in the side. It was a beginning of the repayment. Satisfied, he turned back to Cunningham. 'It's as I thought, another cut-out. This is not the one we were expecting; he's not one of Macauley's captors. But he knows things and he will tell us. He's going to help us – ' He kicked the man on the floor again and spat at him in Arabic – 'aren't you?'

'Does he speak English?' Cunningham asked, unmoved.

Razak shook his head again and then hissed something into Salih's face.

'I will tell you nothing,' responded Salih when he managed to sort his tongue out. 'Kill me. I do not care.'

'What's he saying?'

'Before you came in I asked him whether he knew the name Macauley and whether he knew of Razak. He spat in my face.' He looked at Salih's bloody face again. 'I think he needs a little softening up. I know these people, they think it's very manly – macho, you call it – to have a great deal of pain inflicted before their psyche allows them to say everything you want to hear. Allow me – ?'

'Sure,' said Cunningham. 'Pull out all the stops. Hurt the bastard.' He looked down at Salih, his face impassive. 'But don't kill him – yet.'

Razak smiled. His left hand came away from the inside of his jacket and he held up for Cunningham's inspection the shiny bright stiletto that Badran had given him. Cunningham studied it and nodded in admiration. He wasn't a knife man but it didn't bother him. He walked across the room, picked up the chair from behind the desk and placed it against the wall where he could watch the proceedings. Razak kicked the man on the ground and spoke to him in Arabic.

'Say your name clearly to my friend.'

Salih squeezed his swollen eyes together and tried to loosen them so that he could see his captor. There was a vague shape: nothing of substance, just a shadow. He worked some of the muck around his mouth and spat it at the shadow, but it just dribbled out of his lips and settled precariously on his chin.

338

Razak leaned forward, prized open one of Salih's eyes with his finger and thumb and held the thin blade about six inches from it. He removed it after a second, put his head in its place and stared at the blood-lined eye. It was seeing.

'Say your name clearly to my friend,' he repeated.

Salih tried to spit again but this time his mouth was too dry. Razak made a little sound of annoyance with his tongue then, like a surgeon performing a delicate operation, he placed the point of the stiletto into the split made by the impact of the Desert Eagle at the top of Salih's nose and ran it straight down the length of the bone. There'd been hardly any pressure on the blade but both sides of the nose parted, leaving for an instant an ivory white bone with two segments of flesh hanging obscenely on to his cheeks. Then the whiteness vanished under a flush of blood. Salih screamed, but it was short-lived. Razak grabbed a handful of Salih's shirt, and rammed it into the open, screaming, bloody hole.

Razak studied his handiwork for a moment, remembered he had a spectator and looked up. The two men exchanged glances.

'Was there anything in his pockets?' asked Cunningham.

Razak shrugged. He reached down and patted the side pockets of Salih's jacket. His lip curled. He slid his fingers into the inside pocket and pulled out a new Moroccan tooled leather wallet. He tossed it across the room at Cunningham.

'Is he going to say anything worth while?' said Cunningham as he caught the wallet.

'Any minute now, Jack.'

Razak dragged the bloody shirt tail from Salih's mouth, allowed him several intakes of breath and then touched the point of the knife to the swollen eyelid.

'Say your name clearly to my friend.'

Salih breathed deeply, swallowed a new mouthful of blood and said in a quaking voice, 'Hisham Salih.'

'Louder.'

'Hisham Salih.'

'He said his name is Hisham Salih, Jack.'

Cunningham looked up from the contents of Salih's wallet. 'He calls himself Gilles Talbot here. Must be well paid,' he flipped a wad of 1,000-franc notes and allowed one side of the wallet to tumble down, revealing eight different credit cards. 'It seems he's the driver/bodyguard of a Jordanian named Wasfi Jabr, Managing Director of something or other, import of oriental carpets included, according to this.' Cunningham stared hard at the wording on the card. 'Could this Jordanian be Razak?'

'We shall find out,' said Razak and smiled to himself as he studied his helpless captive.

He made himself comfortable on his ankles and gazed impassively into Salih's mutilated bloody face. 'Tell me,' he continued in Arabic, 'where I can find Mubin Harb, Abu Rashidi and Husam Qadir.'

Salih tried to pierce the shadow but his eyes weren't up to it. 'Go to hell!'

'Think carefully, my friend.'

'I have. You have my answer.'

Razak looked up and shrugged his shoulders at Cunningham. 'I asked him again about Razak. He still insists he doesn't know this man, but he thinks he might know someone who does.'

'Tell me about him.'

'He hasn't told me yet. But he's about to.' He turned back to Salih. 'I am going to ask you again about the names I said earlier. I am not going to accept spitting as a response and lying will bring you more cutting from my little friend here – ' He tapped the point lightly on Salih's forehead. Even that light touch brought a spurt of blood. But Salih

340

was already in too much pain to notice it. He made probably his last mistake – he spat.

Razak shook his head slowly. With a sideways glance at Cunningham he lowered his head and placed his lips close to Salih's ear. He whispered into it for several seconds then swayed back on to his heels. The effect on Salih was startling. He tried to force his eyes open and focus on the man squatting beside him. His colour, a healthy midsummer tan by Paris standards, turned to that of sour milk. His mouth opened, but nothing except blood bubbled out. He tried again but all that came out was a stream of garbled Arabic.

'What was all that about?' asked Cunningham.

'I told him I'd slice his balls off and shove them down his throat. I'd have done it, but he deprived me of the pleasure. He suddenly remembers the name but doesn't know where the man is.'

'Help him remember.'

Razak went down on one knee beside Salih. 'I ask you for the last time. Where are Harb and his friends? I will not ask again – do you understand?'

Salih understood too well. He raised his head and focused in the direction of the foreign voice. 'Help me!' he croaked in English. 'Please help me!' Then he collapsed in front of a startled Razak.

'I thought you said he didn't speak English,' Cunningham said accusingly.

Razak reached down, grabbed a handful of Salih's hair and banged his head up and down on the floor. 'You stupid jackal! You obscenity!' he spat in Arabic. 'You speak only when I tell you to. This American wants to kill you. All I want is information. You fool! You have condemned yourself.' He gave one final pull on Salih's hair then let the head go with a thump. He turned on his heel to Cunningham. 'I asked him,' he said. 'This creature was in

Beirut in the early days. He is a criminal, a terrorist. The only English words he knows are those he heard from the American hostages he ill-treated. This is all he knows; that is how he learnt it.'

Cunningham's face remained set. 'That's the bastard's death sentence. He should have kept his fucking mouth shut. Make him talk about Razak — and Razak's friends.'

Razak nodded. 'He's about to tell us all of those things. Excuse me for a moment — ' He inserted the point of the blade into the crotch of Salih's bright orange Y-fronts and, without taking too much trouble where the blade careered to, gave an upward jab and split the pants apart. Salih howled and brought his knees up modestly to cover himself, but it was only the beginning.

Razak ran the sharp side of the blade across both exposed knees, cutting deeply and causing Salih to straighten them out instinctively. Razak hadn't even broken into a sweat. He studied the bound man's private parts as if they were a delicacy and he was having first choice. Salih began crying as Razak made his selection: he worked the blade under Salih's penis and brought it out from where it had been hiding between his thighs. He stopped crying long enough to plead that he was ready to discuss Mubin Harb's whereabouts. But Razak had closed his ears.

Cunningham hadn't. 'What did he say?'

'He's ready to negotiate.'

'He knows where Razak is?'

'He hasn't said that, but I think he knows the next link in the chain.' Razak looked seriously at the helpless man's penis balanced on the edge of the stiletto. 'He needs just another little nudge.'

'Then give it to him,' said Cunningham. He followed Razak's eyes. 'What are you going to do with that?'

'Cut it off.'

'It's a nice thought, but is it necessary?'

342

'Was your friend Macauley's treatment necessary?'

Cunningham stared him out. 'We don't want the bastard dying on us. Threaten him first. Get some more conversation out of him then we'll think of ways of killing the fucker.'

Razak wiped the blade on Salih's shirt, studied its razor edge and slipped it into its sheath. He stood up resignedly.

'I'm sorry, Jack, I think you'd better come and do this yourself. You've asked me to get information out of this murderous, torturing creature but you don't want me to hurt him and you query everything I say he tells me. You come and talk to him and I'll sit over there and read the contents of his wallet.'

'Cut it out, Robin,' snapped Cunningham. 'And don't get fucking prima-donnerish with me. I didn't say don't hurt the bastard. I just want to see something left for me to have a go at. Cutting cocks off is all well and good; I leave that to the Mafia   it's not my style.'

'It is mine, Jack,' said Razak with a sad smile. 'I am Arab. I understand Arabs. You try stroking this one's hand and the minute your guard goes down he'll sink his teeth in your throat. He understands the knife. I understand the knife. It's the only thing that'll make him tell the truth.'

'Get on with it, then . . .'

'Thank you.' The thin blade came out again and went back to its original position. Salih had followed the tone of the argument between his two captors; he gauged who'd been the winner and drew his stomach in as tight as it would go. He knew what was coming. He tried another 'help me, please' at the shape in the corner but got no response. He reckoned he'd gone far enough. Now he was ready to tell Razak anything he wanted to know, but he knew at this stage Razak would want a little more pain entered into the record book. He swore long and fluently. It sounded to Cunningham as if he were saying his prayers.

343

In a way he was. He felt the sharp thin blade slice his penis from one end to the other. It was not so much the pain, which was bearable; it was the horror, the outrage, the ultimate degradation as his manhood split in two. He bellowed at the top of his voice and fainted.

'Jesus Christ!' Cunningham stared, mesmerized at the obscenity. 'You're a cruel bastard, Robin! I'll give you full marks for that – but how're you going to get him to talk now? You haven't left him anything of value!'

Razak bared his lips in a mirthless smile. 'Thank you for the compliments, Jack.' He pointed the bloody stiletto at Salih's gory penis and tilted his head in study. 'I think if you look closely you'll find there are still a couple of little things he might like to bargain for.' He showed his teeth in a clean white line. 'Perhap's you'd like to, er . . .'

Cunningham shook his head. 'You're doing fine, Robin.'

Razak took time to wipe his hands and light a cigarette and by the time he was ready to go to work again Salih had recovered consciousness. He was crying like a little girl. His legs, restricted by the trousers round his ankles, were opening and shutting to the limit they were allowed as he tried to soften the pain. And as he cried, Razak's unemotional voice put Cunningham's questions and passed on enough answers to keep the American happy; at the same time he added his own, and through his sobs and cries Hisham Salih answered them.

38

After some time Razak stood up. Salih had relapsed into a moaning wreck, answering Razak's questions only in monosyllables, with his eyes tightly clenched and his knees shaking with the effort of keeping his thighs as far apart as possible. As he walked over to where Cunningham was sitting, Razak glanced at the notes he'd made on the sheets of paper he'd taken from M. Bellanger's desk.

'I've finished, Jack. What do you want done with him?'

'What have you got there?'

'Everything you asked.'

'He knows Razak?'

'Sadly, no.'

'The Jordanian?'

'Nothing to do with it. He gave Salih a job, that's all. This poor miserable creature, for once in his life, got lucky and was given a decent job. Trouble is, by his own admission he was heavily involved in the early days of hostage-taking and the cruelty inflicted on those poor people. For that he has a price to pay. But that's your business, not mine. If you think he's already paid enough we'll pull up his trousers and send him back to driving his Jordanian around Paris in his nice car. It's up to you. It's all the same to me.'

Cunningham didn't respond. 'What did he say about Razak?'

'Just that he doesn't know where he is.' Razak paused a

moment to see how the American took this. He needn't have bothered. Cunningham's face was expressionless, he could have been talking to a billiard ball. Razak shrugged and glanced sideways at the man on the floor. There was no question of Salih getting up to run. He was never going to walk properly again, let alone run. Razak pointed at him with his thumb; it seemed a good time to let Cunningham know that the big-secret club was expanding and there were a couple more like Salih to be found. Salih would have been pleased to know of the words Razak put in his mouth.

'He said the people who recruited him live in fear of their lives. This proposition was put to him by one Husam Qadir whom he met in a café in the north of the city. He'd known Qadir in Beirut, during what they called the good days, and they became friends here. Meeting at different cafés this Qadir felt a need to let his mouth run away with him. This one – ' Razak again jerked his thumb at the man on the floor – 'not to be outdone, did his own bit of interrogation and tells me that he discovered from Qadir that there was talk of a big deal being arranged over something that was going on in the Ash-Sham desert – that's a bit of no man's desert on the eastern Jordanian border with Iraq . . .'

'Did he find out what this something was?'

'No. He said according to Qadir the deal was made in Beirut between an American hostage – that could only be Macauley – and this man Razak. But . . .' Razak paused significantly and watched Cunningham's face. Cunningham stared hard at him. This was going to be bad news, he could feel it.

'But, what?'

'Qadir hinted that one of the men here in Paris, Mubin Harb, knows as much about it as Razak; apparently he

346

tortured the information out of Macauley. Qadir told him
he's the only one of the gang who speaks English.'

'D'you know this Harb? D'you know what he looks
like?'

'How could I, Jack? It was just one of the names of the
people who'd been guarding Macauley.' He glanced down.
'He says he's never met him either. His only contact was
with this Husam Qadir.'

Cunningham frowned, first at Salih, then at Razak. 'I
thought you said this one was going to be Harb?'

'That was what I was led to believe, Jack,' replied Razak
glibly. 'But Harb has been too clever for us. He put this
creature in as a cut-out; it's another dead end like the
answering machine. This – ' he kicked the groaning Salih in
the side then wiped the side of his shoe on Salih's trousers –
'is probably the only way we can break into Harb's cover.'
He stopped and thought for a moment. 'There are two
more: one Abu Rashidi and the already mentioned Husam
Qadir. But according to that – ' he indicated with his
thumb again – 'Harb is the one, other than Razak, who has
all the details of the deal . . .' He tailed off. 'Whatever that
is . . .'

'And they're all afraid of Razak?'

'How d'you make that out, Jack?' Razak frowned.

'Why are they all in hiding? Why are they running? Why
have they got a cut-out system between Beirut and here?
Of course they're bloody frightened – they're blackmailing
the bastard. They've got something on him and they're all
waiting for him to deliver.' He got up, walked across the
room and stood over Salih. 'Ask him if Qadir told him what
it is these people have got on Razak.'

Razak smiled again. 'All right,' he said, getting out his
knife again. But the cutting edge of the blade wasn't
necessary. Razak had only to hold it up in front of Salih's
face for Salih to go into an endless tirade of abjuration and

penitence, apology and cries for forgiveness. Razak gave the impression of drinking in every word, which encouraged Salih to even greater depths of abasement. After a while Razak held his hand up and turned to Cunningham, and with the serious, intense look of the born liar, he said, 'He says he learnt that they're protecting Mubin Harb. Apparently this man Razak wanted to negotiate only with the United States over the information Macauley had given him, but these other people, urged on by Harb, say the information, which apparently is of enormous significance to the peace and tranquillity of the Middle East, should be offered to such countries as Israel and Iran on equal terms . . .'

'Just a minute!' Cunningham glanced down at the man on the floor, then raised his eyes to Razak in disbelief. 'You're not going to tell me that miserable little bastard said "enormous significance to the peace and tranquillity of the Middle East"!'

Razak smiled genuinely. 'My interpretation, Jack. It's what he would have said if he'd had the education or the intelligence to say it! What he actually said was that the information is something to do with nuclear warheads.'

'What about them?'

'Just that.'

'Is that all he said about it?'

'He was not a member of the Beirut group that held Macauley. This is merely what he's picked up from Qadir. He says that's all he knows about it and if we want to know any more we must talk to Mubin Harb – something about map references and things . . .'

'And how the hell do we do that? We've already got here a double cut-out which shows the man's no goddam fool. We don't even know what he looks like, let alone where the bastard's hiding himself.' Cunningham stared down at the cringing man on the floor. 'You sure this bastard can't point a finger at Harb?'

'You didn't let me finish, Jack,' said Razak smugly. 'He's already pointed his finger. They're all in hiding here in Paris.'

'How does he make contact with Harb?' said Cunningham.

'Through Qadir,' replied Razak. 'Salih, here, puts a postcard in a shop window – he renews it and changes the date at each visit. This, he says, is passed on to Harb and indicates when he reads it that everything is normal. It's a good system,' admitted Razak, reluctantly. 'Nobody meets, nobody talks – it's a dead-letter box every time – it's the perfect cut-out.'

Cunningham agreed, but didn't say so. 'Has he given you the wording on this card?'

'Yes. And the name of the shop and the district.'

'Where is it?'

'I've no idea. I don't know Paris. Here, the message is written down.'

Cunningham took the sheet of paper and read:

Readings from the Koran in Arabic for non-Muslims.
Enquire in shop for literature.
Date:

'This is in English,' he said suspiciously.

'He copies it from the sample left by Harb,' replied Razak glibly. 'The date is the key; it's usually the first or second of the month.' He studied the date on the gold Rolex he'd taken from Robin Gouda. 'That's in five days' time – Tuesday. The words are the same every time. Do you know this place?'

Razak gave Salih a back-heel kick and looked over his shoulder. 'You sure this place is in Paris?'

Salih groaned.

'He said yes. The shop is easily found. It's a shop that sells wine and fruit and milk and suchlike. That's what *he* says. And the shop owner is Algerian . . .'

'Let's go, then,' said Cunningham.

'What about this?' Razak pointed with his chin at the man on the floor.

'Can he walk?'

'Where do you want him to walk to?'

'Down to his car.'

'You're letting him go? This is not advisable, Jack. He might not have a prick but he still has a tongue – '

'Get him down to the car,' repeated Cunningham coldly. 'I'll follow you down.'

He locked the office door. M. Bellanger was going to have a nasty surprise when he came in to do some translations; the area in front of his desk looked as though a ritual goat sacrifice had taken place on the carpet. On the way down the stairs Cunningham took Salih's silenced .38 out of his pocket. He put his hand round the threaded suppressor and gave it an extra twist, then he flipped open the chamber and inspected the three remaining live rounds.

'Stick him in the trunk,' he said to Razak when he joined the two men at the BMW. 'Can you drive this thing, Robin?'

'Sure.' Razak picked Salih up as if he were a baby and dropped him unceremoniously on his face in the large boot.

'Out of the way.' Cunningham leaned slightly forward into the boot, took the .38 from his coat pocket and held the suppressor about four inches away from Salih's ear. He squeezed the trigger three times in succession. Each time Salih's head bounced off the carpeted floor of the BMW's boot. He made no sound; there was no need for closer inspection. Cunningham reached forward again and thoroughly wiped the spattered blood from the gun on the tail of Salih's shirt, then stuck the revolver into the dead man's coat pocket. Razak blinked several times as he studied Cunningham's face. It was cold and impassive: there was no feeling for having blown a man's head apart, a man a short time earlier he'd complained was being given too much pain. Funny people, Americans. At least this one was.

Cunningham closed the lid of the boot with a soft thud. 'I suggest you take this thing somewhere out of Paris and set fire to it,' he said calmly. 'Make sure the bloody thing goes all the way. Can I trust you with that?'

'You're a man of many surprises, Jack,' began Razak.

'Sure. But just do as I ask. Get this car out of here and turn it into a heap of burnt metal, then go out of sight. We'll arrange a meet for tomorrow. OK?'

'Whatever you say, Jack.'

'Right. I'll check this address out. I don't want to see you hovering around while I'm doing it. Keep away from it. Give me a number where I can get you.'

Razak took out a small notebook, glanced through it and read out a number to Cunningham.

'Where is this place?' asked Cunningham.

Razak shrugged his broad shoulders. 'A contact,' he said enigmatically and left it at that. Cunningham didn't press him.

'If I want you in a hurry?'

'No problems there, Jack. You ring that number and say what you want.' He opened his jacket and tapped the butt of the Desert Eagle. 'What do I do about this?'

'This is France — you can do anything you like. But you'll be on your own if they pick you up — I won't be able to help you.'

'Can I tell them I'm CIA?'

'You can tell them any fucking thing you like, but whether they'll take any notice is something else.' Cunningham turned away. 'If I don't contact you I'll see you

351

tomorrow afternoon, 3 p.m., at the place we agreed on. OK?'

'OK, Jack.'

Cunningham waited until the BMW had disappeared round the corner before turning in the opposite direction. His expression betrayed nothing. He'd just killed a man in cold blood. It didn't touch his conscience – Hezbollah, Islamic Jihad and the rest of the bastards, as far as he was concerned, had opted out of the civilized world. As with all other terrorists, they had no rights, they could be put down like rabid dogs. But there was something else on his mind – Robin Gouda. The man was too smart, too smooth – everything with the miserable little bastard in the office had been too pat. Too many perfect answers – too much detail. He doesn't know Harb, yet he was able to describe him to Sylvie. As he said, how could he know him when he only came into the picture after Harb and his scruffy pals had slipped out of Beirut? And the dead chauffeur? Mr Hisham Salih seemed to know an awful lot of what was going on for a locally recruited courier. If he didn't know where the Beirut gang was holed up how did he arrange to meet the one named Qadir at regular intervals in different cafés? And what sort of fugitive tells his courier, especially one of the old Beirut gutter brigade, all the details of a multi-million-dollar scam? It was all too glib; it was all too bloody clever. Cunningham didn't like it. Robin was beginning to smell.

39

Cunningham signalled the waiter from his corner seat in the bar of the Crillon and ordered another large whisky for Frank from IBM. So far he hadn't broken the good news to him. If Frank thought this was a friendly social he was about to be disillusioned.

'Can you do something for me, Frank?'

Frank wasn't an idiot. 'Two whiskies don't get you a lot, Jack. I had a private bet with myself that you'd go to three at least before you sprang it on me. Go on, ask away, I won't hold out for the third. I still owe you from way back.'

'Can you run a number through your computer and come up with an address?'

'No probs. That wasn't worth even one whisky.'

'I haven't finished.'

'I didn't think you had. Shoot!'

'I want someone who's not affiliated to go to that address and check whether the guy I'm going to describe lives there.' Cunningham gave a pinpoint description of his partner, Robin Gouda. 'Then I want him followed. He's —'

'Just a minute, Jack. If this is company business why aren't you using the embassy facilities?'

'It's not. And it's not official either, Frank. I'm doing this for love. I don't want our people involved.'

Frank sniffed deeply. 'I don't think I like the sound of that.'

'You don't have to. All you have to do is look up that address and ask one of your local assets to follow my guy.'

'No interference?'

'Nope. All he does is follow. When the target goes to ground he rings me up and tells me where. Then he can go home and work out how much he wants to be paid for the job.'

'I don't know, Jack,' said Frank, doubtfully.

'Nothing's going to bounce, Frank. It's straightforward. You don't have to know who or what. You're just a middle man helping an old friend. You did say you owed me. And Frank – '

'What?'

'I'd like it started now – immediately.' Cunningham studied his old friend's face. 'And I'll buy you that other whisky!'

'That's the bit that swings it! You're a very persuasive operator, Cunningham. Order the whisky, I'll be back in a second.'

The call came just as Cunningham was about to launch into the large wedge of Brie that had been placed on the table in front of him. He spurned the use of the restaurant's portable phone and followed the waiter out into the lobby where he shut himself in a private booth.

'Your man took a taxi to La Muette then the Métro to Porte de St Cloud. He gave the impression he was expecting a tail . . .'

'Did he spot you?'

'No way! He then walked to a place called Place Léon-Deubel and went into an apartment block there.'

'Did you say that was the 16th? Bit of a smart area, isn't it?'

'Supposed to be. But it's not as posh as it sounds. You get all sorts around there. Your man looked around the area for a time then paid particular attention to this place I mentioned. He went in. He came out. Matter of minutes. Looking at it I reckon whoever he was looking for wasn't in.'

'You sure it's the right man?'

'It fits exactly the description I was given.'

'Where are you now?'

'In a café on the same side of the road as the apartment block.'

'And the target?'

'In a café on the other side of the road watching the entrance of the building. I think that's it. I think this is as far as he's going.'

'OK. Can you keep him covered until I get there?'

'Sure. How will I know you?'

Cunningham described himself and what he was wearing. 'I don't want to be seen. Is there somewhere we can change over?'

'Get a cab to drop you off on the corner of Avenue de Versailles and Rue Marois. There's a café/bar called Leon's. We can see if he leaves his café and crosses the road from there. I'll approach you, OK? The name's Claude.'

'What's the traffic like, Claude?'

'Rough.'

'See you in about thirty minutes then.'

As soon as he'd left Cunningham, Razak wrote down the real address of Harb, Qadir and Rashidi he'd prised out of Salih. The card in the window would do for Cunningham; gullible people, the Americans. Razak was quite satisfied that Cunningham had swallowed everything he told him Salih had said. He fully expected Cunningham to come back from his abortive checking out and suggest they try something different. Like he said — gullible people, the Americans.

He got back to Paris late that night after destroying the BMW and set out just before lunch for Harb's address near, as Salih had said, a square called Place de la Porte de St Cloud. He studied the map of Paris and went halfway by taxi. This would throw off anybody who, for reasons he could only imagine, would be interested in his activities. You never could tell – and old habits die hard. By the time the taxi dropped him off at the Métro station he was quite sure nobody was following him. He took the train to Porte de St Cloud and wandered around until he found Place Léon-Deubel. Once there, it was a simple matter to find the address that Salih had given him. Nothing special, a narrow building with a heavy wooden door covering a small cobbled yard and an entrance with an iron-framed door on an electric push button on either side of the yard. Flat 12 *bis*. Right-hand door.

Razak went up the stairs; wooden ones that creaked and groaned with every step. After two flights he drew the Desert Eagle from its pouch, screwed on a six-inch suppressor and cocked it. On the third floor he stopped, caught his breath and listened. There was no sound up here but by leaning over the banister rail and straining his ears he could hear the traffic in the square and the odd raised voice from the other side of the block. He found what he was looking for on the fourth floor.

He rattled his knuckles against the door.

Nothing.

He did it again.

Still nothing.

He waited a second then pressed his ear against the panelling. Dead silence. Mubin Harb and the other two were out. He sprang the simple lock with ease, slipped round the door behind the Desert Eagle and closing the door moved quickly through the flat. It was as untidy as he would have expected but it took only a few minutes to establish that the three former Hezbollah gangsters were living here. He left everything as he found it, relocked the door and went back to the street. He studied his surroundings for a moment, settled on the café opposite and found a table in its interior but with an unrestricted view of the building opposite.

Razak didn't move, he didn't even look up, but ten minutes later he watched Abu Rashidi scuffle along the pavement on the other side of the road and disappear through the wooden door of the apartment block. Another eight minutes and Mubin Harb and Qadir came from the same direction.

Razak studied Harb without a flicker of an eyelid. Harb had made little effort to change his appearance. He must feel safe, thought Razak. His thin shapeless beard, little more than a boy's first growth, was intact and his head was still covered with a mass of oily black curls. He'd changed the green combat jacket and canvas bandolier he'd worn until its dirt and grime had made it as stiff as a bulletproof waistcoat for the more Paris Arab-style baggy trousers with turn-ups that concertinaed around the ankles of his down-at-heel laceless shoes. Under an ill-fitting shapeless navy blue jacket he wore a once-white shirt buttoned tightly at the neck. He walked, seemingly without purpose, but to Razak's knowledgeable eye he was nervous and as shifty as if he was making his way in the old days across Beirut's rubble landscape.

Razak allowed himself a quick glance round the square before settling his bill and crossing the road.

Advancing cautiously up the stairs he waited for a few moments outside Harb's door and listened. He could hear the television. His face right up against the fish-eye set in the door, he rapped officiously on the frame.

Silence. The TV sounded louder, as if it had been turned up. He knocked again.

'Oui?' The voice came from very close, puzzled, inspecting the blurred shape through the spyhole.

'Le facteur laisser un pacquet pour vous à la conciergerie . . .' It wasn't perfect but Razak doubted that Harb was a French scholar.

He wasn't. 'Mettez le dehors la porte.'

Razak tried again, 'Désolé, monsieur – j'ai besoin de votre signature . . .' He kept his face covering the spyhole and listened to Harb trying to make up his mind.

Curiosity got the better of him. The postman hadn't come to shoot him.

'Moment!'

Razak heard the chain being unhooked and the lock turned. The door opened slightly. The suppressor on the Desert Eagle slid through and came to rest just below Harb's nose. He studied it for a fraction of a shocked second then tried to close the door; the automatic jammed it and Razak's weight threw the door wide open. Harb lost his balance and crashed across the room as Razak came in and kicked the door shut. Abu Rashidi, sitting in a torn and ramshackle armchair, occupied one corner; he was frozen with shock, his hands held out in supplication as stiff as two dead branches. Qadir, sitting at the table with a half-eaten doner kebab level with his open mouth, turned to stone. Only his eyes moved. The television blared out to its uninterested audience. Razak strode across the room and stood above Harb. The automatic pointed two inches below his left ear.

'Don't move an inch: don't even blink, my good friend, Harb,' Razak said.

Harb closed his eyes. The voice he knew; the man he didn't. He heard three heavy compressed thuds just by his head, and jerking his eyes open saw Rashidi, just in the act of raising himself from his chair tip over the back, his legs flailing the air. Three bullets, .44 magnums, two in the head

358

and one in the top of his neck, almost decapitated him. He was dead before his head touched the floor. Qadir came to life, but too late. The hand with the doner came up to cover his face in a futile attempt at protection as two bullets thudded into the side of his head and threw him against the wall.

Harb hadn't moved. His eyes were closed tight, his back sagging against the wall behind him. The killing had no effect on Razak's expression. His eyes were even and cool and his mouth relaxed; the huge Desert Eagle, made long and uglier by the extra six inches of suppressor was back in its place by Harb's ear. He'd lost interest in Qadir and Rashidi.

Then Mubin Harb came to life. He'd put all the pieces together.

'Razak! Razak!' he cried, 'for the love of God; for the love of Allah – '

'On your hands and knees!' he hissed to Harb. 'And beg for your life. Pray, Mubin Harb.'

'Please, Razak!' Harb threw himself to the floor and sought Razak's feet with his hands.

'Please, Razak!' mimicked Razak.

'Yes – don't kill me!'

Razak spat drily. 'I forgive you. Get on your feet and look me in the face.'

Harb remained where he was, his face pressed into the filthy threadbare carpet. His body shook with an ague that came from deep inside. He was never going to move. This was safety. It was dark and he was safe. Razak's pointed boot thudded into his side.

'Get up, Mubin Harb, or I'll kill you where you are. I've said I forgive you. Get up!' He kicked the cowering man hard again.

Slowly Harb brought himself to his knees. Any moment he expected the blinding flash, the searing pain and everlasting night. But it didn't happen. He kept his eyes tightly closed and carefully, slowly rose to his feet. He refused to meet Razak's eyes. 'Let me help you, Razak. I've always been your friend . . . We've had good times together – remember? I can help you now that we've rid ourselves of these scum . . .' He waved his hand blindly behind him. 'It was they who betrayed you. They forced me to go along with them. . . But now it's all right – isn't it?' His head still bowed, he stared at Razak's feet; a look of cunning was quickly concealed. 'Razak, my brother,' he murmured hesitantly, and then, gaining confidence, 'I have information that will enable you to more than double the American money.'

Razak feigned ignorance. 'What information? How did you come by it?'

Still without raising his head Harb told him of how he'd extracted the locations of the Iraqi dumps in Jordan from Macauley. He spared no detail. 'I wanted to share this with you. It was only fair, you were our leader, but those . . .' he tailed off and waited. 'Am I to be with you?' he asked when there was no response from Razak.

'I said you were forgiven. Go on,' said Razak calmly.

'Erm – by sharing this information – my er . . . ?'

'Tell me the locations.'

Harb sighed. 'They are written as map reference numbers; they are precise with the serial number of the map section and the contents of the dumps detailed.'

'Paper and pen,' snapped Razak. 'Where?'

'In the drawer, but – '

'Don't move!' Razak opened the drawer and without taking his eyes off Harb rummaged around with his free hand. A crumpled sheet of paper, then a ballpoint. 'Sit down at the table,' ordered Razak, 'and write down every detail.'

'But – '

The Desert Eagle touched the top of his head, slid down over his forehead and came to rest in the corner of his eye. Harb shivered violently. Razak said nothing.

Harb began to cry, but it had no effect on the silent Razak. He put the slightest pressure on the automatic and forced Harb's head up.

Harb brought himself partially under control with a series of hiccups and then said, rapidly, the words running into each other in his hurry to get them out, 'I haven't got the information. I don't know the reference numbers. I don't remember any of the details. My mind is not educated. Everything was written down . . .'

The Desert Eagle's suppressor thudded down on Harb's cheekbone with force. The skin split open like a ripe tomato, but other than a scream of pain it had little effect on Harb. He kept his hands on his knees and his head bowed, and shook with fear.

'And where is this writing?' hissed Razak.

'Forgive me!'

'Harb,' said Razak conciliatorily, 'if you don't answer me you will, in a very few moments, join your two friends in whatever hellhole they've arrived at. I am running out of patience.' The conciliatory tone vanished and the words came out like bullets: 'Where have you hidden the information?'

'I-n A-m-merica,' Harb whispered.

The announcer on the television droned on, the only sound in the room. No movement. They looked like figures in a waxworks. After several long moments Harb lost his nerve and risked a sideways glance. Nothing had changed. Razak stood like a statue, his face registering only disbelief. For once he seemed lost for words. But it didn't last.

'America? What are you saying? Have you lost your mind, Harb?'

Harb lowered his head again. Just in time. Razak need time to think. And while he thought he gave Harb's head two mighty thwacks with the Desert Eagle. Harb howled. More blows rained round his neck and shoulders, hurting, but causing only superficial damage. 'I'll forget that stupid remark,' Razak grunted at length, 'and give you this final chance to redeem yourself. Where have you put this information?'

Harb tried again through the ringing in his ears from the blows. 'It was Macauley's idea . . .' he gasped.

'What was?'

'To send the information to America. He said it would be safe . . .'

'You fool!'

But the tap was open. Harb couldn't stop himself talking even if he wanted. 'He said that as long as the information was in Europe it was at risk from the Iraqis, and worse, the Israelis. Macauley said one whisper of the existence of these details and the full force of Baghdad would fall on our heads to prevent this information reaching the Americans. He said should the Israelis learn of these dumps they would leave no stone unturned to locate them. Either way, he insisted, we would lose. The Iraqis would kill us all to preserve the secret and the Jews would torture us until we told them everything. The only people who would pay for the location of these dumps would be the Americans. The only way we would benefit, and save our skins, Macauley said, was to deposit the information in a special place in Washington and negotiate direct with American authorities there . . .'

'What special place?'

'Amex, Macauley called it. He gave the address in Washington and a number. The information was sent by special post to this place in a packet addressed to Macauley.

362

There was a note attached saying that it was to be held in safekeeping until his representative called for it . . .'

'The name of this "representative"?'

Harb gave a deprecating cough.

'Your name?' Razak stared hard at the top of Harb's oily head. 'You have written authorization to collect this packet?'

'Macauley wrote such an authorization.'

Apart from the odd interruption Razak had listened in silence. There was sense in what Macauley had told Harb. He looked for the catch. He couldn't find one. Keeping the map references safe in Washington but at hand where he could reach them whilst negotiating their sale, dribbling them into the dealings bit by bit until all his conditions were met, seemed a much better proposition than using Jack Cunningham to open doors. But Harb had left out an important factor.

Razak's tone was reasonable. 'How did Macauley suggest that a gutter rat from the debris of Beirut like you should approach people in authority in America — people in a position to negotiate?'

Harb kept his eyes away from Razak's. 'He gave the name of a very high-ranking official and a personal phone number known only to him. At the mention of Macauley's name this official would open all the necessary doors.'

'The name of the official? His phone number?'

Harb turned his head sideways and pointed his chin at the corner of the room. 'Under the corner of the carpet under the television is an envelope . . .' He lowered his head back into its submissive position. 'Everything is there: the name, the number, the address of this Amex place — everything is written. A strange name, this official,' he added as a tiny injection of confidence gave him new hope. 'Macauley wrote it down in his own hand. He said it would help open the door ... Is everything going to be all right now, Razak?'

At last he was able to look Razak in the eye. He saw no evil there – only a man deep in thought. He was going to live. He was going to breathe the sweet air of life; he was Razak's brother again and Razak needed him. Everything was going to be all right. Razak gazed down at him and held his eyes for several moments. Then he nodded. 'Yes, Harb, my friend, everything's going to be OK.'

The hollow-point Silvertip .44 blew the inside of Mubin Harb's head to smithereens. For a few seconds he continued staring at Razak. Only his lustreless eyes and the small bullet entry hole just above his eyebrow, still raised in expectation, showed that he was dead. The tableau held for a few seconds, then, in slow motion, he toppled sideways on to the floor, the remains of his head on the dirty carpet as he settled into the attitude of a man saying his prayers.

Razak studied the dead man without a great deal of interest. Harb had solved all the problems for him. He was back now where he'd started: he had Macauley's money banked in a secret account; his own account, and it was intact – all his. Harb had done him a favour. He'd shown him how to double his huge fortune; he now had secrets for sale and a high-ranking contact in Washington. All he had to do now was to get to America and begin the negotiations. So far, so good. Razak had reason to look contented.

He recovered the envelope from under the carpet, switched off the television and all the lights, then came back to the centre of the room and stood beneath the single bare bulb suspended from the ceiling. He reached up and, holding the socket in his fingers, tapped the bulb very gently with the muzzle of the automatic until it shattered. He looked closely at the element. It was unbroken. Carefully he let go of the broken bulb so that it hung

naturally. The cooker was gas; he turned on all the taps.
The heater in the fireplace was also gas; he did the same and
then closed the curtains so that the room was in darkness.
Leaving the door on the latch he walked down the stairs at a
steady, unhurried pace.

He walked across the courtyard and tapped on the
concierge's window. The curtain was pulled aside and the
window slid open half an inch. A face, a mouthful of
saucisson, studied him.

'My friend wished to pay you some money,' he said in
his execrable French.

'Quel argent?'

'I am not sure. You will have to go and see him. I have
just brought him money from his family. I believe he wants
to pay several months in advance.'

'C'est bien! J'irai dans quelques minutes . .'

'Thank you. Er – can you take a spare light bulb. His
seems to be broken. Perhaps the switch?'

'Toute de suite, monsieur. Je m'en occuperai immédiate-
ment. Merci! Au revoir!'

Still without hurrying, Razak stepped out on to the Place
Léon-Deubel and headed towards the Métro at Place de la
Porte de St Cloud. He'd barely turned the corner on to
Avenue de Versailles when the explosion rent the sky over
Auteuil. There was a shocked silence; a smell of ancient
dust and broken timber and smoke as a cloud of debris
soared into the sky. And after the silence the screaming
started: the screaming of people, the screaming of car horns
and the horrendous nose of crumbling masonry. Razak
pressed himself against the wall as people rushed towards the
sound of the explosion. Only three of them took any notice
of him. He threw away the cigarette he had just lit, crossed
the road and descended into the Métro at Porte de St
Cloud.

He didn't look round. He knew that little bit of ruthless

demolition had earned him several days' grace before forensic discovered the three Arabs' bits and pieces; they'd be mixed up with the concierge. And it would take them even longer, if they were at all interested, to discover that three of their corpses had died with bullets in them.

Claude was waiting on the pavement outside Leon's when the taxi drew up. He hovered nearby while Cunningham paid it off.

'Cunningham?'

'Yeah.'

'Claude. Your man's gone back into the building again.' He glanced down at his watch. 'About twenty minutes ago. He hasn't come out yet. D'you want me to show you exactly where?'

Cunningham followed Claude's eyes. It didn't really matter what was going on in the building, though it was worth having a look – after Razak had left. Cunningham was almost certain of what he would find and it didn't bring one tiny touch of remorse. He was going to find one or more of the bastards who'd worked Thurston Macauley over, and he was going to find them dead, hopefully in as nasty a way as he knew Robin was capable of. But what he was mostly interested in finding was that Robin Gouda, in as silly a mistake as possible, had blown his cover. Admittedly, it was a lucky mistake – Sylvie didn't have to have told him that Robin had described Mubin Harb. Robin wasn't supposed to know what Mubin Harb, or any of the others, looked like. A simple mistake by a man who couldn't afford *any* mistake, and the cards had all been reshuffled and redealt. What Cunningham had suspected for some time – that Robin Gouda and Razak were coming closer and closer together – had become a certainty. Gouda was Razak and Razak was blown and now we all know where we stand – except Razak!

366

'Let's wait until he comes out then I'll go and have a look – see what he's been up to.'

'How will you know where he's been?'

'I'll use my nose!'

'I'm not with you.'

Cunningham continued looking down the road. Claude was one of today's protected youth; he was too young to have inhaled the mix of blood and cordite. Cunningham reckoned if Razak had done the business properly he'd smell it from a hundred yards.

'Don't let it worry you,' he assured the young man. 'I'll attend to that place, you stick with the target. You know where to reach me?'

'Sure. Oh, by the way, have you got someone else on the job as well?'

Cunningham looked at him sharply. 'Why?'

'There's a short-arsed pro had his eye on your Arab. Dark-haired fellow, height about 160, well dressed, fit. I might be mistaken – but I rarely am.'

'Where is he now?'

'If he's working, he's good – '

'Well?'

'I've lost him.'

'Thanks!'

The Frenchman shrugged his shoulders. These things happen. 'If you had asked me to follow him as well – ' He stopped and touched Cunningham's arm. 'There's your man – just come out of that entrance . . .'

They watched Razak as he disappeared in the direction of Porte de St Cloud. Cunningham was halfway out of his seat when the explosion from the building sent a shock wave up the street. Both men instinctively ducked as they watched the building come apart. They were far enough away to feel only the gentle wave of heat and the faint rumble under their feet but neither of them moved. They stared into each other's eyes, waiting for the noise and the flying debris to stop. The Frenchman stared, transfixed. Cunningham recovered quickly.

'Jesus!'

The Frenchman was aghast, but not for long. He grimaced and lit a cigarette. His hand shook. Nothing dramatic, just enough for him to need both hands to hold the match. 'What now?' he asked at length.

'We get out of here quickly,' snapped Cunningham. 'Follow him. I'll deal with him later. Keep your mouth shut. OK?'

'What about that?' the Frenchman waved his hand at the smoke-covered debris-littered street. 'What a bloody mess!'

'Not your business! Forget it. Talk to Frank about it. I'm off. Get after him.'

Cunningham turned on his heel and walked casually in the direction of Boulevard Murat. He glanced briefly over his shoulder. The Frenchman had gone.

40

It didn't take Razak very long to note that he had a tail. Claude was good, but not good enough for a man who'd spent most of his life under one form of surveillance or another. But having marked Claude, Razak let him come. He wasn't curious, but he had a fairly good idea. Jack Cunningham was the only person in Paris who would be interested in his movements and Razak had already read the signs. Cunningham had his doubts about him. These would be turned into cast-iron facts when he turned up at the address Razak had given him and found that the shop and the secret message was a figment of Razak's imagination. But he missed the Israelis. They had the resources and used them. Mullins handed Razak over to the local organization, who with a team of eight men and women, had no difficulty staying with him. For Razak, Claude was one thing; a bunch of Mossad agents was something else.

He stripped the Desert Eagle down to its components and dropped them one by one into different parts of the Seine. He disposed of the weapon without regret: it had served its purpose. That much lighter he made his way out of the city and, in a roundabout route, to Charles de Gaulle airport.

Making sure that Claude – and he'd now definitely decided he was Cunningham's man – was nearby he booked a late evening flight to Jordan's capital, Amman, then, having lost Claude he booked an Air France club class to London. He moved into the departure lounge, ignored the repeated calls for M. Gouda to present himself at the departure gate for Jordanian Airways Amman flight and tucked himself into the shower room in the Air France club class lounge until his flight to London was called. The Mossad team noted his departure, brought in a new face with a ticket to Heathrow and dispersed. Claude, for the fifth time, rang Jack Cunningham's Paris number.

At Heathrow Razak went underground and circumnavigated the airport. Surfacing at Terminal 4 he made a booking with United Airways for the 10.30 a.m. flight to Washington, and once again tucked himself in the far corner of the business class lounge where he dropped into a shallow and wary sleep. The Mossad agent found herself a spot overlooking the lounge entrance and spent the night drinking undrinkable coffee in polystyrene cups. She watched him disappear into the boarding tunnel and, thankfully, dragged out her Motorola ready to report that Razak had boarded his flight for Washington.

But Razak had done it again.

And she was too good an agent to let him get away with it. She waited for the boarding gate to close, and watched the charade.

Moving with the crowd under the covered ramp, Razak suddenly turned as if he'd forgotten something, retraced his steps and presented himself to a United Airlines ground steward. United weren't happy. In fact they were downright suspicious, but the fact that he had no luggage and was travelling on the US passport that Cunningham had given him, along with a hint of his CIA affiliation, persuaded them. He wanted to go, after all, not to Washington but to New York.

The phone stopped ringing just as Cunningham came through the door of his room.

He sat on the edge of the bed and lit a cigarette. It would ring again. It always did.

But he had to wait nearly half an hour.

'Mr Cunningham? It's Claude. I've been trying to ring you all evening. The target's at Charles de Gaulle. He's got himself a ticket on Royal Jordan, destination Amman. Flight leaves at 22:45 – they're boarding now . . .'

Cunningham let out a whoosh of cigarette smoke. But it wasn't agitation, it was something he'd half expected. Razak had completed his demolition job. He'd killed the rest of his team and stopped any leakage of information. He'd achieved what he'd set out to achieve, now he was going safe and tomorrow Cunningham reckoned he could expect a call from Amman telling him the good news and opening up the negotiations. Cunningham reckoned he'd just about summed it up. That's the way he would have done it. Give him a couple of days. Razak knew where to find him when he was ready.

'. . . You still there, Mr Cunningham?' asked Claude.

'Yeah. Have you still got him in sight?'

'No. He moved into the departure lounge. I can't go in there without a ticket. D'you want me . . . ?'

'No, don't bother. Thanks. You can go home now. See Frank in the morning. OK?'

'Goodnight, then.'

'Yeah, sure.'

41

Lou Mullins wasn't surprised when the message arrived at his hotel.

Nothing pretentious to look at, L'hôtel Stade was a small insignificant place, no restaurant, just rooms, sitting on the Boulevard Poniatowski near Vincennes. The fact that it was a Mossad safe house was neither here nor there.

The message was verbal, from the messenger to Mullins, direct, no intermediaries — it couldn't be safer: *Be in tonight at half-past seven*. No problem. If it wasn't urgent they wouldn't have bothered.

Mullins carried on sipping his brandy ginger ale when the Coordinator was shown into the private room at the back of the hotel. That too was safe. Israeli intelligence had an obsession with safety and security, which is why they rarely made the headlines in national newspapers. But Mullins was taken aback. He didn't show it, he never did, but for the Coordinator to leave Israel and meet him in the back room of a small Paris hotel Mullins was prepared to lower his glass and offer him a light smile.

He didn't get one back so he dismissed the smile and carried the glass back to his mouth. 'I read your report from Beirut,' said the Coordinator. 'I'd like to hear a bit more detail.'

'Is that what you came all this way for?'

The Coordinator nearly smiled. 'Get me a drink, Lou. A large Scotch, ice and water, not too much water. No, I came to see my sister — she lives in Montparnasse. She's not well.'

'That's as good as anything I've heard for getting out of the sun.' Mullins reached behind him and pressed the bell. The two men just looked at each other while they waited for the whisky to come. When the finely tuned waiter put the glass down in front of the Coordinator and left, Mullins lit a cigarette and began.

'The man Cunningham and Gouda killed was known. He was a former Hezbollah heavy who was used in the early days for booting Western hostages around. His name was Hisham Salih; he was on our Wet List. He was down for take-out. Gouda took his body north of Paris, drove into a wood and incinerated him and his car. He came back by train.'

'Why did they kill Salih?'

'I haven't put it together yet.' Mullins took another mouthful of brandy ginger ale and savoured it before swallowing. His cigarette lay smouldering in the ashtray; apart from lighting it, he hadn't touched it. 'But now comes the funny bit.'

'Not again!'

'Still peculiar. You won't want to laugh at this one. Cunningham put a local freelance on to following Gouda; looks like the honeymoon's over and jealousy has set in. Gouda thinks he's got Cunningham in his pocket — looks like the other way round. Either way, things are beginning to look mighty interesting. I went — '

'Just a minute.' The Coordinator stopped Mullins in full flow. He leaned forward and from his jacket pocket brought out a small folder. 'Before we go any further with Robin Gouda I want you to look at this.' He flipped out a postcard-size picture of Robin; it was one of those taken by Mullins in Beirut. 'That's Robin Gouda. Correct?'

Mullins looked at it. It didn't need a reply.

373

Another picture, same size, came out of the file. 'And that's Razak.'

It was the same picture but a beard had been technically superimposed and the hair, straggly and lengthened, altered the outline of Robin Gouda's head.

Mullins studied them closely. His expression hadn't changed but his eyes, previously bored-looking, were now sharper and keen. 'What made you do this?'

'Your mate Dahti. When you sent him back to Tel Aviv, he said there was something about this Robin Gouda that made his back itch, so he spent quite a long time playing with stacks of these pictures. This is what he came up with.'

Mullins pulled a face. 'Very technical, very professional. Some clothhead with nothing better to do draws beards and moustaches on photographs and pronounces that he's solved the crime. Come off it! He's just making himself useful.'

The Coordinator sipped his whisky carefully. There was a slightly mocking glint in his eye. 'We had Robin's flat done over again, this time properly ... We've also discovered who the real Robin was from the same source.'

'Source?'

'Fingerprints. Apart from those you picked up we collected a whole batch of more of the stuff and isolated the two most prominent. Dahti is still a member of GID, Iraqi Intelligence; he's reported himself still active and under-cover and given himself a codename. Baghdad's accepted him. He sent a packet of fingerprints for identification but they came up with only one name – '

'Razak?'

'Yeah.'

Mullins picked up his smouldering cigarette from the ashtray and puffed it back into life. His reaction didn't fool the other man and he paused for a second. Mullins put the cigarette back.

'Razak's his code name?'

374

The Coordinator nodded. 'Razak, under his real name, got into serious international trouble during the Gulf War. The British SAS want him for the torture of their people. He also murdered one of them . . .' The Coordinator lifted his glass for the first time but didn't drink. He raised his eyebrows. 'Doesn't surprise me in the least, although the British seem put out by it. Didn't they realize they were fighting Arabs?'

Mullins shrugged. He wasn't interested in the British or their little brawl in the Gulf. 'Did he get his knuckles rapped?'

'Who?'

'Razak.'

'Oh, no. Baghdad was quite pleased with him and promoted him after pronouncing him dead. He resurfaced with the codename "Razak" and infiltrated SAVAK . . .'

'Interesting man,' pronounced Mullins, sardonically. 'And Mr Dahti, I presume, came out of the business without a stain?'

The Coordinator shrugged. 'As far as we're concerned he's got a clean slate. If he was involved in chewing the bollocks of the SAS that's their business — we're not letting on. He's one of ours now.'

Mullins didn't bother commenting. 'What's the little hero up to now?'

'You don't really need to know, do you?'

'No,' said Mullins emphatically. 'So we know all about Razak and Robin Gouda. D'you want to hear the rest of my story?'

'It can't be half as interesting as mine.'

'Wanna bet?' Mullins drained his glass and rang the bell. He appeared to enjoy his second brandy ginger ale much more than the first. 'Razak found three of his old mates tucked up in a flat in the east of the city. I reckon he got the address from Salih, the guy he and Cunningham put down.

375

He seemed to know exactly where to go and didn't take Cunningham with him. Make of that what you will. But he took me, and I reckon I saw the contact he was looking for quite some time before he did.'

'Known?'

'Sure. His name was Mubin al-Harb – a very nasty bit of terrorism all on his own. He was due for the mad-dog treatment by me after the bag bomb in Hakirya but he dropped out of sight. He crops up in Paris meeting his old master from Beirut, Razak. Small world!'

'Any idea what they talked about? What they were planning?'

Mullins snorted. It was almost a laugh. 'I don't think the meeting was amicable. Razak blew the bloody building up. I hung around with a couple of hundred other rubberneckers to check the body count. Razak's sort don't do these things by half. Four men, two women and two children went up in that block of flats. One of the men was the concierge, I reckon the other three were Mubin Harb and his two pals. It looked to me like a gas and candle job; either that or the light switch and bulb. Nothing original. But however he did it, it was a very short fuse, he didn't give himself much time. He left the building and turned the corner and up it went – whoof! Before it happened Cunningham's man must have sent for him. Cunningham arrived just in time to see the bricks flying. Neither of them hung around.'

'D'you read anything into that?'

'Cunningham not hanging around? I reckon first of all he's blown Gouda; knows he's Razak and is taking him along – maybe Razak's got something Cunningham and his people want; maybe he's got some other sort of vendetta; maybe he wants to kill the bastard slowly! I honestly don't know at this stage. I'll tell you something though – '

'Go on.'

376

'I reckon he knew Razak was going for blood yesterday; he was almost encouraging him to wander off.'

'How d'you make that out?'

'Well, he didn't take his eyes off Razak until they'd laid Salih out. He wanted to be in on every part of the act. But then, suddenly he goes off with a chum and lets Razak loose — well, not really loose, with a French watcher dogging his footsteps.'

'What do you make of all that?'

Mullins shrugged. 'Nothing. He was going through the motions of a man with a tail. But then he's a suspicious bastard. And so he ought to be with his track record. I haven't sorted it out in my mind yet.' He smiled genuinely. 'But you'll be the first to know when I do. In the meantime I think I might consider taking out Razak and just watch Cunningham at play.'

The Coordinator stared hard at Mullins then nodded. It was almost agreement. But not quite. 'Don't take out Razak yet, Lou. He's stuck himself alongside Cunningham for a reason. It must go back to the American hostage, Thurston Macauley, Les Cohen and whatever it is Cunningham was briefed to find out. It may affect us. Personally I don't think it's anything to do with PLO, Hezbollah or any other local gang. My guess is it's something bigger; something international. Something like Iraq.'

Before Mullins could comment there was a discreet knock on the door.

The young man in a waiter's jacket entered, excused himself and handed Mullins a slip of paper. Mullins glanced at it and dismissed the man then slid the note across the table. 'Razak's on the move. I was right. Cunningham's blown his Robin Gouda cover. Razak booked himself a flight to Amman but didn't take it up. Instead he took one to London. From there he booked to Washington and played the same game. Now he leaves Heathrow by United Airways at half-past ten in the morning for New York.'

'What the hell's he going to New York for?'

'His destination's Washington. He's just making sure nobody's going with him. I don't blame him for that; it's frightened man stuff – we all do it.'

'OK, what's he going to Washington for?'

'Got something to sell. He must have dug something out of these three shit-heads in Paris before putting 'em down – now he's going into the market-place.'

The Coordinator stared at Mullins again. 'Is someone going to pick him up in New York?'

'He'll have a tail the minute he steps off the aircraft until he crawls into his hole. It'll be Washington. I'll stake my life on it.'

'Then you'd better go to Washington as well.' The Coordinator folded the note and handed it back to Mullins. 'What about Cunningham?'

'Let him run on his own. When he finds out Razak's done a bunk he'll be heading in the same direction – Washington. I'll stick with Razak and pick up Cunningham when he arrives. That shouldn't be too difficult.'

The Coordinator glanced at his watch. 'You get out to the airport now, Lou, I'll look after the rest of it. I'll have a word with Home to have some people waiting for Razak at JFK. If he reaches Washington the Al people can take it from there. I'll warn them to expect you.' The Coordinator picked up his glass and emptied its contents down his throat. 'I think you might need a bit of help.' He tapped his stomach and gave a discreet belch, 'I can feel it – in there!' He stood up. No handshake, no smile, no goodbye. 'I hope I don't read about you in the papers, Lou!'

42

From New York Razak caught the Business Express to
Baltimore and from there the Greyhound into Washington.
He hadn't spotted the AI watcher team who presented
Mullins, when he arrived at Dulles airport, with a complete
rundown on Razak's behaviour and a note of where he was
staying in Washington. Two Mossad agents booked into the
same hotel. Razak wasn't going to be able to spit without
Mullins being informed.

'Take it easy,' Mullins warned his opposite number.
'Don't crowd him. As soon as he feels secure enough he'll
be in touch with Cunningham.'

'You sure about this, Lou?'

'I'll tell you in a couple of days! In the meantime, get in
touch with Paris and tell them to keep a tighter than usual
watch on Cunningham. I want him tagged the minute he
arrives in Washington. No balls-ups, please.'

Razak allowed himself the rest of the night in bed. First
thing in the morning he took a cab to the junction of M
Street and Connecticut and drank coffee opposite the
American Express building.

At nine o'clock the building came to life. By half-past
nine the place was humming and Razak presented himself
at the enquiries counter. The formalities were simple.
Macauley's membership number, his handwritten note

authorizing Mubin al-Harb to take possession of an envelope left in American Express safekeeping were sufficient.

It required only the additional proof that Razak was indeed Mr Harb and the envelope was handed over on his signature.

'Did you get a sight of what it was that came over the counter?' Mullins asked Razak's watcher.

'Only that it was an envelope. Bulky. Had come in from abroad by the look of the number of stamps on it.'

'And that's the best you can do?'

'Sorry.'

'Try and get a look. But don't hassle him.'

Razak returned to his café, ordered more coffee and broke open the envelope. It was all there; everything Harb said Thurston Macauley had told him was in the envelope, clearly in black and white.

He stuffed the sheets of paper back in the envelope, folded it and stuck it in his inside pocket, then made his way back to the hotel.

With the door locked and a DO NOT DISTURB sign hanging from the outside knob he settled himself at the writing desk. Macauley's friends would want proof of possession. He selected one of the sites and copied them on to a sheet of plain paper. When he'd finished he compared it with the original and shook his head admiringly. Respect where respect was due – Razak pursed his lips. Macauley must have had a magnificent brain; that, and a great gift of recall. A beautiful memory.

He checked the copy word by word, figure by figure.

Letter Identification:

$$\frac{64w}{100,000 \text{ M.SO}}$$

32° 10' N × 37° 10' E
Code coverted to Grid
Zone
0128–0135

Below this he added the basics of the components stored in the depot. Even with his unscientific eye it looked a serious list of nuclear hard and software, and this one was the least important of the three major dumps. Satisfied, he folded the copy and placed it in a separate envelope. The rest went back into its original packet. Checking that he'd left nothing incriminating lying around, Razak left the room and locked the door behind him.

The two Mossad agents watched him leave the hotel. As soon as he was out of sight they went over his room with a fine toothcomb. Razak was a professional. It didn't take them long to admit it to themselves. There was nothing of interest: the waste basket was empty, the blotter unmarked. They reported their findings to Mullins. He wasn't surprised.

The taxi dropped Razak off at Union Station where he made a photocopy of all the documents he'd collected at American Express. These copies he put in another envelope, sealed it and, with a brief handwritten note, placed this inside another, stronger envelope which he addressed to the Securities Manager of Kaiser & Kaiser et Cie, Zurich, Switzerland. He dropped this in one of the mail boxes in the station. That done, and with relief etched on his face, he left the station, crossed Massachusetts Avenue and walked to the post office on the corner of North Capitol Street. Pausing for a moment to get his bearings, he found what he was looking for and handed the originals, in their sealed packet, to the pretty girl at the counter for stamping. It was prominently marked TO BE COLLECTED and addressed to himself at General Delivery, Washington DC 20090. Well satisfied with his morning's work he caught a yellow cab to Dfouny's Lebanese restaurant in Alexandria.

He kept lunch going until half-past two with numerous cups of thick, sweet coffee. After a quick glance at the sheet of paper in his pocket to remind himself of the name and telephone number Macauley had given Mubin Harb, he left the restaurant and went in search of a public phone.

Razak dialled the number. The phone was picked up at the other end almost immediately. After a short pause a voice grated in Razak's ear.

'Doerflinger.'

43

Mullins bit a huge lump out of his hot salt beef sandwich and chewed. The man and woman sitting at the counter with him watched and drank their coffee. He took his time.

'So, whatever it is, there are now two copies of it?' He took another bite and continued talking and chewing at the same time. 'One's in a mail box in Union Station being watched over by our Ron and the other's locked up in a box in the Post Office. Tell me again, where's this one in the mail box going?'

The woman agent answered. 'Switzerland.'

'That's the best you can do?'

'You said not to hassle him.'

Mullins finished his sandwich, wiped his mouth with a paper napkin then rubbed his hands together. He swallowed a mouthful of tea. 'So what's Ron's plan?'

The woman took a deep breath. 'When the mailman comes to collect Ron's going to plead with him before he opens it that he's posted a packet and forgotten to put something important in it. Ron knows how to play this game, he can lay it on very thick – he's got a sympathetic face. He'll tell the collector that it's so important he'll lose his job if the packet goes without this important addition. I'm not sure whether there's any law against the guy digging it out and letting him have it – there probably is. But Ron can describe the packet, he knows where it's going . . .'

'He only knows it's going to Switzerland,' said Mullins. 'What if the guy's agreeable but wants the rest of the address?'

'He'll have a $50 note sticking out of his fist.'

'And if that doesn't work?'

'Ron'll duck out of the picture and David and Rafi'll go in hard and put the mailman down. They'll make it look like an ordinary heist and clear off with everything he emptied from the box.'

Mullins pulled a face and swallowed more tea. 'Messy,' he pronounced when he replaced his mug on the counter.

'What would you do?'

Mullins smiled. 'Exactly what you've done.'

44

Cunningham kept the taxi driver waiting while he dropped his bag off at his apartment then jumped back in and had him drive to Dupont Circle.

He dispelled any suggestion of tiredness with a brisk head-clearing walk down 19th Street to Sam & Harry's and brought it back again with two large gins and tonic. They banished any suggestion of jet lag. He consulted his watch to see how far away from lunch it was. His watch was still set at Paris time; he should be having his dinner. He reset his watch for Washington time and joined everyone else at lunch. Maine lobster and a massive, rare dry-aged Château-briand. It was a more than adequate substitute. While he was waiting for his coffee and a large Hennessy he slipped out to the telephone.

It was Doerflinger's hard luck again. Cunningham caught him just as he dropped over the edge. 'Joe, I want to see you before I start dealing with Razak.'

Doerflinger dragged himself awake. 'Sure. Meet me in the Sitting Duck at McLean — what's the time now?'

'Twenty past two.'

'Gimme half an hour. I'll see you there.'

Doerflinger was already in place when Cunningham's taxi dropped him off outside the imitation English pub. He was halfway down his over-chilled glass of lager and, as usual, hadn't touched the double measure of Jack Daniels.

It was a much more effective kick-start after an afternoon nap than a cup of Lipton's tea and a Nice biscuit.

'D'you want one of these?' he asked, remaining firmly perched on the leather-topped bar stool.

Cunningham shook his head. 'Coffee, black, hot, large.'

'One of those, is it, Jack?'

Cunningham grunted. He tasted his coffee and pulled a face. It was too hot and it wouldn't do any good. He caught the barman's eye. 'Bring me a Johnnie Walker Blue Label – no water, no ice – and a cold bottled beer.' He turned back to Doerflinger. 'Did you mention my name to Razak when he rang you?'

Doerflinger shook his head. 'He opened the bidding by saying that he'd been in contact with Thurston Macauley, who'd given him my name and my listed number, and he had certain information that Macauley would have liked to pass on. I didn't interrupt. I didn't encourage him. I just said go on, to let him know he'd got the right place. He said this information concerned the Ash-Sham desert in Jordan and he was the only person, other than a select few principals in Baghdad, who had this information.' Doerflinger took a large swig of Jack Daniel's and continued staring straight ahead into the mirror behind the bar. His eyes were locked on to Cunningham's. 'After a long pause he said he'd like to negotiate the transfer of this information. I gave him your phone number – no name, just the number – and told him to say nothing more but to ring that number in two days' time and the person who answered would be fully empowered to discuss and negotiate as necessary.'

'What'd he say to that?'

'Not a lot he could say, Jack. He thanked me and hung up. Very polite, no histrionics – sounded to me like a man very sure of himself and the holder of extremely good cards.'

'Why didn't you deal with him yourself, Joe?'

Doerflinger swallowed a mouthful of beer to chase the whisky. When it had caught up he turned his head from the mirror and glanced sideways at Cunningham. 'For the simple reason, Jack, that you're supposed to be handling the bloody thing. Like I told you at the beginning, any fallout stops with you. I don't want this coming anywhere near the President, and that means me too; any shit that hits my fan is bound to splatter him. That's why, Jack. Now, you had the bastard in Paris and you let him give you the slip. You could have burned the bugger there and then – '

'Wrong, Joe. Killing him wouldn't have done us any good. Paris is where he finalized his game. He ran down the only other people who might have known the locations of Saddam's Ash-Sham desert project and put them out of business. It's my guess that Thurston, before blacking out gave your number and name to one of them. I doubt he'd have given it to Razak because that would definitely have meant the end – Razak would have killed Thurston and lost his body. No question about it. And Mac knew this. So, as I said, he compromised you so that the information about Iraq's nuclear position wouldn't be buried. He didn't want to waste his life or that of his Iraqi contact so that a bunch of ignorant Palestine *jundies* could sit on this time bomb and not know what to do with it. OK, so Razak gave me the slip. That doesn't worry me. If he hadn't turned up here I'd have gone after the bastard some other way. He still owes us for Macauley.'

Doerflinger's expression remained blank. 'Jack, I don't think there's room in this affair for grudge. It's too big; the stakes are too high. The information first, the assurance that no one else has been, or is going to be, offered it and then action to neutralize the problem. Grudges come a long way behind that lot.'

'I'll go along with that,' said Cunningham, equally blank faced. 'But when it's finished I want the bastard to suffer.

Razak is the last of the team that operated on Mac – he's the one who rolled him up at Rome airport, brought him to Beirut and did most of the work on him; he's the one who tied up Mac's stake money and has got it spread around in accounts of his own choosing. Now, with details of the locations of these nuclear holding or component dumps containing Iraq's entire stock of plutonium he's sitting pretty. If you leave this up to me, without interference I'll strip him of all that and still make the bastard pay for what he did to Thurston.' He turned fully on his bar stool so that he faced Doerflinger. 'Will you give me that, Joe?'

'What?'

'A free hand.'

Doerflinger knocked back the remains of his Jack Daniel's then finished his glass of beer in one go. He pointed to Cunningham's untouched drinks. 'D'you want another of those?'

'Answer me, Joe.'

'No answer necessary, Jack. You've had that from the word go. How d'you propose, as you say, to make this bastard suffer?'

'I'm not sure you'd agree . . .'

'D'you want to try me?'

Cunningham went to work on his whisky; it didn't really need anything to help it along but the ice-cold beer gave it that tiny little edge. He wiped his lips.

'I want to bury him.'

'Why wouldn't I agree with that?' said Doerflinger.

'You know what Razak did to Thurston?'

'Sure. You told me. And I've seen him. I've watched him and I've cried for him He just gazes blankly into space, can't talk, at least he can't talk any sense, just makes sounds. He won't walk again properly – he's going to have about as much quality of life as a bunch of fucking grapes. Does that

tell you enough? Tell me what you want to do with this
Razak guy and I'll come and dance on the bastard's grave
with you.'

Cunningham looked Doerflinger in the eye and told him
what he had in mind for Razak. He even drew him a
diagram. When he'd finished Doerflinger stared hard at
Cunningham and for some time said nothing. When he
finally spoke it was short.

'Jesus Christ!'

'I want your help with it.' There was no plea in
Cunningham's voice; no appeal in his expression. Doerflinger studied him closely. Cunningham had every intention
of going ahead with his plan, with or without the help of
Joe Doerflinger.

'Give me the alternatives?'

Cunningham didn't have to think about them. 'When
we've sucked him dry we hand him over to the legals and
within ten minutes every newspaper in the world will
know about the nuclear dumps. Iraq'll have their stuff out
of the Ash-Sham desert before Razak's first hearing. The
money? Great stuff for Iraq if that comes out. Everything
you've been trying to avoid – the President of the United
States tried to bribe a member of Saddam Hussein's family
to betray his country. That'll rank fairly highly against the
Iran/Contra affair. You can't afford that – neither can the
President. And what are you going to charge Razak with?
Beating up a member of the President's staff who, with the
President's explicit approval, moved huge sums of money
around Europe in concealed accounts? Razak would walk
out of the court laughing. Those are the alternatives.'

'But, Jesus, Jack, it's still a bit extreme, ain't it?'

'Sure,' said Cunningham over the top of his glass of
whisky. 'But, political considerations apart, so was what
happened to Mac. All I'm interested in is making the
bastard pay; your interests go further. The money Razak

389

took from Thurston goes back into the Treasury; the information that that money bought goes into the President's ear; the man who caused the damage is punished. That's the sum total.'

'But, Jesus! What a fuckin' way to go!'

'Talk to Thurston about that.'

'See what you mean. OK. You won't mind my saying, Cunningham, that in my opinion you ought to be a fucking Arab! You've got a more twisted mind than any of the bastards involved in this business.'

Cunningham shrugged. 'I want a safe house – ultra safe. A new one known only to you and a caretaker, and this – ' he tapped the scrap of paper he'd been drawing on – 'ready in, say, three days. Also, no one else in on it, Joe. Is that a deal?'

Doerflinger brought his right hand over his left and held it out. Cunningham shook it. 'Got a caretaker in mind?'

Doerflinger nodded. 'D'you know Sam Keble?'

Cunningham shook his head.

'Safest pair of hands in this business. He'd swallow razor blades for me. I think this job's right up his street. I trust him.'

'OK. Can I leave the details up to you, then?'

'Sure – but . . .'

'But what, Joe?'

'It's extreme. What if it got out?'

'Of course it's fucking extreme – and how's it going to get out? I'm not going to tell anybody. Are you?'

Doerflinger considered his misgivings for the best part of a minute. 'Maybe we could get this Razak into a negotiating position and discuss a deal. He keeps the money and his life, we get the information?'

'I thought we'd decided what happens to him,' said Cunningham coldly. 'No deals, Joe. We'll get what we want our way. I'm not negotiating with this shit.'

'Second thoughts, Jack. I don't want to sound wet on this but we've got to consider flexibility. He's sure to have covered his ass against exactly what you propose for him; he's not going to walk up to you and start negotiating without first telling you, look – you try any funny stuff with me and copies of this go straight to Baghdad. That happens and Saddam'll have his stuff out of the fucking desert quicker than you can say shit! and we'll be back where we started. We've gotta be interested in a deal? If there's one in the offing that doesn't reduce us to the status of animals like him we'd have to think about it.'

Cunningham didn't even consider it. 'Trust me, Joe.'

'Trust you, Jack? The security of the biggest fuckin' secret in the world – that that mad bastard Saddam Hussein will shortly be in a position to scatter nuclear warheads around the place like fuckin' confetti – is now dependent on the ball-catching ability of another fuckin' Arab! And you say "Trust me." Great! I think I'll move my bed into the nuclear bunker for the next five years!'

Cunningham didn't share Doerflinger's fun. He stood up, tipped the rest of his whisky down his throat and said, 'Start putting that safe house together. Could you put half a dozen all-rounders on standby on an emergency number – just in case. If I need them they act on my word, code – ' Cunningham thought for a moment – 'Thurston. Might not need them, but you never can tell . . . I'll be in touch, Joe.'

It all happened so quickly. 'Hang on, Jack! We haven't finished yet – where you going?'

'See you, Joe!'

45

With no sign of smugness or triumph on her face the Mossad agent placed on the table in front of Mullins the packet Razak had dropped in the mail box at Union Station. It was unopened.

After she'd left, Mullins slit the thick envelope, emptied its contents and spread them out in front of him. He read Razak's letter to the Kaiser & Kaiser Bank with the merest twitch of his thick black eyebrows. He wasn't prepared for the contents of the second envelope but it didn't take him long to work out what it was all about. '*Shit! Shit! Shit!*' he swore vehemently, as he grasped the implications of the references and details of the locations in the Ash-Sham desert. 'So this was what it was all about; this is what Cohen and Lev went up the spout for. I wonder if it was all worth it? As if it ever was . . .' It didn't worry him that he was talking to himself; he knew he was bordering on lunacy. But this was something else! He let out a couple more ripe expletives, stuffed everything back as it was and put the whole lot into a special file.

He took it himself to the Israeli embassy on International Drive and was shown straight into the Ambassador's private room. A safe room – it had to be, with Jordan's embassy sitting just on the rise behind them and the microwaves bouncing off the blanketed windows.

The Ambassador – who knew more than Mullins about coded map references and what would constitute a major

392

nuclear surprise in Tel Aviv – wasted no time. Within an hour he had a private jet on the tarmac at Washington National waiting to whisk him to New York and an El Al 747 Tel Aviv direct delayed for his arrival at JFK.

The following morning Mullins was summoned to the embassy.

He stuck the red telephone to his ear and waited.

'This man Razak,' said a voice he knew well, 'has to be taken out of circulation. No mess, nothing wet, nothing to upset our friends in Washington. Understood?'

'Yes, sir.'

'He's to be brought back here with a sack over his head. No publicity. It's your responsibility, Mullins.'

'I understand that, sir. But the Americans have been after this man and have one of their top people dealing with him. I think they're about to open negotiations with Razak on the contents of the packet that has just been delivered to you – '

The interruption was curt, and abrupt.

'They are not to talk to him. Play them out of the game, Mullins, and get that man here. Is that understood? I repeat – play them out of the game . . .'

The phone went dead in Mullins's ear.

There was another surprise for him when he got back to his hotel.

'We've lost Razak.'

'What the hell d'you mean, you've lost Razak?'

'Just that, Lou. The guy's a pro, we knew that. We thought we had him covered from every angle; he must have marked one of us. It was the simple switch. He just left his hotel, taxi to the station, on to a Greyhound, off first stop, through the ticket office and round the back and a last-minute hop. We managed to get a taxi behind the Greyhound and went the distance with it but he wasn't on it . . .'

'Surprise, surprise! Dickheads!' But Mullins knew the form. Losing a target was always a fifty-fifty option; with a professional the odds went up in his favour. 'Go out and look for the bastard, and don't go to bed until you find him. He's wanted at Home – urgently. Go on! Get out there! Simon – ' he jerked his thumb at a smooth-skinned young man lounging in the corner watching his fellow AI agents getting stick – 'you come with me. Bring your stuff. I've got a job for you.'

46

It was several weeks since Cunningham had spent any time in his apartment but it was spotless, tidy, and welcoming.

He pulled his tie off, threw his jacket on a chair and walked through to the kitchen. There were no surprises, Mrs Lamazares had done her stuff. Every other morning she cleaned the apartment; every other morning she put in a new quart of milk and a carton of fresh orange juice; every other morning she took out the one she'd put in before and threw it away. She would never take it home for herself; for a poor Hispanic she had expensive hygiene values – anything more than two days old was not worth having.

He opened the fridge and poured himself a pint mug of full cream milk, flipped off his shoes, and propped himself up on the bed. The milk did a very good job. He awoke with a stiff back and a sore neck at nine the next morning. His mouth felt like a well used bird's nest but three cups of scalding black coffee brought some feeling back into it and jerked his mind back on to last night's closing subject.

Everything was still there, flicking away at the back of his mind like the jumbled images in the tube of a child's kaleidoscope. It just needed the right twist to sharpen and highlight the pattern.

He finished the last of the percolated coffee, stripped, and stood for fifteen minutes under a lukewarm shower allowing the pressured water needles to bring his brain back to life. He shaved, draped himself in a towelling robe and went back and sat full length on the bed and waited for the phone to ring.

Razak had no idea who was following him. That he had a tail had taken him by surprise; no one knew he was in Washington, certainly not Jack Cunningham, not yet, and even if he did, Washington DC was far too big a place for him to have been marked so quickly. It worried him that somebody was interested in his movements but he had no doubt of his ability to shake them off.

He spotted the first at a clumsy handover. A brief eye contact, a quick glance away and he was marked. After that it was easy – he logged four of the Mossad watchers and promptly lost them and went to ground for two days in a third-rate hotel in the dilapidated north-east quadrant of the city. It was from here he telephoned the number Doerflinger had given him.

The monosyllabic 'hello' gave him no clues.

'Mr Doerflinger gave me this number to ring,' he said after a reflective pause.

'OK, Razak,' said Cunningham. 'Let's hear what you've got to sell.'

Razak's mouth clamped like a trap. He stared hard at the phone in his hand as if expecting Jack Cunningham to crawl out of it. It took him several seconds to recover his composure. 'Is that you, Jack? Jack Cunningham?'

'You know it is. Get on with the business.'

'We've a lot to talk about, Jack . . . When did you realize who I was?'

'We've fuck-all to talk about, Razak, except the merchandise you discussed with Doerflinger. Talk about that and the conditions for its exchange. That's all.'

'Jack, there are things I'd like to explain . . .'

'Razak,' barked Cunningham, 'if you don't start talking business in ten seconds I'm putting the phone down.'

'Don't do that, Jack.' Razak glanced up and down the scruffy corridor and jammed more coins into the payphone on the wall. His voice hardened. 'You know what I'm selling, but I'm not doing it over the phone. We'll have to meet . . .'

'Name the place. Bring something with you and I'll give a decision on the spot.'

'It's not as easy as that, and you know it. There are some conditions that need to be discussed.' He glanced up and down again: nothing moved, there was no sound, he could have been the only person in the hotel. But he knew he wasn't – it was that sort of hotel, nobody drew attention to themselves. He lowered his voice. 'I want to see you on your own in a public place; if you bring anybody with you I'll spot them and the whole thing's off. A word of warning, Jack. I've taken every precaution; I've covered myself with foreign insurance. You know what that means. If anything happens to me and I can't make contact with my insurers everything becomes null and void – the information that you are negotiating for will go back to Baghdad and you know how quick they are at shifting evidence.' He smiled to himself at the thought of Saddam Hussein's people scurrying around the Ash-Sham desert digging new holes and new caves before the Americans arrived. 'You understand what I'm saying, Jack? No tricks, or no deal. OK?'

Cunningham had got it all worked out.

'What are you bringing?'

'What Doerflinger asked for – evidential collateral. I'm bringing references and details of one of the dumps.'

'OK. Meet me at the Pomona Hotel – it's in George-town, M Street end of Pennsylvania Avenue. The main foyer between four and five.'

'Pomona Hotel,' repeated Razak. 'If I don't like it, or the atmosphere, or if there's anybody there I don't like the look of I won't make contact. But you only get one chance after that, Jack. Make sure it's clean or you lose the deal.'

Razak allowed himself a brief smile as he hung up the receiver and collected his unused coins. As he walked down the gloomy passage he glanced at his watch. Not far off lunchtime. A good time for a preliminary reconnaissance of the Pomona Hotel in Georgetown.

Cunningham's jaw was set tight when he replaced the receiver. He walked across the room to the heavy colonial chest of drawers against the side wall and pulled open the right-hand top drawer. From the back of the drawer he took an almost new SIG-Sauer P229, unused in anger but well tested. It wasn't something he normally carried around Washington but when he held his fingers up and counted the number of Razak's killings in the last couple of weeks he decided a little discomfort might be a small price to pay. He threaded a leather thong on to his belt to house the gun, checked the twelve-round magazine, slid a round into the breech and topped up the magazine again. Thirteen rounds of .357 SIG in Washington DC was enough to start and finish a small war.

When he'd dressed he went back to the phone and dialled a local number. He gave his name and said, 'Book me two, please. Yeah, me and a friend – couple of hours, OK? Thanks.'

On his way out he stepped into Mario's delicatessen, said a quick hello to Mario's wife, went into the office at the end of the shop and picked up the phone. He dialled the number Doerflinger had given him.

'*Thurston,*' he said.

'Hold on.'

'What is it, Jack?' Joe Doerflinger came on the line.

'What the hell, Joe!'

'I wasn't going to miss out on this one. I'm blocking for you; I'm running this team. Say what you want.'

'Fuck you, Joe! You're out of date.'

'Sure, but you're stuck with me! Get on with it.'

Cunningham gritted his teeth at himself in the mirror on the wall. 'I'm meeting the target at the Pomona Hotel – M Street end of Pennsylvania – somewhere between four and five. It's just a feeling. I'd like to have someone watch my back, but it'd better be somebody good – very good. He's no slouch is Razak, he can smell a watcher a mile away. When I've finished talking with him I'm taking him away . . .'

'What about the – '

'Fuck it, Joe. We agreed to do it my way.'

'Go on.'

'He may object. Got the picture?'

'Got it.'

47

Lou Mullins wound down the window of the car and let the smoke out. Simon breathed a sigh of relief, but kept it to himself. A non-smoker, he'd be glad when someone else got the job of driving the chain-smoking Lou Mullins around Washington.

'What's special about the Pomona Hotel?' asked Mullins. The driver was busy flipping through a small, hard-covered book on his lap. 'Nothing. It's just a hotel. Usual thing. Rooms, bars, couple of restaurants, health club, sauna — normal run of stuff. He's arranged to meet with Razak there and that number he's just rung is the Pomona Hotel.'

'And he booked two,' murmured Mullins. 'Two of what?'

'Whores?'

Mullins shook his head. 'I've decided Razak's a shirt-lifter, as far as I know he doesn't like cunt.'

Simon shrugged and bent his head over the open suitcase on the console between them. He fine-tuned one of the dials. It was unnecessary: the sounds coming from Cunningham's flat were as clear and crystal as a newly cut CD.

'Find out what it was and book me two as well,' said Mullins to the top of Simon's head. He brought his flat eyes back to the windows of Cunningham's apartment which overlooked the road. Their car was at the top end, neatly enclosed in the long line of parked vehicles; the only thing that distinguished them from their neighbours was the regular winding down of the passenger-seat window for the evacuation of Mullins's used smoke. He studied Cunningham's windows inexpressively. It was all very clever stuff. Technics always amazed him. Mullins wasn't technical, his trade was death not devices, but he was fascinated, nevertheless.

'Where've you got this stuff arranged?'

The driver *was* technical, as was the rest of his team. They belonged to a Mossad Al group brought out from deep undercover only in exceptional circumstances; all specialists in their own field, each of them a *katsa*, they were the highest rated of Mossad intelligence agents. This one was Simon; just Simon, nothing else, not even to Lou Mullins.

'We've got a special facility on his phone. It's activated by this – ' he tapped the now closed briefcase. 'We send out short-wave high-frequency megacycles – '

'You've lost me,' remarked Mullins in a bored voice. 'Why doesn't he run a check over the place?'

'It's permanently on check,' replied Simon smugly, 'but they haven't come across this refinement yet.' He took Mullins's yawn as an indication of tiredness and overwork, and jet lag. He couldn't imagine anybody being bored with the technicalities of listening to other people's conversations. But Mullins was.

'OK, I'll take your word for it. We can hear everything that goes on up there whether it's on the phone or not – and he doesn't know we're doing it?'

'Not unless they've discovered a counter-beam in the last half-hour!'

'Very smart!' said Mullins caustically. 'What about the Arab – Razak?'

'We've lost him, haven't we?'

'Don't remind me. Can't you find where he's staying from that call?'

'No way! Anyway, from what I've seen of the guy it'll be a public phone. It ties in with Cunningham's opening conversation. Razak's too smart to use his own phone, it's all part of his upbringing – he's too shifty a bastard to use a phone where he's sleeping.'

'He was very free with Cunningham,' said Mullins.

'Sure. But you know the Arab mind – this is Washington USA, and Cunningham's an American. The poor schmuck can't see the Americans bugging their own and doesn't think anybody else would want to! That's why he thinks he's in a medicine box when he's in a Washington public phone.'

'Very enlightening!'

'What d'you think Razak's going to do now?'

'He's going to pull a fast one over his American friend – ' Mullins lit another cigarette and crushed the end of the previous one into the little ashtray – 'and I want to be near before he even starts.' He dragged half an inch off the end of the cigarette and pointed it at the briefcase. 'Will this thing work anywhere?'

'Only on phones. But I've got other stuff that'll pick up medium- to short-range voices.'

'Indoors?'

'Depends.'

'On what?'

'Circumstances.'

'Which tells me precisely fuck-all!' Mullins wound down the window and helped the smoke out of the window with a heavy exhalation. 'Keep the close watch on Razak and carry on with Cunningham. Have someone behind me as well – at all times. Go and give that hotel Cunningham mentioned a good going over. I want to know all about it – its exits, back doors, side doors, downstairs arrangements, everything. This is where we're going to pick the bastard up and take him Home. I want the whole place covered and, if something does go wrong and he gets close to Cunningham, I want you to get their conversation . . . OK?'

'No problem. You walking now?' Simon said hopefully.

Mullins stretched his short legs as far as they would go and folded his arms across his chest. The cigarette he left between his lips but had to narrow his eyes to avoid the steady stream of smoke that corkscrewed past his nose. He looked contented.

'No, not just yet. I think I'll stay here a little longer with you, son. I'm enjoying your company.'

Simon smiled. It was a forced, sickly smile.

Mullins made himself look invisible in the main lounge of the Pomona Hotel. It wasn't difficult. It was a popular hotel and it was crowded, and after spending all day in Cunningham's shadow he was glad to settle down with a pot of coffee and selection of Danish pastries.

From where he sat he could see Simon, every inch the thrusting salesman in his navy blue pinstripe with his well worn hard leather briefcase, glancing nervously at his watch as he waited for a late client. Simon was a great actor. He put everything he had into the part he was playing.

Mullins chewed a lump out of one of the plate-size Danish pastries and played spot-the-rest-of-the-Mossad-team. They were the best in the business. Apart from Simon he spotted only one other, but he knew that somewhere in the vast atrium another four pairs of Israeli eyes were either watching Cunningham or searching the crowd for Razak.

Mullins wouldn't have bet money that he was the first to see him.

Razak didn't make the mistake of standing inside the door gazing around him. He did it all properly, as though he'd been going in and out of the hotel most of his life. He walked purposely, but not hurriedly, with a couple who

403

were making their way obliquely across the open floor towards one of the reception areas. Without changing pace he glided to the left and walked into the book shop; he did a round of the shelves, ending up on the inside of the main window where he stood with the latest Princess Di book open, his eyes not looking down at the words but quartering the atrium.

Razak spotted Cunningham sitting openly in one of the scattered armchairs against a wall reading the *Washington Times*. He spent another five minutes leafing through his book and taking in the ambience of the auditorium. He saw nothing to disturb his equanimity, and finally replaced the book on its pile and left the shop.

Cunningham didn't see Razak until he sat down beside him.

'Don't say anything,' Cunningham said without lowering the paper. 'Not yet. Let's go somewhere where we can't be overheard.'

'You have a room here?' said Razak without turning his head.

'Something better,' said Cunningham, 'the safest place in Washington. Follow me when I get up . . .'

'Remember what I said, Jack.' Razak swivelled his eyes round the foyer and back to Cunningham. 'No tricks.'

Cunningham folded his newspaper and got slowly to his feet. Turning to the right he walked past the stairs leading to the overhanging mezzanine with its fine salons and perfumeries and took the wide corridor leading to one of the banks of king-sized elevators. Razak dogged his footsteps and when the bell pinged and the doors hissed open he joined Cunningham and six or seven other people standing with their eyes glued to the flitting floor indicator. For a second he lowered his eyes and met those of Cunningham. Cunningham gave the merest blink and at the fourth floor stepped out into the plush landing. Two other passengers did the same.

'Wrong floor!' Cunningham stole a glance at Razak as the other people walked off, leaving the two men on their own. Cunningham pressed the button on the opposite side and leaned casually against the wall as he waited for the down lift.

Followed by Razak, he entered the new lift and stood nearest the doors. He reached over and pressed the button marked HEALTH CLUB. The only buttons below it were to the three basements of private parking.

Mullins and Simon, standing out of the way at the back of the crowd of passengers, wandered unhurriedly out of the lift and followed Cunningham and Razak into the health club while the female member of the team carried on down to the garage. She immediately went up by another elevator to the atrium where she reported to the senior Mossad *katsa*, who began calmly reorganizing his team.

Mullins stood at the reception and waited while Cunningham and Razak were each handed a cellophane-wrapped towelling robe and a giant-sized bath towel in the hotel's pale blue livery. Razak looked doubtful but allowed himself to be drawn into the club by Cunningham.

Mullins didn't glance round as he went through the door of the sauna. He knew where Cunningham and Razak were going; he hoped everybody else in the building knew too.

Simon said 'Shit!' when he saw the towels and robes being dished out, but Mullins just marched in, and on, as though it was his regular late afternoon sport. One of the girls had booked 'two for Mr Mullins'. Simon cursed her under his breath. She'd said it was a health club – she hadn't mentioned a room full of fucking heat and sweat and half-naked bodies! 'Can you do anything?' asked Mullins when, naked, he joined Simon in his changing room.

'It doesn't make it easy – '.

'If everything in life was easy we'd all be lying on the beach sucking oranges. It ain't – so get your bloody finger out and do something. Do these sound intensifiers work in steam?'

'This is not steam. It's just fucking sweat, and I can't take my box in there with me . . .'

'Got anything else?'

'I might have. But I hope nobody's lying around in there with a short-wave box. I'll have to put this robe on to hide the lance; I can stick it down the sleeve . . .'

'Come on, don't get carried away. I want to be in there before them.'

'Won't my dressing gown look out of place?'

Mullins grinned. 'You've been in civilization too bloody long. There'll be at least one other guy dressed like you in there – that bloody Arab. Remember? They don't like flashing their pricks, or any other bit of skin around – '

'That's a great comfort!'

'Come on, stop fucking around – let's go and listen to what they've got to say to each other.'

The individual changing rooms were luxurious by any standard and Razak's natural Muslim reticence in displaying his unclothed body was assuaged by their privacy.

'Sauna,' grunted Cunningham. He was waiting outside Razak's changing room and watched while he turned the security lock on the door: 'then we'll finish off in the Jacuzzi. You can talk here. No one can listen in. Just a minute – ' He turned and stood in front of Razak. 'Put your hands up.'

Razak stared at him, his face darkening. 'What?'

'You either take that robe off or put your hands up and let me assure myself you've got nothing more than your body in that thing.'

'Ahhh! Always the suspicious one, Jack. Good! You're learning . . .'

Cunningham's expression didn't alter as he made Razak open his robe and turn round. 'OK, let's go.'

'After you,' said Razak curtly, and tightened the belt of his robe round his shapeless waist. He was uncomfortable. This wasn't his choice of scene; he felt he'd been hijacked and was at a disadvantage but he followed Cunningham along the thickly carpeted corridor and through the door marked SAUNA.

Cunningham had no difficulty finding a discreet corner in the dry heated room. He was comfortable and relaxed here; he had no security hang-ups. How could he? He was in the heart of the capital of the United States, deep in the bowels of one of its most plush hotels and there was no reason, from his reading of the game, for Razak to take fright. If Doerflinger and his men were anywhere around they weren't making themselves obvious. Cunningham settled back in his chair.

But Razak saw it all differently. Inured to a lifetime of double double-cross, of cheating and lying, of ducking and weaving, he was never relaxed in surroundings not of his own choosing. Surreptitiously, he studied the people that he could see. A short hairy man in a towel that barely covered his midriff; he glanced into the face. No eye contact. The man wasn't interested in anything but his sauna. Razak slotted him. He'd been in the lift. Beside the hairy man another one: black hair, pale face glistening with perspiration and, like himself, modestly wrapped in his towelling robe. But he wasn't with them; he lay back in a slatted chair his eyes, trancelike, on the ceiling above Razak's head as he beat time with his left hand to the sound from the Walkman plugged into his ears. There were a few other people, none of them interested in anything but the sweat pouring from their out-of-condition bodies.

Cunningham turned his head and studied Razak's heavily sweating head. 'Start dealing, Razak.'

Razak didn't look round. 'Jack, if I wanted to lie in the heat and cover myself in sweat I'd go and squat in the desert. I don't like this place. I'm going.' He made to get up but Cunningham's hand pressed down on his arm.

'We made a deal, Razak. Stay where you are and start talking.'

Razak lowered himself back into the lounger and studied the sauna room again. 'Are you sure we can't be heard here?'

'Talk, Razak – I'm the only one interested in what you've got to say. Give me something to think about.'

Razak still wasn't happy, but he was now anxious to get the bargaining under way. Greed took over from his inherent caution. He lowered his voice until it was little more than a deep whisper and said, 'Macauley mentioned three specific areas in the Ash-Sham desert and I have the actual map references that he bought from the Iraqi general. I am the only person, other than the Iraqi High Command, who has the exact details of this desert project. You are aware, of course, what I mean by "desert project"?'

'Keep talking.'

Razak continued searching the room with his eyes. 'And you must realize the value of this information. Doerflinger says you are empowered to discuss terms. Then let us discuss them. I am prepared to offer your government first refusal on the exact locations, layouts, and identification of the entire protection capability of the forces in the area.'

Cunningham glanced sideways at Razak. 'How much d'you want?'

Razak's lips began to smile. He controlled it and gazed up at the ceiling as if seeking inspiration there and a figure that wouldn't be over the top. But he'd already worked it all out.

'Two hundred and fifty million US dollars.'

Cunningham's expression didn't change. He turned on his elbow and studied Razak's face. 'And if we decide not to take you up on this offer?'

Razak brought his eyes down from the ceiling and met Cunningham's. 'You'd be fools not to. But, yes, there is an alternative buyer. I am prepared to offer it to Iran, who are very interested in moving into the nuclear age, particularly if it's detrimental to their neighbours, Iraq. They wouldn't destroy the dumps, as you would — they'd use the components — and then you'd have another problem in that area.' His lip curled. 'I would, of course, accept a much lower offer from them. You would not get a second bid.'

'Is this information secure?'

Razak smiled. 'You mean if you kill me here and now will the information die with me? No, Jack. I've covered every eventuality. I told you on the telephone. If you remove me, the fact that the locations have been blown will immediately be transmitted to Baghdad.' The smile tightened into a hard, cruel line. 'Then you lose all round — and Macauley's ordeal was for nothing.'

Cunningham stared hard at him. 'Assuming I pass on your price what guarantee do we have that the information is original and you're not going to try this one on someone else?'

'No point, Jack. The details are complex, I couldn't possibly remember any part of the project. And besides, I wouldn't jeopardize this deal. I'm a professional, Jack, not a card sharp. The information, in fine detail, is in a safe place but can be handed to you within twenty-four hours of agreement. My insurance copy will remain unseen until you have destroyed the dumps, after which it becomes useless. This is a straightforward deal, Jack. Your people would be mad to turn it down. I must insist you now make a decision.' Razak looked hard at Cunningham but could read nothing in his expression. 'A simple yes or no. That's all I want at this stage.'

Cunningham lay back and stared at the ceiling for several minutes. He looked as though he'd gone to sleep. Razak lost patience. He stretched. He'd had enough of expensive sweat: he wanted to get out of this suffocating heat and somewhere where he could control his own movements. He wanted his clothes on; this room was oppressing him, and it wasn't just the heat.

'Well?'

Suddenly Cunningham stood up. Razak, taken unawares, leapt to his feet a fraction of a second behind him. 'What's going on?' he snapped.

'You want a decision – I'm going to get you one.'

Razak stared around him quickly. 'How?'

'I'm going to ring Doerflinger.'

Razak grabbed his bare arm in a vice-like grip. 'No telephones,' he hissed into the side of Cunningham's face. 'Not from here. You wait until I've left.'

Cunningham removed Razak's hand and smiled coldly. 'That sounded a bit like uncertainty to me, Razak. Looked like a little bit of fear. How does it feel?'

Razak made no reply. He glanced around the steam room once more. 'I want to get out of here. We'll finalize the arrangements somewhere else. I've had enough of this place, I need to cool off.'

Cunningham agreed, and so, apparently, did the short, stocky man on the other side of the room who stood up, flexed his hairy shoulders and arms and with his towelling robe thrown casually over his arm pushed through the door as Cunningham turned his back on Razak.

48

Cunningham had overestimated the security of the Washington Pomona's sauna room.

On the other side of the room Lou Mullins lay back in his towel-covered lounger and watched Simon's finger beat out in Morse the basics of what Razak was telling Cunningham.

He was jerked out of his concentration when the finger stopped tapping.

'Oh shit!' hissed Simon and discreetly ripped out his earplugs.

'Wassa matter?' Mullins's voice cut like ice but his lips didn't move. 'What the fuckin' hell're you doing?'

'They're talking about leaving. They're going to cool off. Looks like the Arab's had enough heat for the time being.'

'I'll go in front of them. Wait a couple of minutes then follow me out,' snapped Mullins. Meet me in your changing room – '

'What about a little whirl in the pool?'

'Fff—!'

In the safety of Simon's changing room he lit a cigarette but had hardly got it going when Simon appeared. 'They followed you out,' Simon grimaced at the taste of Mullins's smoke. 'They've gone through a door marked "Pool Suite." Very grand!'

'I know where they've gone. Gimme a contact,' Mullins said abruptly. Then, 'We'll take the Arab now,' he murmured into the small button microphone Simon handed to him. 'Is everything in position?'

'We're ready outside,' replied the AI leader from the atrium, 'and we're moving into position inside now. Give me five minutes and we'll be ready for your "go" sign. Repeat. It will be *your* "go". OK?'

Mullins glanced up at Simon. 'Acknowledged,' he said and handed the button back to the younger man. Mullins was still dressed in his hotel towel robe, his feet bare, his hair, what was left of it, rumpled and disarrayed. He looked as though he had just strolled into the dressing room for a quick smoke and was about to return to the peace and quiet of the sauna.

Razak appeared to be enjoying himself. He was installed in solitary splendour in a large circular bath of swirling warm water. The pressure of the jets was almost lifting him out of the water; he looked like a table-tennis ball being bounced up and down on a water jet in a fairground shooting gallery. He gazed up at Cunningham, his huge fleshy arms spread out like two hairy tree branches on the rim of the Jacuzzi, but he wasn't relaxed.

Cunningham lowered himself into the water at an angle to Razak. He closed his eyes, raised his head to the ceiling and revelled in the fierce pounding before adjusting the water pressure to a more gentle soothing massage. After a few minutes he moved closer to Razak, his face still impassive. To anyone on the other side of the water suite or in the other Jacuzzis and water treatment pools they looked like a couple of friends having a quiet chat about girls, politics or food. But then they couldn't see Cunningham's eyes. Razak could.

Cunningham kept his voice even. 'Assuming I get agreement to your terms, how do you want this transfer effected?' He didn't give Razak a chance to answer. 'And,

412

bearing in mind you already have $150 million of our money that you stole from Thurston Macauley – '

'That doesn't come into the equation. That money, as far as your government is concerned, has been written off. We're talking a whole new ball ga—' His voice tailed off. For a brief moment his eyes glanced over Cunningham's shoulder and hardened.

Cunningham resisted the temptation to swing round. He kept his eyes glued on Razak's.

'Jack, you've set me up!'

'What d'you – '

'You've blown it, Jack!' Razak was almost shouting. 'You've blown it! You've blown it!' He began to clamber out of the Jacuzzi, but Cunningham dragged him back in.

'What the hell are you talking about?'

Razak became icy calm as his brain went into overdrive and his eyes quartered the pool area. 'Fair-haired man on the far side of the pool – red swimming pants.' Razak never forgot a face. 'Another on this side – black pants – they're your people.'

'You're paranoiac, Razak – you're imagining things. I haven't got any people here – '

'Don't fuck with me, Jack! Those two followed me around Washington . . . I know them . . .'

Mullins's two Mossad agents read the signs. Razak had blown them. They moved quickly – but not quickly enough. Razak wasted no more time. His searching hand found the Jacuzzi's pressure gauge and, with one smooth movement, spun it to maximum pressure. Hauling himself upright he turned on his left heel and with his hand open and cocked lunged forward, aiming for the tip of Cunningham's nose.

Had the blow landed correctly Cunningham's nose bone would have been rammed into his brain, but he'd anticipated the move and shifted his balance. A sharp hand

413

jab to Razak's jugular, found its mark and brought a strangled gasp from Razak's open mouth; another jab – the finishing stroke to the back of his neck as he went down – landed on his fleshy shoulder just as the water pressure responded to its gauge and Cunningham was caught at the base of his spine with the full-blooded pressure of an open water jet. But he recovered quickly and ducked as the full force of Razak's killing blow caught him high on the forehead. Not a lethal blow, or a disabling one, but enough to leave an opening for Razak. With his instinct for the kill, he saw the opening and brought a sharp hand-edge cut to the side of Cunningham's exposed neck. Hasty, badly judged. It landed too low, on the collarbone, but with enough force to send Cunningham slipping and tumbling backwards to the other side of the Jacuzzi. Unable to retain his balance, the back of his neck hit the hard edge with a jarring shock. He slipped and went under the raging water and for a moment blacked out. Somebody shouted from a nearby pool, but it was a shout of indignation from a lounging client as the farthest Mossad man leapt over his body and hurtled towards the struggling men. Cunningham opened his eyes and instinctively threw himself to one side.

Razak had gone.

Simon, fully dressed, stood with his finger pressing the plug into his ear.

'Something funny going on,' he murmured to Mullins.

'Funny like what?'

'Razak and Cunningham are rolling around in the Jacuzzi. Hold on! It's a bloody scrap!'

'What's Cunningham doing?'

'Beating the fuck out of the Arab!'

'Our people ready?'

'Not yet.'

'Too bad. Go! Go! Go! Where's Razak now?'

'Clambering out of the bath!'

'Fuck it! Cunningham?'

'Still there . . . No he's not! He's disappeared – '

Mullins moved like lightning. The three Mossad people burst through the door with him and without ceremony one whacked Razak across the head with a short leather sandbag. 'Stick something in the bastard!' hissed Mullins and moved round the other side of the Jacuzzi. He drew the automatic from his towelling robe pocket, cocked it and pointed it at the back of Cunningham's head.

Cunningham looked up, and then felt the hard pressure of metal digging into his collarbone. 'Stay still. Don't move!' snapped a voice in his ear. He half turned his head. 'I said don't move!' The metal dug deeper, bringing a hiss of pain from between his teeth.

And then he saw the three men, the two in swimming briefs and one in a long white coat, dragging Razak along the slippery floor. Even as they manhandled the struggling figure Cunningham could see the white-coated man pulling an empty hypodermic out of Razak's thigh. Cunningham twisted sideways and felt the heat of the bullet sear across his shoulder as the man behind him automatically squeezed the trigger. 'Stay still, you bastard!' shouted Mullins. 'We're on the same bloody side . . .' He fired again into the water, deliberately missing Cunningham. But Cunningham threw himself out of the water and managed to get his hands round Mullins's throat. Mullins went with the weight, brought his feet into play and threw Cunningham over his head. He'd misjudged. Cunningham crashed down on top of him knocking the wind out of him and landed a decisive blow on Mullins's head with his foot. Mullins dropped the gun and collapsed into the Jacuzzi. By the time he'd recovered, Cunningham was throwing himself at the door of the pool suite.

He went through the pool suite doors with a rush, but he

415

didn't expect to see Razak or the men who'd taken him. He hadn't had time to think who they might be. One thing he was certain of: it wasn't Doerflinger and his crew who'd done the business. It was very efficient. Very professional. He slipped and slithered down the corridor to his changing room, crashed through the door and threw himself at the locker. The SIG/Sauer fell into his hand. He depressed the de-cocking lever and, pressing himself against the door jamb, slid round with the automatic in a double hand grip.

Mullins was rushing in the other direction, heading for the doors leading to the lifts and stairs. Cunningham didn't give him a chance. He squeezed the trigger, but Mullins, with a quick glance over his shoulder, didn't pause. The .357 SIG bullet thwacked into the top of his thigh, throwing him forward on to his side. The next shot smashed noisily into his wet chest. The blood from the two wounds began streaming like a bizarre watercolour as it mixed with the water from his dunking in the Jacuzzi.

Cunningham brought the SIG-Sauer up again and aimed for the kill – the T, the head and neck – but as he staggered against the wall it gave Mullins that fraction of a second to drag himself over. With a strangled shout he raised his hand and bellowed: 'You stupid bastard! You're killing the wrong bloke. I'm on your side – I want *Razak*, not you . . .' He collapsed in a heap, his head in his arms and his legs pulled up like a baby hiding itself from the dark.

Cunningham hesitated, raised the pistol and stared cautiously at Mullins's curled-up figure. The short man in Paris who'd been following Razak . . . and was still following him . . . He wasn't dead; Cunningham could see him breathing with difficulty. But, whoever he was and whatever he was doing, he'd have to wait.

He dressed quickly and rushed for the phone.

'*Thurston*,' he snapped.

'Control's in touch,' replied an anonymous female voice.

416

'Just a second . . .' then: '*Thurston* leader – through,' she said after a brief pause.

'Joe,' said Cunningham. 'Somebody's snatched Razak . . .'

Doerflinger's voice came calmly over the line. 'I know. I was there. I don't know who they are – yet. We're following a State Hospital ambulance heading north. Get out of that hotel and go to Control. I'll lead you into the action when you get back in touch.'

It had been the perfect take-out.

As the three men rushed Razak through the glass doors four other men dressed in white paramedic uniforms – having jammed the escalators and blocked the upstairs access door – moved into position at each corner of Razak's unconscious body. Without ceremony they heaved him on to a collapsible stretcher and, with a nurse holding a clear liquid drip feed above him, hurriedly carried the body down the exit stairs to an ambulance waiting at the garage entrance. With just a single toot of its siren to clear the garage exit, the ambulance filtered into the traffic and without fuss made its way along M Street and turned north into Wisconsin Avenue.

The ambulance turned into a deserted side street where the men piled out and took up casual stations while Razak was transferred, still unconscious, into a dark-screened station wagon. The ambulance returned to its hospital; the team, after changing back into their normal clothing, dispersed and the station wagon reversed as far as the Wisconsin Avenue and headed north again.

After joining Rockville Pike they continued until about fifteen miles the other side of the 495. There the vehicle turned off the highway and began cutting across country. After several twists and turns it arrived at a small stock car and rally ground. Among the litter of ramshackle work-sheds, tin lean-tos and wrecked jalopies was a large open space. The wagon was met by two men with a large aluminium trolley. Razak's twitching body was bundled on to it and the trolley was pushed, almost at a trot, between two of the tin sheds. Hidden behind these stood a pale grey civilian helicopter with a fair-haired pilot. There was no logo on it, just a registration number. No gossip, no chatter, no backslapping or congratulations, it was just another job: a Mossad take-out operation. Tomorrow they'd all be back at their jobs, undercover, and honest citizens of the United States of America – and that's how they'd remain until Israel sounded the tocsin again.

But this time, for once, they'd got it wrong.

Doerflinger's team showed they meant business. Cutting through the wood they moved across the ground like shadows. One man shot the pilot dead; half the team surrounded the wagon, and one of the Mossad men who made a tentative gesture towards his waistband took a 230grs .45 Auto SXT in the chest. It almost cut him in half. The rest of the Mossad Al team preferred the diplomatic way out: they stood with their backs to the metal shed and their hands on their head while Doerflinger spoke to Cunningham on the phone.

By the time Cunningham arrived in the first of the group's helicopters Doerflinger had sorted out his prisoners and isolated the Al leader. 'Come and have a chat with an interesting guy, Jack. You might learn something.' Doerflinger was in his element; the smell of cordite and the scent of danger had brought the sparkle back into his eyes and the spring to his heels. He looked twenty years younger. 'And by the way – who said something about being out of date?'

'You got lucky, Joe,' said Cunningham tersely. 'Who's this guy, then?'

'He's something to do with the Israeli Mossad. He'll only

answer to the name Henry. He's got a tale to tell but I wanted you here to see how far we could go. Prompt me if I slow down . . .'

Mossad's senior agent in Washington was sitting on an old box in one of the tin shacks smoking a cigarette and watched over by two heavily armed US agents. He showed no sign of remorse; he was relaxed and comfortable. He could have been the leader of the winning group. But he wasn't.

'OK,' began Doerflinger. 'You're a senior Israeli agent and the rest of your crew are from the Mossad.'

'Is that a guess?' replied Henry.

'Don't get cute, my friend,' Doerflinger said without venom and jerked his thumb over his shoulder. 'You're looking at about twenty-five years without option for that little lot out there. D'you want to talk intelligently with a possibility of some sort of arrangement, or board one of those choppers and take your chance in a court of law?'

Henry gave a half-smile. 'Let's talk about arrangements.'

'Questions and answers first. What d'you want Razak for?'

'I'm a freelance bounty operator. I was contracted to the Israeli government to find him and take him to Israel. He's wanted there to answer charges relating to the death of two Israeli secret agents.'

'Bounty operator my bloody ass! That's bullshit! If Razak's killed any Israeli agents you would have knocked the bugger off when you first clapped eyes on him. What you wouldn't do with a fuckin' Arab murderer is go to the lengths you lot went to to kidnap the bastard. Last chance, Henry. Try again.'

Henry crushed out his cigarette and lit another. He stood up and leaned his back against the tin wall. 'Razak has certain information concerning Israeli security. He's wanted

419

in Tel Aviv to help identify certain areas of this information . . .'

'You want him to cough up some map references relating to the Ash-Sham desert,' said Cunningham.

Henry shrugged.

'Lock the bastard up, Joe. We're not going to get anywhere like this. Incidentally,' Cunningham turned back to Henry, 'there's a little hairy guy named Mullins with a couple of bullets in him back in Washington. He's in hospital. Sick. But he'll live – unless I go back there and pull the plug out. He's a friend of yours, I believe?'

Henry managed to keep his expression flat. But it hurt. Mullins's life wasn't negotiable – neither was his, come to that. And he was already squirming at the thought of the Godalmighty stink this little episode was going to make when it hit the streets. It didn't take much imagination to see the impact here and in Tel Aviv when it came out that a whole Israeli Mossad unit operating in the capital of the United States was not only involved in highly messy shootout and kidnap of an Arab but was rounded up by half a dozen American secret agents led by an old man! It didn't bear thinking about.

'What were those arrangements you mentioned?' he said to Doerflinger.

Doerflinger didn't hesitate. 'Tell me everything about this show, without bullshit, and I'll guarantee that your crew out there can go back to Washington and melt back into the shadows. I don't want to know about them, but if any one of their faces appears in the future in any dubious situation I'll round the whole lot up and shove 'em away. That's for starters. You can go back to Israel without a blemish and there'll be no publicity on tonight's theatricals. A word of warning before you start unloading, Henry. If this episode becomes political the damage that could be caused to relations between our two governments would be

beyond calculation. You've got that, have you? Good. OK
– shoot.'

'Mullins?'

'He'll be repaired and sent back to wherever he wants
to go.'

'Fair enough.' Henry sat down on his wooden box and
lit a new cigarette. He took his time crushing the remains of
the old one under his foot, then looked up into Doerflinger's face. 'Razak was carrying a set of map references
detailing Iraq's nuclear bomb potential hidden in Jordan's
Ash-Sham desert . . .'

Doerflinger and Cunningham exchanged glances.

It wasn't lost on Henry. 'You were after them as well, I
know. We relieved him of one set – '

'What d'you mean – one set?' asked Cunningham.

'He made a copy and sent it off to an address in
Switzerland. My guess is that that copy was his insurance
while he bargained with you. It didn't get there . . .'

'Where's the original?'

Henry shrugged. 'Academic, isn't it? I've just said we –
Israel – have the copy. Our people will take care of
anything that needs taking care of. You don't want to get
involved – not now. I think you should wash your hands of
it and let us pick up the original.'

'Why do you think that?' asked Doerflinger.

'These map references will be physically located by us.
They'll be pinpointed and placed under full-time surveillance. When my people judge the time is ripe these dumps
will be obliterated – '

'After you've taken all the goodies back to Israel,'
growled Doerflinger. But he did it with a straight face.

'Israel wouldn't pose the same nuclear threat to the
Middle East as Iraq, and besides, we're your best friend
there.'

421

'Why should we not have this other copy?' asked Cunningham. 'We've paid our whack for it.'

Henry looked at Doerflinger. He could see Doerflinger understood – after all, Doerflinger might still have the energy and know-how to chase people all over DC but this was a bit on the side. He wasn't in the game any more and it showed. He was now in politics and he was way ahead of the play. 'When the remains of these dumps are eventually attacked and destroyed it would be understood, if not condoned, by the rest of the world as self-preservation by Israel. If it got out that the US was also involved, or had known of the existence of these dumps, the whole ethos would change to one of condemnation of America and its lackey, Israel. That's the way the world thinks. Better there's no evidence that you knew anything about it.'

Doerflinger didn't agree. Neither did he disagree, but it was manifest that he wasn't going to pursue the where-abouts of the other document. 'You're quite sure Razak made no other insurance commitment?'

'Quite sure. The man's naked, he's unprotected. We can do what we like with him.'

'Not "we", my friend,' said Doerflinger quietly. 'Razak's mine, not yours. Come with me.' He led Henry out of the shed and into the open space. Henry's men were still lined up, Doerflinger's two helicopters, their blades idling, standing like dark green shadows a distance apart from each other. A smaller helicopter ticked away under their cover. Doerflinger pointed to the two heavy-duty body bags. 'One of those is your man. Who's the other?'

Henry, for the first time, allowed himself a puzzled frown. 'The helicopter pilot.'

'Israeli?'

Henry shook his head. 'Local.'

'He's neither of those,' said Doerflinger. 'It's an Arab terrorist by the name of Razak.'

Henry was quick on the uptake. 'Who killed himself accidentally while planning an assassination in Washington . . .'

'You will inform Tel Aviv accordingly?'

Henry nodded. 'Provided you're not going to let him go at any time? He killed two of our people in Beirut.'

'I've just told you – Razak is dead, he's in that bag.'

Henry and the rest of the Al unit loaded their dead colleague into the back of the station wagon and climbed in around him. They were a subdued crowd. Henry sat in the front passenger seat, and as the vehicle manoeuvred out of the clearing he gave the briefest of nods to the two Americans. Neither returned it and they watched in silence as the car's rear lights disappeared up the track.

Cunningham was the first to break the silence. 'That seems to tidy things up, then.'

Doerflinger said, 'Give me a cigarette, Jack.'

'You don't smoke, Joe, you gave it up seven years ago.'

'I've started again. Just give me a fuckin' cigarette, will you!' When he'd lit it, and coughed his lungs up with the first drag, he said, 'How were you going to take Razak, knowing that the bastard had covered himself for just such an event?'

Cunningham glanced sideways at Doerflinger. 'Don't ask, Joe. You wouldn't believe me if I told you!'

'In other words, you hadn't got a fucking clue!'

'Think what you like. Now the excitement's over, what about that house?'

'Everything's arranged. Rush job. It's an old communication centre we used to use in the good old cold war days. Very, very safe and your modifications have been carried out. No explanation was given; internal renovations. Sam Keble's already installed. I've told him we're on our way.'

Cunningham glanced over his shoulder at the remaining

423

members of Doerflinger's assault team. 'How many of that lot coming with us?'

'None. It's just you, me and Razak. The pilot's one of those "deaf and dumb" characters. Blind, too. Let's get going.'

Following another large dose of thiopentone sodium, Razak had already been loaded into the back seat of the helicopter. Joe Doerflinger gave a brief wave to the men on the ground then tapped the pilot on the shoulder.

After they had left the ground Doerflinger leaned forward and from a piece of paper shouted directions into the pilot's ear.

'Head north towards Frankerick . . .'

'Got it.'

'. . . then make a south-westerly arc in the direction of Duncansville . . .'

The pilot stuck his thumb up. A short while later he turned his head. 'That's Duncansville ahead.'

'Go south towards Bedford. About twelve miles . . . You'll see some people in a field with an orange panel.'

Several minutes later the pilot touched Cunningham's knee and pointed ahead.

'Got it,' said Cunningham. He looked over his shoulder. 'OK, Joe?'

Doerflinger lifted Razak's limp hand and let it drop. 'Yeah. Let's go say hello.'

Another car, another change and another winding drive before Razak's journey came to an end in a middling to large house on the edge of a small town. It was nicely isolated: there were no guards, no snarling dogs, no broken-glass-topped walls. This was a gentleman's house with all comforts. The garage doors closed behind the car and Razak was humped by Cunningham and the pilot into the main part of the house.

When he eventually came out of his thiopentone-sodium-induced slumber he would find himself in a nightmare: a nightmare that even he, in the cruellest of his excesses towards his prisoners, couldn't possibly have envisaged.

49

Sam Keble wasn't the chatty sort – which suited Cunningham. He wasn't curious either; he was doing a job of work and he was doing it for someone he owed a great deal. 'Help yourself to drink, Joe,' he said to Doerflinger, 'while this young man and I attend to the business. The cabinet's full, you'll find everything you want there.' He turned to Cunningham, 'OK, let's get on with it, Mr Cunningham,' he said by way of greeting.

Twenty minutes later Keble rejoined Doerflinger. He poured himself a decent-sized glass of Jack Daniels and drank half of it. 'He's a hard bastard, your boy Cunningham, Joe. I thought we'd stopped making 'em like that. That lad hates. Very dangerous thing in our game is hate . . .'

'It takes all sorts, Sam. Did you never hate?'

Keble emptied the rest of his glass. 'Not like him. Come on, bring your drink with you, I'll take you down.'

He led Doerflinger through the main drawing room of the spacious house. Under the wide, curving staircase was a door; it could have been a broom closet or the entrance to Keble's wine cellar. But it was neither. Another door, three-inch steel on hydraulic hinges, led to concrete stairs that descended two floors. The first was a large, air-conditioned communications centre. Once thriving, it was now an empty shell.

They stopped for a moment while Keble manipulated the

426

combination on another steel door. 'Any special reason why this guy Razak needs hurting?' he asked. He didn't expect a reply. He didn't get one. Doerflinger kept his own counsel as he followed Keble to the small landing at the top of the next flight of steps. A dim light shone down from the concrete ceiling. It showed, except for two chairs, in one of which sat Jack Cunningham, a totally empty room.

'OK, Sam,' said Doerflinger, 'is everything working?'

'Perfectly. I've switched the sound off but there's a permanent video on the go.'

'Don't record anything, Sam.'

'I'm not a bloody idiot, Joe!'

'Silly me!' smiled Doerflinger.

He took the lighted cigarette from between Keble's fingers, drew on it and watched the smoke being dragged upwards into the filtering system, then, followed by Keble, he walked down the steps, across the concrete floor and sat down in the chair beside Cunningham and studied his profile. His jaw set, he showed no expression: no pleasure, no gloating, no satisfaction as he looked down. It was impossible to know what he was thinking. Doerflinger too lowered his eyes.

Razak's face was staring up at him through the bars of a grille set in the concrete floor.

Keble stood behind Doerflinger's chair. 'I saw something like this in England once . . .'

'I'm not surprised,' said Doerflinger acerbically.

Keble continued to look down at Razak's face. 'Ever visit Warwick Castle in England?' he asked.

'No.'

'I did once. There was this bloody great circular prison cage where they used to pen the guys they captured during their Civil War. Right up my street, I thought. I went in and it frightened the life out of me. They ought to have some of these places around now, I reckoned. That'd make some of the evil bastards think twice about going wrong . . .'

'This leading up to something, Sam?'

'Yeah. Set in the middle of this dungeon was a little grille – ' he touched the one near his foot – 'a bit smaller than this one. What's it for? I said to somebody. To piss in, I should think, said somebody else, and then some character said it was for putting naughty prisoners in. Apparently if one of 'em got on the guards' nerves they squeezed him into this thin drain and fed him slops through the grille . . . I looked around, there was nowhere else – I reckon that's where they pissed as well! The poor bastard who got stuck into the hole was kept there until he died.' Keble lit a cigarette and glanced down into Razak's staring eyes. 'Until he died,' he repeated. 'It put the fear of bloody God into me!'

'How'd you get him into this drain?' asked Doerflinger. 'Squeeze him in like toothpaste?'

Keble smiled happily. 'Taking the dimensions you gave, and without having to use a lot of imagination on what it was going to be used for, I made a few modifications.' He looked down at Cunningham's bowed head. 'I hope you don't mind, Jack. The basics are as Joe told me you wanted.'

Cunningham looked up over his shoulder for a moment. 'Tell me about them.'

'Four-inch concrete lid; it jacks up on an electric motor just wide enough to roll the body in. There's no leeway. In there he can't move; he certainly can't get out – ' He tapped the concrete with his foot. 'Doesn't need people with guns watching him all the time. We don't have to use iron to chain his ass to the wall. It's clean, it's neat – they knew how to make people suffer, those English!'

'What about – '

'Flushes out twice a day.' He jerked his thumb over his shoulder – 'When that door opens it activates the flush system.' He pulled a face. 'I can't stand the smell of shit. And it switches the light on. Every morning we have to allow a little shaft of light to play on his face. The psychologist says it's good stuff; it'll make him think it's sunlight and get his mind working on what it used to be like outside where the normal people are . . .'

'You're a cruel bastard, Keble,' said Doerflinger, admiringly.

'Not me, Joe. I just follow instructions.' Keble continued: 'The rest of the time it's pitch dark; it'll get him ready for what it's like to be dead and buried.'

'Let's have a chat with him, then.'

'D'you want a cup of coffee or tea while we're doing it?'

'Why not? Nice cup of coffee would go down well.'

Keble spoke softly into a small hand radio and at the same time depressed a switch. The single light above brightened and shone down in a cone over the grille. It showed up every detail of Razak's tormented face.

Cunningham continued to stare down, without feeling. So far he had said little. All the conversation had been carried out between Doerflinger and his friend Keble. But he spoke now.

'Let me hear your voice, Razak,' he said.

There was no reply.

He repeated the question.

Still no reply. He sat back in the chair and lit a cigarette. Keble returned carrying a tray with three cups. 'You trying to make conversation?'

'Jack wants him to talk,' replied Doerflinger, 'but there's nothing coming up from the drains.' He sipped his coffee. 'Good coffee. How can I get the toe of my boot into this fucker's bollocks?'

'Let me have a go.' Keble raised his voice slightly, 'Are you going to talk to us, Razak?'

A hawking sound came from below the grid.

'We've got ourselves a tough guy, Joe . . .'

Cunningham stood up. 'OK, Sam, thanks. D'you mind if I have a chat with him? Would you leave us for a bit?'

Keble wasn't put out. It was all part of the business – do that, do this. 'Sure! Give me a wave if you want anything,' he pointed up at the ceiling, 'Camera . . .'

When Keble had gone Cunningham turned his back on Doerflinger and gazed down into Razak's eyes. Razak almost seemed to accept the situation. This was how it happened, thought Cunningham. Sometimes it was 'them' taking the comfortable view and screwing the bollocks off one of 'us' and other times it was the other way round. Last time it was Thurston Macauley; this time it was Razak; next time it might be him; he was well on the debit side of the law of averages. He studied Razak's face beneath the grille. He wouldn't like to be in his skin; not in this one. He reckoned he would have held his breath until he died rather than go into that fuckin' pit.

'Razak,' he said lightly. 'You're going to stay here until you end up like Thurston Macauley. D'you understand?'

'You've got the wrong man, Jack.' Razak's voice was surprisingly strong. Doerflinger stood up and approached the grille. He lit his second cigarette of the day but said nothing.

'Give it up, Razak,' said Cunningham, 'and listen. If there were any rules to this game I'd be breaking your legs by now; I'd also be kicking your brains into the back of your head. You, as always, are the lucky bastard. You've fallen into civilized hands. I'm not going to break your legs. But I'll tell you what I am going to do . . . You still listening, Razak?'

'You're wrong, Jack. Give me a cigarette, please.'

'. . . I'm going to keep you here until you die. Think about that, Razak, and think about what you did to

Thurston Macauley — how long is it going to be before you die?'

Razak didn't reply. His eyes were closed. Perhaps he was thinking how long for ever was. After some time his eyes opened. He was a fatalist. 'Would you do a deal over the money?'

Cunningham and Doerflinger exchanged glances. Cunningham said, 'What sort of deal?'

'You get the money and I go free.'

'I'll tell you what I'll do,' said Cunningham. 'I want all the money returned. I'm not interested any more in the map references you screwed out of Thurston Macauley, so don't bother mentioning them. There's no bargaining. That is it. You can stay in this coffin for the rest of your life; or you can go free. The decision's yours. I don't want to talk to you any more. I shall send someone here to see you tomorrow and you will say yes or no. Have you understood?'

'Just a minute, Jack. Don't go away. How do I know that if I do as you ask you will keep your word?'

'You don't.'

'Give me something.'

'I've already given it. I'll let you free when you deliver the goods.'

'You give me your word of honour?'

'I've given it.'

Cunningham turned his back on the face in the pit and waved his hand at the camera in the ceiling. The strong beam was replaced by a dim light that enabled them to find their way to the door. When they went out even that tiny comfort would be switched off and Razak would be left in his nightmare. Doerflinger breathed a heavy sigh when the door closed behind them. 'You really going to deal with that bastard, Jack?'

431

'I'll do what I said. But he's going to suffer for a long time first.'

Doerflinger crunched his cigarette out and stared at the closed door. In his mind he could see the face; he could see the eyes and he could feel the horror. 'A couple of months in that bloody thing to me would be worse than a lifetime of death.' He looked up. 'Let's go and have a very, very stiff drink.'

Epilogue

Almost two years to the day that Cunningham put Razak in his living tomb Thurston Macauley died in his troubled sleep. Three days after the military funeral in Arlington and with the clear notes of the Last Post that had echoed across the hallowed ground still ringing in his mind Cunningham went back to the other tomb.

He ordered a final and prolonged sluice before Razak's tomb was opened and he was prised out. It meant nothing to Razak. He felt no relief; he felt nothing. His brain, like his body, was dead.

Cunningham and Keble placed him on a stretcher and two young men carried him up the stairs, through the length of the house and out into the crisp winter air. The weak sun was too much for him. He clenched his eyes as tightly as they'd go but still the searing red flashes cut through his eyelids. He tried to bring his hand up to protect his eyes but the movement was feeble and his arm fragile and by the time his hand flopped on to his face they were out of the sun and he was being bundled into the rattling, juddering helicopter waiting to take off from the lawn in front of the house.

He raised his chin and looked into the unsympathetic eyes of the man who was responsible for a nightmare that had lasted two years. The two men stared at each other, each with his own thoughts, until with a vague movement of his hand Razak asked Cunningham to come closer.

Cunningham studied the gaunt figure for a moment then leaned forward. It was difficult to hear what he was saying. The engine increased power and the blades lifted with a whoosh, then clattered to maximum revs.

Cunningham, watched by Keble sitting on the other side of Razak, straightened up. He met Keble's eyes. His own were expressionless. He shrugged, settled back in his seat and watched the ground fall away.

After some time the pilot turned his head and held a map up to Cunningham. He tapped it with his finger then pointed down. Cunningham stared out of the window. There was nothing but water below them and as he looked he could see a gentle ripple running across the surface of the sea with here and there tiny white ridges breaking up the purity of the dark green expanse. He stuck his thumb up to the pilot and leaned forward to shout in his ear.

'Keep on course. Don't go up or down – radar . . . !'

'You don't have to tell me that, Jack. Say when!'

Cunningham nodded to Keble and pointed between Razak's feet. Razak's eyes were half open but what little was showing was blank; nothing seemed to be going in. It upset Cunningham that Razak wasn't fully aware of what was happening.

Keble's head vanished between his legs. After a couple of minutes it reappeared and, flushed with exertion, he nodded to Cunningham and sat back.

Cunningham tightened his seat belt, slipped the catch on the door and slid it back. The wind rushed and blew Razak's straggly beard in all directions but it didn't disturb either him or Cunningham. The noise of the helicopter's engine and the rotors just above drowned out any attempt at speech but that didn't deter Cunningham. He opened his mouth and at the top of his voice bellowed, 'Pass me that thing there – ' He accompanied it with gestures and took from Keble a coiled-up length of half-inch nylon rope and threw it out of the door. There was about twenty feet of it; caught in the slipstream it trailed behind them in a huge stiff loop.

' – weight!' bellowed Cunningham.

Keble was ready with it. With an effort he shoved Razak's legs out of the way and pushed the heavily loaded canvas sack towards the door. Cunningham tested that the nylon rope was securely fixed to it then pulled in a short length of the trailing line. He secured this to a stanchion with a loose knot, ran his hand along it behind him and tested it with a gentle pull. It was firmly roped round Razak's ankles, then came up between his legs and tied again round his waist. There was no slack round the emaciated waist.

With both hands Cunningham pushed the weighted bag out of the door. Hanging on to the side he watched the arc of line pull almost straight by the weight and then take a slight curve as it followed the movement of the helicopter.

'Pass him over here!' he shouted to Keble and leaned back to allow Razak's skinny body to lie across his knees with his feet hanging out of the door. Cunningham looked once into Razak's closed eyes and slipped the rope off the stanchion. It took a fraction of a second for the line to tighten and Razak was whipped off Cunningham's knees as if by a catapult.

Cunningham leaned out of the door as far as he could go and watched until the bag hit the water. Fractionally later and with hardly a splash, Razak disappeared under the blue-green sea.

When he'd closed the door Cunningham rubbed his hands together as if ridding them of something unpleasant, then, unconsciously, he rubbed them on his trouser leg. Keble sidled up against him in the seat earlier occupied by Razak. He put his mouth to Cunningham's ear.

'What was it he said to you as we were taking off?'

Cunningham thought about it for a moment then looked the other man in the eye. 'He said, "Thank you for keeping your word." '

'What did he mean by that?'

'I gave him my word two years ago that I'd set him free. I think he was showing me he still had a sense of humour.'

MORE BESTSELLING FICTION FROM ARROW

☐	Skydancer	Geoffrey Archer	£4.99
☐	Shadowhunter	Geoffrey Archer	£4.99
☐	Eagletrap	Geoffrey Archer	£4.99
☐	Scorpion Trail	Geoffrey Archer	£5.99
☐	The Double Tenth	George Brown	£4.99
☐	Ringmain	George Brown	£4.99
☐	Pinpoint	George Brown	£4.99
☐	Sacrifice	George Brown	£4.99
☐	The Andromeda Strain	Michael Crichton	£5.99
☐	The Terminal Man	Michael Crichton	£4.99
☐	Congo	Michael Crichton	£5.99
☐	Rising Sun	Michael Crichton	£5.99
☐	Jurassic Park	Michael Crichton	£5.99
☐	Disclosure	Michael Crichton	£5.99
☐	The Day of the Jackal	Frederick Forsyth	£5.99
☐	The Devil's Alternative	Frederick Forsyth	£5.99
☐	The Odessa File	Frederick Forsyth	£4.99
☐	The Firm	John Grisham	£5.99
☐	A Time to Kill	John Grisham	£5.99
☐	The Pelican Brief	John Grisham	£5.99
☐	The Client	John Grisham	£5.99
☐	The Chamber	John Grisham	£5.99
☐	The Rainmaker	John Grisham	£5.99